# DEATH STORM

# STORM

ISLAND OF FOG LEGACIES #5

# DEATH STORM

by Keith Robinson

Printed in the United States of America
First Edition: November 2018
ISBN-13 978-1723931383

Cover design by Keith Robinson

Visit www.UnearthlyTales.com

## Chapter 1
## A storm Brews

"And there's nothing else?" Miss Simone persisted, looking at them both in turn. "You've told me everything?"

Travis and Melinda stood before her, pretending to think hard in case they'd missed a vital detail. "I *think* so," Melinda mumbled, wrinkling her nose and casting her gaze skyward. She went on to recap a few things, choosing her words carefully.

It was a warm Monday afternoon. School had finished thirty minutes ago, and Miss Simone had been waiting for them, sitting on an old tire swing hanging from an ancient oak in Melinda's front yard. The house stood nearby, a cozy, picturesque, one-story log building.

"Travis?" the blond scientist said, fixing him with a blue-eyed gaze. "Do you have something to say?"

Just when he thought she'd given up asking questions, here she was again, ambushing the two of them. And despite being in her mid-fifties, she still managed to disarm him with her mermaid enchantment spell.

*Don't say a word*, Travis told himself. He'd agreed with Melinda to keep some of the finer details of their last mission a secret. Their weekend visit to the so-called Haunted Fortress just off the coast of Hemlock had been an eye-opening experience to say the least.

Sensing Melinda's fierce stare boring into the side of his head, he evaded Miss Simone's question and instead offered some random theories and somewhat vague ideas about what *might* have happened to the naga on the beach. Quite honestly, he was tired of thinking about it.

Miss Simone considered his words before answering. "I'm done for now," she said finally. "I still feel something is off, but

I can't put my finger on it. Something has changed." She glared at Travis. "*You've* changed. You look the same, but . . ."

Both Travis and Melinda stared back at her, saying nothing.

Miss Simone abruptly stood. "Well, let's move on. I have another task for you both next weekend, if you're willing? It involves—"

But they never discovered what their next planned mission would have involved because, at that moment, a shout came from the street.

"Lady Simone!" A small, agile nine-year-old ran toward them. He was a recognizable face around the town, one of many messengers. "The council needs you! There's something coming—something really weird, a storm on the horizon."

"A *storm*?" Miss Simone repeated. "So we need to fetch umbrellas?"

The boy halted in front of her, his face flushed from running but his breathing regular. "It's not that kind of storm. It's like dust, only it's blue. The council said you need to check it out. They're getting word about other settlements north of here."

"What about them?"

"They're gone," the boy said with wide eyes. "Completely swallowed up."

While the statement sent a chill down Travis's spine and caused Melinda to suck in a breath, Miss Simone simply raised an eyebrow. "Swallowed up? Really? And I presume those towns miraculously reappeared once the storm had moved on?"

The messenger looked off to the side, his brow creasing. "Um . . . well, I don't know, exactly. The council just said they'd been swallowed up. By a weird blue dust storm."

Miss Simone turned to Travis and Melinda. "It's going to be one of those days. Thank you for your service this weekend. Well done, Travis, for melting the ice. Fascinating stuff . . ."

She addressed Melinda then, but Travis was distracted. This wasn't the first time today he'd had the distinct feeling of being spied on. He peeked over his shoulder, half expecting to spot someone hiding behind a bush.

"I think a trip to Hemlock is on the horizon," Miss Simone finished.

The messenger spoke up. "That's not the only thing on the horizon, Lady Simone. There's this weird blue dust storm—"

"Yes, yes, I heard you. Thank you. I'm on my way."

She left with the boy soon after, and Travis felt an immense sense of relief. "I really think she's done with us now."

Melinda's dad popped his head out of the nearest window. He often took a midday break from his ogre-sized construction duties to collect Mason from school and make lunch, so it wasn't a surprise to see him home. "Something to eat, Travis?"

"No thanks, Uncle Robbie," Travis called. "I'm just gonna head home and crash."

It sometimes sounded funny calling him 'Uncle' when he and Melinda weren't actually cousins. Their parents had always been very close, though. The Franklins and the Stricklands—perhaps the most famous of all the shapeshifters in Carter.

"Simone waited an hour for you both," Melinda's dad said. "I invited her in, but she seemed quite content swinging alone, so I left her to it. Did she drill you enough?"

"Plenty."

"Well, I'm sure there are plenty more questions to come. Your mom won't be giving up that easily." Robbie grinned and vanished inside.

Travis turned to head off home, but he paused when he glimpsed a figure disappearing behind one of many trees lining the property. There! He *knew* he was being watched. He squinted. Was it Nitwit the imp? He couldn't be sure, but the figure had seemed bigger, more like a man. He'd seen the same mysterious figure as they'd left school earlier.

"What?" Melinda asked, twisting around.

"Somebody's spying on us."

"Who?"

"How should I know? Some guy. Hard to tell. I catch him moving out of the corner of my eye, and then he hides."

Melinda made some sweeping arm gestures. "Well, go see!"

Travis balled his fists and steeled himself. "I will."

He started up the garden path, keeping his eye on that one particular tree in case the figure darted away. Whoever it was, they'd better have a good reason for stalking him!

He paused and turned back. "Are you coming or what?"

"Me?"

"Well, yeah." Travis shrugged and looked away. "I mean, this isn't a mission, but we're a team, right? I need you."

When he glanced back at Melinda, she had a faint smile on her face. "Yes," she said. "I guess you do."

As she caught up to him, he couldn't help mulling over the past few weeks. His first mission had been kind of unofficial, more like falling into a situation by accident. He'd single-handedly dealt with Mr. Braxton, a tycoon who had built up a secret zoo of fantastic, exotic creatures from New Earth—all completely illegal, of course.

Travis had taken on his first *official* mission with his best friend Rez along for support. They'd become entwined with sinister walking, talking trees and thousands of scorpion-like critters, and Travis had seen firsthand *the brain* that his dad had been feeding for years. Unfortunately, the underground monster had marked Travis for execution and set a demon on him, a terrifying headless horseman known as the dullahan.

A gargoyle incursion in the quaint town of Garlen's Well had been Melinda's first mission, and she'd taken over the reins on that one, partly because Travis had to remain incognito until the dullahan lost interest in him. But Melinda had done well, settling the problem with the gargoyles *and* taming the wild Goji creature.

But it was their most recent mission that had brought the two 'cousins' together as a team. They'd had some ups and downs during their stay at the Haunted Fortress, a few quarrels here and there, but the incredible events and life-threatening situations had seasoned them into full-blown shapeshifter emissaries of New Earth. They were ready for anything now.

"Hello?" Travis called ahead. "Is someone hiding there?"

He circled the tree and came face to face with a stooping, lanky, white-haired man with a heavily lined forehead. His eyebrows were just as white, and he had clear, grey eyes.

"Shh," the man whispered, standing up straight. He had to be six-and-a-half feet tall, and he wore a grubby black suit. "Don't let on that I'm here."

He gestured toward Melinda's house, and Travis glanced over his shoulder. Robbie had reappeared on the doorstep and was looking all around.

"We have to talk," the man said hoarsely, stooping once more as he peered around the trunk. "But not here. Perhaps—"

"Who *are* you?" Melinda asked, her voice loud and clear.

Travis had to smile. She wasn't one to be trifled with. This mysterious old man wanted them to keep secrets and play cloak-and-dagger games, but he was a complete stranger to them.

"Shh!" the man hissed again.

"Melinda?" Robbie called. "Are you coming in for lunch? Is Travis joining us?" He paused. "Who are you talking to over there?"

The old man cursed under his breath and glared at Melinda. "We have to talk," he repeated through gritted teeth. "Come and find me—quickly and quietly. There isn't much time. I'll be in the library."

Melinda opened her mouth to say something else, but the man abruptly ducked away and strode off at a remarkable speed on his long legs, head down and shoulders hunched.

Travis and Melinda stared after him, then gave each other a perplexed glance.

"Weirdo," Travis muttered.

"Have you ever seen him before?"

"Nope."

Robbie called again from the doorstep. "Kids?"

His eyes were narrowed as Travis and Melinda hurried up the garden path to the house, and he raised a hand for them to stop. "Who was that you were talking to?"

"Don't know," Melinda said. "Some creepy old man who wanted to talk to us in private."

Her dad huffed noisily, causing his nostrils to flare. "And?" he said with a deepening growl.

"And nothing. He hurried off."

"He didn't say who he was? What he wanted to talk about?"

Melinda shrugged. "Well . . ."

She paused. Travis studied her face, pretty sure he knew what she was thinking. The right thing to do would be to tell her dad what the man wanted: to urgently discuss something at the library. But then Robbie would order the two of them to stay home while he went to investigate, and that would be the end of it.

"He didn't say much of anything," Melinda said. "Didn't tell us who he was or what he wanted to talk about. Kind of weird, really. Anyway—I'm hungry."

She pushed past her dad, then stopped in the doorway and waved for Travis to come in.

He'd fully intended going home to crash, but now he felt a need to talk about the strange old man. Besides, he was hungry.

He stepped around Robbie, who remained staring off into the distance with suspicion written across his face. He'd inadvertently started an ogre transformation and was a little taller now, his shoulders wider judging by the way his silky magical shirt was busy adapting to fit.

Melinda went ahead and made a pile of sandwiches before her dad had the chance. He tended to lather them with too much butter for her liking. "Mason, come eat!" she yelled.

The boy came running. He was like a miniature version of Robbie, taller than most other seven-year-olds, thin and bright-

6

eyed, eager for something to poke his nose into. He didn't share his dad's love of bugs, though; instead, he enjoyed learning about the stars and planets.

"How's it going, buddy?" Travis asked.

"Good. There's no school tomorrow!"

Travis glanced at Robbie, who'd just entered the kitchen. "Is that true?"

"That's what I'm told. There's a storm coming. I might not be at work tomorrow, either. That's why I need to get going— we have to finish that roof, otherwise everything'll be water-damaged in the rain."

"Huh. We heard a messenger boy say it's more like a *dust* storm."

Robbie grabbed a sandwich. "Well, just in case, I'm taking Mason with me. Your friend Rezner lives across the street from the jobsite, which is handy because his dad's working with us, and his mother's offered to babysit."

Mason swung around. "Dad! I'm *not* a baby!"

He looked so indignant that everybody laughed. "Sorry, son. I mean kidsit. Here, bring your sandwich, and grab some cookies while you're at it. We have to go."

"Can I help build?" Mason said, rummaging in the cookie jar.

"Uh, maybe."

Mason sighed. "That means no."

"Trust me, you'll get to help when you're older. Why do you think I named you Mason? So you could follow your old dad in his footsteps and build stone houses!" Robbie winked at Travis as he headed out. "I'll tell you, this town will be bigger than Louis before we know it."

"Have a nice day!" Melinda called after him.

Robbie paused in the doorway and turned back, staring at his half-eaten sandwich as he chewed. "Did you butter this?"

Melinda rolled her eyes. "Of course I did."

He shrugged. "All right, well, I'm outta here. If you see that old man again, be careful. You're not shapeshifters right now. That means you're vulnerable."

"We know, Dad."

"Mmm. Come on, Mason."

Robbie and the boy left the house, and a silence fell.

"Speaking of shapeshifters," Travis said with his mouth full, "I wonder what Miss Simone has planned for us next weekend."

Melinda rolled her eyes. "I don't think I can wait that long. School is so boring and pointless after saving the world."

"Saving the world . . ." Travis laughed. "I don't think *you've* saved the world yet. You saved a town from gargoyles, and maybe we saved the naga from extinction, but that's not saving the world. Now, when I dealt with those walking, talking trees and scorpions—"

"Oh, not that again," she complained. "Are we going to keep comparing missions? We'll just have to make sure our next one is really, really serious—like world-in-jeopardy deadly serious. When Miss Simone asks us to go on our next mission on Saturday, let's tell her we don't want any silly little tasks like negotiating with centaurs over who owns which patch of forest, or persuading elves to leave hikers alone, or—"

"Or asking lycans to quit howling at the moon," Travis added.

They laughed. "Yeah, that's really getting old," Melinda said as she finished her sandwich. She grew serious. "I'm kind of worried about that, actually. There's a pack of them out there somewhere. I heard the goblins have stepped up their nighttime guard duty. They wouldn't attack, would they? The lycans, I mean, not the goblins."

Travis recalled what he'd learned from his dad about lycans. "They could if they wanted to. They're seven feet tall and pretty wild at this time of the month. It'll be a week or more before they're back to their human selves—so yeah, right now they're dangerous. And if there's a pack out in the nearby woods . . ."

Melinda sighed. "Well, that's why Lucas is in town. Have you met him?"

Travis shook his head. "I hear he's pretty grim."

Lucas had arrived in Carter over the weekend, called in as an emergency measure. His presence didn't sit well with most, but nor did the sound of howling overnight.

"Well, eat up," Melinda said, standing and taking her plate to the sink. "We don't want to keep him waiting."

Travis pushed his chair back. "Lucas? You want to meet him?"

"Not him, silly. The creepy old man in a black suit. Let's go see what he wants."

## Chapter 2
## The Creepy Old Man

The tiny library stood on the corner of a dusty street in the heart of Carter. An old lady had once lived there, but after she'd passed away, the place had stood empty for months until someone suggested turning it into a volunteer-run library.

Travis and Melinda peeked in the front door.

"This isn't the best place to meet," Travis murmured, glancing around at the array of freestanding bookshelves.

Melinda nodded. "Yeah, he should come outside."

They stood in the lobby and called for the old man, tentatively at first, then louder. A beak-nosed woman popped out from behind a bookshelf and huffed at them. "Why are you yelling? There's nobody here but me. Go away, you noisy children!"

They hustled back outside.

Melinda sighed. "Well, that was a waste of time. Now what?"

Travis didn't feel like wandering aimlessly searching for a creepy old man. "I guess I'll head home. I might see if Dad will take me to meet Lucas. You wanna come?"

She pursed her lips. "Well, if I'm going to meet him at all, I'd rather it was with you and your dad, so . . . yeah, sure."

But as they headed off, a hand snaked out from around the corner of the building and clamped onto Travis's shoulder. He let out a yelp and jerked away, spinning around and bumping into Melinda.

"Shh," the old man said, looking annoyed. "What is it with you kids always yelling? Be *quiet*."

"Well, don't jump out at me from dark alleyways, then!" Travis complained.

The old man raised a bushy white eyebrow, turned to study his surroundings, and said, "This is not an alleyway, nor is it dark. And I didn't jump out at you."

The man had been waiting in a small grassy square sandwiched between the library and the next house. A couple of wooden benches offered a place for readers to sit outside with their borrowed books.

Travis doubted the stranger had been sitting on a bench. He was too shady to do something so ordinary. He'd probably lurked in the shadowed area under the eaves, or perhaps knelt behind the trash cans by the library's side door.

"So what do you want?" Melinda asked.

The man drew himself up straight and tall, taking a long, deep breath through his nostrils. He placed his hands behind his back and glared down his nose at them. "I am Mr. Grimfoyle. I won't bore you with my history; just know that I am here to help you. To help us all, actually." He gazed over Travis's shoulder for a moment before refocusing. "Something is coming, children. Something terrible. I believe you may be the best person to stop it."

Travis swallowed. "Me?"

"Yes." Mr. Grimfoyle studied Melinda. "And you, young lady. You'll be a great help also, of that I am certain."

"But . . . who *are* you?" Melinda demanded. "You don't live in Carter, do you? Where did you come from?"

"Ah, well, that's a very long story." Mr. Grimfoyle rocked on his heels before answering. "I'll be honest. I met your father once, young lady, back when he was . . . well, about your age. Your mother, too. I met them both. They dragged me out of the water and saved me. And then—" He frowned. "Well, never mind. I'm not sure how amiably they would greet me today, knowing who and what I am, and where I came from, hence why I wanted to meet you privately. Now—"

"So my mom and dad know you?" she persisted.

"That is what I said, yes."

"What about Travis's parents?"

Mr. Grimfoyle shrugged. "I have not had the pleasure. Still, I'm sure they are wonderful people. Now, if I may, there are things I need to tell you. Let us sit down over here. You will need to be sitting, for what I'm about to tell you may come as rather a shock."

But before Travis and Melinda could decide whether or not they wanted to sit on a bench with a creepy old man in a black suit, three men ran past, panting hard and kicking up a lot of dust in their wake. They were followed by a couple of women and two more men, and yet more random people, all harried and scared.

Startled, Travis went to the corner to see where they were coming from. It quickly became apparent that didn't matter as much as where they were headed. "Town hall!" a woman shouted in answer to someone's question. "Urgent meeting. Something is happening."

"I heard there's a storm," a man's booming voice cut in. "Dangerous storm on the way. We might need to evacuate."

His words galvanized dozens more people into action, and everyone began jogging or running toward the town hall, which stood quite a few streets away.

Melinda's hand went to her mouth. "That must be what the messenger told Miss Simone about earlier. I guess it's more serious than we thought."

"How serious can a storm be?" Travis wondered aloud. "I mean, it could be a hurricane or a tornado, I guess. But—" He looked up at the sky. "It's about as clear as it can be."

"Let's go see what's happening," Melinda said, getting him started with a nudge.

"Ahem."

The old man still stood there with his hands behind his back.

"Later, Mr. Grimfoyle," Travis said. "Wait here, if you like. We'll be back—unless we have to evacuate, obviously."

The man took a step toward them. "You don't understand. This is exactly why I'm here. And you need to let me help you. It's vitally important."

Both Travis and Melinda faltered. More and more people dashed through the streets, eager to hear the news, and Travis feared the town hall would be way too crowded by the time he and Melinda got there. They'd probably be stuck somewhere at the back around a corner, barely able to hear the drone of a council member as he explained the problem. Or maybe it would be Miss Simone herself, in which case Travis wanted to be nearer the front just so he could see her.

Still, they lingered.

"Tell us quickly," Melinda said.

The old man shook his head. "There is no quick way to tell you. Besides, I need to perform a spell on you both. Forego the visit to the town hall and sit down with me now. I can tell you everything you need to know and more."

He'd taken on a hungry look, his eyes gleaming and his hands clenching and unclenching as though impatient . . . or perhaps in eagerness for what he might do next. Travis had a bad feeling about him. He'd had the bad feeling from the start, but now it was amplified. The man claimed to know all about the approaching storm, more than everyone else, which suggested . . . what? Travis wasn't sure, but he didn't like it.

"Let's go," he muttered, taking Melinda's hand.

She didn't argue and allowed herself to be turned around and led away.

Mr. Grimfoyle's face darkened. He strode toward them. "Do not walk away from me. There is no time. You must—" But then he stopped, perhaps because he'd seen how Travis and Melinda increased their speed in their haste to get away from him. He raised his hands and put on a smile instead. "Children, please. If you must go to the town hall, hurry back straight after. We have urgent business. I'll be right here waiting."

"Okay," Travis said over his shoulder as he and Melinda finally broke into a run.

The old man wasn't done. He raised his voice to be heard. "It's very important that you choose a new form, both of you, to ride out this storm. Something that flies, and something that swims! Do you hear me?"

His voice trailed into the distance, but Travis had heard him just fine. He shivered.

"Crazy," he said as he and Melinda dashed along the street and turned a corner. Ahead, people surged *en masse* between the houses, already far too crowded to get close to the town hall.

"We won't hear a thing," Melinda groaned. "We'll get tidbits passed back to us."

They joined the mob anyway, falling into a sheeplike formation and shambling along until they reached the town hall and came to a halt. Travis hopped up and down, annoyed that everyone in front of him was an adult. Like his dad, he lacked height. Melinda was perhaps an inch taller despite being a year younger, but she couldn't see either.

In the end, they gave up and just listened, staring at the backs of those in front.

A voice floated down the streets, faint and elderly: ". . . The village of Follen's Glen has gone. I repeat, *gone*—swallowed up in the storm. Numerous farmsteads, too. This storm is sweeping across the land, an unstoppable force, and it's headed our way."

"What do you mean *gone*?" someone yelled. "Destroyed? Washed away? What?"

A brief pause followed, and then, "I mean the *people* are gone. The buildings remain, but everyone has vanished."

Travis almost felt the ripple of consternation as it swept through the crowd. He glanced sideways at Melinda and saw her puzzled expression mixed with fear. Everyone had *vanished*?

"The storm is coming out of the northeast, headed this way—straight for us." The elderly councilman's voice seemed to have strengthened as the crowd grew more restless. "We don't

*14*

know what it is yet, but we are urging preparations for a full-scale evacuation."

"How long do we have?" a woman called out.

A hush fell as the councilman answered. "Our phoenix friend estimates the storm will be here in a few hours. I urge you to go home, pack what you need, and head for the mines. Find shelter underground until we know what this is."

A man right behind Travis shouted, "What about Old Earth? Can we use a portal?"

Another ripple of murmurs, this time agreement. "Yes, all portals will be opened up for general use, no restrictions. The portal police will be standing down during this emergency. Old Earth welcomes you if that is preferable to the mines."

*Preferable to the mines*, Travis thought. *Anything's preferable to the mines.*

But was it, really? Most of the people here loved New Earth and scorned the other world with its technology and fast-paced way of life. Travis suspected many, many people would sooner ride out the storm cooped up in a cold, dank mine than step across into Old Earth.

"We have to find Miss Simone," Melinda said, grabbing his arm. "I bet our parents are out right now, investigating. My mom, your dad—they're probably flying about as we speak!"

Travis nodded. "Yeah, we need to help. We need to be shapeshifters."

They turned around and pushed their way past people. The crowd thinned as they went, and the councilman's voice faded. Travis thought he heard Miss Simone's name mentioned, but by that time, they'd found a clear spot and started running.

The thing about everyone congregating outside the town hall was that the rest of the streets were unusually empty. It was almost like the evacuation had already happened.

Breathless, they made it all the way to Miss Simone's science laboratory on the edge of town without stopping to rest. Some of the resident shapeshifters had amassed there.

Travis's mom spotted him and came over. "Your dad's flying around assessing the storm from above." She glanced at Melinda. "Your mom, too."

"I hope they don't get blown away or sucked in!" Melinda said.

"It's not that kind of storm."

Travis saw worry in his mom's face as she absently fiddled with the red scrunchie holding her ponytail in place. "Have you heard from them?" he asked.

She nodded toward a man in the crowd. "That's Blair. He's flown halfway across the countryside already and seen what's happening. He says your dad and Lauren are fine, just flying around."

"*My* dad only just went back to work," Melinda said. "With Mason."

"I'm sure he'll have heard the news by now and will be along shortly."

Old family friends were present in the crowd. Miss Simone was currently talking to the shapeshifters known as Darcy and Dewey, one a dryad, the other a centaur. Nearby, Blacknail the goblin had brought along a few of his surly, stout colleagues. Though Blacknail was really a shapeshifter by the name of Riley, he had voluntarily remained a goblin from an early age. He just naturally loved to tinker, and that was what goblins did.

Travis spotted Canaan, the resident shapeshifter elf. She usually kept to herself or disappeared for weeks visiting elven clans, but today she was here.

He recognized Orson and Ellie, too, both human right now but frequently in their equine forms. Orson was a pegasus, Ellie a unicorn—a couple of pretty spectacular creatures.

And the fierce, wolfish man with a limp—was that Lucas? Travis peered at him, a shiver of fear running down his spine as he tried to imagine what a full-blown werewolf might look like . . .

Being a lycan shapeshifter, Lucas followed the slow-changing lycan cycle throughout the month, fully human for two weeks but increasingly angry and monstrous closer to the full moon. He was a true werewolf, the legendary kind, the sort of person who could shift from man to beast at any time—but who found the full moon's effect almost impossible to resist.

"We want to help," Travis said to his mom. "We can't just stand around and do nothing."

"I think that's wise," she agreed. "And I'd rather you had some ability to shift. We don't know what's coming."

"Let's see if we can interrupt Miss Simone," Melinda said. "Come on, Travis."

She took his elbow and guided him through the friendly, familiar crowd. All the shifters were discussing the storm, figuring out how they could help in some capacity while most of their winged friends were high in the sky.

"Travis!" Melinda snapped. "Wake up. You're awestruck—or dumbstruck, one of the two."

He shook his head and followed Melinda as she weaved her way through the crowd.

"Miss Simone," Melinda called, tugging on the scientist's cloak. "We want to help. Is there time to do the procedure?"

"Hello, sweetie," Darcy said before Miss Simone could answer. "Haven't seen you in a while. You should come visit us in the forest sometime."

Melinda couldn't help smiling. "I'd love that!"

Dewey was busy transforming behind her. In centaur form, he tugged on Darcy's sleeve. "Let's get going."

She climbed onto his back and gave a cheery wave as the centaur galloped away.

Miss Simone gave a nod and turned to face a man Travis had only met a few times. "Blair, you were saying Follen's Glen is empty?"

"The storm smothered it," the man said. "A bunch of farmsteads are gone, too. I saw it with my own eyes as the storm swept in—one second people were there, then they weren't."

Miss Simone pursed her lips and thought for a moment. She touched the man's elbow. "Go back and keep watching. But stay clear!"

Blair nodded and stepped into a clear space. Then, in the blink of an eye, he transformed—into a brightly colored phoenix standing the height of a man, with massive wings and startling golden feathers. Almost lazily, he beat his wings a couple of times, ducked low, then sprang off the ground and launched into the sky.

"Miss Simone?" Melinda said again.

The woman turned to her and Travis. "No time to rest, eh?" She steered Travis and Melinda away from the crowd and toward the lab building. "I can do the procedure; I just hope you can recover quickly. Now, any thoughts on what you'd like to be? I haven't had a moment to figure out what we really *need*. We're all still investigating at the moment."

Travis shot Melinda a glance. He knew she was thinking the same thing.

*Something that flies, and something that swims.*

## Chapter 3
### Transformations

Travis thought quickly. Something that flies . . .

There were plenty of options, but he had to subtract certain creatures like a dragon, wyvern, and a harpy, all of which he'd done before and couldn't do a second time thanks to his super-strong immune system. Melinda was the same way. They had forty-eight hours at most to enjoy their latest chosen forms before their antibodies restored normality. It was a "once and done" kind of deal.

Several of Miss Simone's friends were flying creatures—for instance Blair the phoenix, Orson the pegasus, and Charlie the griffin. No point repeating those. His own mom was a faerie—not that he'd ever choose to be such a girly thing.

"What are you thinking?" Melinda whispered as they followed Miss Simone along a corridor. "I have to say, I'm not sure I want to fly. I had enough of heights over the weekend. When you're hanging in the air hundreds of feet up with nothing supporting you . . ." She shuddered. "I want to be the water thing, if that's okay?"

Travis grinned. "Perfect. Anyway, I'm used to flying."

"So what are you going to be?" she persisted.

"Don't know yet. What about you?"

"Well, we don't know why Mr. Grimfoyle wants us to be something that flies and something that swims, so I don't know where I'll be swimming—in the sea, a lake, a river, or whatever. So I probably shouldn't choose something like a hippocampus, because they're too big."

"Maybe a mermaid, then," Travis said.

"Hmm."

She didn't seem convinced.

Miss Simone gestured for them both to enter a room to the left. "I'm going to work on the two of you at the same time. Let me wheel another gurney in."

As Travis and Melinda entered, Miss Simone yelled for some assistance. The sounds of scurrying footsteps in the corridor suggested there were plenty of willing helpers. After a few quick orders, Miss Simone came back in and got started brewing the weird hot tea she always sent her patients to sleep with.

"I trust you haven't eaten anything?" she asked.

Travis could still taste his sandwich in the back of his teeth. "Uh, no."

"Not *much*," Melinda added. "Just, you know . . . lunch."

This caused Miss Simone to put her hands on her hips and stare at them both. Just when it seemed like she might forbid the procedure on a silly technicality, she sighed and went back to her brewing, setting the burner as high as it would go so the short blue flames roared under the metal pot. "I suppose we'll have to risk it. If you feel sick afterward, try to make it to a bucket or something."

"Yes, ma'am," Melinda said, shooting Travis a relieved grin.

She perched on the side of the gurney while Travis waited for his to be wheeled in.

"So what's the deal with the storm?" he asked.

Miss Simone shrugged. "I honestly don't know yet. Several small settlements have been reported as . . . *empty*. Blair said there's a blue haze over everything."

"A blue haze?" Melinda gasped. "That's weird."

"Indeed." Miss Simone swished the small pot around on the burner. "This is taking too long. Do you care if it's cold?"

Neither of them did, so Miss Simone simply handed the pot to Melinda, who drank half the cold tea and gave the rest to Travis. It definitely tasted better warm, but he gulped it down and tried to refrain from grimacing.

The second gurney arrived, and Travis lay down. The tea worked quickly, and he started to feel drowsy.

"Oh!" he said, struggling up onto his elbows. "We need to tell you what we want to be. Can I be something that flies? And Melinda wants to be something that swims."

Miss Simone was already rummaging around in a cabinet full of tiny vials of dark liquid. Each was a creature's blood, and the label indicated from what it had been extracted. "Well, I was thinking more along the lines of something indestructible, like a gargoyle or a golem."

The room was beginning to rotate. "No," Travis said, finding it took a great effort to open his mouth and force a word out. "Must be . . . something that flies . . ."

"And something that swims," Melinda added sleepily.

Travis was aware of the curious stare Miss Simone gave him as she paused in her rummaging. But already he felt too tired to argue his point.

The scientist's voice drifted across the room like a muted echo. "Well, we don't have an awful lot to choose from . . . and I'm not sure how useful a swimming creature will be when it comes to investigating or dealing with this storm. I think the larger sea creatures are out of the question. Maybe . . . let's see . . ."

And that was that. Travis dozed off.

\* \* \*

*A gigantic wall of blue mist stretched across the horizon, rumbling and wailing its way over the landscape, swallowing everything in its path . . .*

Travis jolted awake to find Melinda still sound asleep beside him on her gurney. Miss Simone had left, probably ages ago.

He sat up. The dream had been vivid, but it wasn't surprising considering what the messenger boy and Blair the phoenix had reported to Miss Simone. Blue dust? A blue haze? The storm probably looked nothing like that.

His chest was a little sore. The procedure itself wasn't bad, just a couple of needles in the arm and a dose of magic. His dad had told him about it. Blood and DNA and all the medical stuff were essential, but none of it mattered without the *secret spell*.

"So what am I?" he wondered aloud.

He found a note in Miss Simone's handwriting: *Travis— when you wake, go straight home and take Melinda with you.*

Travis rubbed his chest, thinking he'd probably woken a little quicker than normal.

Melinda groaned and rolled onto her side. She blinked, pulled her hair out of her face, and focused on him. "Are we baked?"

"A little underdone, but good enough," Travis agreed. "I have no idea what she made us into, though." He showed her the note. "Why do we have to go straight home? Let's go find her."

They walked unsteadily from the room and into the corridor. A white-coated doctor dashed out of a room and nearly bumped into them. She gave them a smile as she hurried past. "Glad you're awake early! Less for us to deal with. Head on home, okay? Simone and your parents are there."

"Okay, but—" Travis started.

The doctor called to them over her shoulder. "No time to chat. Evacuation in progress, patients being mobilized and wheeled out, medicines to pack—go on, now, hurry home."

Travis and Melinda headed to the front entrance. A couple of goblins stood there, peering out through the glass, deep in a grumbling conversation. They glanced around with their usual grimaces and tiny black eyes. Outside, a couple more goblins marched past.

"How long were we asleep, do you think?" Melinda asked as they stepped out into the warm sunshine. "There's no sign of the storm yet."

"Well, the building and the trees are in the way. Let's find somewhere higher up."

A goblin called out to them from inside the building. "Hey! Simone told me to tell yer to head home."

"Thank you, we know," Melinda said politely.

"You're all evacuating to the mines," the goblin added.

Travis frowned. "Everyone's really going there?"

"You heard me."

"Yeah, you heard him," Melinda whispered with a giggle.

"Wait," Travis said. "When you say 'you're all evacuating' . . . You mean goblins as well, right?"

The goblin shook his head. "Naw, just humans. Turns out only humans are going missing."

Travis stared with his mouth open. Only humans . . . ?

Melinda tugged at his arm. "Come on."

The outskirts of the town were almost always calm and peaceful, but not *this* quiet. A few people hurried from one place to another, loaded down with baskets and sacks. If they were indeed evacuating to the mines or even to Old Earth, it made sense to take food and essentials with them.

Travis and Melinda left the perimeter and set off across the meadow. They saw probably a dozen other people way ahead, loaded down with supplies as they climbed the gentle hill. But another stream of townsfolk followed a dirt road along the bottom of the slopes, heading toward a pulsing black portal by the trees. It was dome-shaped, the perfect crossing point for authorized Old Earth vehicles. A yellow bus came through twice a week. Right now, it looked like a bunch of people were going the other way, heading into Old Earth until the storm was gone. The portal police that normally guarded the smoking mass were conspicuously absent.

Travis might have opted for the portal himself if the mines weren't so close to his house. Then again, all those people heading into Old Earth would have to find lodgings or camp out in fields. At least the mines provided shelter.

The meadow had never been so crowded. Travis's house stood just over the rise and across another field. The entrance to the old mines lay buried in the woods somewhere behind the house. It was strange seeing all these people. He walked this same route every day after school, and normally he was alone. Everything was different today. Ever since school had ended—

Sucking in a breath, he almost stopped dead as he gripped Melinda's arm. "Hey! We forgot Mr. Grimfoyle."

"*I* didn't," she said. "But first things first. Let's go find Miss Simone and everyone else, and find out what we *are*. I don't want to deal with Mr. Grimfoyle just yet."

"But what if we run out of time and the storm hits us?" Travis slowed to a crawl. "I don't know, Melinda. Maybe you should go on ahead, and I'll go find Mr. Grimfoyle. If I can fly, I can be back here in no time—".

She spun around, her expression fierce. "Not happening, Travis. We stick together. Let's just see what's what, then come back."

Travis caught movement to his left and was surprised to see a woman striding up the hill like a seasoned hiker. She gave a nod as she passed him. He mumbled a greeting, then glanced over his shoulder to see many dozens of people not too far behind—men, women, children, dogs, goats, a donkey, even a few cat baskets. Horses brought up the rear, pulling wagons and smaller carts. There were even a couple of people in wheelchairs, probably the patients the doctor had mentioned. And beyond them, yet more people marched into the open from the woods. It seemed the entire town was on its way to the mines.

"So what *are* we?" Melinda said, her eyes still on the brow of the hill ahead.

"Let's change and find out."

"How? It's hard enough when I know exactly what I'm supposed to be. I can imagine it, which helps me *become* whatever I am. But this time I have no idea what to think about, what to concentrate on."

"Yeah, I guess I'm the same way."

They both lapsed into silence, trying to initiate a change. Travis knew only that he had wings. At least he *hoped* he did. He concentrated on that, stretching his arms wide and willing them to alter, to grow feathers . . . or perhaps a leathery skin that stretched across long bones . . .

Thick, grey fur suddenly sprouted down both forearms. "Whoa!" he exclaimed. "Look!"

The transformation ended there. As he watched, the fur slowly withdrew as if shy and reclusive. He willed it to stay, to grow *more*—

"It's here!" a voice screamed.

They both jumped. The woman who had just passed them had reached the brow of the hill already. She was pointing down the other side.

Travis broke into a run and joined her, Melinda right behind. He could see his house at the foot of the slopes, on the edge of the sprawling forest that swept around from the south. The forest stretched for miles, all the way to the blue haze on the horizon . . .

He squinted. "Do you see it?" he whispered.

After a pause, Melinda said, "Yeah. I see it."

The woman turned and yelled down the hill. "Hurry! It's here! The storm is here!"

## Chapter 4
## Trouble on the Horizon

"What *is* that?" Travis whispered.

He and Melinda stood and watched the approaching storm in amazement. Carter had its fair share of storms in the summertime, some of them pretty violent and terrifying, with deafening lightning blasts that stood hair on end, and endless rumbling thunder as if a restless giant were stirring from a deep slumber. These storms normally came with almost-black clouds, twisting gusts of wind, and a deluge of rain.

What they saw on the horizon wasn't like that at all.

Travis had never seen a desert sandstorm, but he imagined it would be something like this—except sand was normally a pale tan color rather than an unearthly *blue*. The wall of dust stretched across the northeastern horizon, towering a few hundred feet high, approaching at what seemed like a snail's pace but in reality had to be pretty fast.

A desert sandstorm would have been terrifying enough, but this eerie bank of rolling dust filled Travis with dread. The unnatural color of it scared him the most.

And it was *exactly* as he'd pictured in his dream right before waking up in the lab.

"Why's it blue?" Melinda asked, her voice sounding strangely loud in the silence of the meadow.

"Something to do with the color of the sky," Travis guessed. "Like how the sea is blue when it's sunny but green when it's cloudy."

"It's cloudy now."

She was right. "Well, maybe the light refracting or . . . or bouncing off the atmosphere . . ."

Melinda tore her gaze from the approaching storm to glare at him with one eyebrow raised. "Seriously? You're actually trying to explain this?"

Travis huffed out a breath. "Well, *you* explain it, then."

"I can't."

They fell silent, aware of panting and murmurs behind them as men and women arrived at the top of the hill and voiced their concerns. They spread out in a long line so they could get a good view.

The storm—or whatever it was—was still many miles away, yet Travis could hear a low, distant rumble. Even that seemed unnatural. A sandstorm, blue or otherwise, was nothing but wind, yet the rumbling seemed to carry through the ground itself, a faint trembling that brought with it a queasy feeling in the pit of his stomach.

"We have to go!" a man shouted.

His voice broke through the mesmerized paralysis that had swept across the large group. People started surging forward down the hill, toward the storm, heading for the mines behind Travis's house. Most of the townsfolk had backpacks and baskets, and some pulled small four-wheeled handcarts. One man had piled his stuff into a wheelbarrow, and he weaved dangerously through the crowd.

Horses whinnied as their riders urged them to hurry. They trotted around the far edges of the crowd, the carts bumping and jiggling. Droves of men, women, and children picked up their pace, dragging their pets with them.

This wasn't all of Carter. Back the way Travis and Melinda had come, a stream of townsfolk walked directly into the pulsing portal at the foot of the slopes near the woods. They were all gone seconds later. Travis guessed many others were staying home, perhaps hunkering down in storm shelters. But the majority rushed toward the woods behind his house.

"We'd better hurry," Melinda said.

They scurried down the slope of the field, veering off from the group a little. Travis's house stood alone in a stand of trees just outside the forest, and he knew a shortcut to the mines directly from his back door. But everyone else headed for a narrow lane a short distance away.

Travis saw figures standing outside his house. Miss Simone was there, and so was his mom, and a few others. He could see goblins, too, scurrying to intercept the evacuees and guide them to safety.

Panting from the hasty trek home, Travis wished he had a moment to stop and concentrate, to *transform*. The first time was always a little awkward, and really hard to do while running across a field to escape impending doom.

Anyway, he couldn't fly off and leave Melinda.

They made it at last. The storm had dropped out of sight by now, which was somehow worse. Not seeing how close it was scared him. With all these trees, nobody would know it had arrived until it loomed directly overhead.

"Mom!" he yelled. "Where's Dad?"

"Not back yet," his mom shouted back. She sprouted her faerie wings and came buzzing to meet him. "Where's *your* dad, Melinda?"

She stopped dead. "What? He's not *here*?"

Travis's mom dropped lightly to the ground before them and stilled her wings. "I'm sure he'll be here soon. You know how involved he gets with his work."

Melinda looked up at the trees with her eyes wide. "He'd better hurry! He has a long walk—and Mason isn't as fast."

"Your dad can take great strides when he's a thirty-foot ogre. Mason can sit on his shoulder. They'll be fine."

But Travis knew his mom well enough to see the anxiety etched into her face. He was worried, too, not only for Melinda's dad and little brother but also for his best friend Rez, and *his* parents . . .

He took a moment to glance around. Miss Simone, Blair, Canaan, and Lucas. An odd bunch. "Where's everyone else? Darcy and Dewey and Orson and—"

"Busy," his mom said, distracted as she gazed across the meadow. She sighed. "Okay, despite what I just said, I'm going to have to go and find Robbie and Mason. Wait here."

"Mom—"

But she was already zipping off across the field.

Melinda shook her head. "I can't believe they're not here already. Mom would be mad at him if she knew." She clicked her tongue. "But she's not here either."

Her voice wavered. Travis reached for her and gave her a nudge on the arm. "Your dad and Mason will be fine. The storm's way off yet. Let's go ask Miss Simone what she made us into."

His diversion tactic worked. She nodded, and they went to interrupt her conversation.

"Miss Simone?" Travis called as they approached.

Miss Simone, Blair, Canaan, and Lucas turned to them, and suddenly he lost his voice. Just for a change, it wasn't Miss Simone's enchanting gaze that caused his throat to seize up, nor Canaan's ethereal pale-blue elfin skin and long white hair.

What got him tongue-tied was the ferocious glare from the huge wolfman named Lucas.

The shabbily dressed lycan—currently presenting in an advanced wolf state—could tear him to shreds in a heartbeat if he wanted to. He was tall and muscular, easily six-and-a-half feet, and his fingers were long with deadly claws. His unkempt dark hair, unshaven face, and thick eyebrows somehow went with his natural wolfish stoop. As he turned, one of his hands absently clasped his thigh. Travis remembered something about an old injury, though the details eluded him.

"So you're Hal's boy," Lucas growled in a startling deep voice. "You resemble him."

"Uh, thanks," Travis croaked.

After a brief pause, Canaan reached out and tugged on one of the wolfman's earlobes, causing him to frown. "Lucas here pretends to be scarier than he is," she said to Travis in a soft, melodic voice. "He's really just a big teddy bear."

Lucas growled.

Blair gave a short laugh. "Yeah, a teddy bear with sharp claws that could rip your throat out."

Miss Simone cut in. "Well, I think you all know one another. We should probably—"

"And you're Robbie's girl?" Lucas said gruffly. "Pretty little thing. You got your mother's looks."

Melinda smiled. "It's nice to meet you."

Travis pulled himself together. "Miss Simone, what kind of shapeshifters are we, exactly?"

She frowned, clearly puzzled. "Oh—sorry, yes, I should have said in my note."

Lucas barked a laugh and shook his head. "So Simone turned you into shapeshifters and didn't bother telling you what you were?"

"They were asleep before I had a chance to decide," Miss Simone retorted. "Why don't you all make yourselves useful? Canaan, help the people find their way into the mines. We'll have to let the horses and goats run loose outside. Lucas, that pack of lycans in the woods around here needs to be warned. Blair, please go back to the storm."

"Again?" he said. "Do you know how many times I've—"

"You have wings. I need you flying back and forth, reporting on things. Please do your job."

"Yes, ma'am," Blair said meekly. But he made no effort to move, instead glancing from Travis to Melinda. "So you really don't know what you are? I can't imagine how that must be. I have to admit, though, that the idea of being something different each weekend . . . Man, that has to keep things interesting."

"Blair."

He bowed. "Sorry. I'm off."

Once again, he transformed into the spectacular phoenix and proudly spread his wings, turning in a slow circle while giving them all a sharp-eyed glare. Then he launched in a flurry of feathers, leaving one or two to flutter down to the grass.

"Show off," Canaan muttered.

Lucas pointed at the feathers. "Those are worth a fortune."

"Miss Simone," Melinda said rather impatiently. She spread her hands. "Please?"

"Of course, of course."

Despite being told to get to work, Lucas and Canaan hung around to watch as Miss Simone approached Melinda and reached out to lift her chin. "You wanted to be something that could swim. The kelpie and hippocampus aren't human enough, which would make communication frustrating. The naiad is too timid; you'd probably flee rather than help. And my naga sample fell into the sink and leaked out weeks ago. In the end . . ." She looked almost sheepish. "I hope you don't mind, but I gave you some mermaid blood."

Melinda's eyes widened. "Some of yours?"

"Not mine specifically. I'm a shapeshifter, remember. No, you have true mermaid's blood. You'll be very fast and agile in the water, but you'll be human enough to talk to us should the need arise." She glanced over her shoulder as if checking on the progress of the storm—not that anyone could see it over the trees. "There's a river not too far from here. It flows roughly northeast, straight under the mines and toward the storm. I'd like you to take a swim and get close—but *be careful*. Your job is to report back, do you hear?"

Melinda nodded, apparently awestruck. She'd seemed uncertain about being a mermaid before, but now she had a beam of delight and wonder.

"Aw, look at that," Canaan said with a smile. "We have another mermaid on our team."

"Maybe this one will actually *be* a mermaid for more than five minutes," Lucas growled. He winked at Melinda. "Simone bosses us all about and tells us to use our talents, but she never mingles with her kind."

"Lucas," Miss Simone said in a low voice. "Please go find those lycans and warn them away from the area."

Travis could barely contain himself. "And what about me? What am I?"

She glanced over her shoulder again, distracted by the stream of townsfolk hurrying past. A couple of horses with wagons trotted along at the tail end. That, it seemed, was all of them for now.

"I made you into a mothman," she said absently. "You met one recently, didn't you?"

*A mothman!*

Travis remembered all too well. Just a few weeks ago, he'd discovered and rescued all those prisoners in cages at Mr. Braxton's estate. The mothman had fascinated him.

He stood there digesting the news, thinking about all the things he'd read or learned directly. Mothmen could prophesize. That surely explained his brief dream! He'd seen the storm in his mind before it had arrived. Also, mothmen could fly. That was vital, at least according to Mr. Grimfoyle.

*Mr. Grimfoyle!*

He snapped out of his reverie. While Lucas and Canaan drifted away, and Miss Simone marched over to talk to the stragglers at the back of the evacuee procession, Travis turned to Melinda and fixed her with a stare.

"Okay, so we know what we are. I guess you need to follow that river. I can fly, so . . ."

"You're going to find Mr. Grimfoyle."

She said it like it was a fact—which it was.

"Hurry back," she said. "I don't know how long we have, but that storm's moving pretty fast."

"I know. You hurry, too." He narrowed his eyes. "And steer clear, okay?"

She nodded, her eyes bright and her jaw set. "See you soon."

## Chapter 5
## Something that Flies

As Melinda hurried off in one direction to find the river, Travis turned back toward Carter. His mom had gone hunting for Uncle Robbie, and his dad was off somewhere with Lauren, flying over the storm. Miss Simone and the other shifters had duties to attend to, and hordes of townsfolk had already disappeared into the woods to find the mines.

Travis figured nobody would miss him if he went on a quick flight into town to find Mr. Grimfoyle.

He hurried to the top of the hill so he could get a good view of the storm. The sight of it on the horizon caused his stomach to lurch. He couldn't tell how far it had come in the last ten minutes, but it had definitely advanced. The sheer breadth of it astonished him, stretching as far as he could see. He thought it had a curve to it, closer in the center than at its far edges . . . but he couldn't be sure.

He forgot what he was supposed to be doing as he stood there taking it in. He suddenly felt very alone and vulnerable perched atop the hill.

Melinda had quite a swim ahead of her. He judged the storm to be fifteen or twenty minutes out. Maybe more. It was hard to tell. She'd have to swim fast, meet the storm head-on, take a good look, and return immediately—and hurry to the safety of the mines.

He shook himself. *He* had to hustle, too!

Focusing on his outspread arms, he forced the transformation to kick in. After a brief pause, grey fur sprouted on his arms again—and this time it spread fast, thick and dark on his hands and forearms but paler across his shoulders and chest beneath his smart shirt. The material rippled like fluid. He imagined his magical clothes were assessing the situation, trying to figure out what he was turning into so they could adapt accordingly.

Being a mothman, he knew his arms wouldn't turn into wings. His arms were simply arms. The wings were extra, growing out of his shoulder blades.

The change picked up speed. The first time always took longer. He grew in height but remained standing on two legs. His pants stayed intact, but his shirt finally decided to split apart and reform around his neck, simply hanging down his back so that his wings could grow unimpeded.

*I have a cape!* he thought with excitement. *How cool is that?*

He felt a crawling sensation all over his body as fur continued erupting. He had a pale-grey pelt, darker on his wings and arms. His fingers were almost black. When he touched his nose, he felt something unfamiliar there. He remembered the mothman he'd met weeks ago had been rather ugly, a kind of insect-creature—hence the name *mothman*.

With the transformation complete, he let out a shudder. Somehow, this particular species gave him the creeps.

His wings were much longer than his arms. When he gave them a gentle flap, he felt ready to lift off the ground. Amazed, he gave them a couple more lazy beats, and he rose easily. Continuing to flap while letting his legs and arms hang limp, he floated upward and made a few turns.

Flying was *easy*.

He marveled at the experience, picking up speed as he headed toward Carter. He'd been a dragon before, and a wyvern, and a harpy, but flight for those creatures had required physical exertion. As a mothman, a couple of gentle flaps was all it took to stay airborne. There had to be a healthy dose of magic involved here.

As he circled high over Carter and glanced back, he gasped at the sight on the northeastern horizon. His elevated altitude offered him a staggering view of the blue storm. The sheer scale of it was mind-boggling. As he'd thought, the wall wasn't perfectly straight after all; it was merely the outer edge of a gigantic circular mass that faded into a haze beyond. And from what he could tell, the storm wasn't simply moving southwest toward them. It was *growing*, expanding outward from a distant centerpoint somewhere over the horizon.

*Quit hanging about and get to work,* he told himself.

He turned his back on the storm and dropped toward the center of the town, aiming for the library. He saw nobody in the streets at first, but then spotted an old woman boarding up her windows. A couple strolled by, hand in hand, apparently content to face whatever was coming.

Travis noticed a few more people on his way down, but the rooftops cut off his view as he landed lightly on the dusty road outside the library.

The white-haired old man had said he'd be waiting, but it was still a surprise to see him sitting stiffly on the bench seat, his eyes closed.

"Mr. Grimfoyle?"

In mothman form, his voice sounded like he spoke through a tube, with a distant, nasal quality to it.

The man didn't move. He didn't even appear to be breathing.

"Uh . . . are you okay?" Travis gave the man a gentle prod.

Mr. Grimfoyle woke suddenly. "What?"

Travis jumped back in alarm. "I thought for a second— Never mind. I can't believe you're still here. Aren't you worried about the storm?"

"I walked a long way to find you, boy. I deserved a nap. Besides, the storm won't harm me." The white-haired man looked him up and down. "I'm glad you followed my advice. And I assume the girl is something that swims?"

"A mermaid," Travis agreed.

Mr. Grimfoyle nodded. "How long do we have?"

Travis shrugged. "Maybe fifteen minutes? It's hard to tell."

"And where did everybody go in the end?"

"Some went through the portal to Old Earth. Most are in the mines."

The old man shook his head. "The mines won't help them. Old Earth would have been a better choice." He climbed to his feet. "Where's the girl? We need to stay together."

"Well, she's probably underwater by now, swimming along a river toward the storm, going to check it out."

Mr. Grimfoyle glared at him. "What the dickens for?" He rolled his eyes skyward. "Never mind. Take me with you. We must find her at once."

"But you said you'd explain—"

"I'll explain when we're all together. We must *go*."

Before Travis could figure out how he was supposed to carry Mr. Grimfoyle, the old man simply raised one hand high into the air and waited. It took a moment to figure out what he was doing. Then Travis got it.

"You want me to . . . just grab your hand and carry you like that?"

"You would rather we embraced? Or should I ride piggyback?"

Travis felt his furry face heating up. He beat his wings a couple of times and rose off the ground. He still wasn't sure he could carry so much weight, but he reached for Mr. Grimfoyle's hand anyway, grasping him tight around the wrist.

To Travis's surprise, the old man's weight made absolutely no difference at all. *Definitely a good dose of magic*, he decided as he soared higher and higher.

Mr. Grimfoyle let out a sigh from where he hung limp. "My goodness, this is quite spectacular. Yes, the storm will be here shortly. We must hurry, boy."

"My name's Travis."

He put on some speed. He had only one plan—to find the river and follow it in the hopes of spotting Melinda swimming along. But she'd be in mermaid form, probably underwater. He had his doubts about locating her.

Then again, her job was to get a good look at the storm, which meant he was bound to find her right up next to it. Spurred on by his simple logic, he accelerated some more, at first zipping high over the treetops, then zigzagging in great, sweeping arcs over the open ground until he found a glint of light. *There!* A meandering ribbon with a mirrorlike surface.

Keeping it in his sight, he flew toward the storm, his nerves jangling. *What am I doing?* But he had nothing to fear as long as steered clear. Maybe he'd find his dad and Aunt Lauren circling around, along with Orson and Blair.

He saw a speck in the sky—a phoenix! Or maybe a harpy? No, definitely a phoenix. It swooped and soared above the storm, staying clear of the smoky mass. Travis did a double take. The closer he got, the more obvious it became that the storm wasn't a vicious maelstrom of sand as he'd thought; it was simply a mass of fog, a gigantic cloud that seemed to have fallen from the sky.

And turned blue?

Besides the unusual color, the storm was accompanied by a deep, rumbling roar and an eerie wailing.

Travis suddenly spotted a familiar figure approaching from the west. "Dad!"

But the dragon couldn't hear him. Travis hung back and studied the stormcloud from a safe distance. He'd imagined a sandstorm tearing through clothing and flesh, hammering against glass, battering walls . . . but this was no more than a dense fog whipped up by a ferocious wind. Still, even a tornado picked up dust and debris from the ground, whereas this storm did not. And from what he could tell as he flew a little closer, the blue mist swirled around without moving a single blade of grass.

Travis dropped lightly to the ground, carefully depositing Mr. Grimfoyle as he did so. The old man flexed his wrist, then absently smoothed his black suit while staring up at the towering wall of mist.

Someone lived out here. An old farmhouse stood close by, with a small enclosure for a dozen goats. They bleated and ran about in panic as the rumbling, wailing storm approached. Travis watched with fascination as the mist swallowed the fence posts one by one . . .

Then, seconds before the farmhouse was engulfed, he spotted a figure in a window—a man leaning out to stare at the enormous wall of murk that loomed overhead.

"Watch out!" Travis yelled.

The man didn't hear. As the mist rolled over the roof and smothered the nearest windows, Travis thought he saw the man vanish into thin air—but he might have imagined it.

The front door opened, and a boy ran outside. He froze, gawked, and bolted straight back in again.

An instant later, the entire house was gone, completely swallowed up.

Travis backed away, shaken.

He half expected the storm to tear the roof off the house and rip up the yard, but that didn't happen. People were missing, but they hadn't been swept away or sucked into the atmosphere. "I don't get it," he shouted over the noise. "It's not like a tornado or anything. It's not even stirring those trees!"

He pointed to the cluster of oaks in the field. As the storm swept over them, the blue mist did absolutely nothing to move a single leaf. Travis figured he could stand perfectly still with his eyes shut and not have a clue when the storm surrounded him.

Not that he was about to test his theory.

Mr. Grimfoyle said nothing for a while. The fence posts continued to vanish, one by one, until there were just a few left—and after that, the storm would be no more than a barn's length away.

"We must go," the old man said. "Take me somewhere far from here, then find that girl!"

"But . . . those people!" he said. "And those goats!" He watched them huddle together against the nearest fence. One hopped up onto the backs of the others and promptly escaped the pen with a triumphant bleat. The rest seemed too frightened to think clearly.

"We must leave *now*," Mr. Grimfoyle roared.

Travis rose off the ground and grabbed the man's wrist again. He watched as the storm rolled over the goats—but he saw nothing catastrophic happen. Unlike the farmer and his son, the goats seemed unaffected. He even heard their bleating above the rumble and wail of the storm. They were still alive and well in there . . .

He carried Mr. Grimfoyle well away from the storm and put him down. "I'll be back," he said, rising into the air. "Stay here."

The old man stood with his hands on his hips. "Be careful."

Travis got back on task, headed once more toward the mist, and located the river. Melinda had to be down there somewhere—or would be soon.

He just had to keep an eye open for her.

## Chapter 6
### Something that Swims

Melinda found the river easily thanks to some astute directions from one of the tail-end townsfolk. "Through the trees over yonder," the gnarly-faced, middle-aged woman said, "and keep walking."

She hadn't been wrong. Melinda entered the woods, weaved between trees, and didn't stop until she blundered through some bushes and almost fell into a fast-moving river. It was deep and narrow, flowing toward the town. Streams and rivers like these were the reason the town had been built in a bowl-shaped depression in the countryside—plenty of fresh water.

But it meant she'd have to swim upstream if she wanted to investigate the approaching storm.

She stood on the bank and watched the clear water bubbling past. Was it a river or a stream? She remembered something her mom had said a long time ago: "You can step over a brook, jump over a creek, wade across a stream, and swim across a river." She wasn't sure she could safely jump across this one, and it seemed far too deep to wade, so . . . a river?

*Get it together, girl.*

If she transformed into a mermaid, she'd have no legs to stand on. She'd end up toppling over, maybe even damaging her fishtail. So she sat down on the grass and dangled her feet over the rushing water.

*Change.*

It didn't happen immediately, but she was pleased to see scales popping up on the backs of her hands less than a minute later. And the scales sparked the rest of the transformation. She leaned back with a gasp. It felt like someone had looped a noose around her ankles and was slowly tightening it, drawing her feet together. Just for a moment, she felt trapped.

She'd worn a single knee-length dress today. The silky material was light and breezy in the summertime. It turned out to be quite convenient. If she'd worn pants, the magical material would have adapted just fine, but it was even simpler with a dress.

She watched, fascinated, as her legs fused together. She could see below her knees where the skin *stretched*, the flesh of each leg reaching for the other until they met in the middle. Then the flesh liquified and reformed, and two legs quickly became one thick appendage. Her knees sank out of sight, the joint between her upper and lower legs losing its definition. Her contours softened, and she shakily pulled the dress up to her thighs, amazed at the new fishtail that had developed.

The best part, though, was her feet flattening out and lengthening. They stayed the same color but stretched so thin that she could almost see through the flesh. Her smart shoes rippled and warped, trying to figure out how to adapt. They ended up thinning and melding with her scaly skin. And when her feet had finished changing and were beyond recognition, they unfurled and expanded, spreading sideways into the most spectacular fins full of vibrant blues and greens.

Enthralled, she sat there and watched the rest of the transformation. She felt the shapeshifter magic was showing off, giving her something to savor this first time. Though her skin remained the same color, her scales hardened and took on a vaguely green sheen.

The sleeves of her dress stopped just above her elbows. Her forearms looked no different. Her hands were the same. Her skin was the same. She plucked at her dark hair, noting how it seemed thicker and maybe longer.

"I'm a mermaid," she said out loud. Her voice hadn't changed.

With a sigh of happiness, she half rolled into the water, wishing she didn't have a mission to deal with. The river was cool and refreshing. Lying flat on her belly, she could stretch out in the water with the flow bubbling around her chin.

She kicked off, heading upriver. To her delight, she shot forward far quicker than she ever could have expected. A few quick flips of her tail was all it took to get some speed up, and she spent the next few minutes sluicing along with almost no effort.

The river quickly widened. She darted from side to side, turning over onto her back, then continuing the roll onto her belly again. Swimming was so easy in this form. Her human upper half had nothing to do; her fishtail did every bit of the work. But that didn't stop her pushing her hands out in front as though steering around the bends.

The trees ended abruptly, and the river widened even more. It wasn't as deep as before, but the banks were too high to see over. She imagined fields stretching out on both sides.

Melinda held her breath and ducked under. As far as she knew, mermaids couldn't actually breathe underwater. They enjoyed hanging around at the water's edge, sliding out onto the banks and basking in the sun awhile, then dipping back under . . .

She couldn't remember whether this was something she'd learned from Miss Simone or was just some kind of gut feeling.

The river had a sandy bottom and plenty of reeds swaying in the current. There were rocks, too, great piles of them, and all kinds of fish darting in and out. She swam on, wondering how long she could hold her breath, counting the seconds in her head. *Thirty . . . sixty . . . ninety . . .*

Amazed, she counted slowly and methodically, not feeling the slightest bit of discomfort in her lungs.

*Two minutes . . . two and a half . . . three . . .*

At around four minutes, she began to think mermaids didn't even *need* to breathe. And when she reached five minutes, she completely understood why legends spoke of mermaids as being primarily underwater creatures.

*Seven minutes . . . eight . . .*

She shook her head in sheer wonder and delight. She was human from the waist up, yet clearly something very magical was going on within her body.

The river suddenly grew dark.

Slowing, she remained deep down, a good four or five feet below the surface. Was she back in a forest? It seemed the sun had been blotted out. The rippling water made it difficult to see what was up there, but suddenly she felt afraid. She could hear—or perhaps sense—a deep, continuous rumbling noise.

*I'm under the storm*, she thought with a jolt of fear.

She remained still, staring upward. The river's strong current warped her view of the outside world. But at least she was out of harm's way. It might not be quite so safe above the surface.

Miss Simone had said to get a look at the storm but don't go near. Travis had said the same. Well, she was about as close as she could be, but the water protected her. What would happen if she reached up and broke the surface, stuck her hand into the raging wind above?

She resisted the urge.

Her chest tightened. Alarmed, she clutched at it. Was her breath about to run out? Now, of all the times? She spun about and headed back downstream, driven by panic. As soon as sunlight lit up the river again, she broke the surface and gasped for air—amid the sudden, deafening roar of the approaching storm.

She frowned. After treading water for ages, sucking in lungfuls of fresh air, now her panic seemed like a false alarm. She took in a single breath and felt fine. "Huh," she muttered.

Aware of the deep rumbling and terrible wailing, she turned to face the storm. She'd surfaced just ahead of it, but it was fast catching up. This was a perfect moment to study the blue, swirling monstrosity.

"Huh," she said again.

Not sand, then. Just some kind of mist. *Blue* mist. It was thick and whipping about like a hundred clashing tornadoes, yet she felt no wind, not even the slightest breeze despite how close it was. Another twenty feet and it would be upon her. She prepared to duck under . . .

A movement in the sky distracted her, and she glanced up. She saw the most hideous creature, a pale-grey winged thing with a ghastly insect face. It took only an instant for the image to sear itself onto her brain—and then she dipped her head under and sank low just as the mist rolled overhead.

*That was Travis*, she thought. *That had to be a mothman. Ugh!*

Melinda thanked her lucky stars she'd chosen to be "something that swims." She suspected a mothwoman would be even creepier.

*So, now what? Head back downstream some more and keep popping my head up to watch the storm?*

She wasn't exactly sure what other information could be gleaned, but this was her mission after all, so she surfaced again ahead of the storm, daring to face it until the very last second, curious to see if she could *feel* the mist in any way. Even up close, not a single breeze. It felt neither cold nor warm, nor even damp. It had no smell. Yet the thing wailed like a banshee and rumbled like the tremors of an earthquake.

On her third study, she made sure to watch the bushes lining the riverbanks. Perhaps they'd sway and blow about the moment the storm rolled over . . . but no, not a single leaf stirred. In fact, the opposite occurred. When a real breeze moved some long weeds, Melinda kept her eye on them—and sure enough, they became still when engulfed in blue mist.

It seemed the storm sucked the life out of the air.

Armed with that alarming theory, she ducked under again and headed a little farther downstream. What if that was exactly what the storm did? What if it sucked the life out of the air? Details about the aftermath were sketchy. The messenger boy, and then the councilman, had suggested nobody was left after the storm had passed by, that people had *vanished*.

Shuddering, she rose to the surface one more time and faced the storm.

Movement in the air caught her attention again. There was Travis, swooping in from above, getting dangerously close to the moving wall of mist. She refocused, trying to find something useful to report back to Miss Simone.

Just how big was this thing? Travis would know; he'd probably flown high above already.

What if she swam underneath again? Like, *all the way* under?

It was an interesting idea—except that her breath might run out too early.

Shaking her head, Melinda knew swimming beneath it would be stupid. The water would protect her, but the mist would brush against the surface of the flowing water, and there would be no way to stick her face out and suck in lungfuls of air.

*My mission is over*, she decided.

Anyway, the storm would be hitting the town soon. Best to head back.

"Melinda!" Travis yelled over the wailing wind.

She glanced up. That awful mothman face of his gave her the creeps even from a distance. She cupped her hands and shouted, "What's up?"

Travis descended on her, face down and wings spread wide, reaching out with one hand. His eyes glowed red, adding to his creepiness. "Grab hold!"

She wanted to tell him no way, to leave her alone. She wanted to swim back on her own and enjoy her mermaid form a little longer. Who knew when she'd get the chance again with this storm swallowing everything in its path? But Travis swooped in so quickly that she had no time to complain.

So she reached up, and he slowed enough to grasp her wrist with a ghastly black-furred hand before yanking her out of the river.

Screeching, Melinda hung helplessly as Travis rose into the air and circled over the treetops with the storm raging behind them.

"Travis, what are you *doing*?"

"Need you!" he yelled back. "No time to wait. And I need to pick up Mr. Grimfoyle again."

Mr. Grimfoyle! For a moment, Melinda forgot to be annoyed and allowed Travis to carry her over the fields away from the storm.

"I saw you in the water," Travis explained, his voice much clearer now they had distanced themselves from the wailing and rumbling. "I put Mr. Grimfoyle down and came back for you."

"You couldn't have carried us both anyway," Melinda retorted, her annoyance returning. She glanced down. How long would her fishtail remain now that she was out of the water?

"You wanna bet?" he said. "Flying has never been this easy. You're as light as a feather."

She realized his grip was oddly gentle considering he was supporting her entire weight. And it didn't hurt or strain her shoulder in any way. She felt like she might be only half her normal weight, perhaps less.

It was hard to see Travis's face from where she hung one-handed. Probably a good thing, too.

Soon after, he descended toward the grassy fields where a black-suited figure waited. He put her down near Mr. Grimfoyle, and she slumped sideways, unable to support herself on her fishtail. Squirming to sit up, she adjusted her dress a little. At least the magical material was practically dry already and smothering her with a gentle warmth.

She touched her hair. That was dry, too. *I can do one of Miss Simone's mermaid tricks!*

Despite the noise of the ever-approaching storm, a strange silence had fallen over the field. When Melinda looked up, she couldn't help recoiling at the sight of the mothman's furry face and bulbous, glowing red eyes. He had weird little nubs on his forehead as though feelers or antennae might sprout at any moment. His hair was gone, his entire face and head covered instead with a fine, grey, fuzzy coating. His mouth hung open, revealing tiny pointed teeth.

"Gross," she couldn't help exclaiming before she could stop herself. "I mean—Wow, you're just—"

She cast a glance up and down his creepy body. He had on his smart pants, but his shirt had become a *cape*, of all things. Though not normally thin, right now his narrow chest, bony shoulders, and skeletal arms had the same grey fur as his face, with patches of longer, thicker, darker fur down his arms to his black fingers.

Travis said nothing. He just stared at her.

"I'm sorry," she said. "I didn't mean to— You're not *gross*, just . . ."

But no matter how hard she tried, she couldn't bring herself to fib. There were no two ways about it—he was hideous.

Melinda frowned. "What's wrong? Why aren't you saying anything?"

Travis swallowed and forced his mouth to start working. "Sorry. It's just . . . well, you're . . ."

Suddenly self-conscious, Melinda checked that her dress was still intact. It was. She fingered her thick hair and glared at him. "What?"

Mr. Grimfoyle let out a short laugh. "My dear, you're a mermaid. Your enchantment spell is active. The boy is infatuated with you."

## Chapter 7
## On the Fringe

"We should get to the mines," Melinda said, her cheeks flushing.

Travis couldn't tear his gaze away. She was the same eleven-year-old girl he'd known all his life, but somehow she was . . . different. He couldn't figure out exactly what had changed. Maybe her hair was thicker, but so what? Her eyes might be a tad larger and brighter, but big deal. Something about her face fascinated him. Her lips? Her cheeks? Chin? What?

"Travis!" she snapped.

"Huh?"

"Quit staring. You're weirding me out."

"Right."

He finally tore his gaze from her . . . but it drifted back a second later. Melinda was cute when she got angry like that. She had a fire in her eyes, and her nose wrinkled. A locket of hair fell across her face, and she absently pushed it aside, tucking it behind her ear . . .

"Travis!" she yelled.

He sucked in a breath and blinked. "Sorry. What?"

Mr. Grimfoyle chuckled. "My dear, the storm is approaching. In order to make haste, I suggest you revert to your human form."

"So I can walk, right," Melinda agreed.

"Yes—and so this boy here might return to his senses."

She tossed her head, threw her hair back, then frowned and concentrated. Her tail began to morph into human legs, and somehow she lost something. Whatever magical glow she possessed faded, her hair seemed to lose its luster, and the sparkle in her eyes dimmed. Suddenly she was Melinda again, plain and ordinary.

She stood and faced Travis with a grimace. "Is that better? Can you function now?"

He nodded. "I, uh . . . You just looked . . . It was like . . ."

"Whatever. Can we go?"

Travis gently beat his wings and lifted off the ground. He reached with both hands, and though Mr. Grimfoyle grasped his wrist without question, Melinda raised an eyebrow.

"Are you sure?" she said with obvious doubt.

Travis nodded. "I can carry you both."

To prove his point, he ascended with ease the moment she offered her hand for him to grab hold of. Carrying two people made no difference to his flight at all. He dangled them below as he leaned forward and headed home.

"What is it you need to tell us, Mr. Grimfoyle?" he called down to the black-suited man as the meadows rushed by.

Mr. Grimfoyle clicked his tongue. "This is hardly an ideal time to explain, young man, but I'll do my best. You see, I've lived a very long time, and so has the faun. Or rather, the faun *appears* to have lived a very long time, but in actual fact she's—"

"Wait, *what* faun?"

"A faun. She goes by the name of River. She's at the heart of this menace we face, and very few people will survive. I'm indestructible, of course, and some shapeshifters have the advantage of flight—but every human is vulnerable, shapeshifter or not. You two are as well, but I can help with that. And then, together, we will put an end to this foul plot."

Travis felt like his brain was about to explode. "Whoa, slow down. A faun is responsible?"

"Every human is vulnerable?" Melinda cut in.

"Including shapeshifters?" Travis added.

"What do you mean you're indestructible?"

"How can *we* put an end to this?"

"Yes, why us?"

Mr. Grimfoyle sighed. "I believe we've arrived already."

Travis's house loomed ahead. Standing outside, a group of familiar faces waited—his mom, Miss Simone . . . and Robbie with Mason pressed against his side. He delivered the old man and Melinda safely to the ground and landed lightly between them, folding his wings in one smooth action.

"You found them!" Melinda exclaimed, rushing over to her dad and little brother.

"I sure did," Travis's mom said. "Not that I needed to."

"Sorry, sweetie," Robbie said, hugging Melinda to his chest. "But I wasn't still on the jobsite. I was being an ogre and carrying some old people to safety."

"I sat on Dad's shoulder with Mrs. Pendleton!" Mason said, his eyes shining. "She nearly fell off! I think I saved her life. Right, Dad?"

"Sure, Mason." Robbie smiled, then frowned. "Is that you, Travis?"

Travis allowed them all to get a good look at him before shifting back to human form.

"Delightful," his mom said with a raised eyebrow.

Travis smiled. "Aw, come on, Mom. A mothman might not be very handsome, but flying has never been so easy."

"Where's your father? And Lauren?"

"I saw Dad, and Blair, but I didn't see Lauren or Orson. And I didn't get a chance to talk to Dad, so I don't know where the others are."

Miss Simone huffed in annoyance. "I hope they didn't land anywhere. They were supposed to report back."

"Who are *you?*" Robbie demanded suddenly, glaring at the old man.

A silence fell.

Robbie edged closer, frowning at Mr. Grimfoyle, his rather terse question hanging in the air. He stepped all the way up to the old man and studied him closely, even reaching out to prod his shoulder.

"I know you," he said softly. "*How* do I know you? We've met before."

"There's no time for this," Mr. Grimfoyle muttered. "Do you see the storm? It will be here in a matter of minutes. Unfortunately, there's nothing you can do to avoid it. It is not an ordinary storm. There is no wind or rain. It is merely a mist—but a deadly mist."

He paused there, allowing everyone to absorb his words.

"Wait . . ." Travis's mom said at last. The color had drained from her face. She turned her wide-eyed gaze to Miss Simone. "A deadly mist? A deadly *blue* mist?"

Miss Simone had the same horrified realization on her face. "And only humans are going missing! Abigail—"

"It has to be her."

Miss Simone clutched handfuls of blond hair. "But . . . the *scale* of it! This is a far cry from a few silent puffs of mist in the woods. This is a *raging storm*." She clamped a hand over her mouth, and after a moment spoke in a soft, almost unbelieving voice. "How could we have forgotten? It's been a long time. What, twenty years? Yes, you and Hal and the others were—well, about Travis's age!"

"She came back!" Robbie said, apparently catching on. "Is that who we're talking about? That *faun*?"

Travis shared a puzzled glance with Melinda. The adults seemed to be remembering something from their past.

Mr. Grimfoyle nodded. "The faun, yes. Her name is River. She is back, and this time she's very, very serious."

Travis's mom let out a cry and immediately sprang into the air with buzzing wings. "Hal and Lauren! They're not safe! We have to warn them!"

Miss Simone reached out and grabbed her ankle before she could fly away. "*You* are not safe, Abigail. If I recall, shapeshifters can't be harmed as long as they're in a completely non-human form—like a dragon or a harpy. Being a faerie, you're a little too close to human for my liking. The mist might be dangerous to you. We should head into the mines."

She turned and started to march off.

"The mines won't save you," Mr. Grimfoyle said, causing her to halt. "By all means hide in them if you think it'll help, and block every opening you can find—but the mist will creep in somehow. And even if it doesn't, you can't stay in the mines forever. Did you think to bring biosuits?"

"Of course," Travis's mom said. "Enough for twelve, anyway. That's all we have."

Mr. Grimfoyle made a scoffing noise. "Best keep those hidden, then, or you'll have a riot on your hands."

Miss Simone spun to face him, suddenly angry. "If you know so much, why didn't you warn us? We could have headed through a portal to Old Earth and been safe!"

The old man sagged at the shoulders. "Alas, I fear Old Earth may not be safe, either. The portals have a delicate membrane that will deflect the mist to a certain degree, perhaps for days, but a sustained presence—"

"The fog-hole," Robbie interrupted, his jaw tightening. "Back on the island, the goblins pumped fog through a portal. It's possible. He's right, Simone—Old Earth is in danger, too." He stared again at Mr. Grimfoyle. "I remember you now."

"There's really no time to reminisce about the old days."

"Dad?" Melinda prompted him.

Her dad answered without taking his eyes off the old man. "You might remember I told you kids about him a few winters ago. That night during the snowstorm? I told you stories, and we ate cookies?"

"Tails of a shapeshifter!" Travis said, the memory popping into her head. He grabbed Melinda's arm. "Remember? Mason got 'tails' and 'tales' mixed up. He thought it meant . . ." He trailed off, regarding the old man again. "Mr. Grimfoyle. Yeah, it's coming back to me." So this was the creepy fellow her parents had pulled out of a *bag*?

They had all been raising their voices bit by bit over the past few minutes as the storm drew steadily nearer.

The old man rolled his eyes. "How nice that I'm the subject of a wintry evening's tall tales over cookies and cream."

If Melinda remembered Mr. Grimfoyle's story, she didn't let on. "Most of us shapeshifters are safe as long as we stay in form," she said, changing the subject. "So let's stay in form."

It was just like her to speak so plainly and cut through the squabbling adults. "What about mermaids, though?" Travis said. "Aren't you maybe a bit too human?"

"I can go underwater. I already did that in the river. The water will protect me. You too, Miss Simone."

Travis noticed that Mr. Grimfoyle was shaking his head, but before he had a chance to question him about it, Miss Simone put on her most commanding voice and started issuing orders.

"Abigail, I'm afraid you'll need to head for the mines. It may not be safe there, but it's far too late to get everyone out. Please do what you can to seal up the tunnel. Robbie—be an ogre and help. Bring the roof down if you must—but safely. That mist *cannot* get through."

"And you?" Travis's mom asked, her wings still buzzing intermittently as she stood there. "And my husband, and Lauren? And Blair, and Orson? We have to warn them."

"Travis can do that." Miss Simone drew in a sharp breath, her eyes widening. "My goodness. We need the reversal potion."

Robbie smacked a fist against the palm of his hand. "Yes! Where is it?"

"Hal and I have a small bottle." Travis's mom frowned. "Except I never saw where he hid it. It was a long time ago, and—"

"We have some at the lab," Miss Simone said. "I got a supply from a witch in the south a long time ago. It cost me dearly—but it's been worth it. I've used it sparingly, and we have a good supply left."

"*Reversal* potion?" Melinda said.

"It's actually a powerful healing potion in its liquid form," Miss Simone told her. "It resets the body back to its former state. But in mist form, it does the opposite and *transmogrifies.* That's what the faun conjures with her bare hands. Still, I can't see how she managed to conjure an entire storm . . ."

"We have biosuits in the mines," Abigail said. "I can fly in and fetch you a set."

Miss Simone shook her head. "I can't transform wearing one of those. Just get in there and seal that place up."

Travis could almost hear Miss Simone's mind whirring as she stood there weighing up her options.

She turned to Melinda. "You and I, my dear, will take to the water and head into Carter. It's not far from the river to the lab. We have time. And even if the storm is too fast for us, we can stay underwater and wait it out. It'll pass over, and when it does—"

As if taking umbrage at her plan, the storm wailed harder and rumbled more violently. They all turned to stare up at the colossal bank of mist as it swallowed up the trees and rolled toward them.

"I can fly you to the lab," Travis suggested. "It'll be quicker than—"

"No, you need to find your father." Miss Simone gave Robbie a shove. "Go now, you two—get to the mines and seal yourselves in. Travis, get airborne and find the others. Warn them, and find that faun!"

Travis suddenly found himself being hugged as his mom whispered that she loved him, and that he should be careful and find his dad straight away, and a stream of other things— and then Robbie pulled her away and marched her off into the trees, following the trail toward the storm. He started to transform as he went, growing larger in the shoulders.

"The river," Miss Simone said to Melinda, grabbing her hand.

But Mr. Grimfoyle, quick as a flash, shot out his own hand and stopped them. "Just one moment." Turning Melinda to face him, he leaned over her and shoved his face close to hers. She recoiled a little but stared back with round eyes.

"What are you doing?" Miss Simone said, sounding annoyed.

He began mumbling under his breath, closing his eyes as if trying to remember the words. Miss Simone glanced up at the towering storm and tried to pull Melinda away, but Mr. Grimfoyle grasped the girl's head in both hands and clamped on so tight she couldn't move even when she struggled.

"Let go of her!" Miss Simone yelled.

Her hair started whipping about, and ordinarily this wouldn't look odd at all—not with a storm raging a mere fifty feet behind her. But the storm produced no wind, and Miss Simone's hair sometimes acted up when she got mad. One of her peculiar mermaid tricks.

Just when it seemed she would slap Mr. Grimfoyle across the face to get him to let go, Melinda arched her back and stiffened all over, arms out to the side, a surprised expression on her face. It only lasted a second, and then she staggered and blinked.

Miss Simone grabbed her arm. "Melinda, are you all right?" She shot Mr. Grimfoyle a terrible glare. "What did you do?"

"There's no time to discuss it," the old man said, sounding a little shaky as he edged away. "Go! Get out of here!"

For a second, Miss Simone acted like she would stick around and interrogate the man. But Melinda took her hand. "I'm fine," she said with a puzzled frown. "We have to go."

Clearly disturbed, Miss Simone glowered at Mr. Grimfoyle with her cold blue eyes before reluctantly allowing herself to be dragged away.

The two mermaid shifters hurried off together across the meadow, angling away from the wailing wall of mist. They disappeared into the trees soon after.

Travis transformed—but even as he did so, he remembered what had been said about being non-human. He didn't *need* to take to the sky. He could simply stand here and let the storm swallow him up. He'd be fine. And he might then be able to find out a little more, perhaps go hunting for the faun . . .

Mr. Grimfoyle swung toward him and grasped his arm. "What are you waiting for? Get us into the air, boy! Take us to safety."

"But I'm a shapeshifter. I don't really need to—"

"Do as I say!" the old man roared.

The mist was so close now that Travis could take a single leap forward and be smothered by the stuff.

Instead, he spread his wings, took hold of Mr. Grimfoyle's arm, and shot into the air.

## Chapter 8
## The Storm Rolls In

"What did you do to Melinda?" Travis yelled as he left the storm behind.

A quick glance back showed him the gargantuan blue cloud had rolled over the mines and was now swallowing his house. He watched with alarm as the building vanished. It wouldn't be long before it smothered the dome-shaped portal across the other side of the meadow—and after that, the entire town of Carter.

Mr. Grimfoyle was either too distracted to reply or he just couldn't be bothered. Travis put on some speed, swooping low and almost dragging his passenger through the treetops. "What did you do?" he demanded again.

"I saved her life."

"Saved her *life*? I don't believe you."

"I don't expect you to. But you'll see."

Travis hung about in the air, letting Mr. Grimfoyle dangle. Was Melinda all right? Saved her *how*?

He dumped Mr. Grimfoyle by the river where it entered the town. It was a nice spot surrounded by grass. The mermaids would have to pass this way soon. Maybe the old man could assist in some way.

"I have to find my dad," Travis said, giving his dark-grey wings a shake as he studied them in turn. Not pretty, he decided, but easily the most efficient he'd tried so far. He paused. "Tell me what you did to Melinda. How did you save her life?"

The old man sighed. "I simply took part of her soul."

Travis felt his mouth fall open and almost reached up to close it. He swallowed and gasped, then began to shake with anger. "You did *what*?"

"Oh, don't worry, boy. You see—"

"My name is Travis," he said through gritted teeth.

Mr. Grimfoyle studied him, then gave another of his nods. "Travis, yes. Well, you see, that storm is looking for human souls. It will extract the soul, then disintegrate the body. Soon after, it will reintegrate the body and restore the soul. But it will pass over anyone who is, shall we say, *lacking*."

"Lacking?" Travis repeated, his mind whirling.

"Any human with less than a full soul will be considered not quite human. Therefore, the storm will ignore her." Mr. Grimfoyle glanced over. "You, too," he added pointedly.

Travis took a step backward. "You're not doing that to me."

"Then you will fall victim to the storm."

"You're saying I'll die?"

"No. Indeed not. But you will be *changed*."

"I'll be changed if you take half my soul!"

Mr. Grimfoyle folded his arms. "I wouldn't take half. That would be foolish. I don't have a soul of my own, which means the storm will ignore me—but if I take half a soul from the girl and half from you . . ." He raised an eyebrow. "Well, if my math is correct, that would mean I end up with a full soul. Not a *complete whole*, you understand, but the storm might not be so discerning. It might think two distinct halves is enough in terms of volume alone—"

"Stop!" Travis yelled suddenly, rising off the ground with just the tiniest flap of his wings. "You're talking about souls like it's no big deal!"

Mr. Grimfoyle took a few steps closer. "Listen to me, boy. For this to work, I need you both. You'll never reach the place without the girl's help—and she'll never be able to return without yours. Do you see?" He narrowed his eyes. "Maybe returning isn't essential. She could do this on her own—except it would be much easier with the two of you working together. You must let me help you."

"I'm fine as I am," Travis argued. "I'll stay in mothman form. Then it can't hurt me."

"That was true twenty years ago. Today—not so much." Mr. Grimfoyle raised his hands. "I'm going to do this. Stand still, please. And don't worry—you'll get your missing piece of soul back when all this is over."

He immediately began mumbling, closing his eyes in concentration, his hands either side of Travis's head.

But Travis ducked away from him and backed off. He raised his wings. "No way. I'm going to find my dad."

"Boy—" Mr. Grimfoyle said, his eyes snapping open.

"My name is TRAVIS!"

He shot into the air and soared away, leaving the old man yelling in frustration.

*Am I doing the right thing?* Travis asked himself as he flew along the leading edge of the storm as if surfing a tidal wave. *Does he mean well? Is he really trying to help?* Logic told him the old man had to have a plan. Why bother, otherwise? But no matter how he reasoned things out, voluntarily giving up part of his soul just seemed like a stupid thing to do.

Poor Melinda, though. She'd had no choice. She hadn't had time to ask what the heck the old man was doing. Was she okay?

A barrage of images suddenly flashed through his mind, and he gasped and almost fell out of the sky: *The muffled thump of an explosion within a tunnel, rocks tumbling down, people yelling* . . . Travis gripped his head and tried to see more, to make sense of it, but the images were already fading.

He clearly remembered what he'd seen, but the details were a little too scarce to be helpful. But maybe it was just Robbie blocking the tunnel into the mines as Miss Simone had told him to do. That made sense, although it seemed weird getting an image of something that had already happened.

Relieved, he focused on where he was headed. The storm wailed and rumbled and swirled nearby, already eating its way through the first buildings at the edge of Carter. From above, he saw nothing through the thick mist below. However . . .

He frowned, seeing the vague outlines of hills on the horizon. The storm was expanding outward from a center beyond those hills, a gigantic circular mass with the thickest mist around its outer edge. Travis could picture it clearly now—like a ripple in a pond spreading wider and wider, only this was a huge ring of thick mist, growing ever larger.

Where had it started? Maybe the dead center would be worth investigating. Maybe there he'd find this faun the adults had mentioned.

*That's for later*, he chided himself. *Find Dad first.*

He tore across the town—then spotted the lab building below. He was instantly tempted. It was *right there*. If Miss Simone and Melinda were going to dash in and grab the potion, they should have been here by now. Where were they? They didn't stand a chance of making it before the mist swallowed the place up. Travis wasn't even sure *he'd* have time. But it was worth a try, right? A quick visit, in an out, and then off to find his dad while clutching some reversal potion.

As he landed on the lab building's lawn and took a quick sideways glance at the approaching storm, he figured he had three minutes tops. That was doable—assuming he could find where the potion was stored.

The place was deserted. He yanked the door open and almost rushed through in with his wings spread wide. He paused and folded them back—

And at that moment, a tremendous explosion shook the building, almost knocking him off his feet. He gasped and staggered as, from deep within, timber groaned and glass shattered. Then a shuddering roar swept down the corridor, a shockwave that blasted him backward.

Dust followed moments afterward, rolling toward him like the great storm itself, only this was dense, grey smoke and debris. He stumbled outside to escape it, flying up into the air just as the cloud billowed out onto the lawn.

Rising high, he was appalled at the sight of a gaping hole in the building's roof. Not just a hole but an entire section *missing.* Papers fluttered everywhere, and smoke rose from the damage, making it difficult to see down inside—but he had no doubt the entire Shapeshifter Program was demolished, that wing of the complex completely flattened.

Thoughts of an accident gave way to a far more sinister and logical explanation: *sabotage.*

"The faun," he muttered. "She got to the potion first."

He might have been making a huge leap in his assumptions, but it felt like the right answer. If the faun had returned to spread her blue mist across the land, it wouldn't do her any good to have a lab full of potion that could reverse its effects—whatever those effects were.

Travis flew around and around, looking out for the faun in case she were loitering somewhere. *Someone* had set off that explosion. He didn't know anything about bombs or explosive magic spells, but he was fairly certain they had to be detonated from nearby, at least in New Earth with its limited technology . . .

He let out a yelp as a fireball shot past him.

Spinning wildly, he flapped and fluttered to get away as another flaming projectile whooshed by his head. He could feel the immense heat on his face.

Then he saw it—a chimera standing perfectly still on the grass at the back of the building, glaring straight up at him with three pairs of eyes. The chimera resembled a lion but with two extra heads. The goat-head stuck up from its back, spitting fireballs at him and bleating. A serpent formed the chimera's tail, and that smooth reptilian head twisted around as Travis flew by, its unblinking eyes staring at him.

Travis had been a chimera before in an earlier shapeshifter mission. He knew what they were capable of.

Veering away, he almost plunged straight into the bank of mist. Letting out a cry, he shot upward and away, breathing hard. *Watch where you're going, idiot!*

The lab was half-destroyed. The potion was almost certainly gone unless Miss Simone had hidden it someplace else. And the faun was likely miles away. Her trained chimera had done the work for her.

Travis wanted to warn the mermaids to stay away, but he couldn't bear the thought of flying around in circles waiting on them. They'd just have to watch out for themselves while he did something useful. Making up his mind, he set off toward the northeast, high above the mist.

Everything appeared so different now. He'd been here just a short while ago, above the meadows—but now the grassy hills were smothered, completely obscured. As he flew, the mist thinned enough that he could see the outline of the terrain, the occasional trees, and that farmhouse again with the goats frolicking about inside the fence. One goat trotted aimlessly outside the pen, but the farmer was nowhere to be seen, either barricaded inside the house or . . . or what?

What exactly did the mist do to people? Did it really *disintegrate* them?

Travis squinted, spotting figures in the sky ahead. *Two* figures. Putting on a burst of speed, he aimed for the larger one, hoping it was his dad.

It was. The dragon circled around, descended, then rose again as if trying to pluck up the courage to land.

"Dad!" Travis yelled.

The dragon didn't hear him. The other figure did, though. It turned out to be Aunt Lauren. She spun in the air, peered at him, then yelled something to the dragon. Only then did Travis's dad snap his head around. He had just started on another long downward spiral by now, but when he saw Travis, he gave a quick blast of fire almost like a hiccup.

Travis shot toward them both. "Dad, it's me! I'm a mothman!"

The dragon gave a short roar and flapped hard to turn around. He seemed panicked, urgent. A few more roars suggested he was desperately trying to communicate.

"Don't touch the mist, Travis!" Lauren yelled.

"I won't. But it's harmless to us, right?"

Both Lauren and his dad disagreed vehemently. The dragon couldn't hover as easily as a harpy and a mothman, so he cruised on by with his massive leathery wings beating, his tail stretched out behind.

Lauren flapped closer to Travis and circled him, talking rapidly. "We've been studying the storm, trying to find signs of life. We've seen animals, a goblin or two, a centaur—but no humans. Just clothing littered about where people were."

"I know. It's—"

"We've seen this before," Lauren went on. "It's different now, much bigger, but similar. We figured it out. And it should have meant we were safe. We're *shapeshifters*. It goes after humans. The mist shouldn't affect us as long as we stay in form. Blair and Orson should still be down there somewhere."

Travis frowned. He couldn't help scouring the ground. He could see the meadow quite clearly here, the mist light, more of a blue haze. He saw no sign of a pegasus nor a phoenix. "What—what happened to them?"

Lauren closed her eyes for a moment as she flapped and bobbed before him. "They landed in an area where the mist was thin. They stayed in form. They should have been okay. But then . . ."

"But then what?"

"Then they were *gone*—exploded into dust, like everyone else."

## Chapter 9
### Turned to Dust

Travis listened in horror to Lauren's terrible story. Orson and Blair—both turned to dust by some freaky blue mist! Not to mention everyone else that had been swallowed by the storm. "But . . . are they *dead?*" he croaked.

Now that he thought about it, he vaguely remembered a bedtime story about people exploding into dust and coming back later as something different, *changed* somehow. He'd been young, and the details eluded him.

His dad came tearing past, shaking his head and grumbling. He was gone again seconds later.

Lauren flapped closer to Travis, her yellow eyes blazing. "They're not dead. But they're not all right, either. And we can't keep flying around forever. I'm trying to get your dad to decide one way or another—we get ahead of the storm, or we fly to its center where maybe the mist will be too thin to harm us."

Travis peered down at the meadow. Thick patches of mist drifted here and there, but mostly it was a faint haze. Apparently that haze was deadly. "Mom and the others have gone into the mines."

"I know," Lauren said. "Robbie and the kids, too?"

"Uncle Robbie went in with Mason, but Melinda is with Miss Simone. They're mermaids. Staying underwater is safe."

She looked troubled. "For now, maybe. And as for the mines . . . I'm afraid the mist will still get in."

"Uncle Robbie brought the roof of the entrance down. The tunnel should be blocked and sealed, hopefully airtight."

*Hopefully airtight?* Travis couldn't believe things had come to this. Even if they were safe from the mist, their air would go stale eventually.

"We need to find the faun and stop this mist from spreading across the land," Lauren muttered as she circled him.

The huge dragon came hurtling past again. Travis knew a few bits of dragonspeak, rudimentary grunts that meant "up" and "down" and "stand back," but none of what his dad was saying right now made sense.

Lauren seemed to have a handle on it, though. "I think your dad's finally made up his mind. Thank you, Travis, for showing up. You decided things for him."

"Decided what?"

"Looks like we're heading back to Carter."

Travis jerked, suddenly remembering. "Oh! The lab exploded, too."

His dad had already sped on past by now, but Lauren flapped about and turned to face him. "What?"

He explained what he'd seen—the explosion, the damage, and the chimera shooting fireballs at him—and she closed her eyes and groaned. "So there's no potion. It's all gone."

The dragon roared and huffed. Since nobody could understand him, he let out a sigh and said nothing more all the way back to Carter.

Travis easily matched the harpy's speed. "The town will be half covered by now. I'm hoping Miss Simone and Melinda are swimming out of town away from the storm . . . and not *under* it."

"What?" Lauren exclaimed.

The mist thickened as they approached the leading edge. A column of smoke rose from the laboratory building somewhere deep within the murk. But once they got ahead of the storm, the outlines of streets and houses sharpened. Everything seemed extra clear now. Travis felt like he'd just wiped a lot of gunk from his eyes and could finally focus properly.

"Where are we going?" Travis asked.

"To land somewhere," Lauren said as the dragon chose that moment to head for the ground.

Travis's dad thumped down in the market square, knocking over some empty stalls as he folded his wings and swung his tail around. He immediately reverted to human form and came running as Travis and Lauren landed side by side.

"We have to split up," the sandy-haired man said. He was a far cry from the massive dragon he'd been seconds before. "I'm going after the faun. She has to be at the center of the storm, way over on the horizon somewhere. Lauren, can you deal with that chimera? And see if you can find anyone hanging about in the town and warn them—and anywhere else the storm hasn't reached yet."

Before she had a chance to reply, he grabbed Travis by the shoulders and shoved his face close, scowling with anger and worry.

"Listen to me, son. Find Simone—"

"But she just told me to find *you*!"

"Find Simone," his dad said again, more firmly this time. "She'll soon discover her lab is half destroyed and the reversal potion gone with it—but we have more."

"That's what Mom said!" Travis said, suddenly excited. He reverted to human form, thinking it must be weird for his dad to be staring into the face of a creepy, furry-faced, insectoid mothman. "She doesn't know where you hid it."

His dad's scowl softened. "There's a small vial I kept all these years. I went to see Madame Frost, looking for a cure, and she pointed me in the right direction. You just need to go home and dig it up—but you'll have to wear something to protect you from the mist, or wait until it's cleared and come back later." He ran a hand through his hair. "Never expected to need it, though. Simone got a pretty big batch of the stuff from a witch after the last time this happened."

Lauren looked up at the towering storm as it rolled into view over the rooftops. It would be upon them in less than a minute. "Well, now that small vial is all we have until Simone can get some more," she said, raising her voice above the rumbling and wailing.

"Right," Travis's dad said. "And we should keep it for ourselves—for those who can fight back. Do you understand, son?"

Travis nodded, eyeing the mist as it rolled along an alleyway and crept over the nearest houses. "So we can get Orson and Blair back."

To his surprise, his dad tilted his head and shrugged. "No. I mean for *us*. For your mom, and Uncle Robbie, and you and Lauren, and Melinda, and Simone if she gets caught in this mist. And a handful of witches who know how to make more of the stuff but might already be dust by now. So keep the potion close to your chest while I go and find the faun, and stay safe."

"Okay," Travis said. "So where is it?"

"Watch out!" Lauren screeched.

She instinctively leapt into the air, flapping hard like a startled bird while Travis and his dad swung around to see what was happening.

Something monstrous and brown-haired lurched out of a mist-filled alley, a thirty-foot-tall ogre looming above the rooftops. It let out a roar and swung its huge arms about, and the closest walls on either side of the alley crumbled into a pile of rubble. Roofs creaked in protest as rafters tilted and slate tiles crashed down.

Travis's dad shouted, "Fly!"

Before Travis had a chance to argue, his dad transformed into a dragon and swung around to face the charging ogre. But the angry giant was already swinging its fist around, and it connected hard with the dragon's jaw.

Shifting and leaping into the air in one smooth movement, Travis rose just enough that the ogre couldn't reach him. He joined Lauren, circling around the monster and yelling at it to stop. But the enraged ogre hammered the dragon over and over, so hard that the reptilian fire-breather staggered sideways.

Travis sucked in a breath. He'd never seen such an angry ogre, and he'd certainly never seen one beating up a dragon. He never would have thought it remotely possible, but the giant had sprung out of nowhere and landed a surprise sucker-punch, and now it was nonstop blow after blow.

His dad didn't even have a chance to roar. He opened his mouth to breathe fire, but just the tiniest flame shot out before the next punch whacked his head sideways. The ogre roared and struck with both fists, *bam-bam-bam*, hitting harder and harder . . .

"Stop!" Travis yelled.

There was nothing he could do to stop the onslaught. Lauren was screeching as well, and the two of them flew in and kicked at the ogre, though a mothman and a harpy were nothing but annoying flies. One fist came very close to Travis's face, and he almost felt the full force of that weighty, rock-solid hammer-blow. It missed by inches—but his dad took it on the snout so hard that something cracked.

The dragon went down, falling sideways in a motionless heap. The shaggy ogre roared in triumph and advanced with meaty fists raised . . . and then paused, chest heaving.

With a grunt of obvious disappointment, the ogre straightened up and dropped its arms to its sides. The fight was over. Only then did it notice Travis and Lauren circling just above, and it lashed out in a vain attempt to knock them out of the sky.

With a sigh, it stomped away, heading down a random side-street, trailing its fingers along the rooftops and dragging tiles off.

"Dad!" Travis said with a heavy heart.

He dropped to the ground and fell to his knees by the enormous dragon's head. Listening intently, he heaved a sigh of relief when he heard shallow breathing.

"He's unconscious," he told Lauren as she landed.

"The mist," she cried.

Travis gawked at the towering storm. He'd barely noticed the wailing and howling, not to mention the deep rumbling. Already he'd grown used to the noise. Glancing from the wall of blue mist to his dad, he guessed they had thirty seconds to wake the dragon—or physically drag him away.

*Yeah, right.*

"Dad, you have to wake up!" Travis yelled in his dad's scaly ear.

Lauren joined in too, slapping her hand against the reptilian face and neck while screeching at the top of her voice.

The dragon groaned—but it was way too late.

Lauren abruptly quit yelling and, with wings spread wide, dragged Travis backward just as the first tendrils of mist curled around the limp monster.

"Dad!" Travis yelled again.

The storm rolled over the dragon. Through the thick mist, Travis saw a myriad of fine cracks appear on the reptile's belly. They lasted less than a second before the entire dragon exploded into dust. Then the twisting, wailing, smoky wall was too thick to see through.

Travis cried out and sank to his knees, but Lauren gave him no time to dwell and dragged him farther backward, grunting with the effort, until he lashed out and yanked free. Angry and heartbroken, he launched into the air.

"Travis, wait for me," Lauren called.

He didn't even look back. He couldn't bear to see his dad— his strong, invincible, heroic dad—swirling around like a cloud of dust, swallowed up in the blue mist.

Lauren hurtled past and swung around, wings flapping like crazy. "Travis, listen to me! Your dad will be fine. This is what the mist does. It disintegrates people—and then *puts them back together*. He's alive. His soul is floating around in the storm, but he'll be back."

Her words gave Travis hope. Still, he glared at her. "Back as what? I heard the mist *changes* people." He pointed back at the town. "That ogre! Was that a *real* ogre—or someone who had been put back together?"

"Never mind that now. We have work to do." Lauren ushered him higher. "Since your dad's not here, I'm going to the center of the storm myself. I'll find the faun and stop her somehow. You have to find that potion your dad mentioned."

He frowned at her. "But . . . he didn't say where it was!"

"Find it anyway," she repeated. "I have to go." With her wings flapping dangerously close to his, she reached out and grasped his face. "Be safe, Travis."

And with that, she flipped and tumbled away, then soared higher, her white wings gleaming in the sun.

At a loss, Travis watched her go. Her purpose was clear—find the faun and stop her. His, on the other hand, seemed aimless. How was he supposed to find a potion that his dad had hidden in the ground somewhere at home? It could be anywhere.

And what was he supposed to wear to protect himself from the mist? All the biosuits were in the mines with his mom and Robbie.

*Find Simone. She might have some ideas.*

With a feeling of purpose at last, he circled around until he got his bearings and located the river on the west side. The storm had covered two-thirds of the town by now, but the river flowed on past, meandering off into the forest. Miss Simone and Melinda should have made it that far already—assuming they hadn't decided to go the other way, *under* the approaching storm.

He shook his head. They wouldn't have done that.

Would they?

## Chapter 10
### Mermaids in the Mist

The moment they leapt into the river, Melinda and Miss Simone transformed and hung just below the surface as their fishtails completed the morphing process and unfurled. The blond-haired scientist normally removed her cloak before jumping into the water, but this time the silk material separated into long shreds rather like seaweed. The lower half of her dress did the same. The effect was mesmerizing.

Melinda fingered her own dress. It hadn't changed much at all. She liked Miss Simone's tattered style better. *So* much more natural and aquatic.

To her surprise, Miss Simone began swimming upstream away from Carter and toward the storm. All Melinda could do was bite her tongue and follow. The river wasn't wide enough for them to travel side by side, so she had to stare at a fishtail the whole time.

After a minute or two, Miss Simone slowed and turned around, floating vertically with her hair splayed out. "The storm is thinner here," she said softly. "I can see sunlight."

Melinda recoiled in shock.

Miss Simone smiled. "Yes, we may speak. Do you think mermaids spend their lives not talking?"

"But—" Melinda clamped a hand over her mouth as bubbles floated out. Then she tried again. "How is this possible?"

"How is anything in this world possible?"

It had never occurred to Melinda that anyone could talk underwater and not sound like a garbled, gurgly mess. Yet here they were, two mermaids conversing, the words floating from their mouths amid a stream of small bubbles.

"I can hear you so clearly," she said, amazed.

Miss Simone nodded, then turned her attention skyward again. She'd apparently lost interest in the conversation. She floated mere inches below the surface, then pushed her face out of the water. Two seconds later, she withdrew and sank to the bottom where Melinda waited.

"There's a lingering haze. I'm not certain if it's enough to affect us or not. To get to the potion, we can swim into Carter, but then we'll have to run through the streets to the lab. I wanted to see if we could do that safely *after* the wall of mist has passed by."

"And?"

"I think not. We'd have to be in human form, and the haze will prevent us. Which means we'll need to stick to the plan and get to the lab *before* the mist. Come on. We can make it."

But just then, Melinda glimpsed something tearing downstream toward them. "Miss Simone!"

The lady swung around. Together they stared at the fast-moving creature. It was big and black, an equine of some kind, though with flippers instead of hooves. Its nostrils flared wide as it bore down on them.

"A kelpie!" Miss Simone cried. "Swim!"

The two of them almost jostled for the lead as they fled. Speeding toward Carter had been their plan, but not like this! The aquatic horse was catching up.

"It'll kick us to death," Miss Simone snapped. She abruptly halted and turned to face it, leaning forward and raising her hands, her hair fanning out again. "Go, Melinda—I've got this."

Melinda had the sense not to argue at a time like this, but she wasn't leaving Miss Simone alone either. She backed away and watched with terror as the powerful horse hurtled toward them.

A scream pierced the water—a deafening mermaid screech that hurt the ears and curled the toes. The kelpie backpedaled and reared up amid a torrent of bubbles and froth. Its gigantic flippers smacked against the riverbanks, causing mud to dislodge and cloud the water.

Miss Simone never let up with the screeching. It was one impossibly long high-pitched wail that sent fishes and other river creatures skedaddling for cover. The kelpie flailed, then kicked and lunged for one of the banks.

To Melinda's amazement, its flippers turned into hooves just as it leapt out of the river. Something was odd about those hooves, and its pure-black coat was oddly dull—but then the creature was gone.

The scream cut off. Miss Simone gasped and sagged, then smiled weakly at Melinda. "And that, my dear, is how a mermaid keeps danger at bay."

They rested awhile. "I've never seen a kelpie before," Melinda said. "Was that normal? They chase after people in rivers?"

"Not quite. It shouldn't even be here. The river is too narrow for such a thing. And too shallow."

"Too shallow?"

Annoyingly, something else interrupted them—a cluster of creatures coming *upstream*. Melinda gaped at the sight of half a dozen silver-grey eel-like creatures, perhaps serpents, with pale-green eyes. Except . . .

She let out a cry. "They're all *attached* to something—"

"It's a hydra," Miss Simone said, entirely too fascinated for Melinda's liking. "It's so young, so slender . . . Absolutely beautiful."

It became apparent that the short-legged, six-headed dragon would be upon them very soon. The jaws snapped hungrily.

"We should go," Miss Simone said with a sigh. "I could study this creature all day. I know it's not what it seems, but . . ." She trailed off. "Come on. Let's head back upstream."

As vicious as those six fang-filled snapping jaws looked, at least the young hydra was slow-moving. Mermaids would have no trouble escaping.

But just as Melinda turned away, she caught sight of something out of the corner of her eye and glanced back. The hydra was still twenty feet away, easily out of range, only just visible in the gloomy depths of the river . . . but all six heads were spitting something.

She watched with mounting horror as the water began to freeze.

"Miss Simone!" she cried.

Melinda had seen plenty of ice lately. Her last mission involved a maddening, indestructible block of the stuff, and the last thing she wanted was to be encased in a frozen river. She spun around and shoved Miss Simone to get her moving, and when the blond scientist spotted what was happening, she jerked into action.

They dashed away from the stream of ice. But it pierced the water like a series of jagged lances, tearing after them, the vicious points lunging and thrusting. Melinda knew one would stab through them in a matter of seconds.

"Out!" she yelled.

She veered toward the surface so fast that she shot from the river, sailed through the air, and half landed on the grassy bank, grasping with her hands to pull her tail out. As she rolled away from the edge, Miss Simone splashed out in a froth of water, twisting and turning to wrench her tail free.

The knife-edged spears raced past, followed by a creaking, cracking sound as the river froze into a glass-like sheet.

Melinda watched in amazement, lying on her belly on the grass bank and leaning over the edge. The water was already solid enough to walk on, rippled and rough, full of frozen froth and bubbles—but not far behind, it melted again as the hydra stalked after it. She could see its six heads jabbing forward with each deadly blast of icy-cold breath.

She rolled aside just in case the dragon leapt out after them.

It was then she realized where they were. She sucked in a breath and stared at Miss Simone, who stared back from where she sat with her tail curled around. She'd gone from elegant to awkward, almost exactly like a fish out of water.

The blue mist surrounded them, but it was light, no more than a haze as Miss Simone had suggested. Instead of the wailing gale and thunderous rumble, everything seemed peaceful now, the leading edge of the storm having left an eerie serenity in its wake. Still, dangerous little puffs drifted here and there, and Melinda had the feeling one particularly lengthy wisp was sniffing the air like a ghostly snake as it eased between the two mermaids.

"We're safe," Melinda whispered.

Miss Simone said nothing as she slowly turned to study their surroundings. There wasn't much to see, just another meadow . . . but visibility was down to a stone's throw. Melinda guessed this must have been what it was like for her parents to grow up on the famous Island of Fog—except this fog was blue.

"I think," Miss Simone started to say as she reached out to run her hand through the long, ghostly, serpentine wisp, "that we might be all right in mermaid form. So I suppose we'll wait until—"

She broke off.

Melinda watched her, noting how the woman's eyes had glazed over. She appeared utterly still.

"Miss Simone?"

To her horror, a fine crack appeared on Miss Simone's forehead, starting at the top and working its way down to her nose, then past her nose and spreading across her cheek. As the crack widened, the edges crumbled into tiny particles . . . which rose into the air. More and more cracks appeared, her face literally breaking apart until it was a mass of fragments and pieces floating up into the blue haze.

Then she *dispersed*, the same way a mass of bees swarmed into the air and spread wide and far, only in deadly silence. Her silky smart dress and robe fluttered onto the grass.

Miss Simone was gone.

Melinda could only stare in trembling silence. She sat absolutely still, too terrified to move, watching every puff of mist that drifted too close, ducking low once or twice as she stifled tears.

She felt completely lost. If being a mermaid hadn't helped protect Miss Simone, then reverting to human would almost certainly be the kiss of death. Or would it? Would it make the slightest difference whether she was human or mermaid?

She couldn't sit around on the grass all day, though. Walking on two legs through the haze toward Carter, following the storm as it moved on, seemed like madness. She was better off in the water, crowded with monsters though it was.

Leaving the silky garments exactly where they'd fallen, Melinda rolled toward the river and was about to throw herself in and swim downstream when she paused, seeing something in the mist.

*What now?*

A large shape moved through the haze, not quite heading her way but certainly veering toward the river. *A horse*, she thought. *With a rider.*

The horse drew closer, its outline clearing. It was dark, perhaps black, and the rider fairly small . . .

"Hey!" Melinda shouted before she could stop herself.

Her voice startled the horse. It whinnied noisily, then picked up its pace—still heading to the river. As it neared the bank, it came into view at last. Melinda sucked in a breath. It was the kelpie again—only this time it had a passenger.

Puzzled, she watched it step up to the water's edge. She became aware that the rider was saying, "No, not this way. Wait, what are you doing?"

The kelpie gave another whinny, then picked its way down the steep bank.

"Stop!" the rider shouted. It was a boy, but a very odd-looking one. He had a strange wooden texture to his skin, like the bark of a tree, and the top of his head stretched into a weird crown of splintered wood. He wore pants but no shirt, and his arms, shoulders, and chest had a wood-grain pattern complete with knots.

Melinda still couldn't move, paralyzed with fright and astonishment. And nor could the boy. He struggled and yelled, but it seemed like he was glued to his perch, his pants firmly stuck to the kelpie's dull-black, rubbery skin.

Mesmerized, she watched the kelpie reach out a hoof. Even that was odd, turned backward for some reason. All four were. But then the raised foreleg morphed into a flipper, which was also pointed backward. Perhaps that was its true form. The kelpie leapt in, taking the screaming boy with it.

*A dryad stuck to a kelpie*, Melinda thought, still dazed.

Then she threw herself into the water after them.

Even though she knew the boy was stuck to the kelpie's back, she still wanted to scream *Just let go! Jump off!* as the black horse sank to the bottom of the river and floated with its flippers mere inches above the soft bed. There it waited.

On its back, the terrified boy struggled and punched to no avail. He tried to undo his pants and slide out of them, but his legs were splayed too wide, and he couldn't seem to struggle free. He quickly gave up, eyes bulging, reaching in vain for the river's surface above his head.

Angry, Melinda swam closer and made sure the kelpie noticed her. It did, and it backed up hurriedly, causing a cloud of silt to plume around its flippers.

Melinda opened her mouth and screamed as hard as she could.

## Chapter 11
## Strangers in Town

Though it didn't seem possible, the power of Melinda's scream cut through the water and battered the kelpie so hard it reared up with a gurgled whinny. Panicked, it clumsily spun around, slipped and skidded its way up the bank, and finally shot away—leaving the boy to float free.

Melinda quit screaming and rushed to him. She gripped his arm and pulled him to the surface, where he broke free of the water and sucked in deep breaths.

She helped him onto the grassy bank, where he rolled over and lay with his chest heaving. Meanwhile, Melinda fearfully watched occasional puffs of mist drift by. Was she still in danger from it or not? Miss Simone had touched one of those puffs and *bam!* Well, not *bam*, exactly. She'd silently broken apart and drifted away.

Tentatively, Melinda reached for a trailing wisp and paused. Should she dare? Best not. She withdrew her hand.

At last, the boy sat up. He focused on Melinda and stared, his gaze lingering on her fishtail before returning to her eyes. "Th-thanks," he croaked.

She smiled. "You're welcome. I'm Melinda Strickland. And you are . . . ?"

The dryad frowned and cast his gaze away as if trying to remember. "Um . . . Flynn, I think."

"*Flynn?*" Melinda pursed her lips. "Funny name for a dryad. And how come I can see you? Dryads are normally invisible, right? Or well-camouflaged, anyway." She scrutinized him. Why was he wearing such ordinary pants? Even if he faded out and blended in with the background, mundane clothing like that wouldn't. Something else occurred to her, and she pressed a little harder. "How come you didn't know that was a kelpie?"

"A what?"

"The black horse. It was a kelpie. You should never sit on a kelpie, because you'll stick and get dragged under. That's how they catch their prey; they act friendly and offer rides, then drown their victim. Being a dryad, one with nature and all, you should have known that. Its hooves were turned backwards. Didn't you notice?"

He retained his puzzled expression as he peered around the blue mist. "I need to go home."

Melinda waited for him to elaborate.

Eventually, he climbed to his feet. "Thank you for saving me, Melinda Strickland. That horse came trotting up and acted like it wanted me to climb on, so I did, thinking it could take me home. But . . ." He shuddered. "It tried to *drown* me. Why would it do that?" Shaking his head, he sniffed the air, turned in a circle, and pointed. "I have a feeling my home is that way."

"Mmm, there's nothing that way except fields," Melinda told him, "and maybe a farm or two."

Flynn started walking anyway. Impeded by her fishtail, Melinda couldn't decide whether to risk changing back and going after him or not. What if being human made her more vulnerable to the mist? Then again, being a mermaid hadn't exactly helped Miss Simone.

Melinda sighed, reverted to human form, and dashed to catch up.

He glanced sideways at her, then did a double take and looked her up and down. "You're . . . you're *not* a mermaid?"

"I'm a shapeshifter." She peered ahead. "Seriously, nobody lives out this way except Old Earthers making a new life."

The boy didn't answer.

The rough outline of a building loomed out of the mist. "See, there's a house," she said.

Flynn slowed. "I thought this was my home, but . . . it doesn't seem right. That place is for humans."

"Yeah, it's a farmhouse. Like I said, probably Old Earthers. I'm pretty sure *you* don't live there."

Still, he shuffled onward until a goat came ambling up. It bleated at him and frolicked away.

Flynn watched it go, a frown on his face. "I know that creature. There are more goats in the pen. But . . ."

Sure enough, five more of them danced about in a fenced enclosure. The house was clear to see now, old and ramshackle, built from stone with a weathered but sturdy oak door.

"So this *is* where you live?" Melinda asked. "That's kind of strange. I never heard of a dryad living in a house. Don't you miss the forest?"

Part of her knew what had happened, but she found it hard to believe this dryad was anything other than what he appeared. She didn't *want* to believe it.

They walked up the path to the front door. Flynn lagged behind, clearly uncertain, so Melinda knocked on the door for him. "Hello?" she called. "Flynn's home. I think he's confused. Anyone here?"

As they waited, Flynn whispered, "Why were its hooves turned backwards?"

"The kelpie's? They're normally fins, which kind of angle the other way . . ." She remembered something about backward-pointing feet, though. They weren't unheard of. Some creatures of New Earth were sneaky like that; they robbed or killed, then relied on their weird physical deformity to throw trackers off the scent.

The door creaked open a few inches. A very tall, frowning man peered out through the gap. He had shoulder-length, dark-grey hair and a gaunt face. He said nothing, just stared at them.

Taken aback, she struggled for words. "Er, hello. I'm Melinda. Um . . ." She stared through the gap, puzzled. Obviously this wasn't Flynn's father, but he could be a guardian. "Flynn was in trouble with a kelpie. He's okay now, though."

A strange pause followed. The man glared down at them. Flynn shuffled, gazing off across the field. Then the man opened the door a little wider and slithered out onto the porch.

*Slithered.*

His thick serpentine body was dark-brown with tan-colored zigzagging stripes.

"You're a naga," Melinda said.

"And you're not," the long-haired man said with a familiar reverberating quality in his voice. Melinda had met a lot of naga recently. He studied her, then Flynn. "I would say you have no business here, except . . . to be honest, I'm not sure I have any business here either."

Melinda felt like she was beginning to understand. "You speak the language of humans. Not too many of the naga can do that. And you're here in this house, which is really odd. And Flynn says *he* lives here—a dryad, away from the forest, wearing ordinary pants and claiming he knows the goats."

Both the naga and dryad stared at her.

She caved, accepting what the voice at the back of her mind had been whispering all along. "Okay, I get it. The mist changes people. It changed you both. You were a farmer and his son, and now you're a naga and a dryad. And you've lost some of your memory."

She could see from their expressions that her words rang true.

On the floor behind the naga, just inside the doorway, a shirt and some shoes lay discarded. "Are those the rest of your clothes, Flynn?"

He shrugged.

"Okay," Melinda went on, talking more to herself now, "so you were a boy, and then you exploded into dust and came back as a dryad with no memory . . . and you put your pants on and wandered outside in a daze, and ended up getting on the back of a kelpie hoping it would take you to a forest somewhere. That means Miss Simone is still out there in the mist. Maybe she'll be back soon—*as something else.*"

Eager to be on her way, she stepped down off the porch. But Flynn turned to follow her. "Wait for me."

"What? Why? You live *here*. You're home."

But Flynn's wood-grained face had darkened. "There's no home for me here. I belong in the forest."

"I'm not going to the forest. I'm going to find Miss Simone and then head for Carter."

"I owe you my life. I want to repay that debt."

Melinda frowned at him, struck by his sincerity. "You don't talk like a farm boy," she muttered, "and especially not like an Old Earther."

"I am of the forest," Flynn said, drawing himself up. He faded slightly, the background showing through his face and shoulders. The effect spread down his chest and arms, but the pants remained opaque.

Shrugging, Melinda turned to leave. "Okay, whatever. But when I get to the river, I'm swimming, so I'll have to leave you behind."

They hurried away from the farmhouse. The naga remained on the porch, watching them go, strangely still and thoughtful. What must he be thinking? Was he glad to see the human and dryad gone? Did he have any clue that the dryad was his own son? Even the slightest hint?

Melinda found herself panting as she jogged up a rise with Flynn close behind. He fuzzed in and out, sometimes almost completely invisible except for his pants. *He needs smart pants,* she thought. *Or whatever it is dryads normally wear.*

They saw no sign of the kelpie, nor the young hydra, but they caught a glimpse of a very large man shambling about in the mist. He had a blanket wrapped around his midriff, and when he glanced their way, Melinda was shocked to see only one eye—a huge eye in the middle of its forehead. Luckily, the cyclops seemed too distracted to bother them.

Seeing the cyclops reminded her that Miss Simone could literally be anything. But not that cyclops. She didn't know much about the mist, just that it dissolved a person's essence somehow, then brought them back in a new guise. The cyclops was male, though. She had to assume—*hope*—that the faun's magic didn't cause people to switch genders as well. That would be too much to deal with.

How long did it take to return to life as something different? Ten minutes?

She glanced back at Flynn as they hurried. "How long were you gone?"

"Gone?"

"After the mist disintegrated you. How long were you away before coming back as a dryad?"

Flynn's frown deepened. "I don't understand."

Melinda sighed. "Never mind."

She stopped dead as a particularly thick puff of mist moved across her path. Snatching her arm away, she cringed and backed up, almost stepping on Flynn's invisible feet. But the mist engulfed her for a second before moving past.

Panting, she stood there a moment and came to the conclusion this probably wasn't the first puff of mist she'd blundered through. The weird blue haze was everywhere, and it was probably deadly enough in itself. Thick puffs or otherwise, she'd wandered around long enough by now to realize she was unaffected by it.

Moving on, Melinda made a point to seek out the thicker puffs and walk through them without exploding into dust. Buoyed by her success, her whirling thoughts turned to Mr. Grimfoyle. That old man had done something to her. He'd cast a spell of some kind, and she'd felt a weird but painless sensation, like a ghost passing through her . . . And then she'd be too busy to think about it.

"I think it was here," Flynn said, pulling on her arm.

Melinda paused and studied the riverbank. He was probably right, but it all looked the same, especially amid the blue haze.

"Miss Simone!"

Her shout somehow echoed through the mist. In the distance, something replied—a throaty roar.

*Oops.*

"Shh," Melinda said to Flynn. She put a finger to her lips and motioned him closer to the river. "We have to go," she whispered.

The dryad refused to budge. "I can't swim."

"Even if you could, you would never keep up with me. But we have to try."

"I thought you were searching for your friend."

Melinda chewed her lip. "Miss Simone could be anything. She might be that monster we just heard roaring. Or she might not. Either way, whatever that was could come after us. And there might be other things in the mist, Old Earthers who used to live in this area who are now *different*. We can't stand around here, and it's too dangerous to walk through this mess."

*Something's probably waiting for us in the river, too*, she thought. But Flynn didn't need to know that.

She sat on the grassy edge and slid into the water, transforming as she went. The water, cold as it was, felt good on her fishtail, a refreshing change from the tired human legs she'd been stumbling about on. Walking was such a chore. Swimming was a breeze in comparison.

"Come on in," she said, offering a hand.

Flynn shook his head. "I can't."

"Sure you can. Come on, Flynn. You won't sink. I'm a mermaid. I can help."

Still he didn't move.

Growing impatient, she huffed and shrugged. "Suit yourself. I can't hang around here. I have to get back. Take care, Flynn. If you see anything big and nasty coming, just turn invisible. And . . . well, find some clothes that turn invisible with you."

She gave a wave—but as she turned to leave, Flynn's paralysis broke, and he ran forward and quickly slip-slithered down the bank into the water. He hardly made a splash, but he gasped and floundered until Melinda reached out and grabbed his arm.

"You're okay," she assured him. "But why are you so hung up on coming with me?"

"I owe you my life," he croaked.

*Well, that's all nice and everything*, she thought, *but now you're slowing me down.*

She gently maneuvered him behind her and reached back for his hands. Placing them on her waist, she glanced over her shoulder and said, "Hang onto me. I won't go underwater, but I'll be moving fast."

His curiously wood-textured face and jutting crown struck her as artistic, somehow—a lifelike carving fashioned straight from a log. She realised the backs of his hands were rough to touch, yet his fingertips and palms were warm and soft. She patted his hands and let go, and he remained holding onto her waist, gazing at her from about two inches away.

"You're beautiful," he murmured.

She rolled her eyes. "Yeah, yeah. Thanks, but I'm a mermaid."

*So was Miss Simone.*

Guilt rose in her chest. What if Miss Simone needed help? She might be stumbling around, lost and upset, confused— maybe even in danger from that roaring monster she'd heard.

This was firmly on her mind as she set off. Flynn let out a small yelp and gripped harder. He was fine after that, holding on while she cruised with her head and shoulders above water. A human on two legs would have to sprint to match her speed, and even that would be pushing it.

But just half a minute later, she slowed.

"I can't leave Miss Simone behind," she moaned.

The dryad spoke quietly just behind her ear. "I'll help you find her."

"Even if it's dangerous out there?"

"I owe you my life, Melinda. I'll help you until my debt is paid. After that, I'll go home to the forest."

"Okay," she agreed at last. "Let's find Miss Simone."

In the back of her mind, she was grateful for his companionship. But more than that, it felt wrong to let him head off into the forest when his home was just nearby. How many other families across the land had been split up like this? How many different creatures were wandering aimlessly or, worse, charging about with anger and fury.

And what of her own parents? Her dad and little brother were in the mines with most of the residents of Carter, but if the mist had leaked in . . .

She shuddered to think what *that* would be like.

At least her mom was free, along with Travis and his dad.

She imagined they were flying high above the mist right now, doing something useful like saving people . . .

## Chapter 12
## Soulless

Travis flew high above the mist, wishing he was doing something useful like saving people.

He'd scoured the ground hunting for his dad, hovering over the place he'd last seen the dragon, watching out for a cloud of swirling fragments that might be preparing to reform. But he hadn't seen anything of the sort.

Melinda and Miss Simone were taking forever. He'd flown ahead of the storm, expecting them to rise from the water, then second-guessing himself and wondering why they would even do such a thing. Why emerge from the river into the path of the approaching storm? It didn't make sense for them to do that.

So where were they?

He sighed. There was only one useful thing he could do, and that was to head for the mines and check on the Carter residents. Except he couldn't do that, either, because the mines were smothered.

He gave a cry of frustration and spun about in the air.

The streets below were deserted except for the rampaging ogre, which had stomped its way to the far end of the town. Travis scrutinized the place anyway, looking for signs of movement. Not a soul. Even the chimera had gone.

Travis changed course again. The rumbling, wailing noise was strongest at the storm's leading edge, the mist at its thickest, but once he was past it and into unclaimed territory, the last remaining streets stood out clear and bright in the sunshine.

He found the river again. To his surprise, he spotted Mr. Grimfoyle ambling along the somewhat muddy bank just outside the perimeter fence, about to disappear into the trees.

Travis put on a burst of speed and landed lightly by the old man's side.

Mr. Grimfoyle spun to face him. "You wretched boy. Why did you leave me?" He scowled and glanced over his shoulder. "Never mind. The mist will be upon us soon. Allow me to help you."

"With your dark magic?" Travis said with a grimace. "No thanks."

"Listen to me, boy—"

"Travis."

Mr. Grimfoyle closed his eyes for a second or two. When he reopened them, he stared hard enough to wilt a plant. "If you think you can be of any service to your friends and family while at the mercy of this infernal storm, then be on your way. I have no use for you."

He turned and stalked into the trees, following the river.

Travis reverted to human form. There was no sense having wings in the middle of the woods. He trailed after Mr. Grimfoyle for a minute, then called out to him. "Fine. Do whatever you need to do."

*What have I got to lose?*

The old man slowed and turned back to face him. "No more nonsense. I'm too old in the tooth to suffer fools." He approached and raised his hands. "Stand still."

Mr. Grimfoyle began muttering an incantation. Travis felt nothing for a while, but then a strange *tugging* sensation swept over him, and he wrapped his arms around his chest as if to keep his essence from being stolen. It didn't work, though. With a gasp, the force yanked him off his feet, and he floated in midair for a few seconds while the pressure built in his chest.

Then it was over, and he dropped to the ground feeling decidedly lighter.

It took a moment to confirm he was alive and well. "So that's it? I'm safe from the storm now?"

"You are," Mr. Grimfoyle grunted.

"And you'll give that back? That piece of my . . . my soul?"

"I will. I have no need for it."

As the man perched on a tree stump and stared down into the river, Travis couldn't help feeling curious. "Why?"

"Because, boy, I was killed many moons ago. Only a witch's spell keeps me walking and talking. I am a soulless corpse. Well, now I have two pieces of soul stored away inside me, but they're not mine and never will be. Nor do I have any need for them."

"You're telling me you're *dead*?"

Mr. Grimfoyle nodded. "Have been for quite some time."

"How long?"

The man scrunched up his already wrinkled face and turned his gaze skyward. "Let me see . . . Well, I was born in 1823, grew up in the slums of Old Earth eking a living by stealing and selling, and turned out to be quite an astute businessman—but not astute enough to make myself filthy rich. One day, I stole from a witch, and she cursed me to live a very long life indeed. From that moment on, I never aged a day, which would have been wonderful if I had been in my twenties." He barked a laugh. "Alas, I was already old."

Travis could barely contain his astonishment. "You've lived nearly two hundred years?"

"I wouldn't call it living. More like lurking. And when I was doubled-crossed by a couple of thieves, they tried to kill me and failed. Or rather they did kill me, but I came back, so they tried again. Since I kept coming back, they resorted to stuffing me into a bag and dumping me in the sea." Mr. Grimfoyle gave a wry smile. "That was 1911. I spent over a hundred years in that bag and ended up on a beach, trapped in a small cove. That girlfriend of yours—what's her name again?"

"Melinda. And she's not my girlfriend."

"Yes, Melinda. Well, that girl's parents found me. They released me, and I immediately tried to dispatch them— because that's the kind of person I am." He pursed his lips. "Or perhaps *was*? I like to think I am a little nicer now. More caring. Crossing into this world, this New Earth, has been good for me. Now I steal from good, decent people instead of cutthroats, braggarts, and witches."

Travis wanted to hear more from this awful but strangely interesting person, but one thing kept nagging at him. "So the mist doesn't affect you?"

"Nor you, now—or your girlfriend."

"She's not—"

"The three of us together are perhaps the only people in the land capable of going after the faun to stop her. We're invincible—unless of course she sends her chimera and other pets after us."

Travis shook his head, trying to process everything. They both watched the slow-moving river for a while. Where were Melinda and Miss Simone?

"If I'm invincible," he said, "then I can go to the mines, right?"

Mr. Grimfoyle shrugged. "You *could*. But what would be the point?"

"To see if everyone is okay!"

"They're not." The man turned to him, a scowl on his face. "On second thoughts, if they've changed already and are still locked in there together . . . Imagine a few hundred squabbling monsters. Perhaps you *should* check on them. I'll stay here and wait for young Melinda to emerge, otherwise we'll all be running around aimlessly . . ."

Travis left the woods, transformed, and was halfway to the mines in two minutes flat. The idea of tunnels and mines crammed with all manner of creatures filled him with terror. Just one furious ogre or worse could result in untold deaths.

The faun might not have planned to kill anyone, but her storm had the potential to be deadly.

When he flew over his house, he hovered for a minute just above the haze where tendrils of mist reached upward. He was putting all his trust in a crazy old man who openly admitted to being a scoundrel. Sure, he'd performed some kind of spell; Travis had felt it. But it might be a trick.

*Why, though?*

He could think of no good reason for Mr. Grimfoyle to go to such elaborate lengths to lie. Taking a deep breath, Travis dropped into the mist and swooped down to his front lawn.

Hardly daring to acknowledge he'd landed safely and was still whole, he peered in the windows in case his mom or dad were somehow home. Seeing nothing, he launched and flew around low to the ground, deliberately aiming for a thick, blue, slow-turning whirlwind and plunging through. When nothing untoward happened, he allowed himself a sigh of relief.

*If only I knew where Dad buried that vial of potion . . .*

He started along the shortcut through the woods to the mines, then decided to use the main trail everyone else had used in case people had emerged and were heading back. The trail was wide enough for a wagon at first, but then he had to fold up his wings because it was so overgrown. Old wheel ruts were hard as baked clay under the trampled weeds, and he stumbled a couple of times.

He spotted a couple of horses grazing and heard the bleating of goats. At least they'd get to run around while everyone was cooped up in the mines.

The entrance loomed ahead, a tunnel cut into the side of a shallow hill. Thick wooden beams formed a sturdy doorway, and a metal-barred gate stood open. Travis entered the darkness, wishing he'd thought to bring a lantern before realizing he could see fairly well. He paused, wondering where the eerie red glow was coming from . . . and then figured it out. He was a mothman. He had bug eyes, and apparently they glowed red. It was like some kind of night vision.

Less than fifty paces into the narrow, square-cut shaft with a low ceiling, he stopped before a shocking sight. He'd fully expected to see this, but still it scared him—an impassable blockage of rocks and dirt. It looked like every tiny gap had been plugged. The debris could be ten or twenty feet thick.

Staring in silence, he felt a glimmer of hope. If the blockage was that impenetrable, maybe the mist hadn't worked its way through. There might be another entrance somewhere, but if so, Robbie would have blocked that, too.

*Just like in my vision.*

Except . . .

Travis frowned. Something was off. In his vision, he'd heard yelling. People panicking and screaming. They wouldn't do that if Robbie was purposefully bringing the roof down to save them from the mist. That part of his vision didn't make much sense.

"They're okay," he reassured himself anyway. "Trapped but alive."

But for how long? There had to be hundreds of people in there. Food and water would run short in a matter of days. Maybe more. Actually, he seemed to remember there was a trickling stream deeper in. Still, being trapped had to be a horrible feeling. Fear and frustration would kick in long before anyone grew hungry. Tempers would flare, fights would break out . . .

He couldn't know for sure, but he imagined people all over the world had suffered a similar experience decades ago when the virus had broken out across Old Earth. Those lucky enough to make it into bunkers had faced the prospect of forging a new life underground, unable to roam free outside until told that the air was clean.

They'd emerged thirteen years later.

And that was what his mom and Robbie and everyone else faced for as long as the mist lingered.

Travis clenched his furry fists, his wings spreading of their own volition. "I've got this, Mom. Miss Simone's out here with Melinda, and Lauren is going to find the faun, and . . ."

*And Dad is gone.*

He swallowed. His dad *wasn't* gone. He was out there somewhere. Travis clung to the belief that the faun, as crazy as she was, would stick to her original plan and bring every soul back as something *different*, with or without a memory of what they'd been. Something was better than nothing. When his dad returned, Travis knew he'd get through to him. It would be okay.

He turned away. Now that he was invincible to the mist, he could actually do something useful—like going after the faun. He just needed to treat this like another mission.

A steely determination crept over him as he headed back to the entranceway. Yes—a mission. He and Melinda could deal with this.

He heard a noise ahead.

Stopping, he focused on the square patch of blueish daylight as something moved into view there. A hulking four-legged creature with a lion's head and something else on its back—another head—and a long, thick tail that curled around and hissed noisily.

Travis groaned softly. The chimera was the last creature on earth he wanted to bump into right now. It had him trapped.

The chimera roared.

Two things happened then. A fireball shot toward him—and a sudden blast of images and noise filled his head, causing him to clutch his ears and throw himself to the ground with a yell.

He was only dimly aware of the fireball whooshing and sizzling as it soared overhead and smacked into the rubble. The explosion of rocks and dirt showered him, but he felt nothing. The only pain he felt was inside his mind as a series of snapshot images flashed and flickered, accompanied by terrible screams and shouts.

*This is it. This is my vision. I didn't see Robbie sealing the entrance. I saw this creature opening it back up!*

Travis cried out as another fireball roared by and hit its target. The explosion spattered him with even heavier debris. He sank into darkness, face down, his hands over his head and his wings spread wide . . .

## Chapter 13
## The Mines

Melinda swam as fast as she could without dislodging the silent dryad from her back. Flynn hung on around her waist, gagging and choking whenever water bubbled up into his face. She slowed each time, then gradually accelerated again.

"Stop complaining," she said when he gagged for the fourth time.

"I'm not!" he protested.

"You're making a lot of noise."

"That's the sound of me drowning. There's a difference."

There was no sign of Miss Simone. On the plus side, there was also no sign of the ice-breathing hydra, nor the nasty kelpie.

"This is hopeless," she said with a sigh, slowing to a leisurely pace so Flynn could catch a breath. "If Miss Simone is out here, she's nowhere near the river. I don't want to go hunting across fields for her."

"I'll protect you," Flynn said fiercely.

Melinda couldn't help wondering how a timid dryad could stand up to *anything*. Wasn't that why they were able to turn invisible?

"Thanks," she said. "But let's just try and avoid—"

A mournful moan sounded from a stand of trees. She whipped her head around and craned her neck to see. Sometimes the grassy bank was low enough to peer over, but here it was too high, so she eased herself up out of the water and wriggled onto the grass, staying low.

She gasped at the sight of a huge wolfman. Correction: wolf*woman*. Melinda hadn't seen any lycans except for Lucas. This one was slender with a long snout. Because of the lunar cycle being at its fullest, the lycans were in their fiercest, wildest state. This one loped along on two legs, stooped forward, arms swinging, nostrils flaring, and ears twitching, her long body hair covering a lean but muscular physique. She looked more animal than human now, an upright and rather large wolf.

Melinda opened her mouth to shout "Miss Simone!" . . . but refrained. What if it wasn't her? There were actual lycans in the area. That was why Lucas had come to visit.

But even if this *was* Miss Simone, suddenly Melinda had doubts about approaching her. Flynn hadn't even recognized his own father beyond a few dim, random memories. Why would Miss Simone recognize anyone she was merely acquainted with?

Melinda sank into the river, raising a finger to her lips and motioning for Flynn to be quiet. She indicated he should grab her waist again, and without a word, they resumed their calm river cruise—this time heading toward Carter.

As they drew close, Melinda glimpsed an opening to her left masked by reeds and overhanging grasses. A stream, very narrow, flowing in from somewhere beyond the fields . . .

She stopped and spun around, almost throwing Flynn off. "Hey," she said, not bothering to elaborate.

"What?"

Melinda pushed through the reeds. The offshoot stream stretched ahead, winding through the fields. It was *very* narrow, though. She could barely squeeze her shoulders in. Maybe if she swam on her side . . .

"Oh!" she exclaimed. "This goes to the mines. Or comes *from* the mines. It's the stream that flows underneath. It gave the old miners a fresh water supply back when they worked there."

"Miners," Flynn repeated, screwing up his face.

"Goblins. They used to mine for geo-rocks. Just one of many places. It's a dead place now, though—all the good stuff, the magic, the *sparkle*, has been dug out. But anyway, this stream . . ."

It didn't take her long to realize she had to follow it. But not with Flynn on her back. She turned to him and placed her hands on his wood-grained shoulders. "I'm going on alone."

He immediately turned invisible and fuzzed back in again, his face a picture of alarm. "No!"

"*Yes.* I'm sorry. I need to do this. But I need a favor."

Flynn narrowed his eyes. "That sounds suspiciously like you're trying to make me feel better."

"No, actually it's a pretty big favor. I'm almost afraid to ask you."

He drew himself up. "Ask, Melinda the mermaid."

"Well, Flynn the dry—" She paused, then said firmly, "Flynn the *human.* I need you to go to Carter and find Travis. Tell him I'm going to the mines, and I'll maybe see him there somewhere."

"I don't know this Travis person."

"You can't miss him. Look for the ugliest flying creature you can imagine, a human-shaped, grey-furred creature with dark wings and the face of an insect. He's got red, glowing eyes." She considered a moment. "And if he happens to be in human form, look for a boy a bit shorter than me wearing silky clothing like mine, with a clueless look on his face." She giggled.

It took a little longer to convince Flynn she needed him to do this. Eventually he agreed. He stood and watched as she turned on her side and plunged deep into the water. Then she was off.

Swimming on her side wasn't difficult, even heading upstream, but her fishtail kept batting at the narrow banks. She continued anyway, expecting the river to widen out. It didn't. It went on and on, cutting deep through the hills, sometimes completely underground for a while before emerging close to the surface. She passed under a small bridge at one point.

A human could never make this journey. When the river passed underground, the water filled the narrow tunnel to the top. She only stayed submerged for a minute or two, but she was a mermaid; a human would be much slower, probably half the speed.

The hazy sky above darkened as she entered the trees. Then the stream plunged underground again. Everything grew very dark, and she slowed her pace, feeling for the walls. Easily holding her breath and confident she had plenty of time, she pushed on against the flow.

What little light there was faded, and she swam in pitch-black darkness, using her hands for guidance. *Just don't dead-end*, she thought with a sudden panicky feeling. The idea of trying to reverse didn't appeal to her. But if she had to, the flow would help.

After a lot of sideways twists and turns, a vague light appeared ahead. It was deep here, and she guessed she was emerging from a fissure in the bottom of a tunnel or chamber. Realizing the walls had finally opened up, she spread her arms wide and smiled, seeing the light of lanterns glimmering through the clear water above.

She broke the surface at last and found herself in an expansive cavern filled with noisy people. The stream cut through the middle of them all, a water-filled crack in the flat rock floor. Any of the townsfolk could take a large step across the water if they wanted, but right now, with so many people present, the stream seemed to divide them into two squabbling factions.

Melinda waited, keeping her hands underwater, feeling like she might get stepped on if she gripped the rocky floor on either side. A pretty heated argument was in full swing.

"But we can't stay here forever!" a man shouted above the noise. Many in the crowd voiced their agreement.

"We've been over this," a woman said. Melinda pricked up her ears. Was that Travis's mom, Abigail? "Look, nobody has a right to decide for others. The exit is sealed, and the mist isn't getting in. We're safe right now. But if some of you want out, then it means pulling rocks out of the way and letting the mist in—and that's not going to happen."

Another part of the crowd cheered in agreement, clearly the majority.

"And how will we find out when it's safe?" another man demanded. "Is there a plan for that?"

"Yeah, has anyone really given this evacuation some thought?"

"Seems like we escaped one danger and walked into another."

"I'm from Old Earth," a calmer voice said. The noise died down a little. "I escaped the virus and spent thirteen years in a bunker. The last two decades have been bliss—the best time of my life. My wife and two children are with me right now. Do you think we want to be cooped up in another hole in the ground while a deadly virus spreads around the planet? No—we don't."

Voices started rising again.

"BUT," the Old Earther interrupted, "I don't want to die, either. So if we have to wait it out for a day or two, I'm okay with that. You should be, too."

Disgruntled murmurs suggested some disagreed, but his words had obviously made an impact on many others.

"And what about *him*?" a small, round-faced woman demanded. She averted her gaze. "No disrespect, sir, but you're dangerous."

The crowd parted a little to reveal Lucas lurking by the wall. He looked even more fearsome in the shadows, tall and broad, perhaps more wolfish than before.

"It's a full moon tonight," the woman said. "Just because we're in the mines doesn't mean he won't turn."

The murmurs started up again. Melinda noticed that Lucas made no attempt to respond. Maybe he knew she was right.

"Hey," a voice just behind Melinda said.

She turned to look up at a sweet-faced woman in her twenties. She wasn't the only one who had noticed Melinda in the water.

"Hello," Melinda said with a smile.

"What are you doing in there, girl?" an old beak-nosed man asked. "That water's gotta be freezing."

*Not really*, Melinda thought.

Someone whispered, "I didn't see her jump in, did you?"

"Uh-uh."

As the discussion raised in volume again, she jumped when she heard her dad's familiar voice. She couldn't make out his words, because he was talking quietly to some people up front, but just knowing he was near filled her with delight.

"Excuse me," she said briskly, pulling herself out of the water and sitting on the rocky edge with her dress and fishtail dripping wet.

People gasped and moved away so she had more space. Then someone pointed and shouted, "Hey, Robbie—your girl's here."

It took Melinda a moment to revert to human form. She climbed to her feet, noticing that her dress had dried already. Reaching up, she exclaimed in wonder. Her hair, too!

Her dad pushed through the crowd. He stopped dead when he saw her, then grinned and rushed to throw his arms around her. "Everything okay, sweetie?"

"It's all good, Dad," she assured him. Then, realizing everyone was watching, she struggled free and added, "Well, obviously it's not *all* good. Actually, nothing's very good right now. The mist is all over the place."

"But you're okay," Abigail said, appearing out of nowhere. She gave Melinda a side-hug.

Melinda looked around, seeing a wall of people and staring faces in the subdued light from lanterns. "Where's Mason?"

"He's been trailing around after Rez. Right now they're looking at stalactites in one of the smaller caverns deeper in.

Canaan's with them, along with a bunch of others." She smiled. "Most people have never visited this place. It's huge."

"Didn't even know it existed," a man mumbled from the crowd.

Abigail leaned toward Melinda. "Have you seen your mother? And Hal? Travis? Simone?"

"Haven't seen anyone since—well, since we were all together last."

Her dad said, "You went off with Simone. Where's she?"

"She . . ." *What should I say? Everyone's listening.* "She's somewhere around. Um, I made a new friend, a dryad boy called Flynn, but he's really a farmer's boy, and, uh, his dad is a naga now, and he doesn't . . . um . . ."

The crowd had fallen silent now.

*I'm terrible at this*, Melinda thought. *But telling them Miss Simone exploded into dust will cause a panic.*

As if sensing her reluctance to pass on bad news, her dad changed the subject. "Is the mist right outside the mines?"

She nodded.

"So we're definitely trapped for the time being?"

"Yeah."

"The dryad and naga you saw—are you sure they weren't just an ordinary dryad and naga?"

"Highly unlikely," Abigail muttered. "Just *seeing* a dryad speaks volumes." She sighed and raised her voice. "It's the real deal, everyone. Same as twenty years ago. The faun's back, and the mist is everywhere. We *have* to stay where we are for now."

"For how long?" a man demanded again, only in a softer tone this time. "And if your girl found her way in here, the mist will too—right?"

"Wrong," Melinda's dad said. "This stream runs underground. You'd have to hold your breath for a long time to make your way through. Melinda can do that in mermaid form—but we can't, and the mist can't. We're safe. The mines are good and sealed. We just have to be patient for a few days."

He put his arm around Melinda and steered her through the crowd. Abigail followed close behind. Lucas sidled over to join them, moving quietly for someone so brutish.

Melinda leaned against her dad. She felt safe with him. Her mom was still out there somewhere, but harpies were pretty tenacious. She'd be all right.

When they were away from the slowly dispersing crowd, Abigail leaned close and whispered, "Okay, tell us *everything*. Where's Simone?"

"Abi, ease up . . ."

Melinda took her dad's hand. "It's okay. Well, the thing is—"

At that moment, a tremendous *thud* sounded from a corridor, followed by a muffled yell. The four of them glanced that way. *Everyone* glanced that way. A silence fell.

"What was that?" a man piped up from somewhere.

"Shh."

Another thud shook the hanging lanterns around the place, followed by the pitter-patter of debris on the corridor floor.

Melinda's dad rushed to grab a lantern. "Oh no," he muttered.

"What's going on?" someone screeched. "What *is* that?"

Another thud, much louder now. This one was accompanied by a flash of orange. More dirt and rocks sprinkled the floor.

Melinda, her dad, Lucas, and Abigail inspected the wall of rubble. The roof fall itself wasn't the cause of their concern. Her dad had done that—he'd sealed them in. But now there was an opening near the top where daylight streamed through.

Another explosion made them all jerk backward in fright— a flash of firelight and another spray of dust and rocks.

Screams and yells came from behind her. "Who's *doing* that?"

A calmer voice said, "Wait—is it over? The mist is gone? Is this a rescue?"

His suggestion instantly silenced the panic and evoked a sense of relief and wonder. Melinda almost got caught up in the excitement. Of course! Who else would blow a hole in the carefully blocked tunnel? This *had* to be a rescue.

Everyone started cheering.

Everyone except Abigail, Lucas, and Melinda's dad. They exchanged a glance, then turned to Melinda with questioning looks on their faces.

"You were the last of us to be outside," Lucas rumbled. "Any ideas?"

Her excitement died as quickly as it had come. This wasn't a rescue. She shook her head, feeling miserable. "I—I don't know what's happening."

Her dad immediately transformed, filling the tunnel with his enormous ogre bulk so that he had to bend double. He rushed toward the roof fall, scooping up loose rocks as he went, obviously intent on plugging the holes. Lucas joined him, becoming even more wolfish as he hurried about.

But another explosion sounded, and this time half a fireball came inside and bounced off the walls. The ogre staggered as red-hot embers set his shaggy hair alight, and Lucas rushed to help smother the flames. Moments later, they both went back to work—then paused as they came face to face with the first tendrils of blue mist.

Neither one tried to avoid it. It seemed like time stood still as they stared it down. The mist curled around their necks. They stood side by side, a half-ogre and partial werewolf, standing up to what seemed like a feeble enemy . . .

"Dad, no!" Melinda screamed. "Get away from it!"

And then, abruptly, both men turned to dust and swirled away, their smart clothes falling where they stood.

Panic set in then. Everyone started yelling. Abigail spun around and grabbed Melinda's hand, but they had nowhere to go except to join the rear end of the crowd as everyone surged into the tunnels leading deeper into the mines. People tripped and fell, some plunging into the narrow stream, but most shouted and screamed as they tried to escape the deadly mist.

It seeped into the cavern, absolutely silent, moving slowly but surely.

Seeing the chaos, Melinda was eternally grateful her little brother was ahead of the crowd where he wouldn't be trampled.

"The water!" she cried, yanking on Abigail's hand. "The water is safe! Look, some people are jumping in—"

"We can't hold our breath like you can," Abigail whispered, strangely calm. Her jaw tightened as she stood firm, thinking hard. The mist crept closer.

Melinda shook and tugged at her hand. "We can't just *stand* here! What about the biosuits? You said you had enough for twelve!"

"Yes, and they're right there." Abigail pointed to a stockpile by the wall just inside the entranceway—numerous bags, sacks, wooden boxes, even a few small carts that had been wheeled in. The mist was already creeping over everything. "It's too late."

She glanced upward. The one advantage she had was flight. But the cavern ceiling was low, not much more than twice her height. The mist would fill every square inch.

Abigail had a look of resignation on her face. "There's no escape."

With the tunnels jammed with people and nowhere to go, she sagged at the shoulders and gave a sigh.

Her voice trembled when she spoke. "My husband, my son, your mom, Orson, Blair . . . they can't stay in the air forever. So I really don't know what— "

"Yes, but Mr. Grimfoyle did something to me! Somehow, the mist can't hurt me. Miss Simone disappeared before my eyes, but I didn't. I'm safe! And I think Travis might be, too."

Abigail's eyes widened. "Wait—you're *invincible*?"

"Y-yes!"

"Then there's hope!" She gripped Melinda's shoulder. "It's up to you guys. This is another mission, Melinda, your most important one yet. No pressure, but . . . please bring us all back!"

Melinda could only watch in horror as the mist crept up around her favorite aunt's shoulders and sniffed around her head.

Abigail stared at her the whole time, a grim smile on her face . . .

## Chapter 14
### Awakenings

*A woman towered over him, flames roaring from the top of her head. She grinned and showed her fangs . . .*

Travis woke with a throbbing headache. "I don't want any more stupid visions," he grumbled. "What's the point if I can't use them?"

He recalled a story about the prophecies of a mothman back in Old Earth. A bridge had collapsed in the late 1960s, killing forty-six people, and a mothman had been sighted numerous times beforehand. Travis guessed the creature had been trying to warn them, but nobody had paid attention.

His visions were probably important. Or maybe some were more important than others. But all of them were useless if he didn't know what to do with the information.

When he tried to roll over, he found himself pinned down by piles of dirt and small rocks. He struggled free, amazed that he hadn't suffered more injuries than a few bruises. He sat up, shaking his wings. Crying out with pain, he saw that one was kinked quite badly. It hurt when he tried to lift it.

*Transform a few times. The bone will soon heal.*

Reverting to human form, he found the pain shifted from his wing to a random place somewhere high on his back. Stretching and grimacing, he flexed his fingers and checked himself over, finding nothing more serious than a few aches. The broken wing—currently a sore area on one of his shoulder blades—wouldn't be a problem until he transformed again.

He looked back toward the entrance. The chimera was gone. With a heavy heart, he turned and peered into the darkness toward the roof fall and saw a gaping hole. The pile of rocks was still there . . . but where before the mist had been held at bay, now it had spread into the darkness, seeking out every tiny nook and cranny within.

Travis stared and stared, terror filling his heart. How long had he been out of it? Long enough for the dust to settle. There had to be a few hundred people in the mines, yet he heard nothing.

He climbed to his feet, his mind racing. He already knew what he'd find. *What next? What do I do?*

Clambering over the rocks and through the three-foot-wide hole, his fingers came away covered in soot. The chimera's fireballs had left their mark.

He scrambled down the other side and stood a moment while his eyes adjusted to the darkness. His mothman form would have offered night vision. Still, a few lanterns hung from the walls, glowing softly, and a few more lay on the tunnel floor, their lights extinguished. He heard the gentle trickle of water. But mostly what he focused on was the amount of discarded clothing scattered about the place.

A whisper echoed from somewhere, and he jumped at the sound. "Hello?" he called.

The whispering increased. But a sharper sound caught his attention, a scuffle nearby. He squinted and saw a shape rising from the shadows, standing up and moving toward him. He tensed.

"Travis?" a familiar voice said.

He breathed a sigh of relief. "Melinda!" Then he frowned. "How are you here?"

"I swam in. Travis, they're all gone. Everyone in here— gone."

Travis exhaled loudly. His worst fears had come true. The amount of pants, shirts, dresses, frocks, shoes, and other garments littering the floor was a dead giveaway. "You're saying they . . ."

"Exploded into dust, yes."

"*All* of them?"

"All of them."

"Your dad, too?"

Melinda nodded.

Travis swallowed. "And . . . my mom?"

"Everyone."

He shook his head and squinted into the shadows. His mom. His *mom*. The loss of his dad had been hard enough. He told himself it was a temporary thing. They weren't dead. They were just missing.

"Yeah, but . . . I mean, *everyone?*" he murmured.

Melinda huffed and stalked past him. "They're all gone, Travis. Let's get out of here."

He hastened to follow her back along the passage, still having a hard time believing what had happened even though he nearly tripped on a pair of pants and an upright boot. Was that—was that *Robbie's* boot? He glanced back at it. It could be. But what about his mom? Were her smart clothes here somewhere?

It wasn't until they had climbed back out through the hole in the roof fall and were hurrying toward daylight that Melinda spoke again.

"Who did this?"

"A chimera. The faun's pet."

She slowed and frowned at him. "The faun's here?"

"No, just her pet. At least, I don't *think* she's here." Travis shrugged. "Nobody really knows. We're all assuming she's at the center of the storm, like she somehow magicked it into existence, and it spread out away from her—"

"But she sent a chimera here to . . . to what? Break the mines open?" Melinda wore a deeply puzzled frown. "If she's at the center of the storm, which is way over the horizon, how did she even know people were *in* the mines?"

"I don't know. Same way she knew where Miss Simone kept all her potions. The chimera destroyed the lab, too."

Melinda's mouth fell open. "Destroyed the— What, so all her lab equipment, her latest experiments, her potions, our supplies of smart clothes, all *gone?*"

He'd forgotten about their smart clothes. "Yep. The potions that might have reversed the spell were kept in the lab."

She rubbed her eyes and thought for a moment.

Before she could say anything, Travis added in a dull voice, "My dad's gone, too. I saw him explode into dust."

Melinda slumped at the shoulders, looking pained. "I saw Miss Simone dissolve and float away. Travis—what about my mom?"

Finally, Travis had some news that had an element of hope. "She flew off to find the faun. She's okay. Or she was when she left."

He'd hoped for a spark of relief, but Melinda seemed to slump further. "Just us here, then," she muttered.

After half a minute of staring off into the distance, Travis filled her in about Mr. Grimfoyle's spell and how he'd 'borrowed' part of their souls so they wouldn't succumb to the power of the mist. Her frown deepened, but she nodded. "So *that's* how he did it."

"And here we are. The only two people who can walk around without a problem."

"Mr. Grimfoyle can, too," she reminded him. "And anyone who isn't human."

"Yeah, well . . ." Travis paused, uncertain how she'd take the rest of his news about the old man. Did she or did she not remember the story her dad had told them years ago? Apparently, Mr. Grimfoyle had been dismembered by lions at one point, and yet he'd lived. "He, uh, doesn't have a soul of his own. Because, you know, he's dead."

Melinda simply stared at him, one eyebrow raised. "So we're all perfectly safe as long as we give up a piece of our soul . . . or are already dead?"

"Kind of, yeah. But hey, there's a small vial of potion that my dad hid away twenty years ago. That'll save us."

"Where is it?" Melinda demanded.

"Don't know exactly. He never got a chance to tell me."

"Argh!" Melinda screeched, throwing up her hands in frustration. "Look, Travis, we need to do something. Let's go after the faun. I don't really see a choice, do you? My mom needs help."

"Yeah," he agreed—and then paused. "Did you hear that?"

They both turned toward the passage they'd exited from. Climbing over the rubble was a small tousle-haired figure wearing pants that were too big for him, and clutching a shirt. The creature—a gnome—had an oversized head and a heavily wrinkled face. His bare shoulders looked wrinkled, too.

Travis and Melinda watched in silence as the gnome paused to put on the shirt. His pants seemed to be shrinking to fit, and the reason for that became obvious as he pulled the shirt down over his head.

"Those are smart clothes," Travis whispered.

"Those are my *dad's* smart clothes," Melinda said angrily.

She stalked toward the gnome.

"Uh," Travis said, "hang on, I think maybe—"

"Those are not yours!" Melinda shouted. The gnome jerked around in surprise. "They belong to my dad. Go find something else to wear. There's plenty in there. My dad's going to need those when he . . . when . . ."

She trailed off as the gnome backed away from her. He was now fully clothed, and both silky garments had shrunk a few sizes so they now fit snugly around his small frame.

Travis joined Melinda, and together they watched as the gnome, eyeing them warily, began to edge past them. He was barefoot, his feet rather large compared to his small, thin body.

"Where are you going?" Melinda asked, more gently now. Her anger seemed to have dissipated.

The gnome shrugged and gestured.

Melinda stepped toward him, raising her hands as if to grasp an arm. "You're going into town? Do you remember the way?"

Eager to be past her, the gnome put on some speed and slipped away from her outstretched hands.

"Hey!" Melinda yelled as he hurried along the trail that led through the woods. She turned to Travis, looking troubled. "Do you think that might have been . . . I mean, do you think it's possible . . ."

"You think he's your dad?"

She swallowed. "That seems to be how it works. They explode into dust, then come back after a while as someone else. Some*thing* else. He picked up the smart clothes. He might have remembered they were his."

"But somehow forgot you were his daughter?" Travis argued.

Melinda pursed her lips, watching the gnome disappear along the woodland trail.

Travis reached for her hand. "Look, I don't know if that's your dad or not, but it's a good sign, right? Someone came back. That means they *all* might come back. This was the faun's plan, right?" He struggled to remember the details of the story his dad had told him long ago, and what Mr. Grimfoyle had hinted at. "The faun doesn't want anyone dead. She wants to . . . to *evolve* people into something else."

"So my dad's a *gnome*?" Melinda said, sounding bitter.

"Maybe. But it doesn't matter, because we're going to bring them all back. You and me, Melinda—this is a mission, and we're gonna fix things."

Voices sounded from within the mines, one a soft female cry, the other a deep, guttural, angry roar.

Seconds later, a blue-skinned elf scrambled through the opening in the rubble. She clutched a shabby robe to her chest, and as she spotted Travis and Melinda standing there with their mouths open, she pulled it tighter around her and ran past them in a half-crouch, making sure to twist around as she went so she didn't reveal her bare backside.

Travis averted his gaze. "I think we should probably get out of here."

But before Melinda could reply, that guttural roar came again. This time, a monstrous form appeared in the partially blocked tunnel, peering through the opening. It had muscular human shoulders . . . but the enormous head of a bull.

"A minotaur," Travis whispered. "That's not good."

It let out a bellow and lunged at the gap, dislodging rocks and dust as it struggled to get through.

Travis was about to transform and sweep Melinda away into the sky when another roar came from behind the bull-headed man, distracting it. Some kind of fight broke out behind the roof fall, and a sudden flash of flame lit up the darkness, silhouetting both figures for an instant.

Above the noise, Travis heard that weird whispering sound again, together with the shouts and cries of many different voices—high-pitched squeals, mournful wails, frantic yelps, angry bellows, even fluty laughter. The silence had turned into a chaotic babble, and the noise intensified as more townsfolk returned to the land of the living.

The minotaur let out a grunt of pain and slammed against the opening in the roof fall. It had a look of surprise on its face—and then its eyes rolled back, and the monster slid out of sight.

A second later, a fierce woman stuck her head through the gap. Flames licked up from her hair. She wore smart clothes, and Travis sucked in a breath at the sight of the familiar material. She was clearly strong and agile, and as she sprang from the opening and moved toward the daylight, Travis saw her grey-furred legs below her smart dress, with hooves like a faun.

Only she wasn't a faun. Travis had seen an empusa vampire before. The fiery hair was a dead giveaway, and so were the fangs she bared as she hissed at the dazzling daylight.

"Mom?" he called.

## Chapter 15
## Nothing is The Same

Travis approached the empusa vampire. Deeper in the passage behind her, half-dressed figures were climbing out through the opening and dusting themselves off.

"Mom?" he said to the creature with her hair on fire. Once more, he was struck by how accurate his vision had been. Despite the danger of getting too close, he felt like a moth attracted to a flame—almost literally.

The empusa hissed at him, then went back to glaring at the stark daylight flooding the ground inches from her feet. She lifted a hoof and gingerly stepped outside the tunnel's shadow—then winced and yanked it back again.

Her fangs were long. *Great for sucking blood*, Travis thought as she bared them in his direction once more. At least he felt safe standing in the sunlight.

"Can I help?" he asked. "Maybe a blanket?"

"When will it be sundown?" the empusa snarled.

Travis could only shrug. He had no idea what time it was. "Uh . . . in a few hours."

He absently stepped aside to allow a couple of naga to slither past. Then, with a double take, he paid more attention to a dozen others emerging from the mines and watched the growing crowd in amazement. Three elves, two goblins, four pixies, a gnome, two brownies, and still more clambered through the hole.

He heard another ruckus from inside—an angry roar, anxious shouts, a single commanding bellow, scuffles and grunts . . . Then, whatever had been roaring in anger suddenly gave a yelp and went quiet.

After that, another stream of elves and goblins hurried out, all thankfully wearing something. Travis couldn't help wondering how they managed to recall such a trivial thing as clothing and yet completely forget who they were.

"Hey," Travis said to a passing elf. "What's your name?"

The short, blue-skinned creature—either a boy or very young man—gave him a quizzical look. He shook his head, causing his dust-covered white hair to flop in front of his face. He pushed it back and hurried past.

Other elves avoided Travis's gaze, so he grabbed a goblin's arm instead. "What about you? What's your name?"

"What's it to you?" the goblin snarled.

Travis recoiled, taken aback by the hostility. Goblins were known to be grumpy, but not outright mean.

Other goblins gave him the same hateful glare, and he stepped back and waited for them all to stomp past. Funny how they had gathered and emerged in groups like this. There were hundreds of people in the mines, and he had no doubt there would be many more such groups, but for now the last of the goblins barreled past, each wearing pants that were too long and too tight, and shirts that tore as they struggled into them. Some goblins had attempted to put on slender dresses, and the result was both comical and embarrassing.

Travis stared hard at the ground until they'd passed by.

Melinda joined him. "Mason's in there," she said in a trembling voice. "He and Canaan, and your friend Rez—they were looking at stalactites deeper in the mines. They might be some of the last ones out." She turned to him. "We have to fix this."

She had tears on her cheeks. Travis swallowed. "Sure."

His mom still stood by the entrance, bathed in shadow, inches from the daylight. Perhaps it was a good thing she couldn't go running off. Large groups of elves and goblins might be easy to find, but an empusa vampire would have no desire to stick around.

More pixies came next—humanlike, very small, no taller than chest height. They had long, pointed ears that stuck upward, and thin, serpentine tails. Their clothes were baggy and long, and they had to hold onto their pants to stop them from falling down, especially with their tails in the way.

"It's weird seeing them all together like this," Travis whispered. "Pixies are normally loners, and they definitely don't hang out with goblins and elves."

"They'll probably shoot off in different directions once they're out of this place," Melinda whispered back.

They watched them walk off along the woodland trail. They stayed together, at least for now.

Large-headed gnomes blundered past, along with a random cyclops who towered over them all and didn't seem to care that he kicked a few as he strode among them. He was much taller than a human but fairly short for a cyclops, so he had to be a youngster.

Behind him, a few more naga slithered free of the mines. They looked thoroughly put out at having suffered the indignity of being imprisoned with crowds of 'inferior creatures' . . .

Then a huge stick-and-mud creature held up the procession as it bent and tore a bigger opening in the rubble. Large rocks tumbled loose, then a deluge of smaller ones, and finally the golem stepped through, stooping under the low ceiling, its wooden face giving away no sense of emotion. Once clear of the tunnel and into daylight, it stood up straight, fully eight feet tall.

"How is there a golem here?" Melinda said as a couple of giggling brownies ran past. They looked rather like pixies, small and slight with the same pointed ears, but they had no tails—and their hair was long and black even though these two were male.

"What do you mean?" Travis asked.

"I mean golems aren't real. They're made out of clay and sticks, then animated by magic."

Travis glanced again at the golem as it stalked away. "Looks pretty real to me. Does it matter?"

A manticore came next, pouncing out of the darkness, licking its lips and showing three rows of needle teeth. Travis grabbed Melinda's arm and pulled her aside as the red-furred, human-faced lion looked them up and down and slowed. "My, what have we here? You're an unusual sight."

Frowning, Travis couldn't help responding. "*We're* an unusual sight?"

The manticore sat before them, curling its scorpion tail around and letting the ball of poison-tipped quills and vicious stinger dangle in plain sight. "A rather odd pair, if I may say. What *are* you?"

Travis exchanged a glance with Melinda. "Uh," he said, "we're human."

"*Human.*" The manticore licked its lips. "Many of us have shades of the legendary *human* in us, but we all know true humans don't really exist. So what are you, really?"

"Uh . . ."

As the manticore sat there eyeing them up and down, a centaur ducked and scrambled over the roof fall, then clip-clopped past, giving the red-furred monster a wary glance. A legion of other creatures followed—a few more pixies and goblins, a human-faced, silver-skinned reptilian cat known as a lamia, at least eight fauns, and dozens of tiny faeries that zipped about everywhere.

"So?" the manticore prompted. "What are you?"

Melinda cleared her throat and spoke with a tremble in her voice. "You're the first, um, person that's talked to us. Everyone else seems to look at us like we're something nasty they just stepped in."

The manticore gave a high, fluty laugh. "You *are* rather unsavory. I would love to know what's inside your minds . . ."

The creature narrowed its blue eyes and licked its lips.

Travis knew what that meant. Manticores devoured humans and absorbed knowledge from their brains. That was why they struck up conversation before the kill—to get the brain juices flowing and the thoughts stirred up. Or so he'd heard.

Before the manticore could raise its stinger, Travis transformed and spread his wings. The sudden change caused the manticore to leap backward in surprise, and Travis used that moment to leap off the ground and grab Melinda's outstretched hand. In seconds he was airborne, dodging a volley of poison-tipped quills that shot from the manticore's tail.

"Back soon, Mom!" he yelled down to the puzzled empusa as he shot up between some trees, narrowly missing their reaching branches.

But Travis hadn't reckoned on his wing hurting so bad. The break wasn't completely repaired, and he cried out in pain as he struggled to safety. He eased up and glided in a circle over the trees, resting the injured wing.

"Travis?" Melinda called, dangling below.

"I'm okay," he said with a grimace. "Slightly broken wing."

"*Slightly* broken?"

"Less broken than it was. I'll land somewhere."

He came down a little heavier than he'd planned, causing Melinda to skid and stumble as he swooped down into the meadow outside the woods. He reverted to human form again, noting that his shoulder blade still ached just a little.

Travis's house stood not too far away. He and Melinda watched the line of townsfolk spreading out as they headed toward Carter. Some slithered, some marched, some trudged. The faeries flew in all directions but kept circling back. On the surface, there was no reason for any of these different tribes to stay together, nor even to head toward their old home of Carter . . . yet they did, and this gave Travis hope.

"They remember," he said. "They might not remember who they are or what they're doing here, but they recognize the area, and they know something is there for them. Their town. Their *home.*"

Melinda sighed. "Maybe. I don't think it'll last, though. Flynn was the same way. He felt a need to go home, and he recognized the goats and the house, but when he got there, he just felt it wasn't home anymore, and he couldn't wait to get to the forest."

"Oh."

After a silence, Melinda added, "But it's better than nothing. What if we try to get people to their homes?"

Travis snorted. "We don't even know who any of them are or which house they live in."

"Well, no, but we can at least find our dads and bring them home. And your mom, if we can get her there without having our blood sucked out."

"And Lucas," Travis said. "I've been looking out for his smart clothes, but I haven't seen him yet, which means he must still be inside the mines."

Melinda nodded. "Okay, but it'll be harder to find Mason and Rez. They're not wearing smart clothes. I can't remember what Mason *was* wearing . . ." She covered her mouth, tears welling up. "Is that bad? It *feels* bad."

"I would never remember what anyone else was wearing," Travis said.

"And we'll never find Canaan among the other elves. She could be long gone." Then Melinda huffed and shook her head. "What am I thinking? She's probably something completely different now."

That was a weird thought—the idea that an elf shapeshifter might have been turned into something like a pixie or a goblin when simply a full-time elf would have been a much more logical fit! And if she *had* been turned into an elf and tried to transform, would she have shifted into a slightly different elf, or stayed the same?

Travis mulled this over for a moment while Melinda stared into the distance, lost in thoughts of her own.

"Okay," he said at last. "Look, it's pretty late in the afternoon. I don't think my mom is going anywhere just yet, so let's go into town and find our dads."

Melinda turned to face him, looking hopeful. "And bring them home?"

"Yeah. Maybe to my house. We can keep them together."

Travis shifted back and forth a few times to make sure his wing was fully healed, then dragged Melinda off into the air. He swooped easily over the long procession of altered townsfolk, amazed at how many there were. Hundreds of people changed beyond recognition. The leading crowd of elves, naga, and goblins had almost made it to Carter's perimeter already, but the rear end of the line hadn't left the mines yet.

Travis spotted a couple of sphinxes and couldn't help thinking of Bo and Astrid, wherever they were right now. But that was the problem—it didn't matter where they were. All who stood in the path of the storm would soon be turned to dust. The town of Hemlock on the coast, Garlen's Well, numerous smaller settlements around the region, even as far north as Louis and as far east as Brodon—all doomed to be swept up in the slow-moving but unstoppable blue mist, the human race wiped out.

Suddenly, making sure their dads were safe at home seemed almost pointless. But it felt like the right thing to do.

Travis flew low above the hazy streets, awaiting the first arrivals into town. Slightly ahead of the oncoming crowd, he spotted a single gnome banging his head on the wall of a thatched home. Melinda saw him at the same time and gasped. "There! My dad!"

Landing behind him, Travis remained in mothman form and stood nervously while Melinda quietly approached the gnome. She reached for his shoulder, making him jerk and swing around.

"It's okay!" Melinda cried. "It's just me. You remember me, right? You're . . . you're my dad, I know you are. You're wearing his clothes, and you were first out because you were closest to the roof fall." She nodded as if she'd just convinced herself. "Yes, the mist got you first, and you were the first to come back. And Travis's mom was soon after, along with . . ."

She shot a look at Travis.

"What?" he asked.

"That minotaur was one of the first things we heard. Do you think it's Lucas? He was right there with my dad when the mist crept in."

Travis groaned. "Great. A minotaur who can turn into a werewolf? That's just . . . that's just *great*, Melinda."

She turned back to the gnome, who had resumed his head-banging. "Dad? Will you come with us? I can take you somewhere safe."

The gnome paused and squinted at her. "Safe? No giants?"

"No giants," Melinda agreed.

"Garden with fence?" the gnome urged, stepping closer. He had smudges of dirt and soot on his wrinkled face. "Enclosed? Safe?"

"Uh, right. Exactly, yes."

The gnome nodded his oversized head and gave a grin, the first Travis had ever seen on a gnome—not that he'd seen many gnomes in his life. Melinda smiled and took his hand. "I'm taking him to your house, Travis," she murmured. "Probably safer there away from everyone."

"Okay. I'll be with you in a bit."

Travis watched her lead the gnome away, bemused and more than a little confused.

Giants?

## Chapter 16
## House Arrest

Travis searched for his dad, but he couldn't help being distracted by the new arrivals. The town of Carter was filling up, repopulating.

He flew above the streets, noting how goblins, elves, naga, pixies, and even gnomes spread through the streets apparently with a destination in mind. Many of them stood outside doors, just gazing and scratching their heads, while others tentatively pushed their way in.

Travis focused on one particular goblin. The stout, pig-faced woman, almost wearing a dress that was split in several places, rattled the door knob and entered. She was out of sight for half a minute as Travis circled above. Then she re-appeared, standing on the doorstep, hands on hips. Finally, she left the house, turned this way and that, almost started walking . . . and then paused, looking back at the open door. In the end, she sidled back in again, and Travis could see her nostrils flaring even from where he hovered over the roof.

*Like a confused kid in a new home*, he thought, feeling a pang of sadness.

It was the same story all over the town. Many residents abandoned their homes, opting instead to march back out of Carter . . . only to stand around at the perimeter wondering what to do next. Elves and goblins clustered together. The naga isolated themselves but appeared equally uncertain. Pixies and brownies didn't seem to mind so much; they entered house after house, apparently exploring with some degree of mirth.

Two sphinxes sat together at an intersection, and it seemed they answered a lot of questions as confused townsfolk walked past. Travis wanted to hear what was being said, but he really needed to concentrate on finding his dad.

The manticore loped into view at the outskirts of the town. It—or rather *he*, Travis reminded himself—had cut a path through the woods instead of walking across the fields. Manticores loathed to be out in the open.

The cyclops caused a bit of trouble. As far as Travis knew, the one-eyed creatures could be as temperamental as ogres— big softies one minute, raging monsters the next. This one pounded on a door until the whole thing splintered and fell inward, and then the cyclops rampaged around inside smashing things, even busting out some windows. After a while, he calmed down and emerged to sit on the doorstep.

The golem was no different. He knelt to peer in through a window and seemed to freeze like that for a long while. He was still in that position when Travis flew past a third time.

A pack of gargoyles scampered down the streets, then split up and scaled walls in a matter of seconds, taking up perches on the rooftops. There they froze, much like the golem below.

Travis almost flipped over in joy when he spotted a harpy flying toward him above the houses. Lauren had returned! But his heart sank when several more of the creatures fluttered down from the thickening clouds. He suddenly doubted any of them were Melinda's mom. They'd most likely emerged from the mines together. Or they could be a pack of *real* harpies. How was anyone to tell?

That thought struck a chord of fear in him. Melinda's dad was a good example. It was bad enough that Robbie had turned into a gnome. But how awful that he could walk off into a crowd of *real* gnomes and never look back, and if he changed out of those smart clothes—which he would sooner or later— then Melinda would likely never identify him again.

"Find Dad," Travis reminded himself.

He searched and searched, scared he would never find him. Or if he did, not recognize him. Only magical smart clothes would give him away. Travis tried to ignore what kind of creature he was looking at and focused entirely on what they wore—or didn't wear in some cases. He grimaced at the sight of a naked pixie running about in one street and a waddling goblin in another.

At the far western end of Carter, a massive ogre sat on a rooftop. The roof had collapsed under him, and the ogre appeared to be stuck, lounging there with his arms splayed to the sides like he'd found a well-worn armchair. He looked relaxed, unlike earlier when he'd torn through the streets.

Travis was sorely tempted to fly close and kick the ogre in the face. *That was my dad you beat unconscious. Now he's gone. He could have flown above the mist if you hadn't attacked him. It's your fault he's not here.*

The anger he felt almost overcame him, but he veered away, knowing the ogre might swat at him like an annoying fly. One smack and Travis would be down and out.

In the pond at the center of town, an amazing sight distracted him again—three mermaids frolicking with a large black horse. Someone sat astride the horse's back—a small elf boy who seemed to enjoy being dunked up to his waist as his steed waded into the water. But his laughter turned to cries of terror as the horse sank deeper and deeper.

Why didn't he kick free? Maybe he couldn't swim.

The mermaids rushed to help, but it seemed they couldn't drag the elf boy off, so one went under with him, pressing her face to his as they submerged amid froth and bubbles. The other two mermaids scolded the horse, but it ignored them, sinking lower until only its snout was sticking out.

A piercing shriek filled the air, and Travis nearly tumbled out of the sky in shock. Two mermaids with their mouths wide open, letting out a terrible noise that caused the pond to ripple and froth. The black horse reared up with a frantic whinny and scrambled to get away. In that instant, Travis saw the elf boy tumbling free, clutched in the arms of the third mermaid.

*The kiss of a mermaid*, Travis thought, suddenly jealous. *I mean, he was about to drown, and she was just giving him air, and it was probably horrible and frightening. But still . . .*

He almost wished he were that elf. Just for a moment.

"Find Dad!" he yelled, furious with himself.

He was used to squinting through the blue haze by now, but a strange column of thicker mist caught his attention. He flew around it, curious. It was like a funnel reaching up from the ground. He followed it upward until he emerged from the mist and ascended into clear air. With a shock, he realized the funnel stuck out the top another fifty feet or so. A miniature tornado of blue mist?

As important as finding his dad was, this discovery trumped that mission just for the moment. The faun's storm was unnatural, and the lingering blue haze across the landscape equally so, but this funnel . . . It didn't fit. It didn't make sense.

He thought he could make out a shape within the funnel, a kind of negative space where the blue mist *wasn't*. From this angle, the swirling funnel appeared to be split in two about halfway down, so it looked like a couple of legs.

Just then, a whole section peeled away from the top half, lifting upward . . .

Travis gasped and fluttered backward, reeling with shock. He could see it now, that negative space within the mist—an invisible arm rising toward him, fingers curling open, reaching out to grab him.

Yelling with terror, Travis shot away. Only when he was at a *very* safe distance did he pause to turn back, and then he yelled again, amazed that he hadn't seen this thing before.

*A giant.*

When the monstrous human-shaped figure stood still, the funnel cloud was barely visible through the haze unless Travis rose high above the town. Then he could see it clearly. And when it turned with one arm raised, moving in awful slow motion, its overall shape and size stood out crystal clear: a man of colossal height, thin and gangly, its feet firmly planted in the streets as it slowly turned toward him like a gargantuan tree twisting in a gale.

Travis quaked in his smart shoes. How could he have not seen this mighty beast before? How had nobody noticed? But the truth was, from below, the haze blocked it out. The streets might be impassable, but that just meant a few goblins and elves were puzzled by an invisible obstruction. Just one more bewildering problem on top of the rest.

Travis dared to fly closer to the giant. Thankfully, it hadn't moved its feet. It stood still, its raised arm just now dropping back to its side. The head had no discernible face. The whole thing was merely a three-dimensional silhouette within the funnel mist. How long had it been standing there? It certainly hadn't wandered out of the mines.

*Could this be . . .?*

"No way," he whispered.

*But what if it is?*

He barely croaked out the word: "Dad?"

He couldn't bring himself to call out to the thing. He couldn't bring himself even to believe this monster might truly be his dad.

Travis felt his terror dying and anger building. This was too much. This invisible giant was *impossible* to deal with. And if it decided to take even one step, let alone stamp about the town, then the loss of life—

He tore away, fighting tears. It was time to catch up with Melinda and deal with something real and tangible, something *simple*, a sad-faced gnome who just needed a safe place to hide. After that, they'd go after the empusa. It might be a little darker by then.

"Argh!" he yelled as a new, unexpected, and entirely ill-timed mothman vision flashed through his mind:

*. . . A dragon rested its head on the rocky floor, a shaft of moonlight glinting off a small, blue gem near its paw. In the darkness, the monster let out a low, mournful moan before taking its very last breath . . .*

Travis fought to control his panic. Maybe this vision wasn't so ill-timed. Thinking of his dad had triggered this one. Only it wasn't his dad he'd seen. It *couldn't* have been. And anyway, the beast in his vision had looked smaller and slimmer than his dad.

He shoved the thought to the back of his mind. He had no doubt the vision would come true, but what was he supposed to do about it?

*Just as long as it's not my dad . . .*

He raced away.

\* \* \*

He caught up with Melinda shortly after.

She'd made good progress. Having trudged across the meadows with the gnome in tow, she was almost at Travis's house by the time he landed on his front lawn. He watched them coming, then led the way around to the back of the house where his dad had a fenced-in section for growing vegetables. The fence kept the wildlife and critters away, and right now it would give the gnome a sense of security.

It was hard to believe this mild, fumbling creature with an oversized head was Melinda's father, the famous ogre shapeshifter, or Uncle Robbie as Travis knew him. He watched in silence as Melinda led him into the enclosure like some kind of new pet. Gnomes weren't the smartest of creatures. Ogres were lacking in that department, too.

Yet another horrible thought: Even if he could still transform, Robbie would have to switch between a dimwitted gnome and an even dimmer ogre. How long before his remaining human faculties faded into a murky swamp of stupidity?

The gnome seemed pretty happy right now, though. He threw himself down in a soft bed where corn grew and plunged his hands deep into the soil. Just that act alone calmed him. He grinned at Melinda, and she smiled back, then swallowed and backed away as her eyes filled with tears.

"He's safe," Travis whispered as she joined him by the gate. He touched the upright planks of the fence. "This is solid. We can lock the gate. There are no gaps for small critters to get in, so he won't be able to squeeze out—and it's taller than him, so he'd have to be pretty determined to climb over."

"But he could if he wanted," Melinda said, wiping her eyes.

"Well, let's keep him happy, then." Travis patted her shoulder. "*You* keep him happy. I have to go find my mom."

She sighed and nodded. "Maybe I'll hunt around for that vial of potion your dad buried. Any ideas?"

Suddenly struck by the urge to help her find it, he moved from place to place looking for some kind of logical burial place. It couldn't just be in some random patch of dirt. Nobody dug holes to store something for safekeeping without bothering to mark the spot.

They searched for a while—along the flower beds, near an old disused well, in and around a shed, between some firmly embedded rocks, and in the enclosed vegetable garden. Melinda's dad joined in, digging far more deftly than the two of them combined.

Nothing.

"I need to find my mom," Travis said at last, brushing soil off his hands. "It's getting dark."

Melinda stopped digging and twisted to face him. "She's going to be hard to deal with."

He stared at the rows of corn towering over the gnome. He and his dad had spent a lot of time together shucking cobs until they'd discovered it was better to leave the cobs in their protective casings and boil them as they were, and peel back the layers later. The annoying stringy bits came off easier that way.

"Travis?"

He waved his hand dismissively and said, "Gotta go. As soon as it's dark, Mom will be out of there, gone forever. The sunlight is the only thing keeping her in the mines. So I need to either trap her there overnight . . . or bring her *here* before the sun sets."

"But how are you going to do that?"

Travis gazed at the corn for a long time before answering. "I think I have an idea. The spare room upstairs will do nicely."

"She'll jump straight out the window as soon as it's dark!"

"Not if we trap her."

"And you don't think she'll break the glass?" Melinda said, climbing to her feet and wiping her dirty hands on her dress. Then she paused. "Oh, wait. Your house has reinforced doors and windows. She won't be *able* to break the glass."

Travis nodded. "And there are shutters, too. I can secure them with rope." Warming to his plan, he added, "I just need to find a really big, thick curtain . . ."

## Chapter 17
## Cloaking the Vampire

"Crazy, crazy, crazy," Travis muttered to himself as he flew low over the trees. He had a short length of rope in his pocket and was carrying a folded curtain—an old, thick one from the basement, covered with dust and cobwebs. His mom wouldn't miss it.

The idea of cloaking the vampire had come to him while staring at the corn growing in the yard. *Just wrap her up so she's completely encased.* But the notion had evolved into something more. *And then I can carry her—like a stork delivering a newborn baby. No problem. She just needs to agree to it.*

Travis landed at the entrance to the mines. The place was quiet. It seemed everyone had finally made their way out. He wondered if Canaan, Rez, and Mason were still together. What would they look like now?

The empusa vampire—his mom—lurked in the shadows, her arms folded. The flames on her head had gone out.

"Still here?" Travis said, trying to sound like he had nothing to fear from her. "Thought you would have left by now."

She gave him a withering look. "As soon as the sun is down."

"But why do you need to leave? The mines are huge. You could wander around down there for days. There's plenty of fresh water."

"There's food, too," the empusa agreed, raising an eyebrow at him.

Travis nodded. "Tons of it. Bread, cheese, eggs—"

"I'm not talking about that kind of food."

He studied her, feeling a chill as the meaning of her words sank in. "You mean . . . there are still *people* down there."

The empusa licked her lips. She looked troubled and more than a little puzzled. "I'm getting hungry."

"Mom, you can't," Travis blurted, forgetting himself for a moment. He flung the folded curtain aside and stepped toward her, closer to the shadowed entranceway. But he checked himself, staying in the weakening sunlight.

She tilted her head, clearly puzzled. "Tell me why. I have conflicting thoughts about it. My head tells me there is food down there—I've heard the voices of goblins and a few others, and that minotaur is still here. All of them have thick, pulsing blood running through their veins. If I sealed myself in the mines with them, I could feast for weeks on just a handful of victims."

Travis tried to make out her features, but the fading sunlight caused deepening shadows on her face. "I know of a better place."

"Oh? Where?"

"Your home."

She was silent. After a while, she unfurled from the darkness and eased forward, closer to the daylight. She stood tall, and Travis had no doubt she could pounce high into the air if she wanted—though not in a confined tunnel.

"And where is my home?" she said softly. She tried to sound like she didn't care, but her voice was full of intrigue and longing. "Why don't I remember much of it?"

"What *do* you remember?"

She paused. "I'm not sure. I just have a feeling the place is close."

Travis nodded eagerly. "It is. And I can take you there." He gestured toward the folded bundle at his feet. "I can wrap you up in this thick curtain to shield you from the sun and carry you home. Then you can eat." He quickly added, "Like a sandwich or something."

She stared at him.

"A steak sandwich?" he said.

Deeper in the tunnel, behind the roof fall, an irritated grumbling started up.

The empusa glanced back and scowled. "Now you've set the minotaur off. You'd best be on your way."

"Come home with me," Travis persisted.

"Maybe I will," she said softly, "*after* the sun goes down. I'll seek out this 'home' you speak of."

The idea of a vampire scratching at his window in the night filled him with terror. He wanted her home—but safely locked away.

The minotaur grumbled again, and suddenly his horns showed. He peered over the roof fall, a black shape lit up by glowing lanterns in the background. Could it be Lucas? If so, the best place for him was right there in the mines. Especially when night fell.

*But anyone else left behind had better leave. Nobody wants a minotaur rampaging around tunnels after them—especially one that turns into a werewolf.*

"You can't stay here," Travis urged. He lowered his voice. "That minotaur? He's a shapeshifter."

The empusa said nothing.

"He's a shapeshifter," Travis repeated, a little louder this time. "As soon as the moon is out, he'll start to turn. Probably before then, actually. I think it's a full moon tonight. He's feeling the effects already."

"The *effects* . . . ?"

"The pull of the moon. He'll be a werewolf soon."

"I don't know what you mean," the empusa murmured. "Besides, I handled him earlier. My fists can pack more of a punch than you think."

"Well, if you want to stay right here and take your chances with the minotaur turning into a raging seven-foot-tall wolfman while you're stuck in the shadows of the tunnel, then . . ."

He trailed off, feeling no need to say anything more.

The minotaur suddenly let out a bellow that echoed throughout the tunnel and probably halfway into the mines. He crashed through the opening in the roof fall and stamped toward them, all muscle, thick hair, and a sheen of sweat. But he wore silky smart pants.

*Lucas!*

The empusa raised her fist and stared at it as if expecting something to happen. And, just for a moment, Travis swore her flesh developed a curious metallic sheen, a brassy color . . . but then the color faded, and she hissed with obvious annoyance.

The minotaur advanced. With nowhere to go but into the daylight, the vampire stumbled out, shielded her face, and sprang for the trees on powerful goat legs. The minotaur bellowed and went after her.

Travis grabbed the curtain and shot into the air, narrowly missing the jutting branches of overhanging trees. But the minotaur had his sights set on the empusa and completely ignored him. Maybe the empusa's punch had enraged the bullheaded creature.

Circling around and trying to trace the whereabouts of the empusa proved impossible in the woods. Travis could see glimpses of the forest floor, but she was well hidden, probably cowering under a thick branch somewhere.

The minotaur was much easier to spot. The monster snorted and huffed and tore after her, zigzagging around the trees.

Travis had to assume this was indeed Lucas. He wore smart pants, and he'd been among the first to appear from the mines. And if that was the case, the shapeshifter really might react to the moon in the next few hours.

Werewolf or not, Lucas the minotaur was a formidable monster. He crashed around in the woods below, roaring and panting, hot on the heels of the screeching empusa. Travis kept glimpsing the two of them through the trees but couldn't find a large enough opening to drop in and help her. If he could just reach down and pluck her into the air . . .

Then the woods simply ended. The meadow sprawled below, and his house stood just a short distance away.

Another one of those mothman visions flashed through his mind just then, and he clutched his head and spun in the air:

*. . . A tower stood in the middle of a small lake. The water shone like a mirror, calm and clear, with no sign of the hazy mist that blanketed the landscape. Flying creatures circled the tower . . .*

"Curtain!" the empusa screamed from below.

Travis jerked and cursed inwardly. Just for once, he'd sensed the importance of a vision, and this time it had been interrupted. A tower in a lake? That seemed like a decent clue, something he could *use.*

"CURTAIN!"

He flew down, searching for the empusa, aware that the minotaur had also heard her cry for help. His mom, with her hair on fire again, lingered at the edge of the woods trying to shield herself from the harmful rays of the descending sun. Smoke rose off the bare skin of her hand every time she reached into the daylight, and her face was covered with lesions and welts.

He tossed the curtain to her. It fell open as it twisted and turned in the air, then flapped and spiraled uncontrollably until it snagged on a bush. The empusa grabbed it, wincing as another ray caught her.

Behind her, the minotaur wove around the trees into view, continually snorting. Travis hovered just above the ground and could see the beast blundering through the undergrowth, tearing bushes in two, uncaring of the scratches across his sweaty skin.

The empusa, completely covered by the curtain, stumbled into the open and headed toward the house. But it was clear she would never make it, and she seemed unable to leap when hampered so. Her fiery hair was quickly burning a hole through the fabric.

Travis slammed into her, wrapping his arms fully around her waist and pinching the curtain tight. Rather than tumble to the ground, he lifted off and took her with him. She hissed at the indignity, but she hung limp, allowing him to save her from the raging monster below.

It occurred to him that he was leading the minotaur directly toward the house, but there was no time to rethink his plan. He couldn't hold onto the empusa for long, especially with her flames beginning to rage out of control.

The curtain smoked badly, and a hole developed. As the sunlight made it through to the top of her head, she hissed and swore and struggled to reposition the curtain—but she couldn't with Travis pinning the thing tight around her waist.

He was almost upon the roomy cabin-style building when Melinda appeared in the open window of the upstairs spare bedroom. *What are you doing?* he thought in panic. *Get out of there! Lock the door!* But before he had a chance to vent his annoyance, she promptly disappeared again.

Seconds later, he dumped his mom rather heavily on the steep roof and gave her a push so she stumbled in through the window and landed with a thud on the floor, tangled up in the smoldering curtain. Travis pushed the window shut and slammed the heavy shutters.

He stood panting for a moment, trying to keep his balance and avoid slipping on the slate tiles. It was quiet inside for now. The empusa was probably relieved to be out of the sunlight. She'd be fine until nightfall. After that, she'd probably try to escape.

He dug in his pocket for the short length of rope he'd found in the basement and looped it through the slats of both shutter doors, pulling it tight, twisting it around multiple times. Now she couldn't get out. The glass was unbreakable, the window was impossible to open outward with the shutters closed, and the shutters themselves were tied together. She was trapped— assuming Melinda had locked the inner door.

Gasping, he staggered and almost fell as yet another vision blasted through his skull:

*. . . The horribly distorted face of a woman, stretched long on one side, her eyes mismatched and staring in a ghastly fashion as he knelt over her. He stared impassively, not caring that she might be suffering . . .*

This vision shocked him to the core. It was by far the worst. Was that the faun he'd seen? She hadn't looked like a faun. She hadn't looked like *anything*. But worst of all was the fact that he'd simply stared down at her and done nothing to help.

*No time for this now.*

He spun around as the minotaur stampeded across the meadow toward the house. "Not good," Travis muttered. "Not part of the plan."

Swooping down, he tried to get the beast's attention and lead him away. But the minotaur clearly had the empusa on his mind.

Travis watched with dismay as the monster—Lucas out of control—tore up the path to the house and rammed his horns into the door.

## Chapter 18
## Mr. Grimfoyle Talks

When Travis had gazed for a long time at the corn in the backyard and finally announced he had an idea, Melinda had been skeptical. How could he bring his mom, a bloodsucking empusa vampire, to the house while avoiding her fangs *and* preventing her from burning up in the sunlight?

But he'd come up with the idea of wrapping her like a cob of corn to keep the sun off. All he needed was a large curtain.

She hadn't liked the plan, but—whatever. This was his mom he was trying to save. Travis left soon after, and Melinda went upstairs to open the window of the spare bedroom as instructed. She stood there a while, taking a moment to enjoy the peace and quiet.

The meadow out front was a serene setting. Off to her right, somewhere in the trees, the entrance to the mines stood at the end of a woodland trail. Travis shouldn't be long.

But then she spotted Mr. Grimfoyle striding with purpose toward the house, cutting through the long grass.

"How did he find—?" Melinda whispered.

She left that thought hanging. Of course the creepy old man knew where Travis lived. He'd pretty much admitted to being a stalker. He knew where Melinda lived, too.

She sighed. Whatever it was he wanted from the two of them, he was obviously coming to collect.

As she turned away from the window, the old man suddenly toppled sideways and fell. He thrashed on the ground, almost hidden in the long grass, his arms waving and legs kicking. Melinda stared in amazement. It looked like something had grabbed Mr. Grimfoyle, only he was alone.

Or was he?

Staring harder, she saw a pair of pants floating about . . . as though the wearer were invisible.

"Flynn!" she gasped.

For whatever reason, the dryad fought Mr. Grimfoyle and kept him pinned down while the grass swayed unnaturally around them both. Thick weeds bent low and wrapped around his wrists like thin snakes, pulling tight and restricting his movements.

"No, no, no," Melinda muttered.

She had no affection for the old man, but he'd come here for a reason. Leaving the window open, she dashed downstairs and out the front door.

"Flynn, stop! It's okay, he's with us!"

The dryad paused, fuzzing into view briefly. Pinned under him, Mr. Grimfoyle sputtered and cursed, struggling to free himself from a tangle of weeds and thorns while the long grass whipped about as though caught in a gale.

"I don't like him," Flynn said, panting. "I'm protecting you."

"I don't like him either, but he's on our side."

Melinda stopped a few yards away and watched as the weeds binding the old man's wrists appeared to wither. He quickly wrenched free.

"*What* is the *meaning* of this?" the man roared. He picked himself up and brushed grass and dirt off his black suit. "Who *is* this?"

"His name's Flynn, and he's my friend."

Flynn fuzzed into view, his wood-patterned skin darkening. "Did you see what I did with the weeds?" he said, sounding astonished. "I made them move! I made them grab this old man! How is that possible?"

"Because that's what dryads do," Melinda assured him. She looked across at the trees, spotting the woodland trail leading to the mines. "We need to get inside in case Travis needs our help. And—oops! I was supposed to lock the bedroom door."

Waving at them both to follow her, she hurried back to the house. Behind her, she heard Mr. Grimfoyle voicing his immense dissatisfaction, and the dryad mumbling a short reply. She waited for them to enter the hallway, then slammed the door.

"Where is the boy?" Mr. Grimfoyle demanded.

Melinda paused on the bottom step of the staircase. "He'll be back in a minute."

The old man threw up his hands in obvious disgust. "Do you kids *ever* stop running about all over the place? It's very important that we get our heads together and work as a *team*. The three of us can bring down the faun. With my brains and your shapeshifting ability, we can infiltrate the faun's lair and put an end to her dastardly scheme." He paused to take a breath, then spoke a little more calmly. "The boy will be back soon?"

"In a minute," Melinda repeated.

She started up the stairs, but Flynn distracted her. Being semitransparent, she could see the inner waistband of his pants as he shuffled from the lobby into the main living room. He touched things as he went—the armchairs, the highly polished wood table, the sturdy mantel over the fire, the picture frames that stood there . . . He paused to stare at the little boy in one of them, standing with his mother and father.

Touching the picture, Flynn turned and looked up at Melinda. "This is the one you call Travis? He's your . . . friend?"

He sounded so aloof in that moment, no doubt his dryad nature taking over. "Yeah, farmboy, that's Travis. He's older now—about the same age as me. He'll be back in a minute." Realizing she'd said that three times now, she gestured toward the armchairs. "Why don't you two take a seat."

Mr. Grimfoyle clicked his tongue and tutted and made a lot of other annoyed sounds, but he agreed to sit. Flynn perched opposite, keeping a watchful eye on the old man.

A shout from outside caused all three of them to jump. Melinda ran back downstairs and across to the front door, which she opened a crack. Travis swooped in from above the woods, distracted by something among the trees at its fringe. She couldn't see what it was.

Travis threw the curtain down. It unfolded as it fell, flapping madly before landing on a bush—and then a hand reached out and plucked it off.

Melinda gasped. "Travis is with his mom," she announced for the benefit of the others. "He's tossing her a curtain to shield her from the sun. He's . . . Oh! There's something coming!"

Terror struck her, and she wrenched the door wide open.

Mr. Grimfoyle's cold fingers clamped around her wrist, holding her fast. "Stay inside, girl."

A second later, as she watched helplessly, Travis slammed into the empusa and lifted her into the air—just as a raging minotaur tore out of the bushes.

Mr. Grimfoyle pulled Melinda back inside, slammed the door, and bolted it. He glared at her. "No more running around. Just wait until he gets here."

She gasped. The bedroom door!

Dashing up the stairs, she reached the spare bedroom and ran to the window. A quick look confirmed Travis was heading her way, so she bolted for the hallway, slammed the door, and locked it.

She put her ear to the door and listened.

The commotion was startling, loud and angry. First came a thud and a gasp. Then the empusa scuffled about, muttering under her breath and hitting things. After that, the sound of determined fists beating against the unbreakable glass.

His mom was *mad*.

"Girl!" the old man yelled from downstairs.

She ran for the stairs, but Mr. Grimfoyle and the dryad were busy tearing up them, so she backed out of their way. "What's going on?"

As if to answer her question, something struck the front door with tremendous force. And again. The entire frame shook both times, and dust trickled down.

"He led the minotaur straight to us," Mr. Grimfoyle complained. "Foolish boy."

"He was saving his mom!"

Grunts and snorts came from outside as the minotaur hit the door again and again.

"We need to open another window," Melinda decided. She headed off along the hall, aware that the empusa was just as angry as the minotaur and stomping about in the spare room, turning things over in her fury.

Maybe the master bedroom would work.

It was weird enough running around Travis's house without him being home, but even weirder barging into his parents' room. Maybe Aunt Abigail would recognize the room and calm down a little—but right now she needed to vent, and it was better to do that in the empty guestroom.

Melinda ran to the window and opened it. "Travis!" she called, spotting the mothman circling above.

He swooped down and landed on the steep roof, then crawled closer as if to climb in. But Mr. Grimfoyle appeared beside Melinda, holding out a hand to stop him.

"Time is now of the essence," he said firmly. "I had planned to sit down and tell you this before the storm arrived, but you two won't quit running about everywhere. Now, *listen* to me."

Melinda and Travis froze where they were, one inside the room, the other standing on the steep roof outside the window, clutching the sill to steady himself.

Mr. Grimfoyle spoke softly, commanding their close attention. "You are wasting time and energy trying to make a few loved ones feel comfortable. We should be attacking this problem at the source. The faun didn't do this alone. As I understand it, young Travis, you are uniquely qualified to deal with this situation—and deal with it you must, and quickly, or this storm will continue spreading across the land."

"Uniquely qualified?" he repeated. "What do you mean?"

"There's a . . . *creature*," Mr. Grimfoyle said, lowering his voice. "It lives underground. Your dad knows all about it. You do, too. You've been down there."

Melinda shot Travis a glance. His eyes widened. "The *brain*?" he gasped.

The old man nodded. "That would be an apt name for the monstrosity down below." He paused, apparently struggling for words. "I *connected* with it. Just briefly—or maybe for hours, I'm not sure. I saw what it planned. It took the idea straight from the faun's head. I don't think she was even aware of it."

"But . . ." Travis started.

"The *brain* did this?" Melinda said, finding her voice. "The giant brain under the ground?"

She'd heard Travis's story about that monster. He'd been pursued afterward by a dullahan, a terrible horseman that hounded him across the land. Travis had only survived because he was a shapeshifter, able to disguise himself in another form.

"I don't know for certain," Mr. Grimfoyle said, "but I believe this *giant brain* is responsible for the storm. The faun should be dealt with of course, but to halt this disaster in its tracks, you need to destroy the real monster deep underground."

"No, no, no," Travis muttered, shaking his head, his wings fluttering as he balanced on the roof outside.

"You've confronted it before, young man," Mr. Grimfoyle said. "You can do it again. Destroy that thing—and capture that blasted faun."

"But what about the damage that's already been done?" Melinda waved her arms about. "Everyone around us, all across the land! We need to save them. We need some reversal potion!"

Mr. Grimfoyle hung his head. "Indeed. The faun had a cauldron full, but I fear it's all gone, turned to mist and used to generate this storm. And what Simone had at the laboratory is destroyed." He pursed his lips and spoke softly. "Children, you have to think of the bigger picture. I'm saddened by your loss, of course, but it's not too late to save the rest of the world."

"No!" Travis shouted. "We have to save my mom and dad!"

"We *are* going to save them," Melinda assured him with no idea how that was supposed to happen. "My dad, too. Mr. Grimfoyle, there has to be a way."

Travis leaned in through the window, gripping the frame. He had a fierce expression. "There's still a vial of a potion buried in the backyard, Melinda. My dad can't tell us where it is, because he's a massive invisible giant right now, but we have to find it."

Melinda's ears pricked up. "Excuse me? He's a what?"

He ignored the question. "We *have* to find it—even if there's only enough to save our parents."

Her heart soared. "Yes! Yes, a few drops is all we need for now. And maybe there will be enough left to give to a witch somewhere, so the witch can make *more* potion."

How they'd find such a witch when she'd been transmogrified into something else was beyond her, but they'd cross that bridge later. Her mind raced. Maybe stop the storm from spreading first—then save their parents—then look for a witch, even if they had to travel far outside the scope of the storm . . .

Mr. Grimfoyle reached through the window and gripped Travis's arm. "There's hope, boy. You're a mothman. As a mothman, you can *prophesize*. Do it now. You have only to look deep inside your mind to find the answer. If you want to know where to dig for that missing vial of potion, then ask yourself that very question and sleep on it for a while. Allow your dreams to guide you. We'll leave in an hour or two while it's still dark."

Travis's fierce expression turned to one of doubt. "I've had some weird flashes, but nothing really useful."

"Like what, boy?"

He frowned and stared past them into the room. "I saw the mist before it arrived. I saw an explosion and rocks falling, which at first I thought was Robbie sealing the mines, but it turned out to be the chimera shooting fireballs and blasting the entrance open again. I saw a lady with flaming hair, which was my mom." He looked up at Mr. Grimfoyle. "And there are visions that haven't come true yet. I saw a dying dragon—in a cave, I think. Also a tower on a lake. And something horrible lying in the grass, a twisted creature that . . ." He broke off and swallowed.

The old man brightened. "Tower on the lake, yes! That's where the faun is, at the center of the storm. That's where you must go. But . . . first, tell me about the dragon. A dying dragon in a cave, you say?" He rubbed his hands, a glint appearing in his eyes. "Did you also see a blue gem?"

Travis jerked in surprise. "Actually, yeah."

"Well, my boy, that might be our answer. That's a rare boulder opal."

"A what?" Melinda said.

Her head was beginning to spin. Travis's mom was in the next room, pacing angrily. Her dad was outside in the vegetable garden, hopefully keeping quiet inside his walled hidey-hole. And a rampaging minotaur hammered against the door out front. Just wait until he turned into a wolfman . . .

And now the old man was going on about a rare gem?

"A boulder opal," Mr. Grimfoyle repeated. "It's a very rare gem that allows not just visions but *actual glimpses* into the past and future. It's far more reliable than a mothman's vague, somewhat random prophecies."

Mr. Grimfoyle seemed to have made up his mind as to their next course of action. He pounded his fist on the windowsill several times as he spoke:

"Go fetch that opal. It belongs to the ancient steamer dragon by the waterfall. You said the dragon is dying, so it shouldn't give you much trouble. Take the gem. It might show you a glimpse of yourself digging the potion out of the ground.

Then you can dig up your precious vial of potion, face the brain under the ground, and stop this ghastly storm of death."

Travis looked about as doubtful as Melinda felt.

On the doorstep, the minotaur resumed his endless pounding.

## Chapter 19
## The Full Moon

Melinda watched Travis leave, unable to contain the feeling of hopelessness. A mysterious opal, a buried vial of potion, a sinister creature under the ground . . . It was all too much.

As the sun started to descend on the horizon, she watched Travis fly off over the trees, a creepy oversized bug with glowing red eyes.

Downstairs, the minotaur paused for a while. It seemed even bullheaded monsters grew weary of their furious tirades.

Melinda checked a rear window, looking down on the vegetable garden. Her dad sat on a mound of dirt, hunched over, apparently asleep. Gnomes led simple lives. It was kind of sad, and she missed her ordinary human dad and his goofy stories and enthusiasm for weird wildlife. Tears welled up again, and she angrily wiped her eyes.

*He'll be back*, she told herself.

Mr. Grimfoyle and Flynn were busy checking the front door by the time she made it downstairs. Flynn had single-handedly shoved some of the furniture in front of the door in case the minotaur made it through.

"There's no need," Melinda muttered as she inspected his handiwork. Two armchairs and a heavy dining table! Who knew a dryad could be so strong? "Uncle Hal had a special door installed after Madame Frost came here and tried to take his fire gland."

Mr. Grimfoyle frowned and looked closer. "A special door?"

"It's made of oak—but it's actually two thin layers of oak with a sheet of iron between. Same with the frame. It's all reinforced."

"And the windows?" the old man said, walking over to inspect one. "I trust those are reinforced as well?"

"Imported from Old Earth. It's extra-tough glass. Impact resistant."

"And spell proof?"

She frowned. "Well—"

"Never mind. There are no witches here tonight. Just an angry minotaur. What about the chimney?"

Melinda floundered. "Are you saying someone might climb down?" She shook her head. "A minotaur isn't going to climb down a chimney."

"Well, then perhaps we can rest a little easier knowing we're secure."

"Good," Melinda muttered, "because I want to spend some time with my dad. I need to bring him inside."

As she hurried toward the back door, the old man scampered after her, surprisingly nimble. "Wait—you're not serious, young lady! It's too dangerous. Even if you made it across the yard without that minotaur hearing, that silly old gnome isn't going to come willingly. He'll drag his feet and bang his head—"

But Melinda had already pulled the back door open. It felt heavier than the one at her own house, now that she thought about it. A steel panel no doubt lay within. "Make some noise at the front," she told Mr. Grimfoyle. "I'll be right back."

Leaving the old man to mutter to himself, she darted across the grass to the fenced-in garden. At the same time, she heard Mr. Grimfoyle yelling at the minotaur to stop making so much noise, which of course infuriated the bullheaded creature even more. Before long, the pounding on the door resumed.

Melinda opened the gate. "Hey," she whispered to the gnome. "You'd better come indoors."

The gnome looked up at her. He was still sitting on the same mound of dirt. "Do I live here?" he said in a low, gravelly voice.

"What? Uh, well, no. Not *here*. This is where Travis lives. But you've been here many times. In fact, you helped build this fence."

The gnome looked around, nodding. "It's . . . familiar."

"Our house is closer to the town," she went on. "This place is safer." She tilted her head at the sound of bellowing and thudding from the front of the house. "Well, we *thought* it was safer. It is inside, anyway. Are you coming?"

The gnome didn't move. Melinda watched him closely, studying his lined face, his thin neck and oversized head, the brown-and-grey hair that refused to lie flat, the thick eyebrows, and the jutting ears . . . It was hard to believe he was really her father.

"Dad?" she said softly.

The gnome's frown deepened, and he glanced at her. "Don't call me that. Your face is familiar, but you're no child of mine."

Melinda almost choked on the wail that threatened to escape her throat. She told herself he hadn't said such a thing with malice. He simply didn't remember her.

"Let's go inside," she said again. "You hear that ruckus from the front of the house? That's a minotaur bent on getting in. But he won't. The house is the safest place to be. If he comes around the back and realizes you're hiding out here . . ."

The gnome shrugged. "A minotaur won't bother me. We'll butt heads, and I'll win."

"What? Look, the thing is, he might not stay a minotaur for long. He's really a lycan, and if his shapeshifter magic still works, he'll turn when the full moon shows itself. He'll be a wolfman, and trust me, it'll take more than a big noggin to win against a crazy seven-foot wolf with razor-sharp claws."

Whether the gnome believed her or not, it didn't take much more to convince him. Maybe deep down he wanted to come inside. Either way, he sighed and got up, brushed dirt off his smart pants, and trudged behind Melinda as she led the way back to the house.

When she let herself in the kitchen door, the gnome turned his nose up and paused on the threshold. "What an odd dwelling. This isn't gnomish at all. I certainly don't live here."

"That's what I said. This is my friend's house."

"And your friend is what? Is he like *you?*" The scorn in his voice was unmistakable.

Melinda wanted to grab him by the scruff and yank him inside. "Travis is like me, yes," she said through clenched teeth. "We're human."

"You're what?" The gnome wrinkled his already wrinkled nose. "*Human,* you say? Nonsense. They're but a legend. What are you really?"

"Fine. I'm a mermaid with legs, and he's a mothman."

Her befuddled dad looked like he was remembering something. "Yes," he said after a while. "Yes, I saw him outside the mine—and then in the town. I think I was in a daze. I'm a little clearer now. Still, I feel as though—"

"Dad, please, come inside."

The gnome huffed and stepped into the kitchen. "I'm *not* your dad. Please don't call me that."

"Then what should I call you?" Melinda challenged. "What's your name?"

"My name is . . ."

"Yes?"

"My name . . ."

Melinda would have liked to stand there an extra half-minute to find out if he actually knew his name or not, but a sudden crash and wrenching of splintered wood carried through the house.

She spun around and headed toward it. *The front door! The minotaur!*

To her surprise, Mr. Grimfoyle stood there quite calmly, hands on hips. The front door had not shifted, and neither had the two armchairs and heavy table crammed up against it. But the old man pointed upward to the ceiling, and Melinda knew in an instant what had happened.

She ran for the stairs. Not even halfway up, she froze as the empusa vampire stomped into view on the upper floor. She leaned over the railing and scowled down at them all. "*What* is going on?"

"Aunt Abigail," Melinda said, continuing up, "there's a minotaur banging on the door, but the door is reinforced—do you remember? This is your house, so—"

"I'm not talking about the minotaur!" the empusa screeched in sudden anger. "I punched him hard enough to knock him out, and he's furious, so he followed me here! Of *course* there's a minotaur banging on the door!" She met Melinda at the top of the stairs and towered over her. "What I'd like to know is why you locked me in up there!"

Mr. Grimfoyle folded his arms and tossed his white hair back as he glared up at them. "That's what I wondered. Utterly pointless, if you ask me. We need to get to the source of all this nonsense, not worry about a few individuals wandering off."

The pounding on the door stopped abruptly. A silence fell, and everyone in the house paused to listen. The gnome had appeared from the kitchen. Flynn fuzzed into view briefly. He kind of blended in despite the stubbornly visible clothing.

"Well—" Mr. Grimfoyle started to say.

Just outside on the doorstep, the minotaur let out a strange cry. He had to be leaning on the door with his face pressed to the oak judging by the way the sound filtered through. Despite the thick oak and sheet of metal, they all winced as a mournful wail found its way through the gap around the frame.

The wail started out like a cry of anguish, then turned angry and determined. It went on and on, impossibly drawn out, rising in volume and deepening in pitch. The minotaur had been pretty throaty before. Now his booming voice rattled the windows.

"Uh-oh," Melinda whispered.

Instead of taking the stairs, the empusa leapt over the railing and thudded down on the hard floor of the living room, cracking some of the tiles with her hoofs. Her hair had begun to smolder again, and a tiny flame ignited near one ear.

"The moon," she announced, stomping over to where Mr. Grimfoyle stood on the doormat. "If what the mothman boy said is true, the minotaur is changing. I suggest you all stay inside."

"You too, I hope?" Mr. Grimfoyle said, gazing up into her fierce eyes. "We could use your help if that beast should get in."

"And why should I care?"

Melinda marched down the stairs. With the gnome banging his head on a wall and mumbling, and Flynn trying to find a safe corner to fade into, she couldn't afford to lose Aunt Abigail even if she acted like a complete stranger. The empusa was strong. "Is there anything you can do with that fiery hair of yours? I mean, what's the point of it, anyway? Why does it keeping catching alight?"

If the empusa had entertained ideas of leaving, perhaps out the back, she instantly forgot those thoughts and flared up in anger—literally. With healthy flames shooting upward from her head, she cast an orange glow in the darkening room and generated a lot of heat.

"Why?" she growled. "*Why?* Other than an obvious emotional response to danger and frustration?"

"Yes. Why?"

The vampire woman reached for Melinda and grabbed her by the throat. Lifting her clear off the floor and holding her there to dangle, she shoved her face close to Melinda's and bared her fangs. "Would you like to see, little girl?"

The heat of her fire threatened to melt Melinda's skin. "Uh, sure."

Mr. Grimfoyle raised his hands. "Now, I don't think that's wise . . ."

"Not wise at all," the gnome grumbled as he backed into the kitchen.

Flynn was nowhere to be seen, not even with his pants on.

The empusa dropped Melinda and pushed hard, sending her staggering. Then fire erupted from the vampire's eyes, ears, and open mouth. The flames engulfed her entire head, then spread down to her shoulders and arms, raging hotter as her torso and upper legs caught alight.

Melinda let out a cry of terror and recoiled from the heat, backing across the room, but the empusa wasn't done. With her legs burning as strongly as the rest of her, she stood quite still, hands on hips, and threw back her head to laugh.

Then the flames died, leaving black smoke to roll across the vaulted ceiling. Her silky dress was doing something weird, rippling and melting and reforming again, beginning to slide off but quickly adjusting, morphing and adapting until it cooled and settled.

The empusa was vastly different now. Still the same shape and size, but her flesh had turned to shiny brass—legs, arms, face, everything. When she took a step forward, her foot clanked against the hard tile despite the smart shoes she wore.

"You're made of *brass*?" Melinda gasped. "But . . . why?"

With another laugh, this time derisive, the empusa shook her head and said, "Now that's a question I cannot answer. More to the point, why does a mere *human* exist in a world where humans are long forgotten? How are you here? You and your friends—that boy who became a mothman, and this old fool with the white hair—you are all human, are you not?"

With every passing minute, she sounded less and less like the woman Melinda knew. "Yes, we're human—and so are you, *Aunt Abigail.*"

The brass woman clanked across the floor to where Mr. Grimfoyle stood and threw aside the table and chairs before he had a chance to react. When she reached for the door handle, he shouted "No!" and went to grab her, but she casually backhanded him, sending him spinning.

Melinda ran to help him up, watching with horror as the empusa yanked the door wide open. Though the moon was out, it wasn't quite nighttime yet. Still, the daylight had faded, and the brass empusa stood framed in the doorway, looking out.

The minotaur had vanished. "See?" the empusa said. "Nobody will challenge me when I'm in this state. I'm invincible."

*She's bragging*, Melinda thought. *The minotaur's not here. He probably has no idea she just turned into a walking statue. He's already gone.*

But where?

As the empusa stepped outside, she staggered and caught herself. Hissing, she continued on down the path under the evening sky.

"Are you all right?" Melinda called, weaving around Mr. Grimfoyle and dashing outside. "What's wrong?"

To her amazement, the empusa's skin was losing its metallic luster, fading to a more familiar flesh color beneath her constantly morphing silky dress. One arm changed first, then her neck and face. Though her legs were shaped like those of a goat, only one sprouted fur and returned to normal. The other remained firmly brass.

"Alas," the woman said with a sigh, "my invincible state doesn't last long. Still, I'm far more agile in my natural form."

The brass slowly faded from her face and left arm. She reached down and tapped her solid left leg. "Huh. This one always lingers."

*How does she know that?* Melinda wondered. This was the first time Abigail had ever done this. How could she even know—

She pinched the bridge of her nose as if that might slow the whirling thoughts in her head. "Look, I'm glad the minotaur is gone, and I'm glad you got to show me your . . . uh, well, that fire thing you just did. But please stay. There are things you don't know. Things you don't *remember*. If you could just come back inside, I'll explain everything that's happened, and then . . ."

She trailed off. The empusa had heard it, too.

In the nearby woods, the howling had started. The long, drawn-out howl of a wolf—or, more correctly, a lycan in a frenzied state. Lucas was no longer a minotaur. The full moon had worked its magic on him.

Worse, several other howls answered him. A chorus of them echoed through the evening sky, followed by excited roars and the distinct sound of monsters crashing through the woods.

Melinda grabbed the empusa's hand. "That's a pack of bloodthirsty lycans. *Please* come inside. I know you're fast, but not *that* fast."

Slowly, the empusa turned and headed back to the house, one leg still stiff and clanking. Once inside, Melinda pushed the door shut and leaned on it.

Hearing the howls again, closer this time, she swallowed and decided it was going to be a very long night.

Or worse—a very short one.

## Chapter 20
## Torn Limb from Limb

"Are you sure they can't get in through these doors and windows?" Mr. Grimfoyle asked again.

Melinda gave the table one last shove so it was back against the door. "I don't know! This isn't my house."

"What about upstairs? Are those windows reinforced as well?"

"I think so, yes! Stop asking me!"

The old man shook his head. "How the dickens did we end up stuck here? We should be miles away from here by now."

"It was *your* idea to send Travis off to find the gem," Melinda muttered.

"Only so you'd have a means to save your parents!" the man retorted.

Melinda flared up again. "Are you sure that's the only reason? I saw that look in your eye when you first mentioned it. It's valuable, isn't it? You *want* it."

"Me? Nonsense!"

But something in his voice betrayed him. "You're lying. You're pretending to help us find the potion to save our parents, but really you just want Travis to bring that gem back before we go off and visit the brain under the ground—because you're worried we might not return!"

Breathless, she folded her arms and glared at him, daring him to argue. He merely grumbled and wandered away.

The empusa flopped down in one of the chairs pushed against the door, her goat legs sticking out, any trace of metal gone. "We could just leave now. They're not here yet."

"You had enough trouble escaping one minotaur," Melinda reminded her. "How about ten werewolves?"

She actually had no idea how many there were. She didn't even know for certain they were headed for the house. They had no reason to unless Lucas had told them to come. But all that howling . . . It sure seemed like he was gathering an army to break in.

Melinda went to find her dad. Flynn fuzzed into view and pointed to a shoe closet. The gnome had shut himself in. When she gently opened the door, he was hunched on the floor amid a pile of shoes.

"Dad?" Melinda said, kneeling. "Are you okay?"

The gnome frowned at her. "You are no child of mine. But . . . you are kind."

She patted his knee. "We're going to be fine. We just need to make it through the night." *Yeah, that should be easy enough.*

The gnome grimaced and banged his head sideways against the wall. He did it once, then again, harder.

"Hey, don't do that," Melinda cried. "It's going to be fine, I promise."

He banged his head a third time.

"Stop! Why do you—" She took his hand and squeezed it. "Why do gnomes do that?"

"Sorry. It's just instinct."

"Instinct? But why?"

The gnome patted the wall with his hand. "I know it doesn't work with walls, but as I said, it's instinct."

"*What* is? *What* doesn't work with walls?"

"It's how we escape from undesirable situations."

Melinda stared at him, wondering if he was speaking literally or figuratively. "Escape? Like reading a good book?"

The gnome frowned. "I don't understand."

"So . . . you mean *literally* escape?"

A sudden thud against the front door startled them both. Melinda jumped up and swung around.

The empusa was still sitting in the armchair, but she slowly climbed to her feet. "Sounds like they're here," she whispered.

Mr. Grimfoyle paced back and forth. "Well, this is unfortunate. Very unfortunate indeed."

"I thought you said you couldn't die," Melinda murmured.

"I can't. Which means I'll have to survive this night alone. Extremely tedious."

The empusa smiled. "You're immortal? How interesting. I never age, but I *can* be killed. What about you?"

"Can we save this conversation for another time?" Melinda hissed, trying to keep her voice low as rumbling growls came from outside. "What should we do? Hide upstairs? Barricade the doors up there?"

"Is there a basement?" Mr. Grimfoyle asked.

"Yes. Would that be better? There's only one way in and out."

The old man nodded. "Better than upstairs bedrooms. We'll only have one door to barricade instead of a door and an external window."

Melinda didn't like the sound of being trapped down there, but Mr. Grimfoyle and the empusa seemed to agree on the idea. The vampire sauntered over to the basement door, opened it, and peered down the steps.

"We'll need a lamp. The one hanging down there is broken."

As Mr. Grimfoyle went looking for one, Melinda studied the empusa with interest. How had the vampire known the lamp was broken? How had she even been sure that door led to the basement? It could have been another closet.

"Aunt Abigail?" she said, reaching for her hand.

Flames sparked on the vampire's head as she snatched her hand away. "Don't be ridiculous, girl."

"So what's your name, then?" Melinda challenged.

The vampire bared her fangs and leaned closer. "You'd better ask your *father* to head downstairs. And your invisible friend, too."

Disappointed, Melinda went to fetch the gnome. He grumbled but climbed to his feet and allowed himself to be led to the basement door. He peered down, then quietly took the lamp Mr. Grimfoyle had returned with. Without another word, he started down the steps.

"Flynn," Melinda called softly.

The dryad fuzzed into view from a shadowed corner. He hurried down the steps without question. From one dark corner to another; what difference did it make? Dryads typically had no scent, so maybe the werewolves would have no clue he existed.

"They probably won't even get through the front door," Melinda assured him as he went. "I'm sure it'll be fine."

A heavy thud on the door made her jump. Then ferocious roaring started up, accompanied by scratching and thudding. The frenzy of noises continued for a full minute. Melinda, Mr. Grimfoyle, and the empusa watched the door in silence, looking for any sign of movement.

Nothing. It seemed the basement wouldn't be necessary after all.

A huge shape hurled itself at the nearest window, making Melinda jump and cry out. She clamped a hand across her mouth and stifled her scream as the hulking werewolf slammed again and again at the glass. But, like the door, it seemed unbreakable.

The evening was dark enough now that the monsters outside were hard to discern. Melinda moved closer, her heart thumping, trusting the toughened pane to hold the monsters at bay. She saw three of them out there, one with its muzzle so close that it steamed up the glass with every pant. The glint of its eyes unnerved her. Even in the darkness, she sensed these creatures were driven by madness.

As if to prove her point, they let out roars and hurled themselves at the window again. Melinda flinched as the frame shook.

"They can see you," the empusa said from behind her. "In the full moon, lycans lack control. All they see in you is an animal to tear apart. They're probably not even hungry. They just need to hunt and kill."

"You're not helping," Melinda muttered.

Scrapes and scuffles came from higher on the walls outside. Then the rending of metal as a gutter popped loose, thudding footfalls on the roof, a few tiles crashing down. More roars and thuds.

Melinda and her unlikely companions stood perfectly still, listening intently. There had to be at least four or five of them out there judging by the shapes flitting by the windows and the noises upstairs. Perhaps six if the scrabbling she heard from the kitchen door at the back of the house was another of them trying to get in.

"Why are they so intent on invading?" Mr. Grimfoyle wondered aloud. "These creatures normally roam the woods and tear through anything in their way, but they don't take detours and spend ages trying to access a house."

"They smell you," the empusa said. "Humans. You're something new, something intriguing . . ."

"We're *not* new," Melinda said. "It's because you knocked Lucas out with one punch. He's mad at you." Hearing the empusa's chuckle, she sighed and pointed. "I think we should go down to the basement."

In the kitchen, the back door crashed open.

"Go!" Mr. Grimfoyle urged.

The three of them raced for the narrow basement door. The empusa happened to be closest, and she wasted no time thumping down the steps. Mr. Grimfoyle should have been next, but he waved Melinda to go ahead. She did so—but not before catching a glimpse of movement behind him.

A ferocious, upright, seven-foot-tall wolfman lurched into view from the kitchen. Seeing the old man, it howled, dropped to all-fours, and slammed into him.

Melinda screamed—but a hand reached out and yanked her the rest of the way down the steps, preventing her from seeing what happened next. She heard the noise though, a frenzied growling and the awful sound of claws slashing and ripping. The empusa leapt back up to the top of the steps, paused for just a second, then slammed the door shut and locked it.

"Mr. Grimfoyle!" Melinda exclaimed. "We have to help him!"

"We can't," she said shortly, her hair alight. Although a lamp glowed from the basement below, the empusa's flames did a good job illuminating the top of the darkened staircase where they stood. "Get downstairs, girl. Let's hope they can't break this door open."

From the sound of her voice, she didn't sound too hopeful.

In the basement below, the gnome and the dryad huddled next to the lamp in the middle of the floor. The place was extensive, the length and width of the house and eight feet high, with numerous wooden posts and stacks of stone to provide a strong support system. The walls were made of stone and clay. Shelves lined one side of the room, and Melinda knew without looking they were crammed with canned food and non-perishable items, much of it imported from Old Earth. Travis's family was a big believer in being prepared.

The empusa stared around, her expression unfathomable. Trying to ignore the muffled sounds of roaring and growling in the house above, Melinda sidled across to the gnome. "Are you okay, Dad?" she whispered. "It's gonna be all right."

The gnome muttered something and shook his head. He headed across to a wall and started banging his head.

Flynn, fully visible at the moment, reached for Melinda. "I want to protect you, but . . . I don't know if I can."

"We'll be fine," she said, the words automatically bubbling out of her mouth. Why did she always feel a need to reassure people? "As long as they don't bust the basement door open."

"They broke into the kitchen," the empusa muttered, her flames dying down. "If that reinforced door didn't hold them, I very much doubt the basement door will."

Melinda fought the urge to shout at her. "That's helpful," she said through gritted teeth.

"It's realistic." The vampire woman had a frown on her face as she peered around. "You know, I recognize this place. Why is that?"

"Because you live here. The whole house is yours. You live here everyday—and you recognize the *basement*?" Melinda realized she'd taken on a bitter tone, growing annoyed at the empusa. She eased off, remembering this was Travis's mom she was talking to—Abigail Franklin, the faerie shapeshifter.

Her mind whirled. Would transforming into a faerie be helpful in any way? If Lucas could change from a minotaur into a lycan, maybe Abigail could switch forms as well. Maybe the art of shifting wasn't completely lost.

For that matter, her dad was an ogre!

Trying to contain her excitement and hope, she hurried over to her dad once more and spoke as calmly as she could. "Dad, listen. Stop banging your head for a second. You're a *shapeshifter*. Do you remember? You can turn into an ogre. A huge, thirty-foot ogre—although obviously you wouldn't want to be that big in this basement. But you could be a half-sized ogre. That would be enough to fight off these werewolves if they happen to get ... Dad, can you stop banging your head, please?"

But the gnome ignored her, his hands placed on the stone wall as he thumped his forehead over and over, harder and harder. Melinda wanted to yank him away, but she was afraid he'd lash out. She peered closer, deciding she would physically tackle him if his forehead looked like it might be bleeding or bruised. To her amazement, she saw no sign of injury despite the force of the headbutting.

Upstairs, one of the monsters rammed itself against the door.

"Dad, please," Melinda whispered. "You have to listen to me—"

She broke off.

Squinting, she stared closer as the gnome continued banging his head.

"Uh," she said, "can someone bring me a lamp?"

Flynn hurried over with it. Under its soft glow, what Melinda thought she'd seen became an obvious reality.

She gasped. "Look at this!"

Upstairs, another terrifying thud on the door. This time, something splintered. This set off a chorus of howls.

The gnome continued headbutting the wall, but now his forehead sank *into* the stacked stone instead of connecting with it. It sank deeper each time, inch by inch, until his entire face disappeared into the solid surface. Then he staggered forward as his hands and arms plunged in, too.

The gnome slowly backed out but kept one hand submerged in the wall up to his elbow. He grinned at Melinda and reached for her with his other hand. "Time to go. All of you hold hands and follow."

Astonished, Melinda took his hand. It was solid despite his power to pass through walls like a ghost. Flynn took her other. She was too busy staring in amazement to notice if the empusa joined the end of the line.

Her dad plunged into the wall. Melinda would have wrenched free if he hadn't held on so tightly. The gnome gave her hand a sharp tug. She sucked in a terrified breath and tried to rear back as he yanked her toward the wall.

The last thing she heard was the sound of the basement door splitting open and a volley of triumphant roars.

The last thing she *saw* was the stone wall before she plunged into absolute darkness.

Fumbling around in a pitch-black emptiness, Melinda wanted to scream and yank free of the gnome's hand. But then she changed her mind and gripped it harder, realizing in a flash that if she let go, she might become one with the rock and dirt, a permanent fixture in the earth. Her skeleton would be found one day, perhaps centuries from now, and people would wonder who could have had done her in and buried her so.

Her heart thumped harder than she'd ever known. The suffocating pitch-black darkness, the ponderous sensation of walking underwater, the knowledge she was moving through *solid earth* . . .

Despite that, she felt something under her feet, something to walk *on*. How could the ground under her feet be any more solid than the ground she walked *through*? And, even stranger, why did it seem like she were walking up a gentle slope?

She gripped two hands tighter than necessary—the gnome's in front, the dryad's behind—and continued walking, wondering how her dad could see where he was headed.

Panic threatened to overwhelm her. She needed to take a breath, but she was afraid to try in case her nose and mouth filled with dirt. But as a pain in her chest increased, she had no choice but to try.

To her immense surprise, she was able to take in air—sort of. It felt like inhaling through a thick rag, but it was better than nothing. She controlled her breathing, focusing entirely on that as she walked. Gradually, her panic subsided.

The slope steepened, and suddenly she felt a lightness on the top of her head. Another couple of paces and the moon appeared. Then her nose and mouth were above the surface, and she sucked in deep lungfuls of air as the gnome dragged her onward and out.

Her dad was already clear of the ground above the waist. Melinda followed him up what had to be an imaginary slope and slowly emerged from the ground as though wading out of the sea and up a beach. Amazed, she watched her legs moving through the earth. The dirt seemed to move aside and fill back in after her, and yet there wasn't *enough* displacement for that to be entirely true. Astounding magic was at work here.

As she waded the rest of the way out, the gnome glanced over his shoulder and said, "Keep walking, and keep holding on."

Melinda glanced back. Flynn was behind her, clinging on for dear life, his eyes wide as he trudged up to his knees in dirt. And behind him the empusa, flames shooting out of the ground as her head came into view.

"Don't let go," Melinda warned her.

But the empusa's flames roared higher. "Enough of this!" she hissed about halfway clear. She wrenched her hand free of Flynn's. While he staggered forward with Melinda, the vampire woman suddenly found herself trapped waist deep.

The gnome, Melinda, and Flynn were free. She glanced around, realizing they were inside the fenced vegetable garden. The gate was open, so she went to close it—quietly, because the house stood not too far away, the kitchen door ajar, and all the lycans were inside letting out all kinds of erratic barks and growls as they searched for their prey.

Half buried, the empusa wriggled and squirmed in a frenzy, but her goat legs and waist were so firmly wedged into the ground that she made no headway at all. She looked like a strange and terrifying plant blowing in a gale, fire raging from the top of her head.

The gnome grinned and reached for her. "Take my hand while the phasing lasts."

She reached for him, giving him a glare. "You could have warned us. What kind of dirty trick was *that?*"

Melinda groaned at the pun, intended or otherwise. But despite the empusa's anger, the gnome—her dad!—had rescued them from a terrible fate.

Most of them, anyway. Poor Mr. Grimfoyle . . .

She swallowed and closed her eyes. They were going to have to huddle together and stay very, very quiet until the lycans gave up their search. That could take a while.

"Put your flames out, Aunt Abigail," she murmured.

The empusa scoffed. "Do you think I can control such things?"

Nevertheless, with a bit of effort, the flames died.

"Aunt Abigail?" Melinda said.

"Stop calling me that, you silly little girl."

"Aunt Abigail, do you know where Uncle Hal buried the potion? I mean, you said you never saw where he buried it, but you must have some idea. A clue, maybe? We've dug around in the dirt already."

"I have absolutely no idea what you're talking about. Be quiet."

But Melinda wouldn't be quiet. She pestered the empusa for a while, as gently as possible, mentioning the places she and Travis had dug, trying to spark even the tiniest of hidden memories, the slightest hint as to the whereabouts of the missing vial. She lost track of how many times she asked, and eventually the empusa simply stopped responding.

Hopefully, Travis would return soon with the opal, and it would give them their answer.

On the other hand, Melinda hoped he *wouldn't* return soon, or else he might blunder into a pack of werewolves in the living room.

What exactly was he doing right now? Had he found the dragon and the opal?

## Chapter 21
## Old Steamer

Travis flew straight to the Steamer Cave by the waterfall, the place everyone knew as the home of the old steamer dragon. It was a short journey. If he was lucky, he'd be in and out before the sun went down.

He'd been to the Steamer Cave many times, hanging out on the lower slopes where the waterfall pooled by some rocks, but he'd never ventured into the cave itself. Nobody in their right mind would do so. Nobody except his dad, anyway.

Travis shook his head as he recalled the story. Somebody at school had asked about it: "Hey, Travis, is it true your dad fought the steamer when he was a boy? Did she really bite his hand off? Is it true there were *three* dragons back then, and he battled all of them and won even with an arm missing?"

*An arm missing . . .*

Obviously that wasn't true.

Since Travis hadn't heard that particular story, he made sure to ask his dad that evening. "Oh, yeah. That was *years* ago. I was about your age at the time. And yes, there were three dragons. The parents are dead now, but the young female grew up and stayed put, guarding her jewels."

He'd gone on to tell how he, as a dragon shapeshifter, had needed to borrow something and ended up fighting for it. The blue opal! Travis barely remembered that detail, but it all fit now. Between them, the dragons had chomped his dad's fingers and steamed his eyeballs.

Travis wished he could remember more of the story. It struck him as odd that he was heading to the cave to borrow a gem exactly as his dad had twenty years before. What were the chances? Come to think of it, it had been when the faun had attacked the first time around . . .

He chewed on that. Was it just a coincidence?

Landing at the front edge of the cave, Travis lowered his wings and stood quietly and respectfully. The cave was more of an overhang, but it went back a long way, a huge wedge-shaped chamber shrouded in darkness. The waterfall thundered nearby.

Two decades ago, anyone landing in the cave like this would have been attacked before they took another step. But things were different now. The steamer had grown used to visitors, and though she had steamed quite a few people over the years, she had learned tolerance. Humans were inquisitive. Usually, a few well-placed growls and huffs of steam sent people running. She attacked only when necessary.

Travis waited. In the darkness, he heard motion—the creaking of leathery wings as they unfolded, the scrape of a scaly tail on hard rock, the scrabbling of claws, and of course grunts and growls.

He'd been a dragon shapeshifter once. A dragon could have had an actual conversation with the steamer. But Travis was a mothman, and he had only a rudimentary grasp of dragonspeak thanks to lessons with his dad.

The steamer eased out of the shadows, the setting sun playing across her vibrant green coloring and giving her scaly hide a slight orange hue. She was slender, as all steamers were, and nowhere near as big as the dragons from the labyrinth. And she blew steam, not fire.

She pushed her snout all the way up to Travis's face, and he resisted the urge to tumble backwards off the ledge and fly away. He stood and waited while she sniffed at him, her nostrils flaring. Her breath stank of something dead—not a rotting smell, more like fresh blood, strong and coppery.

The steamer huffed and pulled back, staring at him and tilting her head to one side. The moment stretched out. Travis couldn't imagine what she was thinking. In fact, he never could have imagined standing here facing her like this without being chewed up and spat out. Yet his vision . . .

"I came to borrow the blue boulder opal," he said softly, his voice trembling like crazy. "W-would that be okay?"

The dragon let out a long sigh, which turned into a mournful moan. She lowered herself to the cave floor and rested her chin on the rock, looking up at him through somewhat cloudy eyes.

Travis struggled to understand. "Are you all right?" he whispered. "Are you . . . dying?"

She merely stared at him. In the darkness, he could see her tail sliding around to one side, the pointed tip gently tapping on the floor before coming to a rest. Her sides eased in and out, her breathing slow.

"You *are* dying," he said, an immense sadness descending on him. "Is there anything I can do?" He felt so helpless. "Can you even understand me?"

She stretched out one of her front legs, her paw reaching for him. He fought the urge to retreat.

But she just wanted to show him something. Gripped in her claws was a tiny blue gem. He found it remarkable that she held it at all, being a dragon, but she was slender and dextrous, and she had opposable thumbs like his dad. Most dragons did. Still, she was old and dying, and she must have been gripping the gem for a while. She'd known he was coming.

He reached out, marveling at the size of those curved claws, each the size of his hand and capable of tearing him to shreds in an instant. And yet she was as gentle as could be, and she let him take the gem from her.

"Why?" he whispered. "Why are you letting me have this?"

She tapped the gem.

He studied it, still not understanding. "You *want* me to have this? Or . . . you saw something in it that you thought I should see?"

His excitement rose. Maybe the old man was right and the opal would give him the answers he needed.

He found that he couldn't just turn and leave, though. It felt wrong. The old dragon was dying—of old age, he guessed, since she was pretty ancient. His dad had met this same dragon when she was young, so she had to be twenty-something. That didn't *seem* very old, but . . .

That got him thinking about his dad. How did it work when a human shapeshifter outlived his dragon counterpart? Or maybe the dragon in him was *paused* when not in use, in which case it could live for as long as his dad needed it.

Travis steeled himself. "I'm going to change, okay? Don't be alarmed."

He reverted to human form in the slowest, smoothest way possible, a gradual morphing until his wings and feathers were gone and he'd lost all his fur and insect features. His smart clothes rippled a little, something that didn't go unnoticed by the steamer judging by the way she stared.

But she didn't seem surprised.

He sat down near her, placing the gem by her paw in an effort to show that she was more important to him right now. The rock floor was cold. "I'm going to sit here and talk to you until . . . well, for a while."

The steamer let out the softest of grunts.

And, feeling like he was waiting for a favorite pet to slip away, he started talking. He began with the story of his dad twenty years before, who'd met the young steamer a few times back then and borrowed the same blue gem for a little while—and how the dragons had fetched it back, leaving a trail of destruction in their wake.

The steamer huffed and closed her eyes, and Travis felt sure he detected a snicker . . .

* * *

She passed away several hours later.

Travis had grown pretty tired himself, and he'd stretched out on the rock and rested his head on one of her paws. He talked the whole time, regaling her with tales of shapeshifting, focusing on how it had been as a wyvern, then a labyrinth dragon, and adding how a steamer dragon would be even better . . .

He had absolutely no idea whether she'd understood a word he'd said. Why would she? She was a *dragon*.

He trailed off at some point and fell asleep. When he woke, she was no longer breathing.

A dream lingered as he lay there. Was it true? Had the steamer dragon once witnessed a ghostly image of Travis in his mothman form standing right here in the cave entrance?

*She knew I was coming tonight. She'd foreseen it—probably by looking into the boulder opal. It really does work.*

He frowned at the golden ray of sunshine creeping across the wall, then leapt to his feet. It was dawn already. He should have gone home hours ago, but it wouldn't have been right to just snatch the gem from the dragon's dying paw and leave her alone in her final hours. No matter what, he felt good about his small act of kindness.

But he was *so* late getting back.

He flew home clutching the blue gem.

\* \* \*

Travis stood bathed in the morning sun, unable to grasp what he was seeing. Melinda and a gnome—both sound asleep in the vegetable garden. The gate stood open. There was no sign of the empusa or the dryad.

"Hey, wake up," he called, giving Melinda a gentle kick.

She bolted upright, blinked, and focused on him. Then she sighed. "About time you showed up. Did you fall asleep or something?"

"Yeah. Same as you."

Melinda opened her mouth to retort, then thought better of it. She shook her dad awake.

"Where's Flynn?" she said, looking around. "And your mom?" Her eyes widened. "Oh!"

She jumped up and hurried toward the house.

"What?" Travis asked, running after her. "What's wrong?"

"Mr. Grimfoyle. He kind of stood in the way of the werewolves."

"The—the *werewolves?*" Travis almost stopped dead, but he hastened to catch up as she dashed into the kitchen through the open door. "You had werewolves here?"

"They tried to get in. They *did* get in. We hid in the basement, but Mr. Grimfoyle didn't make it in time."

Travis couldn't make sense of it. He followed her through the kitchen to the spacious living room. "So how did you end up outside?"

He exclaimed in shock when he caught sight of the old man lying flat on his back, legs akimbo, pants in long shreds. He only had one arm; Flynn was holding the other. It still had the jacket and shirt wrapped around it, and the dryad was busy peeling the material aside and offering the limb to the man's exposed shoulder—which thankfully Travis couldn't clearly see from where he stood.

Melinda had halted in her tracks, hand to her mouth. "Flynn!" she cried.

The dryad looked up. "He was in pieces. He asked me to put him back together. I'm just placing the limbs where they're supposed to be."

"A neat trick," a voice said behind Travis.

He swung around to see the empusa lurking in the darkest corner.

The gnome walked in just then, saw the state of the old man, and immediately began moaning and banging his head on the nearest wall.

Mr. Grimfoyle turned his head to glare at them all. "Ah, there you are, boy. Did you get it?"

Travis opened and closed his mouth like a fish out of water. "Uh," he stammered, "sure, yeah. It's right here."

"Splendid!"

Finishing his work, Flynn slowly edged backward. "Is that all right?" he murmured.

"It'll do just fine," the man told him. "Now I just need to wait a while for my legs and arms to reattach."

Melinda let out a squeak. "Your legs as well?"

Seeing how distressed she was, Flynn sidled over to her and looked like he wanted to take her hand. He faded in and out.

"Yes, ripped into my chest as well," Mr. Grimfoyle muttered. "Look at this suit. Ruined!" He lifted his head slightly, then let it thud back to the floor. "Come over here, boy, where I can see you."

Travis moved closer and held up the blue gem between a finger and thumb. "Well, this is it. The famous boulder opal."

"Infamous," Mr. Grimfoyle corrected him. His arms and legs twitched occasionally.

"What's infamous about it?"

The white-haired man let out a cackle of laughter. "Boy, if you knew how many have tried to get hold of that thing over the years. Madame Frost herself tried once, and three steamer dragons tore her house apart. That was your father's doing. He borrowed it much like you are now, and the dragons reclaimed it shortly after."

"I know."

"I'm sure you do. Did you know it spoke to him? Showed him a vision. And if it worked for him, perhaps it will work for you."

Travis frowned. He hadn't heard this part of the story before. "*Spoke* to him?"

"It lit up and projected an image, or so I heard. Now, enough talk. Take it outside in the fresh air and focus on it. See if you can get something out of it—a vision of some kind. Find out where your father buried that potion."

Travis looked around at the strange group. Was this it? The fate of the world depended on this motley crew? A recently dissected old man wearing a black suit, a silent empusa vampire caked in mud up to her waist, an almost invisible dryad wearing completely opaque pants, a gnome who kept banging his head on the wall, and of course Melinda and himself.

Four shapeshifters, two of them faulty. A man who couldn't die. And a farm boy who seemed to have a thing for Melinda.

"Okay," he said. "I'll see what I can do."

He trudged outside. The warm sun was rising quickly, and faint wispy steam rose off the dew-covered grass. The blue haze seemed almost nonexistent this morning. He started walking around the outside of the house, focused on the gem, trying to figure out how he was supposed to get the thing to work.

*Show me something*, he urged. *Give me a vision. Let me see the future where I'm digging up the potion. Or the past when my dad buried it in the first place. That would be better. Show me that, please.*

He reached the front of the house and was distracted by the terrible claw marks all over the cabin-style log wall. The wood was gouged deep in many places. The front door, too—and the windows. Very large pawprints littered the flower beds under the windows, and the plants were ruined, trampled flat. The werewolves had wrecked the place inside and out.

Looking up, he noticed the gutter was hanging low at the corner, and roof tiles were scattered across the grass.

He saw the same kind of disruption to flower beds under the windows around the side of the house, too. And as he moved around to the back, he found where another of the savage beasts had climbed up onto the roof. It had used the recess where the stone chimney jutted out from the log walls, as evidenced by numerous scuffs all the way up.

"What a mess," he muttered.

"Could have been worse," Melinda said from behind him.

Travis jumped. "Yeah, sneak up on me while I'm thinking about werewolves. Great idea."

While he leaned against the stone chimney, she took a few paces back and stared up just as he had done. "Wow. That's determination right there. I'm so glad your dad had the doors and windows reinforced."

"They still got in, though," Travis pointed out. "When he's back, I'll tell him he needs to complain to whoever installed the back door. They didn't do that one very well. The door held up, and the frame is good, but the hinges popped right off."

"May I see the gem?"

He tossed it to her and folded his arms, watching as she studied it closely.

"I'm trying to imagine my dad borrowing that thing years ago," he said. "What do you think he saw?"

"He never mentioned it?"

Travis shook his head. "Not that I remember. I guess it wasn't that important."

Melinda placed the boulder opal on a knee-high tree stump. The tree had been cut down six months ago because it was too close to the house, and ever since then, Travis's dad sat on that stump to rest during yard work. He patted the stump sometimes almost like he missed it. Maybe he still hoped it would shed walnuts if he kept talking to it.

"I miss my mom and dad," he said, a sudden lump in his throat. He swallowed.

"Me too," Melinda said.

They both knew his mom and her dad were just inside the house, but that wasn't the same. What if they stayed like that? A gnome for a dad, and a vampire with flaming hair for a mom? What if Travis's dad remained a towering giant? What if Melinda's mom was struck down by the faun?

"I wish I could see them," Travis mumbled. "Maybe this opal could show me the future—just enough to see them again and know they're okay. You know? That's really all I need right now, some kind of—"

"Shh," Melinda said. She pointed. "Something's happening."

Travis gawked as the carefully placed gem glowed brightly, then started flashing about once every second. It shone like a beacon from the tree stump, so bright he could barely see Melinda on the opposite side.

*What the heck . . . ?* he thought, staring in amazement.

Within a hazy field of shimmering light, two figures materialized, a boy and a girl about his age. Travis had seen enough old pictures to recognize them immediately as his own mom and dad when they were younger. Many people said he looked a little like his dad—the same sandy-colored hair and short stature—and his mom's dark-brown hair and freckles were pretty distinctive, at least to him.

Not a vision of the future, then. This was a scene from the past.

## Chapter 22
## A Blast from the Past

"Hello?" Travis's young mom said, her voice eerily clear from within the hazy projection. "Can you . . . can you see us?"

*Is this actually happening?* Travis thought. *Is this just a vision, or . . . can we talk across time?*

"Yes," he said loudly, his heart thumping. "Wow. This is so weird. I, uh . . . I need your help."

The boy—his dad!— frowned and said, "You need our help? How come? We've never even met."

*He heard me! He answered my question!*

"Travis?" Melinda whispered.

He glanced at her, barely able to contain his excitement. She stood off to one side, squinting toward the projection but perhaps not seeing it as clearly as he was. He waved her closer. "Come here. You have to see this."

She took a few steps, and her expression changed when the light from the projection played across her face, almost like understanding had just dawned. "Huh? Is that who I think it is?"

"Yep."

Travis watched his two young parents for a while. They seemed to be struggling to figure out what was happening. Maybe nobody had told them about the boulder opal's power. And anyway, it was much easier for Travis to look back into the past and recognize his parents than it was for them to look into the future and see—

*Yeah, I'm your son,* he thought. *That has to be weird. I should keep that to myself.*

When the projection flickered, he had a sudden panic attack and got down to business before it could expire. But even as he opened his mouth to speak, he was distracted again.

These were his parents! He couldn't help studying his mom's delightfully young face as he absently said, "You have to tell us what you did with the potion." He looked again at his dad. So, so young!

His dad took a step sideways. Travis followed his gaze. *Trying to catch me out?* he thought with a moment of glee.

"What potion?" his mom asked.

*Okay, enough gawking.* Travis focused on her. "The potion to turn everyone normal. We need it urgently."

Neither said anything. They just looked blank.

Melinda spoke up. "You got a potion from the witch. From Madame Frost. What did you do with it? I know you used some, but there was a bit left over. Where did you put it?"

Again, those completely befuddled expressions. But was Melinda right about that? Travis remembered his dad saying the witch had pointed him in the right direction to find it, not that she'd actually *given* it to him. Still, a vial was a vial. He had to know what she was talking about.

"You have to help us," Melinda went on. "I know this is weird for you—for all of us—but we need that potion. We've asked you a million times already, but you can't remember." She broke off and frowned. "Okay, let me reword that. We've asked the *other* you—the older you. But everything's gone wrong here, so we're asking you instead, the *younger* you. Does that make sense?"

"Who *are* you guys?" Travis's young dad exclaimed.

The projection flickered again. The haze was getting more pronounced. Travis felt panic setting in. This might be their last chance.

"Uh, we're . . . from the future," he said, aware that he had no time to explain everything in detail. They needed some kind of clue, though. "The faun is back, and she's worse now. You have to tell us where you left the potion."

Looking flabbergasted, his dad opened and closed his mouth a few times and finally said, "I—I don't know. I mean, we haven't— *What* potion? Look, what are you saying? What do you know about the faun? I don't understand any of this!"

Travis couldn't help thinking it was like looking in a mirror. The uncertainty, the flustered manner, the somewhat clueless way about him . . .

Melinda suddenly turned to Travis. "They haven't made it that far yet."

She was right. That had to be it. This was a point in time *before* his parents had run afoul of the faun, *before* they'd gone to see Madame Frost. They knew nothing about the potion yet.

Travis thought quickly. There was a workaround. "Okay. Listen, Dad, this is important. When you find the potion, you must make sure to store it safely, maybe in a place that we might find easily? We've looked everywhere, but we can't find it. I mean, all I got from you was that I had to dig it up. But dig it up where? The backyard? The vegetable garden? The flower beds around the front of the house? The—"

Melinda reached out and touched his arm, pointing at the fading image.

Travis shook her off and shouted into the haze. "Mom! Dad! You have to help us! Give us a clue! Just—just tell us where— Argh!"

He ran over to the stump and kicked at the boulder opal. Instead of launching it high into the sky, it only flew a few yards into the grass because he miscalculated and stubbed his toe on the immovable stump. He cried out in pain, sank to the grass, and rolled onto his side, moaning and cursing, clutching at his foot. The thin, magical smartshoe had become dislodged, but it quickly rippled and warped back into place.

"What a waste of time!" he yelled at the top of his voice. "This *whole night* has been a waste of time! We could have been fighting the faun by now instead of hanging around here messing with stupid blue gems!"

"Travis—"

"I mean, *seriously*," he exclaimed, clambering to his feet and hopping toward Melinda, "what was the point of this? I'll tell you what, I'm *done* with Mr. Grimfoyle and his stupid ideas. Let's just go and fight the stupid faun and get this stupid thing over with! We'll deal with the stupid missing potion later!"

She raised her eyebrows and said nothing, and he glowered at her and panted, waiting for a response. When none came, he screwed up his face and winced at the throbbing pain in his toes. He sank to the grass again and started massaging his foot.

"Stupid potions and things . . ." he muttered.

Still Melinda said nothing.

After a while, Travis sighed and looked up at her. "I think I'm done yelling."

Melinda knelt and smiled. "Good. I guess it's okay to get stuff like that off your chest. But you're right—it does seem like we wasted a lot of time. We should have left last night when we had the chance. Let's grab Mr. Grimfoyle and go now."

"We don't need him."

"We *do*."

She was right, of course.

"Well, maybe we'll leave his arms and legs behind and just stuff his head and body in a bag, and we'll unbuckle it when we need to ask him something. Then we won't have to listen to his grumbling and dumb ideas."

Melinda nodded sagely. "Sure, sure, that sounds like a plan. I'll go find a bag while you drag him outside."

"Stop humoring me."

"Then suck it up, buttercup." She stood and offered him a hand. "Ready?"

He accepted her help, and they went indoors to get things moving.

Though he could have transformed a few times and sorted out his painful toes, he chose to suffer the pain. It served him right for losing his cool. He'd be fine once they set off.

To his surprise, Mr. Grimfoyle didn't complain when they helped him off the floor and sat him on a hard kitchen chair.

His arms and legs dangled uselessly—but they were attached, and that was remarkable in itself. His suit, shredded in multiple places, revealed glimpses of his pale flesh. The wounds underneath were no more than pink welts. His missing jacket and shirt sleeves showed the ugly lumps and scars around the joints—but again, they were attached! Just a few hours ago, they'd been lying in different parts of the house.

"I'm afraid I won't be able to walk for a little while," the man said. "But I assume you'll just carry me anyway, won't you, boy? So I'll dangle helplessly no matter what."

"Right," he agreed.

"Dad," Melinda said to the gnome, who was hunched on the floor by a wall, fingers clasped together. Just for once, he seemed relaxed. "We're going—but you're staying here. Don't worry about us, okay?"

The gnome frowned at her. "Why should I worry?"

"Well . . . it might be dangerous."

"And?"

"And, well, you know, I'm your daughter."

"If you say so," the gnome said, giving her a wan smile. "I admit I have grown quite fond of you in the past few hours. I hope you'll be safe."

Travis sought out the empusa. It took a while to find her. She was standing outside an open closet in the master bedroom upstairs. "Hey."

She glanced at him. "I have a strange feeling . . ."

"What kind of feeling? Strange how?"

"The feeling that . . . *these* belonged to me." She waved her hand in an almost disgusted way at the clothing hanging in the closet.

Travis smiled. "They did. I mean, they do. They're yours. See, there's some more smart dresses like the one you're wearing . . . and some normal clothes . . . and some winter things. Those shoes are yours, too. And the hiking boots. And the—"

"Clearly the footwear is not mine," the empusa said rather stiffly. She slammed the closet door shut. "My mistake."

"No, it's not a mistake. Your memories are real—"

"I'll be leaving shortly. I've had just about enough here." She suddenly gripped his shoulder, leaned closer, and inhaled next to his ear. "Although, truth be told, I'm quite hungry this morning."

Travis fought to get free of her grip. "That's enough, Mom."

The empusa's hair suddenly caught fire. The intensity in her eyes and the sudden flush to her cheeks indicated she was caught up in a moment of longing and desire. "The scent of hot blood pumping through your body is exquisite. I've never— There's something about you and that girl. Why am I drawn to you?"

Travis squirmed harder, but her grip was rock solid. "Mom!"

The flames grew hot, threatening to melt his skin as she moved her face even closer and sniffed at him. "No wonder humans were hunted to extinction. How did *you* survive?"

"Is that what you think? Are those the false memories the faun put in your head?" He thrashed wildly until his smart shirt ripped. He pulled loose and backed away, panting. "Mom, that's enough. Just . . . just stay here until it's over."

She snorted. "I'll stay here until I've finished draining your blood."

With a sudden leap, she gripped his throat and slammed him against the wall, lifting him off his feet. Choking, he beat her arms and punched at her face, but nothing he did helped— partly because she'd taken on a metallic sheen, and her flesh had hardened into brass.

"I must eat," she said softly, flames still shooting up from her hair.

With that, she leaned close, baring her fangs and opening wide . . .

Travis transformed. His wings spread wide, pushing him away from the wall a little. Mostly, though, he hung in the same position, feet off the floor, while she gripped his throat and paused with her fangs inches from his neck.

Then her face screwed up into a grimace She recoiled and dropped him. "What?" she yelled. "How *dare* you! You're foul!"

"Insect, actually," he muttered. "*Birds* are fowl."

Giving her no time to recover from her disgust, he raced out of the room and down the stairs. "We have to go, Melinda. My mom just tried to drain my blood."

As he went to hoist Mr. Grimfoyle onto his feet, he heard Melinda say, "That's not something you hear every day." Then she raised her voice. "Flynn? I'm leaving. Please look after my dad."

"But I haven't repaid my debt to you," the dryad said, appearing out of nowhere to her side.

"You can repay it by saving my dad from that crazy vampire upstairs."

Mr. Grimfoyle struggled to sit up. "The gem," he barked. "Where is it?"

Travis shrugged. "Lying in the grass somewhere."

Melinda's tone was far more surly. "And it can stay there until we're done. Right, Mr. Grimfoyle?"

The old man scowled.

They took an arm each and helped him up. Travis couldn't help worrying if they were putting too much strain on his recently attached joints. What if things *separated* in the air?

Outside, Travis looked up to see his mom peering out of the window, keeping to the shadows. Her flames had died down, but she had a hungry look on her face. Her gaze was directed at Melinda now.

He spread his wings wide and launched, repositioning and grabbing Mr. Grimfoyle's wrist as he went. He lifted the man into the air with ease—and nothing came loose.

Next, he reached for Melinda. They locked hands and wrists, and then he soared upward, taking them both with him.

He called out to his passengers as he headed toward the sun. "Next stop—the horizon."

## Chapter 23
## A Journey Northeast

Travis couldn't help glancing back toward Carter. Now that he knew what to look for, he made out the enormous column of smoky mist that spun over the town. Even from here, he could see the man-shaped giant within, standing perfectly still over the houses, arms to his side. Was he as ghostly and insubstantial as he looked? Or could he do some real damage if he took a step this way and that?

Melinda let out a cry when she spotted the monster. "Travis!"

"I know, I know. I think that's . . . my dad."

"No!"

He veered back toward the giant, and Mr. Grimfoyle said, "Fascinating! That, my boy is a jinn."

"A what?" But even as he asked the question, a memory sparked. He'd done a *lot* of research before embarking on shapeshifter missions, and the jinn was something he recalled quite clearly. He just hadn't recognized it.

Mr. Grimfoyle answered the question anyway. "Perhaps you know it best as a genie? But either way, the jinn is a powerful and dangerous creature. Don't get too close, boy. It may change at any moment."

Travis thought about some of the things he'd read—how the jinn usually appeared in mist or sandstorms, often as a combination of different monsters but sometimes, on rare occasions, as a giant human-like figure. They existed between worlds, not quite a ghost and not quite physical. They could touch and feel physical things—meaning it would be disastrous if the jinn started walking about. But it was entirely possible for the giant to change its shape and size. Surely the faun hadn't meant to create a massive smoke-monster, had she?

The giant turned its head toward him as he passed and once more lifted a hand in slow motion. This action had seemed hostile the first time; now Travis had the sense the giant might be reaching out for help . . .

"I'm going to save you, Dad!" he yelled.

The jinn, towering over the town, tried to twist at the waist as Travis circled around, but the smoke monster couldn't reach far enough and started roaring with obvious frustration. The noise carried across the landscape, probably for miles, like the rumble of thunder.

Then it roared again, only this time it sounded as if the giant were trying to articulate the word "stop."

"What?" Travis yelled. "Stop what?"

Another roar, and Travis could have sworn it was the word "stomp." That made even less sense. His dad was obviously confused.

Fighting back tears, Travis flew back out across the town.

Below, he saw goblins marching toward a mass of elves. They looked determined, drawing swords and slapping them against their chests as they went. Travis understood that elves and goblins were rather like disgruntled neighbors—tolerant up to a point. Perhaps this town wasn't big enough for so many of each. Goblins had lived among humans for some time, but the same couldn't be said of elves, who acted aloof and superior toward both goblins *and* humans.

"Trouble brewing," he muttered.

He resumed his journey northeast. The center of the mist storm was out there somewhere. And that was where they'd find the faun.

The blue haze was almost nonexistent when he flew low to the ground, but much more noticeable from higher up. So he ascended, eager to view a bigger picture, to see how far this thing really stretched.

It was pretty staggering. He heard Melinda gasp and Mr. Grimfoyle mutter something under his breath. The higher he flew, the thicker the blue haze seemed—and the outer rim that had passed over Carter yesterday was a thick, impenetrable wall in the far distance.

He flapped harder, finding it increasingly difficult to make progress. The air had thinned dramatically, and not even magic could get around that problem. *Just a bit higher*, he thought, urging himself on.

The clouds were forever out of reach. His dad had far more strength. So had Travis's previous shapeshifter incarnation as a wyvern. It seemed mothmen relied on lighter-than-air magic rather than raw power like dragons.

The outer reaches of the storm were visible in the far distance to the south and west, a gently curving, thick line of solid blue. But the haze blanketed everything else, stretching over the horizon to the north and east.

He gave up trying to climb and began a slow, gentle descent, gliding the whole way. Glancing at his passengers, he suddenly realized how trusting they were. They didn't feel heavy, but still, all of their weight hung in his hands. If he slipped . . .

Did his palms feel sweaty now? He chalked that up to an active imagination.

"Hey, Mr. Grimfoyle," he called down. With the breathtaking view and the near-silence of the altitude, it seemed like a perfect time for the old man to spill the beans. "Tell us what you know about the faun. You said you'd tell us on the way. What's there to tell?"

Mr. Grimfoyle said nothing for a moment, just hung limp with his black jacket flapping in the wind. Then he sighed. "In my travels, doing what I do for a living, I never thought—"

"What *do* you do for a living?" Melinda interrupted.

"I buy and sell."

"Buy and sell what?"

"Whatever makes me a coin or two. I bargain, cheat, steal, and then sell, sell, sell. I make enough to get by. I carry everything I own in a small case. If it's too heavy to lug about, I empty it. I do business, I move on. That's how I live."

Neither Melinda nor Travis had anything to say about that. But what a sad existence.

Mr. Grimfoyle went on with his story. "Doing what I do for a living, I never thought for a minute I would lead a safe, trouble-free life. But I never expected to bump into a faun who started following me around the market square one Sunday morning."

"The same faun we're looking for?" Melinda asked.

"The same, yes. I turned on her and demanded to know what she wanted with me, why she was following me, and she told me I was a thief. Granted, she had seen me pickpocket a little old lady."

Travis scowled down at the man. "You say that like you don't care."

Mr. Grimfoyle twisted his neck to look up at him. "I don't. I make no secret of it. I'm a horrible fellow, and have been for a long time. This is why I have no soul of my own. It withered and died."

"I thought that was because someone had put a curse on you," Melinda said.

"Well, either way, I am a most wretched excuse for a human being. I thought this faun was going to turn me in or try to punish me—but instead she put me to sleep with a spell, and when I woke in her lair, she offered me a job."

"Offered you a—" Melinda repeated. "Wait, what? A *job*?"

"I was intrigued, to say the least. She said she could use a man with my obvious lack of scruples. In fact, she said I was almost overqualified. Or should that be underqualified? What is it when someone has such low moral value that he's too despicable to be a villain's henchman?"

"Get to the point," Travis told him.

Ahead, the mist was definitely thinning. He judged the center of the storm to be about halfway between the two clusters of mountains on the horizon. If he fixed his gaze and made a beeline for it, he should get there in fifteen or twenty minutes, maybe less.

Columns of smoke rose from a small village nearby. Travis felt sure the place was called Follen's Glen, established by a family of Old Earthers ten years ago. It had grown into a tight community of maybe fifty or sixty people—a tiny place, but self-sustaining, with farmland all around. Apparently, they had some amazing basket weavers and blacksmiths there; Travis's mom had commented just recently on the quality of their goods, which were often sold at the market in Carter.

Mr. Grimfoyle bent his free arm, lifted his hand, and stared at his twitching fingers. "Ah, look. There's life left in me yet. Anyway—yes, the faun offered me a job. I accepted because she had a small pouch of coins for me, and the promise of more for each day I worked with her. She called herself River, and she lived in a short tower on a tiny island in a lake. And when I say a tiny island, I mean a mound sticking up from the water, its surface mostly covered by the tower."

"Is this where I come in?" Melinda piped up. "Something that swims?"

"Mmm. Let's not digress."

"What was the job?" Travis asked.

"Whoa, what's *that*?" Melinda suddenly screeched.

Descending from the clouds above was a gigantic monster with four coppery wings and a beautifully fanned tail of colorful feathers. But it was more than just a bird. It had the feet of a lion and the giant head of a dog. It started barking at Travis the moment it saw them.

"Not good," he muttered, paralyzed with fear. Should he go up or down? Left or right? This monster could snatch him out of the air in a heartbeat no matter which way he turned.

He chose down. He already knew his limits in altitude, and that monster had just dropped out of the sky much higher than he'd been able to manage.

*It's a simurgh*, he told himself as he plummeted.

The barking continued as he shot toward the ground. He glanced back once to see the enormous beast bearing down on him, and he beat his wings as hard as he could to put on a little extra burst of speed. Melinda screamed, and even Mr. Grimfoyle let out a squawk of fright.

Travis aimed for a patch of woodland. It wasn't a big patch, but it didn't need to be. He stayed low to the ground while the furious barking increased in volume. The simurgh was closing in.

The trees ahead came upon him fast. He didn't slow down but was careful to tilt his wings so he fit between the trunks. The moment he entered the woodland, plunging in the gloom at top speed, he had to twist and turn to avoid more trees ahead. Melinda slipped free of his grasp. Suddenly off-balanced with Mr. Grimfoyle still hanging on, he spun and veered sharply, grazed a tree, crashed through the branches of another, and smacked hard into a third.

He collapsed to the ground in a heap, groaning, vaguely aware that he still held Mr. Grimfoyle's hand even though the man was nowhere to be seen.

The simurgh barked up a frenzy, clearly furious. Travis lay on his back listening to the sounds of a monster tearing into branches but not getting very far. Splintered wood, cracking and creaking, the rustle of leaves and bushes, angry growls and roars . . . and then a sudden silence as the simurgh flapped away.

"Ow," Travis moaned.

Sitting up, he winced in pain. His wings hurt. His right arm hurt. His chest and face hurt. His stubbed toes *still* hurt.

He threw Mr. Grimfoyle's arm aside with a shudder and slowly climbed to his feet. The old man lay on his back nearby, panting. His other limbs were still attached.

"Go find the girl," the man said.

Travis headed back the way he'd flown in. It amazed him that he'd made it so far into the woods, easily passing between twenty or more trees before running out of luck. He staggered about, wincing and grumbling, searching for Melinda.

He found her lying on her belly, face to one side, staring ahead. At first he thought she was unconscious, or worse—but as he drew nearer, she turned her gaze on him and raised a hand in greeting. "I'm okay."

"Are you sure?" he said, kneeling by her side.

He helped her turn over and sit up, ignoring his own pains while he figured out where she might be hurt. She rolled her arm around, holding her shoulder and grimacing—then pressed her fingers against her side and finally massaged her knee.

"I guess I got lucky," she said.

She had a long scratch on her cheek, and Travis felt a surge of guilt. "Sorry about that," he mumbled.

She squinted at him. "For saving our lives from that giant flying hound? Don't be sorry. You did good."

Travis glanced at her with suspicion. But she seemed sincere.

"Seriously, thank you," she added. Struggling to her feet, she leaned on Travis until he winced, and then she snatched her hand away and looked him up and down. "Wait—are *you* okay?"

"Ugh," he grunted. "I hurt all over. But nothing a few shifts won't cure."

"Well, do some shifting *now*."

They both did, in unison. He reverted to human form while she flopped down on the ground and grew a fishtail—and then she switched back to human while he sprouted his wings—and so on back and forth until most of their injuries had faded. He tried to look away while she was in mermaid form, because each time, in those few seconds, he found himself gazing at her a little too intently. The problem wasn't that they were related, because in fact they weren't. The problem was that . . . well, she was *Melinda*. He'd known her all his life, and they were *friends*. Anything more than that was just plain weird.

"You keep looking at me funny," she said at last when they were done shifting and he'd ended up in human form.

He felt his face heat up. "I was just . . . I'm glad to see that scratch on your face has gone away."

She automatically reached for her cheek. "Oh. Well, good."

Travis sighed. "Let's find Mr. Grimfoyle. I don't think his arm was on properly. It came loose again, so we'll have to reattach it."

## Chapter 24
## Follen's Glen

As it turned out, Mr. Grimfoyle had already reattached his arm. He sat by the tree Travis had slammed into and held his dislodged limb in place, staring into space. When he spotted Travis and Melinda, he struggled to stand, still holding onto his arm.

"Well, that was an adventure," he grouched. "I seem to recall the faun telling me she had no intention of harming humans. 'All life is sacred,' she kept saying. 'I just want to evolve them into something better.' Well, I'd say turning someone into a terrible beast like that is harmful to human life, don't you think? Harmful to *other* human life, that is."

"Maybe it was a real simurgh," Travis offered.

The man had nothing to say to that. Still, he'd made a good point.

"There was an ogre back in town," Travis went on. "It went crazy and beat on my dad."

"Well, my boy, I should imagine it's confusing waking with very little memory of who or what you are. For an ogre, and perhaps for that four-winged monster just now, it might be quite unnerving and scary, liable to send them into a panic."

They threaded their way through the woods until they reached the open ground. Searching the sky, Travis saw no sign of the simurgh, so they moved away from the trees and stood in a circle. It felt strange walking around in human form after being a mothman for so long.

"Ready to try again?" Travis asked, looking at them both in turn.

Mr. Grimfoyle tentatively released the grip on his arm, and it slipped away from his shoulder. Too late, Travis saw the nasty gap that appeared before the old man pressed it back in place. "Well, that's a nuisance."

"Can't you carry it?" Melinda asked him. "You carry your arm, and Travis will carry *you*."

The man stared into space again, his brow furrowed. Eventually, he sighed. "I feel I am no use to you from this point forward. Even if you carried me to the faun's tower, I would be no use other than to point you in the right direction—which, quite frankly, I can do from here."

Melinda looked aghast. "Y-you want us to go on alone?"

"Come now, my dear—I'm sure you can manage just fine without a doddery old fool slowing you down, especially one whose arm keeps dropping off."

"But we don't know—"

"I'll tell you everything I can, and then you'll know as much as I do." The man nodded ahead. "Come now. Let's walk in the morning sunshine while I regale you with my short time working with the faun."

Travis couldn't help noticing there *was* no sunshine. The cloud cover was ominous, and the hint of a blue haze lingered across the fields. But they walked together anyway, circling the patch of woods so they were headed roughly in the right direction towards the faun's lair on the horizon.

"That faun wanted someone with very little conscience," Mr. Grimfoyle said. "And I'll be the first to admit I'm perfect in that respect. So I accepted her bag of coins and stayed, and she set me to work at the stroke of midnight."

"At midnight?" Melinda repeated. "Something despicable, I'll bet."

"Well, despicable is my middle name. And yes, the task was pretty wretched."

Travis couldn't fathom how the old man not only went through life being mean and thoughtless but accepted his shortcomings so readily as well. If he recognized he was a rotten apple, didn't that mean he could change?

"River told me she had stepped out of her tree a few months ago and started work on a new version of her evolution mist, whatever that was. She wanted me to—"

"Wait, what?" Melinda interrupted. "Stepped out of her *tree*?"

"All fauns have a place of solitude, a tree of tranquility. Hers is not far from Carter, out in the plains. She said that place was full of life, once—forestland stretching for miles. It seems the rain clouds stayed away, and over many decades, the forest dried up—but her tree remained, because it's enchanted by magic and cocooned within a shell that protects it from the ravages of time. She and her faun family would seek refuge in the tree whenever danger approached. When they stepped back out, days or weeks or even months would have passed, and so had the danger."

Travis felt a memory stirring. "I remember something about this. My mom and dad chased her, and she escaped into the tree and disappeared—and my parents lost some time as well."

"Indeed," Mr. Grimfoyle said, leaning over and giving him a shoulder-nudge as they walked. He still had his hand clamped onto his other arm, holding it in place. "And so River, who had broken an ankle, stepped inside her tree to escape your parents and rest her foot. She slept, and when she woke, nearly twenty years had passed in the outside world."

"No way!" Travis exclaimed, though this part of the story sounded familiar as well.

They left the field and turned onto a dirt road. Just ahead, thin columns of smoke rose into the sky. Maybe the old man could stay at Follen's Glen for a while. On the other hand, it might be safer to hide out in the woods . . .

It made a nice change to walk on an established road. Many wagons had traveled this route, and probably a few vehicles from Old Earth, too. Follen's Glen had a portal of its own in the center; the village had grown up around it, as new settlements tended to do. From what Travis had heard, the place was picturesque and friendly. A neatly carved and painted sign at the side of the road proudly stated the village name in ornate lettering, and he immediately decided he wanted to come here and explore when everything was back to normal.

*But not right now,* he thought grimly as reality came crashing back down. *I'll bet it's not very friendly at the moment.*

"So what's this despicable task?" Melinda said, apparently not quite so enthralled with the parts of the story they already knew.

Mr. Grimfoyle chuckled. "Ah, well, if you really want to know, she sent me out at midnight to dig up a human corpse from the nearby cemetery. The smallest finger bone from any skeleton is what she wanted—the older, the better."

As Travis and Melinda gasped in astonishment, the old man shook his head and clicked his tongue.

"Now, you see, I'm getting ahead of myself. Why did she want the finger bone, you ask? Because it's an essential ingredient of the transmogrification potion, along with one hundred and sixty-two other ingredients. Actually, it's a healing potion. It only becomes a transmogrification potion when it's turned to mist. Anyway, it's quite a recipe, let me tell you, and many of those items are rather suspect—not the sort of thing you can find in a store. A bat's blood and three live toads are fairly standard in potion-making, but four grams of scraped cerberus skin and three cyclops' eyeballs—those are not so common."

"Plus," Melinda piped up, "it must be hard finding a cyclops with three eyes."

"Three *separate* cyclops," Mr. Grimfoyle corrected her—and then gave a chuckle. "Ah, you're pulling my leg. Don't pull too hard, dear, or it'll come off."

Rooftops appeared over the brow of the hill ahead. Travis suddenly grew nervous. If one of the residents had disintegrated and sprung to life again as a confused simurgh, what else might they find?

The old man didn't seem concerned at all. "So, this despicable task involved going to a cemetery and digging up a corpse. And then, the next day, she sent me off to the nearest village—*this* one—to hunt up some more ingredients: something half-chewed by a very old person, a shiny brooch worn by a woman who had recently suffered a terrible tragedy, the tooth of a twin, the toe of a spinster, a tuft of hair from—"

"What?" Melinda almost yelled as she spun around. "You're making this up! The toe of a spinster? How on earth would you get hold of something like *that*?"

Mr. Grimfoyle nodded sagely. "Exactly. This list of ingredients was a challenge. Witches have very specific needs, and this faun learned from a witch—from Madame Frost, in fact. And a faun prancing about the village market would not go unnoticed, whereas I am adept at blending in. Being 'invisible' was, after all, my livelihood."

"Should have hired a dryad," Travis muttered.

"Anyway, naturally it took quite a bit of plotting to get hold of that toe," Mr. Grimfoyle went on. "A very carefully crafted accident, being on hand to lend assistance to the poor woman, making sure her wound was properly dressed and the bleeding staunched while at the same time collecting up that very valuable toe and depositing it in my capacious pockets before anyone—"

"Oh, stop!" Travis snapped.

"You're despicable," Melinda said. "How does someone like you go from helping a faun gather ingredients for her potion to—to what? Running away? Betraying her?"

They all came to a halt at the very edge of the village, where the dirt track ran between a couple of posts with a sign across the top saying WELCOME. Beyond, the dirt track continued in a more leisurely, meandering way, with stone-walled thatched cottages on either side, interspersed with trees and shrubs. Flower pots hung in windows. The place couldn't be any prettier.

But rather than ordinary people walking about, Travis spotted a naga hissing at a troll, and a harpy looking down on them from a rooftop and cackling. Backing away from the squabbling naga and troll, a nymph clutched a rather large dress to her slender frame. She turned and ran, her eyes wide with fear.

Melinda gasped and pointed. An enormous horse trotted from one backyard to another, but its head was more like that of a dragon—a long reptilian snout, and jaws stuffed with pointed teeth. A spiky crest ran down its neck and back to a serpentine tail. The entire thing was scaly with a silvery sheen.

Travis searched the recesses of his mind for the name of this rare beast. It began with an L, but . . .

He, Melinda, and Mr. Grimfoyle stared in amazement at the magnificent equine as it turned and trotted back, apparently content to pace the backyards of neighboring cottages. A good thing, too. Something like that getting angry could cause mayhem.

Overhead, multiple screeches made the three of them duck. Travis expected a flock of birds, but instead saw a vivid, red-feathered, nine-headed phoenix about the size of a dog. Not an *actual* phoenix but a variation of one. Again, very rare.

"It's a longma!" he exclaimed, spinning back to point at the majestic dragon-horse. "Man, I don't know if anyone's seen one of those in . . . well, forever!"

Melinda gestured to the red bird creature as it soared away. "And what about that thing? *How* many heads was that? Ten?"

"Nine," Travis said, his heart thumping. Despite the seriousness of the situation, this was still pretty amazing. "It's a nine-headed bird."

"But what's it called?"

Travis shrugged. "It's called a nine-headed bird. Some people say it's an early form of a phoenix, but others say it's just a close cousin. There's also something even weirder called a *fenghuang*, which is a mixture of different kinds of birds—"

"This is fascinating," Mr. Grimfoyle said, "but I suggest we part ways. You have work to do. And I have a small village that needs my help."

Travis turned to him. The man had a curious shine in his eyes. "Needs your help how?"

The old man shrugged. "I spent some time here while gathering ingredients for the faun. And I got to know people. I began to enjoy my visits here, day by day, plotting to strike off the next item on my list. I was here several weeks. People grew used to my presence, and were courteous and polite, dare I say *nice*. There's a small bed-and-breakfast that put aside a room for me, because this village is some distance from the faun's tower, and I would often stay overnight."

Travis and Melinda silently waited for him to get to the point. Not so far away, the naga advanced on the troll, ramrod straight and swaying in a threatening manner. But the troll stood just as tall and seemed to be itching for a fight.

"So I will stay, and you will go," Mr. Grimfoyle finished. "Remember—head for the center of the storm, where the mist is at its thinnest. That's where you'll find the tower."

"Hang on," Travis said. "What are you so interested in here?"

"Is it . . . a woman?" Melinda whispered. "Did you meet someone and fall in love? Is that it? Mr. Grimfoyle, the cold, heartless, soulless man who can never die . . . finally found a reason to live?"

Nearby, the troll and naga began hissing and growling.

Mr. Grimfoyle gave Melinda a long stare. "But, my dear, I *do* have a soul now. Part of yours, and part of the boy's."

Travis groaned inwardly. This old man wasn't just out to help save the land from the faun. He had his own reasons, and he was playing two or three angles.

"Do you sense a loss?" Mr. Grimfoyle asked, looking from him to Melinda in turn. "Do you honestly notice a difference?"

"Why did you leave the faun with that underground brain?" Travis asked through gritted teeth. "What made you betray her?"

The man started walking, seemingly undeterred by the squabbling naga and troll, or indeed the cackling harpy on the roof. He made it ten paces, then turned back. "I have my reasons. It just so happens that your mission aligns with mine." As he turned away again, he added in a low voice, "For the most part, anyway."

Travis felt anger bubbling up. He took a step forward, planning to go after the lying, cheating, no-good, cowardly—

Melinda touched his arm. "We'll come back. One thing at a time. He may have a part of our souls, but it's keeping the mist from getting us. So let's go and deal with the faun and come back after."

## Chapter 25
### The Eye of the Storm

The old man's questions haunted him. *Do you sense a loss? Do you honestly notice a difference?*

The truth was, Travis didn't feel any different. He'd have thought losing part of his soul would leave him a little . . . empty? But maybe he was comparing it to a physical loss.

He mulled it over as he flew past the village of Follen's Glen and toward the center of the mist cloud in the distance— the eye of the storm. Melinda hung below, equally silent.

If the two of them failed to notice a difference after losing a third of their souls, would Mr. Grimfoyle feel any different with his gain? But then, he had gained more than they had lost; he now had two-thirds of a soul, whereas before he'd had none. That *had* to feel different. But so what? Would possessing a soul change him? Travis doubted it. Plenty of very mean-spirited people had far more complete souls than him.

So what was the point? "Do you think that old coot took part of us to help himself, or to help us all?" he asked, breaking the silence.

Melinda sighed from where she hung below. "I think both. He *did* save us from the mist . . . but he didn't do it out of the goodness of his heart. I just can't figure out what he hopes to gain from all this. Do you think he just wants to go about business as normal, with people instead of trolls and naga? Did he fall in love? Is there some other reason?"

"I was just starting to think he was all right, too," Travis said mournfully.

They finally spotted the center of the storm. It stood out plain and obvious—a distinctive circle where the haze was nonexistent compared to the surrounding area. That clear patch had to be the diameter of a small village like Follen's

Glen, and Travis blinked rapidly, amazed at the vivid clarity of the green, grassy banks around a flat, mirrorlike lake.

Dead center of the storm, a tiny island protruded from the water just as the old man had said. And a squat tower stuck up in the middle.

Seeing a number of flying creatures circling the tower, Travis veered away in a hurry and landed by the water's edge, ducking down behind a stand of trees. He wasn't sure if he'd been seen or not.

"Are they guards?" Melinda whispered, peering out from behind a tree trunk.

Travis felt the whispering was entirely unnecessary and spoke in his normal voice—or normal for a mothman, anyway. "Gotta be. I see a small griffin, a wyvern . . . and two harpies."

"Mom?" Melinda gasped, jerking upright. She started to move out from behind the tree, but Travis stopped her.

"Wait. Why two? We need to be sure one of them is actually her before you go running out."

They watched a little longer, and after a while, Melinda sighed. "Neither one of them is Mom. They're both male."

"That's probably a good thing. Male harpies are kinda stupid."

"I wonder if my mom's inside," Melinda said, her voice still hushed. "I mean, she has to be a prisoner, right? Otherwise she'd have dealt with the faun by now."

*Or the faun changed her.*

Travis gritted his teeth. "Yeah, she must be a prisoner. We have to get in there somehow. Any ideas?"

"Something that flies, something that swims. Whatever Mr. Grimfoyle's intentions were, I do think he had a plan for us to stop the faun and deal with the giant brain. I just wish he'd been a bit more helpful."

"So what do you think? I fly around and distract them all while you swim underwater?"

They chewed on the vague plan. It was all they had, and it was pretty lame. A mothman against two harpies, a griffin, and a wyvern? He wouldn't last two seconds. He knew for a fact a griffin could fly much higher. And the wyvern was probably faster.

However, he didn't need to face them in hand-to-hand, tooth-to-claw aerial combat. He just needed to distract them.

Somehow.

He sighed. "They won't fall for it. They're not all going to come after me and leave the tower unprotected. If anything, they'll be even more on their guard. I'll have to fly closer and ask to speak to her."

"Speak—" Melinda spun to face him. "Speak to the faun? Are you serious?"

"Do you have a better plan?"

"How about taunting them and flying off? Get them so angry they refuse to let you get away with it. I can swim underwater all the way to the island. All I need is a few minutes to climb out and get into the tower."

He shook his head. "And how do I shake them off? Also, you're assuming there's nothing in the water guarding the place. There might be a kraken lurking in the depths."

She fell silent.

"We both have a dangerous job," she said finally. "But we have to deal with this today. We got our shifting powers yesterday after school. We'll lose our powers sometime tomorrow afternoon."

That was a horrible thought. About forty-eight hours was the limit. Not only would their strong immune systems rid their bodies of the shapeshifting ability and render them *ordinary*, they wouldn't ever get to transform again because there were no scientists to perform the procedure. They *had* to put things right.

A thought occurred to him. "Melinda . . ."

"Hmm?"

"We just got back from the Haunted Fortress, right? That stasis bubble—"

She held up a hand. "I know what you're going to say. You're going to say everything must be okay in the future, that things must get straightened out somehow, otherwise certain events never would have happened at the Haunted Fortress in the first place. A time paradox or something."

"Right. Logically speaking—"

"I know, I know. But I can't think like that. I have to live in the here-and-now. If I start thinking, 'Oh, we already know everything will sort itself out,' then I'm afraid things *won't* get sorted out, because we'll be too busy kicking back and relaxing, waiting for things to sort themselves out—and then what happened at the Haunted Fortress won't happen exactly as it happened, and . . . Does that make sense?"

Travis sighed. "Sadly, yes."

"So . . ."

"So here we go, then."

Melinda gave him a hug. "Be careful."

"You too." He grinned and spread his wings. "First chance you get, do something to sabotage her magic."

*But with what?* he thought as he rose into the sky.

Everything seemed so hopeless. He and Melinda had finally made it to the faun's lair with nothing but a vague suggestion of destroying the brain—which was impossible. The thing was huge. They didn't even have a vial of raw potion to save their parents. They were woefully unprepared. Some shapeshifters they were! This mission was doomed to fail.

It was with a heavy heart that Travis flew toward the tower.

The small griffin had landed on the conical roof and was busy preening itself. The wyvern soared high in the sky. Right now, the harpies were his main concern.

"I just want to talk!" he yelled as the white-feathered creatures veered toward him with yellow eyes blazing.

"Stay away!" one of the harpies screeched. "We have orders to kill anyone who comes close!"

"Just you *dare!*" the other warned.

Travis kept moving. From what he'd heard, females were far worse, more vicious and vindictive.

Still, these males spat and screeched, swooping up and down and around in a frenzy as though trying to create a draft strong enough to stop him. To his surprise, what they were doing worked. Both harpies chewed on something, a fistful of green leaves that Melinda's mom had long ago named *harpy-nip*. Where had they found *that*? It had to grow locally. Or maybe other harpies lived in the area.

As the winged creatures began muttering in earnest, a gust of wind blew in out of nowhere and buffeted Travis from left to right.

He remembered then that males were really good at generating storms, especially when they chewed on those intoxicating leaves to expand their natural abilities. Maybe they'd been responsible for the faun's widespread blue mist . . . but he doubted it. That seemed a little beyond their range of skills even with an endless supply of *harpy-nip* to harness their powers.

The gust turned into a gale. Overhead, pale-grey clouds darkened and rolled, and then the going got really tough as the wind strengthened, pushing against his face.

Both the wyvern and griffin steered well clear of the sudden change in the weather. The localized outbreak turned into a twister, and Travis fought to push through as the harpies continued chewing and muttering while flying at a safe distance.

Travis felt he wasn't getting anywhere fast. He wasn't moving forward at all now, just fighting against the wind to stay airborne. On a whim, he stopped fighting and turned to follow the direction of the rotation. He picked up speed instantly, spiraling quickly outward as he became one with the twister. The speed of his circling quickly made him dizzy, but he kept count of his laps and watched for the tower on every pass.

As he rushed around for the sixth or seventh time, he launched free of the wind and straight toward the tower, shooting directly between the two harpies where they flapped together.

Surprised, they snapped their heads around as Travis hurtled by. He yelled with triumph, knowing he could make it to the tower before they could generate another twister.

Except that the griffin was on his tail. He glimpsed it out of the corner of his eye as it descended at a frightening speed, the giant eagle front section giving him a baleful glare as it extended its talons . . . with the lion's body and rear legs following behind.

Travis began to quake with fear. That thing, small and young as it was, could literally rip him to shreds in seconds. He'd heard a story about a hungry griffin snatching up a horse and taking it up into the sky, then rolling in the air, tearing with its beak, clawing with its talons . . . The horse was dead in no time, and the griffin had landed and feasted for hours.

And to his right, the wyvern roared and angled toward him as well, its beautiful yellow body gleaming, red wingtips vivid in the overcast sky, and long tail tipped with a deadly barb. The tower was *so* close—but not quite close enough.

Racing onward, Travis whipped his head from side to side, keeping an eye on the approaching enemies. The griffin reached him slightly ahead of the wyvern.

Travis snapped his wings up like a pair of sails and veered skyward at a sharp angle, and the griffin's outstretched claws grasped uselessly at thin air as it tried to correct its course. The monster's beak came within inches of Travis's toes, and the golden wings actually brushed his feet so hard that he tumbled head over heels before righting himself.

The wyvern, arriving a split-second later, tried to steer clear of the oncoming griffin but failed. They two crashed head-on with a terrible clacking sound—the griffin's beak—and an awful snap and tearing noise—one of the wyvern's wings.

As Travis spun back onto course, the griffin and wyvern screeched and squawked and roared as they tumbled toward the lake. They hit the water with a heavy splash.

He wasted no time gawking. The harpies were close behind again. Travis saw an open window in the very top of the tower and aimed for it, knowing he wouldn't completely fit but—

He crashed through the glass and frame, got snagged on something jutting out, and jerked to a halt with his feet dangling over a gantry that ran around the inside of the tower.

Pulling himself loose from the broken window frame, he dropped onto the gantry and scuttled clear, afraid the harpies would smash through on top of him. But they didn't. He glimpsed them splitting off in opposite directions and shooting past.

Relieved, Travis collapsed and started mewling like a kitten at the pain in one arm, one wing, and an ankle. He had a cut on his fur-covered cheek, too.

He shifted to human form, hoping that would be enough to heal the injuries. It wasn't. Crying out again, he shifted back and forth a few more times, finally settling back into mothman form when the pain had subsided.

Only then did he take stock of his surroundings.

Aware that the harpies screeched like crazy on the roof, he peered down into the depths of the tower. A single metal ladder stretched all the way down one side of the rounded structure. Other than that, the place was pretty much empty—except of course for what grew in the center, reaching almost as high as the gantry itself.

No wonder the harpies didn't want to come in.

## Chapter 26
### Inside the Tower

Melinda slipped into the lake the very moment the harpies started screeching at Travis. The griffin was busy preening, and the wyvern was soaring high in the sky. She took a chance without stopping to think too hard about it.

The moment she was underwater, she transformed and instantly felt at home. Smiling with glee, she swam at breakneck speed, staying deep in case one of the monsters spotted her from above. She had no doubt a griffin could plunge into the water and snatch her up like a fish.

She would have reached the tiny island in one minute flat if it weren't for the hulking shape ahead. She groaned. At least one monster patrolled the murky depths just as she and Travis had feared.

Something else shot toward her. She hesitated, then relaxed a little at the sight of a mermaid—no, a mer*man*. But as he approached, she frowned. This was neither a merman nor even a triton; this was something else. His ears were pointed, and his eyes were utterly black. Strangest of all, the upper part of his body—torso, arms, shoulders, and face—was scaly, whereas merfolk were very much human.

And this eerie creature *glowed*.

He was bare-chested and handsome, with a square jaw and high forehead. His hair was long and black, flowing in the water rather like oil from a punctured drum, as mesmerizing as his dark, expressionless yet soulful eyes.

*A jengu*, she thought, feeling like she was dreaming.

She tried to remember what she knew of these creatures. Their collective name was *miengu*, more commonly known as lake spirits even though they were just as real as merfolk. That ghostly glow, the eerie aura . . . Anyone spotting one of these creatures would naturally assume it was a phantom.

Melinda shook herself out of her bedazzled stupor. The miengu were known for exactly this—mesmerizing their victims with their beauty and sucking the life out of them.

Gills opened on the jengu's slender neck. Then he spoke— but not before Melinda clamped her hands over her ears and shot away. She felt his voice would be too melodic and hypnotic for her to cope with.

Startled, she realized the jengu had caught up and was swimming alongside. He spoke softly, and she accidentally overheard a few words before humming noisily to herself and blocking it out. His words would be pure poetry otherwise, designed to melt her heart. She would swoon and fall under his spell, and he would imprison her somewhere, and then he would spend the next few days coming up with ways to shock and scare her . . . and feeding off her emotional state. They were a special kind of vampire.

She made a point never to visit the Lake of Spirits. What a horrible place that must be!

Melinda ground her teeth and looked straight ahead, focused on the next hurdle—a giant sea serpent.

It was huge, its head easily the size of a cow, with plate-sized unblinking eyes. The long body floated easily just below the surface, arcing around the tiny island that stuck up from the bedrock. There was no way she was getting past *that*. It seemed to be waiting for her, its mouth gaping open, almost as though it expected her to swim straight in.

When she slowed, the jengu did, too. His hair fanned outward, and he stared at her with those awful yet strangely alluring black eyes . . .

"Go away!" she yelled.

At that moment, something plunged into the water not too far off—*two* somethings that apparently had fallen from the sky. *Travis*, she thought with a jolt of fear. But it wasn't him at all. It looked like the griffin and the wyvern had taken a plunge.

*What in the world . . . ?* Melinda couldn't imagine a puny mothman clobbering these ferocious beasts, especially midair. Something else had happened.

But in that moment, everything changed. With the jengu distracted, and the serpent twisting around to investigate the newcomers, Melinda saw a chance and took it. She tore off as fast as her tail could take her, aiming to shoot past just behind the serpent's head . . .

It must have caught her movement out of the corner of its eye because it suddenly jerked and twisted back toward her. She swam under its massive scaly coils just as the giant jaws rushed closer. Momentarily getting tangled in its own body, the serpent thrashed with anger amid a churning froth of bubbles, then lunged again—but Melinda zigzagged away.

She made it to the rocky bank, glanced back once, and saw the monster barreling down on her with mouth wide and fangs gleaming. She picked up speed, angled upward, and launched straight out of the water, diving onto the slick rocks above.

After rolling a couple of times and scrambling for safety, she cowered under a massive deluge of lakewater as the serpent attempted to follow her out. It slammed down mere feet away, the underside of its jaw smacking the hard rock. She waited until the monster had slid back into the lake before reverting to human form. Once her legs had morphed into shape, she got up and dashed the last few yards to the tower's base.

Running around the curved wall, she hip-hopped over random shards of glass that lay on the smooth rock and came across a door.

Screeches came from above—two harpies on the roof.

Melinda grasped the doorknob and twisted it. To her surprise, it opened with ease. She pushed her way in and slammed it shut again.

It was as she stood against the inside of the door, gasping for breath, trying to take everything in at once that she realized she was not alone. A huge, white tree trunk, thick tentacles everywhere, hundreds of thinner tendrils snaking all over the walls—and a low, ominous growl from the shadows on the other side of the room. A pair of red-glowing eyes blinked at her.

Panting, Melinda sought an escape. A ladder led up the wall to a gantry at the top—and she saw movement up there, a grey-furred, dark-feathered mothman leaning over the railings.

The smooth, white trunk stretched nearly to the top of the tower, stopping short of the gantry. The tendrils reminded her of creeping ivy. The entire place was smothered with them. The ladder was blocked in several places. Even if she tried to climb it, she'd only get a third of the way up.

The tree, or plant, or whatever it was, had sprouted out of the tower's floor, through the rock itself. The island was no more than a raised welt on the earth's surface, from which grew a colossal white—*something*. Water surrounded the trunk like a castle's moat, just two or three feet across. The tower was a later addition.

*The giant brain under the ground*, she thought with awe. *This is one of its feelers.*

Though she'd never actually visited any of these hideous tentacle plants, Travis's dad had studied them for years. And Travis had actually visited the brain below.

The growling creature had been lurking in the shadows under a mass of tangled white vines on the opposite side. It emerged slowly, unsteady on its feet as though waking from a deep slumber.

"Travis!" she shouted to the mothman high above.

"Where have you been?" Travis called in a somewhat sleepy voice. "Did you have any trouble?"

"Not really." She blinked, noticing the hound was halfway around already. It was a hulking giant of a dog, black and shaggy, and its eyes shone red even when daylight fell on it from above. She frowned at the sight of its goat-like hooves. An appropriate pet for a faun.

"Careful!" Travis shouted, sounding a little more animated now. "I've been studying that thing for about twenty minutes now."

*You haven't been here twenty minutes,* Melinda thought, staring uneasily at the approaching hound. It crept one step at a time, each hoof clicking on the rock.

"It's a cadejo. It's black, so it's a bad one. The white ones are good."

"*Cah-day-ho?*" Melinda muttered. She raised her voice. "Is there a white one here as well? If so, now would be a good time for it to stand up."

She heard a slight rattle from above. Glancing up, she saw that Travis had leapt off the gantry and was descending at speed, dodging the smooth, white tentacles as he came. He landed behind the cadejo.

"Hey!" he called.

The black dog swung around, and its growling intensified. It had seemed lethargic before, almost lazy in its stalking. Now it awakened.

"There's something in the corner," Travis called to her. "I'm not sure, but it looks like a cauldron. Can you see it?"

Melinda searched where he was pointing. So many tendrils spread out across that side of the tower that it reminded her of an impenetrable patch of woods, a mass of vines and shoots arcing in all different directions. If there was something buried under all that, she couldn't see it from here.

She didn't need to argue the point, though. She hurried away from the cadejo, circling the plant until she reached the tangled mess. Ducking under the nearest white vines, she threaded her way through, squeezing past some thicker tentacles and grimacing at the feel of them under her hands—warm and somehow tingling with energy.

Deep within the mass, in the center of a shadowed area but bathed in a shaft of light, she found a cauldron just as

Travis had mentioned. A large opening just above explained how he'd seen it from his higher vantage point.

Tucked away in the shadows, she saw a makeshift bed, piles of clothes, bottles of all sizes, a wooden box filled with empty glass vials, a few pots, cups, and other things to suggest someone had been camping out here and *experimenting*.

"Melinda?" Travis called, sounding nervous. "I'm flapping about, trying to distract this thing from coming after you, but I think it's losing interest in me."

She hurried to the cauldron. Peering through gaps in the white vines, she could see the shaggy black dog growling up at Travis, who was indeed flapping about just out of reach.

"What am I supposed to . . . ?" she started to say, then paused as her lazy, slow-moving brain caught up. A cauldron. A cauldron full of thick, blue-colored liquid.

Could this be *potion*? *The* potion? But how could there be any left?

She knew this stuff worked both ways. Turned into a mist, it had the power to transmogrify. But its liquid state reversed the effects. If the cadejo was one of the faun's transmogrified victims, then it could easily be put back to normal.

*And then so can my mom if she's here, and Travis's parents. And everybody else!*

Shaking with excitement, she grabbed a cup from the faun's belongings and scooped up some of the foul-smelling stuff. *Just a couple of drops*, she thought.

Racing out from under the vines, she headed straight for the shaggy black dog and flung the potion directly in its face, spattering its muzzle and eyes. The creature blinked, rearing back in obvious surprise. Melinda stood there and prayed it would revert to human form in an instant.

It didn't.

With a scream, she backpedalled as the cadejo let out a roar and sprang.

But instead of being slammed by the creature, Travis swooped down and yanked her upward by the scruff of the neck, lifting her off the rock floor and shooting into the air as the cadejo hurtled past below. She felt the fabric around her neck tearing, or perhaps stretching, or just adapting to the strong force being exerted. Either way, she was terrified her smart clothes were about to let her down—literally.

Travis ascended with frightening speed, all the way up past the white trunk and splayed tentacles, as high as the windows at the very top, over the railings of the gantry, and down onto the somewhat rickety metal flooring.

She gasped and hugged the metal supports, then pulled Travis closer and hugged him, too. "Thank you, thank you! I thought for sure I was going to die then."

"I had your back," he said, folding his wings as he knelt there by her side. "I stood up here looking down at that cauldron thinking I should give that a try—you know, nip down, fling some potion in the cadejo's face, and fly back up here . . . but I lost track of time, and I just ended up . . . *standing* here."

He looked so crestfallen that Melinda had to laugh. Her laugh turned to a shuddering cry of relief, and she hugged him again. "You saved my life twice in the last . . ." She frowned. "Ten, twenty minutes? Thirty? Why does it seem like we've been here for so long? Oh . . ."

She already had her answer, but Travis replied anyway. "Brain plant," he said, pointing downward. "Sucks the juice out of your brain. It makes you think you've been here longer than you have. That's why the Prison of Despair was such a terrible place. Prisoners stayed a month and thought they'd been there for *years*. They were changed by the time they were released, very sorry for what they'd done, ready to take their lives back, convinced their kids had grown up, their friends moved away."

"But these things were destroyed!" She poked him in the chest. "You made sure of that, right? You and your dad?"

"Well, it's a big job," he admitted. "There's quite a few of these plants around, and they're tough. Each one needs a hole drilled into it, then something like liquid dragonfire poured inside. Then they wilt and die. My dad knows where they all are—except this one." He glanced down into the depths of the tower. "Well hidden, isn't it?"

Melinda gripped the bars and peered down with him. The height terrified her despite having hung a million miles above the ground on numerous trips with Travis. "Why would the faun make a potion but not use it?"

"Well, I assumed that was a second or third batch."

"I don't think so. All those ingredients Mr. Grimfoyle fetched . . . It's not like you can split all those things in half or into thirds. So if everything was thrown into the cauldron and mixed up into a potion—why's it still there, full to the top? It doesn't make sense."

Travis had no answer to that. He changed the subject. "Twice?"

"Huh?"

"You said I saved your life twice? I saved you from the cadejo, but what else?"

"Oh, well . . . I was about to be chomped by a giant serpent when a griffin and a wyvern fell into the lake. It was all the distraction I needed."

Travis smiled. "Glad I could help."

They stared down together in silence for what seemed like ages. The shaggy black dog stalked about, going around in circles, looking up at them once in a while.

"So where's my mom?" Melinda muttered.

"Probably below," Travis said.

"I was afraid you'd say that."

Another silence fell.

Finally, Melinda said, "So the potion's no good, then. That's why it's not been used. It's a dud."

"Mmm," Travis murmured. "Maybe it takes a while to work."

So they waited a bit longer.

And waited.

"It's been half an hour," Melinda complained. "Right?"

"Uh, not sure," Travis said. "It's hard to tell—"

And at that moment, the cadejo abruptly reverted to human—a naked man hunched on the floor in the shadows far below.

"Well, then," Melinda said. "I guess it works after all."

## Chapter 27
### Breathless

Travis felt a little like Jack and the Beanstalk as he carefully carried Melinda down past the sprawling white tentacles. She hung below, limp and quiet.

By the time they'd touched down on the rocky floor next to the thick trunk, the naked man had scurried out of sight under the mass of vines. *Good thing, too*, Travis thought.

"Are you decent yet?" he called to the man.

After a bit of shuffling, the man emerged with clothes on. He was short and sturdy, bald except for a strip of hair behind the ears and around the back of the head. He hadn't shaved in a week. "What happened?" he muttered, his gaze darting from side to side. "Why am I here?"

"We were hoping you could tell us," Melinda said. "This is Travis, and I'm Melinda. And you are . . . ?"

"Conrad." The man blinked, looking surprised. "Yeah, I'm Conrad." He looked Travis up and down, running his gaze over the dark-colored wings. He studied Travis's facial features with an air of disdain. "You're a *mothman*. I've never seen a mothman up close before."

"I'm a shapeshifter," Travis said. He promptly reverted to human form.

The man took a hurried step back. "Whoa!"

"So, Conrad," Melinda broke in, "what happened here?"

As though the shock of seeing Travis shift had knocked a few memories loose, he gently tapped the side of his head and stared wide-eyed at the floor. "It's . . . wait, it's coming back. The mist—"

He paused again. Travis and Melinda waited while a myriad of expressions passed across his face. In the end, he scowled and looked around in disgust.

"I've been here *forever*. I'm the caretaker, and . . ." He shook his head, his scowl deepening as he ran a hand over his bald head. "That faun. She muttered something under her breath, and this blue mist came at me . . ."

"And you turned," Travis said. "Into a cadejo."

The man glared at him.

Melinda sidled closer. "Do you know where the faun is now? Did you ever see a harpy? Not the two males outside, but another one? A female?"

Conrad squinted at her. "My memory is spotty, but . . . I remember the faun and the old man arguing . . . and he left, and . . . the faun was mad, *real* mad. And then, maybe days later, a female harpy walked in. Just walked in and surprised the faun. They fought right here on the floor, and the faun kept yelling at me to help, and . . . I couldn't."

Travis thought about the way the shaggy black dog had stalked him and Melinda. It hadn't exactly been a frenzied attack. "Because you knew it was wrong?" he said.

Conrad shook his head. "Naw. I was just too lazy. Couldn't be bothered."

"That'll be the effect of the plant, then," Travis said.

Melinda sighed. "Okay, but where's my mom now? The harpy, I mean. Where's the harpy right now?"

Conrad turned and pointed.

Following his gaze, Travis suffered a sinking feeling in his gut. Just as he'd feared, the man was gesturing toward the base of the white trunk—the water-filled moat.

"Down *there*?" Melinda said, clasping her face.

"That's where they went," Conrad said with a shrug.

Melinda stepped toward him and gripped his arm. "Wait, what? My mom *and* the faun fell in?"

The man explained himself. Apparently, the two had fought, rolled across the rock floor, and finally tumbled into the water. Well, the faun had tumbled in. She'd maintained a grip on the harpy's arm and yanked her in, too. They'd vanished without a trace.

"Sorry," the man said, patting Melinda's hand. "I guess they both drowned."

"No!" Melinda shouted.

Travis reached for her. "Relax. She's not dead. Neither of them are. Trapped, maybe, but not dead." Actually, he had no proof of that. All he knew was that the narrow channel of water around the plant wasn't exactly as it seemed. "I guess we need to go down there," he said with a heavy heart. "This is why we're here, right?"

Melinda immediately crouched by the water, then sat and dipped her legs in. She transformed, her legs melding together and becoming a fishtail. The rest of the changes were almost too subtle to notice, but when she looked around at Travis, he couldn't help gasping. In his head, he knew mermaids had an enchantment spell . . . but still, in this form, she was even more beautiful than he remembered.

Conrad let out a grunt of surprise, too, but for a different reason. "Hey, what? So you're one, too?"

"A shapeshifter, yes," Melinda said. She looked at Travis. "Maybe you can start bottling that potion up? We have to take it back with us when we leave here."

He broke out of his trance. "I'm not letting you go down there alone!" he exclaimed. "Are you nuts? I'm the one who should go. I know what to expect."

The look of relief on her face was plain to see. Still, she frowned. "Travis, this is *water*. I can do this, but you can't. I don't know how deep this goes. It could be as deep as the lake."

He couldn't figure that out either. He couldn't imagine lakewater filling the shaft as far down as the giant brain under the ground. And there was a massive cavern down there, so the water would have to fill that, too. The entire lake should have drained away long ago.

But he also remembered the strange phenomenon he'd experienced on the way down last time. He chewed on that for a moment, gazing at Melinda as she swirled her hand in the water.

"I think it'll be okay," he said. "I don't think the water will go too deep."

"Well, I could check—" she started.

"No," he said hurriedly. "Don't do that. Let's go together."

Conrad backed away, shaking his head and muttering, "You kids are crazy. You're really going down there? What if that plant thing sways and crushes you against the rock? What if it's deeper than you think?"

Travis turned to him. "Do you think you could do what Melinda said and find a way to bottle up that potion?"

"There's a wooden box with empty vials in it," Melinda said helpfully.

The man shrugged. "Well, yeah, I suppose I—"

"We need *every drop*," she added.

"Sure."

He said it a little too flippantly for Travis's liking. "Where are you from?"

Conrad paused, looking off to one side as though memories were flooding back. His face lit up. "Follen's Glen."

"I thought so. Well, there's nobody left there now."

The man's smile faded. "Wh-what do you mean?"

"The faun got them all—same way she got you, only with a huge mist storm. All of Carter is gone, too. Everybody is a goblin, or an elf, or a gnome . . . or some random animal. That potion is the only thing that can put everyone back."

Conrad stared at Travis for a long time. Then he sucked in a breath and puffed his chest out. "Gotcha. I won't spill a drop."

Travis nodded. He went to sit by the water's edge next to Melinda and dangled his feet in.

"Travis," she said softly, "I'm just not sure you should do this. You could drown. We don't know how deep—"

"It'll be fine," he assured her.

He slid off the rocky edge and went in up to his neck. He immediately felt an undercurrent and grabbed for the rock, his heart thumping hard. "It's pulling me down. I think this is a one-way trip."

"But then how will we—?"

"It's a one-way trip for *most* people. But you're a mermaid. I think you can pull us back to the surface."

She slid into the water up to her neck. Unlike him, she didn't reach for the rocky sides. He imagined her fishtail was flapping about quite easily just below. "Okay, stay with me," she said, offering her hand. "Hang on tight. Close your eyes if you have to, but don't let go."

"I won't."

She nodded, then slowly went under. A second later, her hand tugged on his. He had no choice but to allow her to drag him under, so he took a huge breath and went limp. There was no point trying to help by kicking and splashing; she could do all the work for him if he let her.

The feeling of being pulled under by a surprisingly strong grip sent waves of panic through his chest. He had to summon every ounce of nerve to refrain from yanking free and shooting back to the surface. He reminded himself he'd been flying her around for the past day, letting her dangle in midair high above the ground, and she hadn't complained once. She'd trusted him completely. Now it was his turn to trust her.

Except, unlike her, *he* had to hold his breath the whole time.

Keeping his eyes open was difficult. The water stung, causing him to blink a lot. He could see the smooth, white trunk inches from his face. Behind him, dull-grey rock. It was like falling down a well shaft, and since it was occupied by a giant beanstalk growing up the center, he had very little clearance and bumped against both surfaces as he descended.

It didn't help that he tried in vain to stay upright as Melinda pulled on his hand from below. It was easier once he gave in and flipped over into a dive, head first. After that, her fishtail swished back and forth near his face, and he sometimes felt the translucent fins bat his ear. She maintained her tight hold on his hand the whole time.

His chest was growing tight. Anxiety began to gnaw at him. He needed to take a breath.

Melinda moved pretty fast, descending into darkness, and he could no longer see much even with his eyes wide open—so all he had to think about was the lack of air. He tried to take his mind off it and relax.

The trunk had a soft glow to it. He touched it now and again and felt its vibrant energy. He reached out to the other side and felt nothing. The narrow shaft had opened up into something much bigger.

Then real panic began to set in. He was nearly out of air. He tried to ignore it for a second or two, thinking they *had* to be close by now—but Melinda kept descending, dragging him down and down, and he knew he wasn't going to make it.

He started convulsing, and he couldn't help flailing and yanking his hand free. He kicked for the surface, his heart thudding like crazy, his chest flip-flopping, knowing he was never going to make it.

Melinda grabbed his feet. He thrashed and kicked, and she let go. But then she was right there in front of him, her hands on his shoulders, pushing *down* on them, like she was *trying* to drown him!

She did something really weird then. She leaned toward him, and he instinctively pulled back, but she grabbed the back of his head and pressed her face closer, mushing her lips to his. Before he could even think about how to react, he felt air flowing into his mouth.

Shocked, he held still and let it happen. Air filled his mouth just as his chest felt like it might explode. He had no choice but to take a breath—and when he did, it was an *actual breath*, one that re-filled his lungs. He took two more breaths, and a third, before she pulled away and stared at him, her expression clearly saying, *Are you okay? Did that work?*

He wanted that moment to last forever—that face of beauty, her smooth skin and clear eyes, her dark-brown hair fanning outward . . . He'd never believed in angels before, but right now she was exactly that.

He nodded and gave a thumbs-up.

She smiled. Her cheeks looked a little flushed. He imagined his own were burning a fiery red.

Melinda grabbed his hand again, and they continued their descent.

A dozen thoughts whirled around Travis's head, and not one of them involved an evil faun. Melinda had saved his life. But more than that, she'd *kissed* him.

He shook his head. No, she'd simply saved his life. That was all. Nothing else. No kissing, none of that stuff. She was just being practical. It made sense for a mermaid to share her air.

*I'm alive. She gave me the kiss of life.*

Life at home would be different after all this was over. How would he and Melinda get along now? Would there be a strange awkwardness between them now that she'd kissed him?

He shook his head again. No, because she hadn't kissed him. She'd simply done what was necessary and saved his life.

*Yeah, so get over yourself. Nothing has changed. She's still just Melinda, my cousin, and—*

That gave him pause for thought. She wasn't his cousin, and never could be after this. He vowed to abolish the lifelong family tradition of referring to her parents as uncle and aunt. He'd pretty much grown out of that anyway. And Melinda most definitely was not his cousin.

Somehow, that helped calm his frazzled mind.

*She's not my cousin. She's . . . a friend. A very good friend.*

Melinda suddenly jerked on his hand. Something had changed around them, and it took him a moment to figure it out. Opening his eyes was easier now, the water thinner, no longer pressing against him but instead spattering his face and body from all directions. His clothes felt heavier, more sodden than before. It was like wading out of a rockpool alongside the spray of a waterfall.

Except he was still floating. *Falling.*

He heard an echoing voice as Melinda exclaimed and cried out.

"Travis!" she gasped.

## Chapter 28
## Depths of Despair

Still gripping her hand, they fell together—or rather tumbled slowly through a void. Water droplets floated with them all around. If the two of them had been swimming in a pool high above the ground and the bottom had dropped out, this was what it would be like in slow motion—spinning aimlessly along with tons of water.

It soon became apparent the water was no longer falling. Travis and Melinda descended past the last of it, amazed and awestruck as they watched the last droplets receding into the darkness above their heads. He'd done this slow underground fall before, just not through water. This was way freakier.

"It's okay," he said out loud, suddenly realizing he could breathe again. The shaft felt cold and empty. His voice echoed all around.

They still descended alongside the white trunk, though now it was twice as thick. The rock wall of the shaft that had surrounded it was . . . gone. They saw nothing but blackness. Still, he could see Melinda just fine, and it seemed she could see him.

He was struck again by her beauty. Was she glowing? Could she really be so enchantingly pretty that—

*Oh, wait. It's the trunk that's glowing.*

The ghostly aura wasn't much of a glow, but enough to illuminate the two of them in the darkness. He held out his hands, shuddering at how creepy-pale they appeared.

"What now?" she said, trembling.

He noticed her hair was already drying, as was her smart dress. His own clothes were drying too, but his hair was dripping wet.

"We just keep on floating down," he assured her. "It'll take a while, but we're safe." He looked up, then down. "Mr. Grimfoyle saw all of this just by touching the plant. That's how he knew we should be something that swims, and something with wings. It wasn't just about getting to the tower. It was about *this*. This place below. When we leave here, I can be a mothman and fly us back up to the water, and then you can get us the rest of the way out."

Melinda nodded slowly. "Okay. That might explain why Mom never made it out. She could fly up as far as the water, but not *through* the water. In fact, I'm surprised she and the faun didn't drown on the way *down* . . ."

Her eyes widened. Travis knew what she was thinking. What if her mom and the faun *had* drowned? They might have been already dead by the time they reached the bottom of this awful, despairing place.

Neither of them said a word for a while. Their descent slowed further, at least judging by the huge white trunk standing nearby. Keeping his eyes fixed on it, Travis could see bumps and nodules and scars that seemed to rise at a slow walking speed, indicating he and Melinda were still falling.

But then everything brightened. A ghostly glow from below suggested they were close to landing on the giant brain.

Travis gave Melinda a quick recap. "So it's a massive creature of some kind. I think it started out fairly small and just grew underground—but it's not just some ordinary organism. It's got some serious powers. It carved out a hole for itself down here and kept on growing. It seems really deep down, like it's at the core of the planet, but it's not. It's near the surface, just under the Earth's crust."

It made him feel good to throw in some technical words.

"But not deeper than the mantle," Melinda murmured, peering down.

"Uh . . . right. Well, this creature might stretch halfway around the world for all we know. Or it could just be like a cancerous blob. There could be lots of them. Lots of *brains*, as we call them. Anyway, this one put feelers up, so they poked out of the ground and spread out like tentacles. *Treentacles*," he added with a smirk. "That's what my dad called them."

"And your dad had them all destroyed."

"Is *still* destroying them," Travis corrected her. "Yeah, because after years of thinking they were harmless, I came down here and realized they were dangerous."

The surface of the brain came into view. It was rather like an expanse of smooth, white rock with mounds and dips, glowing softly. The trunk spread even wider at the base. It looked more than ever like a gigantic hair as viewed through a microscope in Miss Simone's lab.

"You'd better lose the fishtail," Travis warned.

Melinda gasped. "I forgot about that!"

She reverted to human form, then flexed her legs and wiggled her toes, ready for touchdown.

"It's no different than landing on the moon," Travis said.

"Like either of us know what *that's* like."

Their feet came down on the softly glowing floor at the exact same time. The weird, somewhat spongy surface yielded over a ten-foot diameter, and silent streaks of light flickered and flashed in an outward zigzagging pattern from where they stood. Travis and Melinda froze as the smooth surface rose to its original level. All around, an ominous rumble echoed about the place as though a giant had just been awakened.

"I don't like this," Melinda whispered.

"Yeah, it's freaky," Travis agreed. "But—"

Before he could say another word, someone cried out from behind him—from behind the massive trunk. He swung around.

Sure that his eyes were deceiving him, he edged closer, vaguely aware of Melinda passing him by then breaking into a run.

"Mom!" she screamed.

Lauren stood almost out of sight around one side of the white Treentacle, her back flat against the smooth surface, harpy wings spread wide. She was apparently glued to the trunk judging by the way she wriggled furiously without budging an inch. But she wasn't standing on the floor; she was suspended a few feet up.

"Mom!" Melinda yelled again, rushing to her. She grabbed her mom's hands and pulled. The only reason her hands were free was because her wings were spread out behind her like a feathered cape, plastered to the wall, utterly immobile.

Travis stared in horror. Thin white tendrils protruded from the trunk and were wrapped loosely around her neck and legs. Even now, another couple snaked around her waist as if realizing its prey was trying to struggle loose.

"Honey, don't get too close!" Lauren croaked, sounding weak and pitiful. "Don't let it get you, too."

"Where's the faun?" Travis asked. "Did *she* do this?"

Lauren's eyes darted to her right. "Not exactly. She's right around there."

Travis dashed around the trunk and stopped, astonished. There she was, the infamous faun herself, just as incapacitated as Lauren, stuck to the Treentacle a few feet off the ground, turned at a slight angle, her arms and goat-legs akimbo.

She looked in worse shape than Lauren. Through half-closed eyes, she stared for a while at Travis as he stood gawking at her.

So much fuss for such a dainty creature. Her skin was coppery brown, and she wore a threadbare furskin tunic that left her scrawny arms bare. Her grey-furred legs were like that of a goat. Wherever her arms, legs, or body touched the white Treentacle, it looked like the surface of the monstrous trunk had melted all over her, then hardened like cooling wax. She was stuck fast.

She had streaks of gold paint on her shoulders, down her arms, on her face, and around the two horns that jutted from her forehead. At first glance she looked bald, but in fact her hair was slicked back, heavily coated in the thick paint and plastered to the back of the head. Sweat had made the paint run. The faun was a mess.

While Melinda struggled to free her mom with lots of futile yanking, Travis approached the faun and studied the tendrils that shifted and crawled over her body. They sensed his presence and tightened, and she moaned as the ones around her upper arms strained to keep her in place. One slid around her neck, too, and Travis paused.

"Get me out of here," the faun whispered.

It hardly seemed the time or place to decide whether or not she deserved to be there. And he knew it would be wrong to just leave her behind.

He reached for the tendril around her neck. He slid his fingers all the way around it, disgusted by the warmth it generated. But, like a snake, at least it was dry rather than slippery and slimy.

When he gently pulled on it, the thing tightened a little more. Others emerged from the trunk as well, sniffing at the air before curling around her limbs.

Travis withdrew his hand.

Melinda seemed to have come to the same conclusion. "What are we going to do?" she cried.

Lauren spoke softly, reassuring her that everything was going to be fine.

"I don't understand," Travis said to the faun after a silence fell. "Why are *you* stuck here? Wasn't this part of your big plan?"

The faun grimaced. "Do you think me capable of such grand spellcasting?"

"So it was the brain, just as Mr. Grimfoyle said?"

The faun hissed with anger at the sound of his name.

"It was her idea, though," Melinda muttered.

Lauren gave a nod and peered at her and Travis with subdued yellow eyes. Her harpy nature seemed exhausted. And if she reverted to human, she'd still be stuck to the trunk, only her arms would be pinned as well.

"This is River's fault. It was her idea. But this . . . this *thing* around us turned her idea into a reality."

As she said that, the floor beneath their feet flickered and pulsed with light.

"It's listening," Lauren said softly. "It's always listening. And sometimes it shares. It shared some of River's memories with me, and mine with her. Here, take my hands, both of you. Let me show you what she showed me. Then you'll know everything that happened."

They did so and waited, looking up into the harpy's white-furred face.

Lauren closed her eyes.

At first, her memories flitted through their minds. Travis couldn't help recoiling at the barrage of images and noises, and he saw Melinda jerk as well. He found himself looking down from overhead as a pegasus and a phoenix landed in the blue mist and stood there—and then exploded into dust. He saw his own dad roaring in anger and swooping past. After a bit of flickering, he saw *himself*—a mothman appearing out of nowhere. Travis remembered that clearly, as well as the ogre beating up his father. He grimaced as that whole scene played out again.

Moments later, seeing everything from Lauren's viewpoint, he flew off across the land, heading for the center of the storm to battle the faun.

She thought of Robbie, Melinda, and Mason when the tower came into sight. She thought of everyone in Carter, everyone in Follen's Glen and all the other settlements, and the farmers who lived out on their own. Feeling an immense burden of responsibility and determined to set things right, she hurtled toward the tower, aware of two other harpies springing off the roof with savage screeches.

They tried to attack her, but she made it to the door at the base of the tower before they did. "How dare you!" one screeched in a cracked, ugly voice as it swooped down toward her.

Lauren pushed the door open, turned, and slammed the door shut just as the first harpy thudded down. She locked it and spun around to face whatever came next.

Panting and sweating, she spent the next moment or two craning her neck to look up at the immense white trunk, its sprawling tentacle branches, and the hundreds of sinister tendrils. What on earth was *this* thing doing here? Did Hal know about this one?

Then she saw the faun.

"You should not have come here," River snarled, ducking out from under a tangle of tentacles that formed a canopy around the backside of the trunk. "You should have accepted your new role in life. You should have let yourself *evolve*."

Lauren screeched and flew at her . . .

* * *

Gasping, Travis pulled himself out of the vision by letting go of Lauren's hand. He backed away. Melinda was still connected, a dazed look on her face.

Lauren still had her hand outstretched toward him, inviting him to join her again, to continue sharing her memories. But Travis found himself wanting to see the story from the faun's point of view. How had she found this place? What made her so hateful toward humans?

"Travis," Lauren murmured, shaking her head as he sidled away from her and toward River. "Stay with me here."

"I have to see this," he whispered.

Coming face to face with the faun, he looked into her dull-yellow eyes and flinched at the fearsome glare she directed at him. He reached for one of her hands, and she snarled and said, "Stay out of my head."

He clasped her hand.

A barrage of new memories flooded his mind . . .

## Chapter 29
## A Faun Named River

River finished daubing herself with gold paint and washed her hands off. She always felt calmer once the paint was applied. "Peace," she whispered. "Love and compassion."

She radiated positive energy. The wildlife would not bother her now. She had, on countless occasions, stood quite still as fearsome beasts sniffed at her and wandered past. A cerberus had left her be. An angry troll had sprung out of nowhere, looked her up and down, then grunted with exasperation and moved on. It seemed even manticores knew she was a force of good and should be left well alone.

Painting herself every morning always brought to mind her family. Maybe that was the true reason she did it. It had been a family ritual, something her father taught them all long ago.

Now they were dead.

Every time she woke with dawn streaming through the trees, anger washed over her at the thought of what *humans* had done. The paint calmed her, gave her peace . . . and ugly thoughts of vengeance transformed into a desire to *help*. Humans weren't to blame. The problem was simply that they couldn't help themselves.

River stared into the pool of cloudy water, seeing the gold paint gleaming off her face and jutting horns. She smoothed her hair back, but it wasn't quite dry, so she had to wash her hands off again.

"Today is the day," she whispered.

She inspected what was left of her blue-colored potion. It wasn't much, all she had left from her time with Madame Frost, but it would do. And she wouldn't need any more if she truly mastered her new spell.

River balanced the potion on a log and removed the top. The smell was as pungent as always. She practiced conjuring, drawing tiny droplets of liquid out of the bottle so they hung glistening in the air. Holding her hands palm up near the floating droplets, she gave it her all, willing the droplets to break apart and turn to mist.

She'd tried this same spell countless times over the past few months, gradually depleting her valuable stash of potion. But she was there now. She had the spell tamed. Madame Frost would be proud.

The blue droplets dissolved into a fine mist and spread outward.

River took a deep breath. That was the easy part. The difficulty was conjuring the same mist with no liquid source to draw from.

She turned away, allowing the mist to drift wherever it wanted. Then she worked on the far more difficult spell— replicating what she'd just done. She had a feel for the stuff now, could sense every tiny molecule of its existence. That had come through endless practice and repetition. Keeping the exact recipe straight in her head had been an impossible challenge at first, but it was second nature now, and her skill with the replication spell was strengthening every day.

She produced a fresh puff of mist alongside the slowly dissipating haze. Comparing the old with the new, she was convinced she had it just right. *Almost* convinced, anyway.

River spent the day practicing, traipsing about in the woods, loitering near the outskirts of the nearby human village and second guessing herself. She couldn't just walk in and start transmogrifying people. They'd pounce on her immediately, and her vengeance—no, her desire to help—would be over. The morning passed, then the afternoon, and her frustration grew.

*Tomorrow then*, she thought as night fell. *My nerve will not fail me tomorrow.*

As it happened, a couple of travelers walked through the woods on their way to Carter. A man and a woman. River watched them with mounting excitement. Test subjects!

She conjured her mist and leapt out at them. The blue, smoky substance engulfed the man, and he halted with surprise. "What—?" he started.

And then the transmogrification began. He dissolved into dust, flew apart, and his clothes scattered. The woman screamed, and River went after her, but she was surprisingly fast. It didn't matter, though. The experiment had *worked*.

At least partially. It would be a little while before the molecules were ready to coalesce.

\* \* \*

Witches had been messing with transmogrification spells for hundreds of years. But the potion hadn't been created for that purpose.

It had started out as a cure-all remedy, restoring the physical body to its former state, cleansing it of illness and injury, even focusing an addled mind. Witches found themselves in demand as people sought to buy bottles of the stuff at often exorbitant prices. Centaurs, elves, and the naga inquired also, but the potion didn't work for their kind; it was full of human ingredients, after all.

Years passed, and the potion was honed to perfection.

The story went that a rather careless practicing witch accidentally evaporated a few drops of the stuff one day. The blue mist swirled around her home. Caught in the middle of it, she disintegrated—and returned to life that afternoon in the form of a cat. Terrified, she leapt into the cauldron of potion and, soon after, was restored to her human form.

This of course sparked a new generation of magic—the beginning of a much darker time in witch history, where the threat of transmogrification defined witchcraft for generations to come. One simple error had reversed the potion's magic and undone years of public image-building.

River had gone beyond what her mentor, Madame Frost, had taught her, learning to replicate the mist *without* the potion being present. Choosing what the victim came back as was a neat but fairly simple trick. But she'd also added an amnesia spell to erase all memory of life as a human.

Buoyed by her success, River tracked the dissolved man through the woods and reintegrated him in the form of something harmless—a dryad. As such, he wouldn't go scampering about drawing unnecessary attention. He would simply hide.

Naturally, humans came to investigate the next morning. And not just humans but *shapeshifters*. That gave her pause. Her spell worked on humans, but what about hybrids? She hid out in her cave, but one showed up there, poking his nose in . . . River waited for him in the darkness, then conjured the mist and blew it up the tunnels toward him.

He fled like the coward he was.

It seemed the local humans were out in force already. "There's no turning back now," she muttered.

The morning and afternoon became a game of chase, though it was unclear who was chasing who. It seemed the shapeshifters *were* invulnerable while in their alternate forms . . . but River eventually caught one of them unawares, in human form, and the girl exploded into a satisfying cloud of dust.

Jubilant, River knew she was onto something. Her spell *worked*. But she needed a way to spread the mist across the land on a larger scale. Conjuring small amounts directly into faces just wasn't practical . . .

\* \* \*

Travis gasped and broke loose, his vision clearing. The faun stared at him from inches away, a sneer creasing her face.

He'd seen his *dad*. In the cave, so young and nervous, sneaking in to find the faun. She'd thought him a coward for fleeing her blue mist, but he'd had no choice.

*That's the second time I've seen him so young*, Travis thought in amazement. *He looked exactly the same in the boulder opal's projection.*

The other shapeshifters had been there, too. He'd seen them all, including his mom, in the forest pursuing River—an *actual memory* of how it had been twenty years ago. As for one of the shifters exploding into dust . . .

Travis shuddered. The faun's blue mist had been a new and unknown threat at the time. It must have been awful for the others to see that happen.

"Let's skip forward a bit," he told River, glaring at her.

She scowled. "Do you think I can control which memories you are snatching from my head? You are a fool."

"Shut up," Travis growled. He closed his eyes. "Let's go forward to the last time you saw my parents—when you disappeared. What happened after that?"

And with that thought in his head, he grabbed her hand again . . .

\* \* \*

"We made a deal," River growled.

"Only because I had no choice!" the annoying shapeshifter girl named Abigail snapped. "I'll save my friends, and I'll save Miss Simone, and I'll save Derek and the other people you turned. Then, and *only* then, can you have the potion back. Or, since you don't need it, I'll promise to pour it out."

River gave up and turned away, trembling with anger and pain. "If my ankle wasn't broken . . ." she grumbled. Hopping around to the other side of the thick tree, she glanced back and said, "Do not disturb me while I rest. I will be gone for some time."

The last thing she heard from the girl was, "How long will this take?"

River ignored her. Her ankle hurt, and she felt defeated. She vowed to steer clear of shapeshifters from now on—or better still, adapt her mist and make it powerful enough to work on them, too.

Still, the plan had always been to develop something on a much larger scale. The past couple of days had been an experiment gone slightly awry. She ducked into the opening in her tree and plunged into darkness, feeling safer with every step she took. Already she'd distanced herself from the outside world. Even if that girl followed her in, she would be days behind.

River rested on some old blankets and gingerly made a splint for her ankle. Tying it with vine, she winced and cried out, then fell back and wiped the sweat from her face. She imagined her gold paint was running, and with it her compassion for humans.

*I'm sorry, Father.*

She thought of his stern but kind face, her mother and two brothers, and tried to block out the way they'd died—murdered by humans for no apparent reason other than sport. "To the tree!" River's father had yelled to his family. They'd gathered there together, joined hands, and filed into the tree as the hunters arrived. River had been first inside, and she'd heard the thud of spears, the gasps of pain—and felt the jerk of her brother's hand as he fell. He'd snatched his hand back, and in that moment, River had lost them forever.

Despite rushing straight back out into the daylight, several days had already passed by outside, and her family was rotting on the ground. Grief-stricken, she'd crawled back into the tree to weep.

Popping her head out again several hours later, she saw that bones littered the place, picked clean by vultures.

Another week passed. The lack of water forced her into the open. There were still bones, but a sandstorm had blown through and scoured them clean. That awful image seared into her mind. Her family—gone forever, their essence swirling away into the vicious, stinging dust . . .

And now here she was again, forced to retreat into her tree, this time with a broken ankle. She lay there for a long time before emerging. To her disgust, a fence had been erected around the tree, probably to pinpoint her location in the plains. But it was already old and falling apart; the humans had likely forgotten her by now. She headed off to find a clear spring and something to eat.

When she returned, loaded down with supplies, she entered the tree and settled in to practice her spellcasting, to figure out a way to expand a small amount of mist to cover a vast area. But despite her aspirations, she couldn't see how it could be done. Her spells became more and more muddled until, with a sigh of exasperation, she decided to go back to basics.

*I need more potion.*

Though her ankle still hurt, she daubed herself with paint, emerged from the tree, and stood under the leafy branches as rain hammered the plains. She couldn't remember the last time it had rained here. Amazed, she felt a sense of hope. Maybe this was her time.

The fence had gone. The bones had gone. The place looked different, more vibrant than it had in a long time. She saw great swaths of grass and surprisingly mature trees that hadn't been there before.

Avoiding the village to the south and the shapeshifters who lived there, she traveled northeast instead, heading out of the plains and across lush meadows. She made good time despite having to limp, but had to pause upon arrival at a small village. This one was new. The sign read Follen's Glen.

Seeing a goblin on the dirt track leading into the settlement, River decided to give the place a visit. She grimaced at the sight of humans bustling about the place, but they were a necessary evil for the time being. It galled her that she required humans to create the potion she needed, but there was a satisfying irony to the situation as well.

The villagers gave her suspicious looks. The goblin must have been passing through or delivering something; it seemed the village was solely for humans, and they didn't take kindly to a faun snooping about.

She loitered out of sight for a while, then spotted a white-haired old man who seemed as out of place as herself. The villagers gave him mildly suspicious looks but welcomed him as a passing traveler. Marketers in particular smiled and offered their wares, and he appeared interested but held up a hand as if to say, "I'll think about it."

River watched him and smiled when he deftly pickpocketed a lady in a small crowd. He just might serve a purpose.

When he passed by the alley she hid in, she called out and waved him closer. She had a tiny wooden box containing nothing but the snipped, thorny stem of a withered rose, its flower shriveled into a brown husk—one of a few curses she'd brought on her journey. Promising glittering jewelry, she lured the man deeper into the alley and gave him the box. He took it greedily and wrenched it open—then scowled.

"What's this?" he demanded. Before she could answer, he plucked it out of the box to get a closer look. "This is nothing but a—yowch!"

He stared at his thumb. River did, too. Curiously, very little blood welled up. Still, he collapsed seconds later, falling into a deep slumber.

She'd always considered herself strong, but it seemed this man was lighter than he had any right to be. When she swung him over her shoulder and escaped the village through backyards, she couldn't help thinking the man was somehow empty inside. It made her journey easier, though. She'd expected to make it to the outskirts of the village at best, but she found herself able to continue onward across the fields— and all despite a delicate ankle.

Sometime later, she came across a tower standing on an island over a lake. Staring in delight, she vowed immediately to make it her new home no matter what spells she needed to wield to get rid of its occupants.

A small boat half buried among reeds, a leisurely row across calm water, and a simple spell to unlock the door. A quick check inside revealed the place was empty, at least for the moment.

She dumped her deadweight on the stone floor and stared in amazement at the giant, smooth-white plant that grew to full height inside the tower like a tree with its limbs severely restricted. And those limbs weren't like any tree she knew of. They were more like tentacles, curling around and pressed against the walls. On the far side of the trunk, a tangle of vines formed a shelter that drew her nearer. She ducked under and smiled. This was perfect. A new place of tranquility. Her new home.

And she had a supply of water. The trunk grew straight out of the stone floor, but there was a gap all around it—a gap filled with lakewater. It was like a moat encircling a castle, the water lapping gently against the banks and spilling over to form small puddles on the floor. Lakewater might not be the freshest water, but it was better than nothing. She could always use her purifying spell.

"I have work for you," she said to the old man as he began to wake. "What is your name?"

The old man called himself Mr. Grimfoyle, and he was naturally quite put out at being abducted, and even more irritated about the jewelry she'd promised. River cut through his bluster in an instant.

"If it is pointless baubles you desire, I can promise you an endless supply."

Mr. Grimfoyle's mouth flapped open and shut a few times. "You can?"

She rose up on her powerful legs, ignoring the tightness in her ankle. "When you finish helping me, you will be able to walk about that village and lift every trinket you can find—with no repercussions. You will walk about the place gathering your riches, and nobody will stop you."

"How is that so, young lady?" the old man demanded.

"I will show you. First, a few conjuring tricks to prove I am capable. Then you will begin fetching ingredients."

"Ingredients? Ingredients for what?"

* * *

Travis wrenched free and staggered backward. "I've heard this part," he gasped.

The faun glowered at him. "Then stop invading my mind and leave me be."

"I can't. I need to know."

He glanced toward Melinda. She was still firmly connected to her mom, now holding both her hands and staring glassy-eyed into space while Lauren looked distinctly groggy and sleepy. Wherever they both were, it was pretty deep.

Travis wiped the sweat from his forehead. "I want the rest," he said.

"Then ask me."

He shook his head. "I want the truth, not a bunch of lies."

He advanced on her again, and she struggled feebly. He touched the back of her hand, then clasped it tightly.

The visions flashed across his mind once more . . .

## Chapter 30
## The Storm is Unleashed

River watched Mr. Grimfoyle as he sat cross-legged on the floor staring at the white trunk, barely blinking, shoulders slumped. How long had he been that way? How long had *she* been that way?

He jerked and clambered to his feet. "Wh-what—"

His voice startled her. It felt like the two of them had been in a stupor for days, though she knew that wasn't so. Ever since she'd arrived in this tower, time had seemed to crawl by at a snail's pace. Or maybe it sped past. She couldn't be sure. Something was definitely off, though.

When Mr. Grimfoyle eventually focused on her, he frowned and glared. "Were you thinking about a storm?"

"A *storm?*"

"Yes, a storm. You were thinking of spreading chaos across this land with a storm."

She had to force herself awake, stretching and yawning, her back aching from where she'd been leaning against a thick, drooping tentacle. "I thought of how a sandstorm took away the remains of my family and left their bones gleaming in the sun. Then I thought about expanding my magic in such a way that it swept across the landscape and swallowed everything in its path, wiping humanity from the Earth." She shrugged. "But these were just thoughts. Why?"

"Have you been down there?" the man demanded.

"Down *where?*"

"There." He jabbed his finger toward the stream of water surrounding the base of the trunk. "No, of course not. You'd never survive the journey to the bottom—and certainly couldn't get back up again. It goes deep. There's something down there."

He spoke in a rather manic voice, and the hairs on her neck stood up. "What did you see, Mr. Grimfoyle?"

But he clammed up, shaking his head and pacing the tower room for a while. Eventually, he returned to the shelter and stood peering into the cauldron. It was bubbling strongly, the fire underneath burning hot, and the rounded iron surface dangerous to touch. "Is it done?" he barked.

"It is done," she murmured.

"Then my work is complete?" Mr. Grimfoyle sounded eager. "And you will uphold your end of the bargain?"

"Of course."

River inspected the bubbling liquid in the cauldron. Yes, it had finished brewing. The fire could be extinguished, and the potion left to cool. Then she could begin.

Yet a major part of her plan still eluded her. She'd put it to the back of her mind, hoping something would clarify, that the answer to the problem would present itself:

How could she spread the blue mist across the land?

While Mr. Grimfoyle had been out gathering ingredients, she'd been alone in the tower pondering this enigma, dreaming of endless clouds of mist raging across the planet like an unstoppable sandstorm. The old man really had tapped into her thoughts. Or rather the strange plant had, and shared it with him.

The answer was just *there*; she could feel it. But she couldn't reach out and grab it. And now the old man had completed his task and wanted payment.

"I feel I am close to an answer," she said.

"Close? To an answer? Answer for what?" Mr. Grimfoyle's face darkened, his scowl deepening. "Tell me you're going to deliver on our bargain. I've gone and fetched the most vile ingredients for your potion over the past few weeks, and I'm sick of it. Now it's done—and you had better deliver what you promised."

River felt anger stirring. "Or what, old man? You are nothing but a human. A strange one, I will admit, but still a human. When I am ready, this potion will mark the end of your kind. All humans across the land will be eradicated, replaced by something better. *Evolved*, Mr. Grimfoyle."

The old man recoiled in shock. "You plan to eradicate all those people at Follen's Glen?"

"I mean *everywhere*."

"You said nothing about *eradicating*. You simply said you would cast a spell, and I would have unrestricted access to all their valuables, that people wouldn't stand in my way as I searched their houses and pilfered things."

"Trust me, they won't. Nobody will."

He stared at her with his mouth open. "And me? This spell—"

"The spell goes after souls. Do you have a soul, Mr. Grimfoyle?"

"No."

"Then you are safe. Those with no soul will be ignored."

"No soul . . ." he murmured.

"My magic requires full souls. I will not evolve a human life otherwise. So you are safe to live out your sad existence."

"Pah!" Mr. Grimfoyle scoffed, apparently recovering from his shock. "Nothing wrong with being soulless."

"I disagree. Have you ever seen sylph victims? Nothing but empty shells. They will still be wandering aimlessly long after my work is done."

"*I'm* an empty shell, but have you ever seen *me* wandering aimlessly?" Mr. Grimfoyle snapped. "A witch stole my soul, but I function just fine."

"Your soul withered and died over time," she corrected him, feeling a pang of sorrow for the man. "A piece here, a piece there. I suspect it took a day or two for you to notice a distinct lack of empathy. Am I correct? You had time to adjust—unlike sylph victims, who suffer a great and sudden shock."

He sighed and rested his hands on the side of the cauldron—then snatched them away as his skin started to blister on the hot surface. He made no complaint, just watched as his skin began to heal.

River curled her lip in disgust. "This is no way for anyone to live. Try a few drops of the potion in your eyes once it has cooled—"

He hurriedly backed away. "I will not!"

"You were cursed by a witch to live a long and soulless life. I cannot recover a lost soul, but I can give your cold, dead body a chance to heal, perhaps to nurture a new soul over many years. *That* is what this potion does in liquid form—it restores a physical body to its natural self. Now, in *mist* form, it does the opposite and—"

"My natural self?" the man gasped, his eyes bulging. "Do you have *any idea* how old I am? My natural state is . . . is . . ." He gestured wildly, clearly flustered.

"Ah, I see," River said. "You are older than you appear. In that case, there is no hope for your physical body." She paused, thinking. "Perhaps if you acquired a new soul first, gave it time to settle in, and then allowed my mist to evolve your body . . . Yes, that might work. I have a spell that will extract a soul."

"So do I," he growled. "In my long life, I've purloined a number of witch's tomes with that in mind. If I'd wanted a soul, I'd have stolen one by now—or a piece of one. But the truth is, *I just don't care.*"

River sighed. "As you wish. Perhaps it is for the best—so you feel no regret when this is over."

He turned and started pacing the small shelter. "But . . . are you saying I'll be alone in the world?"

She shrugged. "Not alone. In *better company.*"

He grew angry again. "My life is meaningless enough as it is! Do you think I want to be the only human in existence? No, this is madness!"

He halted and frowned. It seemed like an idea had just popped into his head. His gaze flitted across to the enormous white trunk, and he stared from it to the cauldron, then back to her, his eyes narrowed.

She realized the old man was no longer her puppet. The look on his face suggested she'd lost whatever blind trust and obedience she'd commanded before.

"Go to the village," she said firmly. "Wait there. When this potion cools, I will perform my magic, and the blue mist will arrive, from which you will be safe. After that, feel free to steal all the valuables you can carry."

Mr. Grimfoyle ducked out from under the shelter. "But at what cost?"

"It is no concern of yours," River said, following.

"It most certainly is." He kept moving toward the door, keeping his eyes on her the whole time. "Those without a soul are safe, you say?" he muttered.

"Perfectly."

"Even if they just have a piece missing—they're still safe?"

She nodded. "A substantial piece. Why do you ask, Mr. Grimfoyle?"

He said nothing more on the subject. But he paused by the door. "Had I known the full extent of the madness you planned . . ."

"What? Baubles and trinkets are of no interest to you now, old man?"

He snarled and slammed the door.

She stared after him for some time, feeling she should have killed him. That wasn't in her nature. All life was precious, even that of a lifeless old man with no soul.

Besides, what could he do to stop her?

\* \* \*

She settled into a funk that lasted longer than she cared to consider. When she reached out to see if the cauldron was yet cool enough to touch, she found it stone cold. She was dehydrated and weak with hunger.

A stranger stood over her, a puzzled look on his face.

*You're a fool, Mr. Grimfoyle,* she thought. *You didn't hide the boat.*

On the other hand, he'd probably left it in full view on purpose.

"You have no business here," the stranger grumbled. He was mostly bald, just an ugly strip of hair around the back of his head. "This ain't no place to squat. Go back to your forest, faun. This place ain't safe." He tapped the side of his head. "This tree messes with your brain."

She slowly picked herself up off the floor, startled at how groggy and stiff she felt, like she hadn't moved a muscle in weeks.

"Whatever this is," the man said, leaning over the cauldron, "you can't be cooking here. You don't live here. You can't make soup or broth or whatever this is and sell it at the local market, if that's what your game is. No, this won't do at all."

He gripped the rim of the cauldron with both hands and put his weight behind it—to no avail. The thing didn't budge one inch.

Still, River's anger stirred. She shook the funk from her mind and stepped closer. "What is your name?"

"Conrad, miss. I'm the caretaker here."

"So the boat is yours. You do not live here, but you frequent the place. You are perhaps the only person who ever visits."

"This place is special and needs watching," he said. "But it turns out it's dangerous, too. I heard these plants have been spewing out scorpions and trying to take over the land! So they're being systematically destroyed by order of the Council of Carter—only they don't know about this one."

"Because of the tower," she murmured, distracted. *Keep talking while I work up a spell.*

He gave a nod. "An Old Earther discovered this plant twenty years ago. He was a scrag, as they were called then. He'd spent time in the Prison of Despair, and when he got out, he found he wanted a plant of his own. He never did tell me why. Anyway, he built this tower to hide it. But he ain't been here in a decade or more. I come by every month." He frowned. "What are you doing? Look, you'd best clear out and let the experts in to set fire to this thing. So, get your things and—"

She didn't let him finish. She'd already begun her spell, and with all the practice she'd had, the blue mist spewed from her hands within seconds, its essence drawn directly from the cauldron.

"What—?" the man called Conrad said right before he froze and exploded into dust.

River waited awhile, then brought him back as something fierce, a *cadejo*, to guard against further visitors. And it occurred to her that visitors might be a very real problem if what Conrad had said was true—that the white-tentacled plant had been deemed a public menace and condemned for destruction.

She vowed to protect it. To protect the plant, the tower, the island, the lake, and especially her cauldron of potion.

The very next people who came to visit were investigators who'd heard rumors of the plant within the tower—six of them, rowing across in a boat of their own. She cursed these humans and their boats and vowed to sink them all.

When they arrived, she turned them to dust. Two she sent into the water—a sea serpent and a jengu—with instructions to destroy both boats and not let anyone else cross the water. The other four she sent into the sky—a griffin, a wyvern, and two harpies.

Then, with a fearsome black-haired hound patrolling the inside of the tower, she settled into her den to contemplate the potion.

River spent a long time staring at it. She drew from it, formed mist, and tried to expand that plume of mist twofold. It was difficult but possible, though she knew in the back of her mind this pitiful effort was far from what she needed. She tried again and again, her experiments diminishing the liquid potion by a few ounces. Keeping a close eye on the level, it became apparent that even if she were successful at multiplying the blue mist and expanding it to a hundred times its size, the potion would be used up long before her work was done.

Frustrated, she stalked the tower for a while, yelling at the hound and then throwing the door open to yell at the harpies, griffin, and wyvern as well. When she slammed the door shut behind her and threw herself into her dark corner by the cauldron, it took a while to calm herself down.

As River sat there breathing hard, she noticed some of the thinner white tendrils moving like snakes, creeping around the low ceiling of her organic shelter. The thick trunk glowed a little, too. She crawled over to it, reaching across the surrounding pool of water to touch the hard surface.

*It's alive.*

Not just a living organism like a plant, but *sentient*. It was listening to her, hearing her thoughts, understanding her desire to evolve every last human on the planet . . .

She wasn't sure how long she stayed that way, leaning over the water with her arm outstretched, her palm flat on the smooth, white trunk. All her anger evaporated. This thing, whatever it was, could help. Enormous power dwelled within, deep down inside—more power than she ever could have dreamed of. If the tentacled creature were a wizard, it could grant her wish to evolve humans with the merest suggestion of a nod and a simple gesture. But it was far more powerful even than that.

With a gasp, she realized her wish had already been granted. She flinched as a wave of energy blasted from the trunk. The pool of water bubbled, tentacles twisted and coiled above her head, the caudron rose off the floor a few inches then thudded down, splashing drops of potion all around, and the black-haired hound let out a howl. Outside, the harpies screeched, and the wyvern and griffin roared in unison.

Then all went quiet.

Shaking herself from what seemed like a thousand-year slumber, River stumbled outside. What she saw filled her with astonishment—and delight.

A wall of blue mist surrounded the tower. It loomed above, too thick to see through and so tall it looked like she were peering up from the bottom of a massive well. But the shaft rapidly widened, the circular wall expanding outward across the lake.

Seconds later, the banks of the lake came into view, then the trees beyond. The mist set off on its journey across the land—an expanding storm she knew would roll over every village for miles around.

*Just like in my dreams. Humans slaughtered my family, and a sandstorm scoured the remaining flesh from their bones. Now my mist will disintegrate humanity.*

She had to admit the image appealed to her: people turning to dust and swirling away, leaving nothing behind—not even bones.

River stood and watched until the towering misty walls receded into the distance, leaving a blue haze in its wake. Was it thick enough to protect her from retaliation? She thought so. The tower stood dead center of everything. Even if humans figured out the source of the mist and came after her, nobody would make it safely across land.

She looked upward, struck by a sudden concern. What if shapeshifters came looking? The haze was thin here. If they got ahold of the potion . . .

Rushing back inside, she knelt across the pool and touched the trunk. "Can you see what is happening? Is anyone coming for me?"

No response.

Sitting with the trunk and allowing her mind to merge with its immense intelligence, she again felt overwhelmed. The creature was vast and ancient. She was a mere gnat—but one that had caught its attention. Her plot to evolve the human race had captured its interest, and now it wanted to assist.

However, its idea of *assisting* was completely taking over and making her unreachable goal a reality . . .

"I know you can hear me," she whispered. Her hands moved across the white surface, and it flickered with faint light under her palms. "Show me what you see."

Still nothing.

She grew angry. "This was my idea!" Biting her tongue, she forced herself to show a little more respect. "You are far more powerful than I will ever be. I just wish to know the progress of the storm. How far reaching is it? Will it neutralize shapeshifters as well?"

After a long silence, the light beneath her palms intensified. She closed her eyes and watched, listened, *felt*, and her heart thumped with excitement. She saw the storm spreading across the land. She saw people exploding into dust and coming back in random forms—not frogs and bugs but ogres, goblins, elves, trolls, and more—exactly as she'd hoped for. She saw everything!

Her mood soured. She also saw shapeshifters rallying to defend humankind . . . and Mr. Grimfoyle *helping* them . . . and people rushing into the mines to seal themselves in . . .

And she heard talk of transmogrification potion in the lab bought from a witch in the south. Or, in its present state, *healing* potion.

"No!" she screamed. "Nobody will escape this!"

The moment she thought about it, the powerful super-intelligence beneath the lake heard her and acted. Astonished, River saw her own wishes being carried out—a confused chimera guided like a puppet toward the science building she had once been held captive in. A series of fireballs blasted the walls. Something inside exploded. Part of the building collapsed.

Done.

Elated, River could barely contain her excitement. She commanded a godlike power. Vengeance was hers. Humankind would end today. And nothing would stop her.

"Open the mines," she whispered, guiding the chimera again. She saw through its eyes as it blasted a hole in the roof fall—just enough for her mist to creep in. In minutes, every last human inside those tunnels would evolve into something else. Something *better*.

She reveled in her newfound power. Her father would be proud. She had avenged their senseless deaths while honoring life. Not a single human would die in this process. They would simply be reborn. It was more than they deserved.

A noise distracted her. She jerked back, frowning. The black-haired hound was growling at someone or something that had burst into the tower. River went to investigate and found, to her astonishment, a harpy standing with her back against the shut door, breathing hard.

"How dare you—" River started before realizing this was *not* one of her airborne guards.

The harpy flew at her. As the two of them rolled across the floor, River caught a glimpse of the hound—the man named Conrad—just standing there watching. Utterly useless! The unlocked door was River's own fault, but had *nobody* tried to stop this harpy from entering the building?

"What are you *doing* here?" River shrieked as the two of them fought.

"I'm here to end this," the harpy panted. "It didn't work last time, and it won't work this time. You're finished, River."

"What—?" Then realization dawned. "You! The harpy shapeshifter!"

"That's me. And I'll break your arms the moment you conjure any of that mist."

The faun and the harpy rolled and fought, scratching and punching and biting—and then they plunged into the narrow moat around the enormous tentacled creature.

Sucked under, River clutched the harpy close. She must *not* get away, even if it meant the two of them sinking into the depths.

To her surprise, tendrils encircled her arms and pulled her downward at a breathtaking speed. Once more, her thoughts had been made a reality. Before she knew it, she was floating in midair, in total darkness, still clutching the harpy, both of them sucking in lungfuls of air as they descended to the deepest, darkest corners of the earth . . .

But River felt a contentment she hadn't experienced in a very long time.

*Humans are no more.*

## Chapter 31
### Escape

"We have to get out of here," Melinda said, tugging on the tendrils around her mom's neck. She hated how they felt, all warm and *alive*, like thin but utterly mindless snakes. Glancing around, she was surprised to see that Travis was no longer by her side. Instead, he was gripping the *faun's* hand. "Travis! Wake up!"

Her shout jolted him awake. He jerked backward from the faun.

Melinda gazed in despair at her mom. She looked so tired and weak, her normally pure-white feathers stained and mussed up. "Mom, have you tried shifting? Maybe if you shift, you'll come unstuck."

Her mom sighed. "I was afraid to. My wings are the only thing keeping my arms free. Otherwise my arms would stick, too."

Melinda leaned closer, her face almost touching the nasty white trunk as she studied the gluelike substance holding her mom in place. The tendrils only did so much. On their own, a person could probably wriggle free. But this glue stuff . . .

She tentatively pulled on a wing. It barely shifted. It really was like wax—as though a giant candle had melted over her mom's wings and the backs of her legs and cooled off seconds later.

"Okay," Melinda said quietly. "Hold on, Mom."

She walked around the trunk to where Travis was busy making sense of the faun's predicament. Same problem—stuck fast. "Hey," she whispered to him, pulling on his arm. "Let's talk."

He looked puzzled as she led him a few paces away. "What?"

Melinda took a deep breath. "Why is my mom still my mom?"

"Huh?" Seconds later, a look of understanding passed across Travis's face. "Well, she flew straight down into the eye of the storm where there was no mist."

Melinda shook her head. "I mean the faun could have conjured mist from her hands at any time. That's how she does it, right? So why hasn't she?"

Travis narrowed his eyes. "She never got a chance? And now she's got other things to worry about? Or—"

"Or the faun *needs* my mom. How else will they fly out of here if they ever get free?"

"Good point. Escaping requires something that flies."

"And then something that swims." She edged closer and lowered her voice. "The thing is, the faun could still conjure mist. Now that we're all here, we could work together to escape. If the faun uses her mist on my mom . . ."

She trailed off, hating her idea. There had to be another way.

But Travis had caught on. "The faun turns her into something else, and when we get to the surface, we use the potion to turn her back. It won't work, though. The faun will still be trapped. There's no way she'd agree to it."

"She'll have to trust us. You tell the faun, and I'll tell my mom."

Melinda stomped back to the trunk, aware that light flickered with every step she took exactly the way she imagined synapses fired in a brain. She spent half a minute whispering in her mom's ear, and as she did so, the harpy's yellow eyes snapped open.

Now fully alert, her mom gave a curt nod. "I had the same idea when we first arrived, but River wouldn't do it."

The faun exclaimed. "No! I will not!"

"You have to," Travis said, stepping back. "Otherwise you'll be here forever. We all escape together, or we stay down here."

"I'd rather die than give you the chance to live as *humans*."

"Fine," Travis snapped. "Die here, then."

Melinda gave a shrug. "It's okay. We can go and get help. It's probably more important to get all that lovely potion bottled up first. A drop in the eyes? There's enough there to fix *thousands* of people. We should get on that, Travis. We'll come back for Mom later."

Though she choked on her own words, they had the desired effect. The faun's attention pricked up, and she narrowed her eyes as though scheming. "All right," she said at last.

*She can't wait for the chance to tip that cauldron over*, Melinda thought.

The faun could barely angle her hands outward, but it didn't matter. Blue mist seeped out of them anyway, rising as two separate clouds and coming together as one in front of her face. She stared at the growing haze and, with a gentle flick of her head, sent it sideways.

Melinda stared in fascination. The faun was directing the mist *with her mind*. The power she wielded was scary—even without the brain's help.

She took her mom's hand. "It's going to be okay."

Her mom wriggled her hand loose. "Stand well back."

Melinda joined Travis some distance away, watching with mounting fear as the blue, wispy cloud engulfed the harpy. Seconds later, with a last yellow-eyed glance toward Melinda, she exploded into fine dust and floated into the air while her silky smart clothes fluttered to the floor.

Fighting back tears, Melinda waited for the mist to clear. It took a while, and finally the faun looked at her.

"Well, now she is free. What would you like her to come back as?"

"It doesn't matter," Melinda snapped.

"Uh, well, actually it does," Travis said quietly to her. "Nothing too big to carry, but something strong enough to get the faun free."

Melinda was distracted by the tendrils wriggling about where her mom had been moments ago. The melted wax had formed a human-shaped scar, and the tendrils protruded from all around, reaching for the missing person and finding nothing.

The tendrils tightened around the faun instead, and more sprung from the trunk.

"It's annoyed," Travis muttered. "Let's speed this up, faun."

River shook her head and closed her eyes. "It is too early. The soul has to find itself. It is a confused mass at the moment, a swarm of bees without a queen. Give it time."

"How much time?" Melinda demanded, fearing some kind of trickery.

"Whatever it takes," River snapped.

They all lapsed into silence. Melinda picked up her mom's clothes and stuffed each piece in a pocket. The various layers of light, silk material squished down very small, but even so, her pockets bulged by the time she was done. She just had room to slide a smartshoe in each.

Then she paced back and forth, watching the light radiate outward underfoot. The heavier her tread, the brighter the zigzagging flashes were.

Melinda couldn't wait to leave. The place gave her the creeps. The softly glowing light from the white, uneven, somewhat spongy floor illuminated a sizeable area all around, but there were no walls that she could see. The floor just faded into the shadows. And she saw nothing above but endless darkness. The cavern could be thirty feet high . . . or three miles! She had no way of knowing. The hideous trunk towered over them, but even its glow faded out higher up and revealed nothing.

She couldn't shake the idea that some kind of intelligence surrounded them. The *dullahan* had chased Travis out of this place the last time he'd been here. Though only he'd been able to see it, that phantom creature had been summoned by the giant brain itself.

Travis kept looking over his shoulder, squinting this way and that. He looked worried.

A whisper lifted out of the darkness.

Melinda pricked up her ears and exchanged a glance with Travis. The faun lifted her head, listening.

The whisper came again, closer and louder this time. If it was the sound of someone speaking, the words were indistinct. "Mom?" Melinda murmured. "Is that you?"

She felt a draft, utterly silent but strong enough to push at her hair and ruffle her sleeves. The whisper came again, and she thought she heard the words "time to go" . . . but she might have imagined it.

"I think she's ready," Melinda said, hurrying across to the faun.

River was already mumbling to herself, her eyes closed.

"Wait, what are you bringing her back as?" Travis said, marching over.

But it was too late to discuss the matter. The faun's chanting rose, and then she snapped her eyes open. At the same time, Melinda felt a static charge in the air, and she turned to see a dark cloud swirling nearby, thin and wide at first but closing in and thickening. It narrowed to a column and stopped rotating, the mass *almost* reintegrating in human form—but then it morphed, shrinking to about chest height and crouching.

Melinda gasped as her mom solidified into something humanoid but thin, with a fiery red skin—but this state lasted no more than a second before she burst into flame.

"Mom!" Melinda screamed.

The creature—her mom—stood up and raised her arms. The flames engulfed her from head to toe, yet she didn't seem to care. As Melinda and Travis watched, the flames died down a little, and her lower legs came into view, the same fiery red as before. From the knees up, bright flames seemed to crawl around her body, and they crackled noisily from her shoulders and head.

The faun called to her. "Burn these tentacles. Burn the trunk. It is not as strong as on the surface. Free me!"

"What *is* she?" Melinda whispered.

Travis, the walking encyclopedia when it came to outlandish creatures, frowned for a long time before answering. "She's an ifrit."

"An . . . *ifrit?*"

The word seemed so small and harmless, yet the creature was a walking inferno.

"Yeah. A sort of demon."

Melinda wasn't sure what to make of that. A demon implied the existence of all kinds of other supernatural things she wasn't quite ready to accept. Then again, this underground place was home to what Travis's dad had called the Lady of Light, some kind of mystical being who channeled dead souls into a pit. And then there was the dullahan and the Grim Reaper. And in the town of Garlen's Well, Melinda had dealt with numerous ghostly phantom creatures called sylphs, who took souls in an effort to gain substance. Oh, and there was Mr. Grimfoyle, a walking dead man.

She gave a shrug. "Okay. So my mom's a demon."

Her mom leapt about as though gravity had no meaning. Melinda had tried a few jumps herself, finding she could reach higher and longer than anywhere above ground. But she couldn't leap about like an ifrit.

Perched above the faun's head and somehow clinging to the smooth trunk, the ifrit pulled back a flaming fist and drove it forward. She punched a hole through the outer skin and plunged deeper, then rummaged around and yanked her hand out grasping what looked like cords and tendrils. Or perhaps arteries. They stretched as she pulled, blackening and bubbling and smoking the longer she held on.

Light flickered and flashed up and down the trunk, and dozens of thin tendrils began twisting and thrashing.

The ifrit blazed brighter, her flames shooting high as she ripped the hole wider. Then she plunged inside, headfirst. Watching with morbid fascination, Melinda could see the glow of the flames through the trunk's thick shell. And when the ifrit clambered all the way inside, it seemed she let rip with her inferno, burning so hot that the trunk began sweating and rippling.

The faun started sliding. The smooth, white surface had become slick, and she simply peeled away from it. Tendrils jerked and flopped, making a half-hearted attempt to grab at her, but River calmly ducked out from under them and tipped forward.

She staggered and righted herself. A slimy white substance dripped off her back as she joined Travis and Melinda and turned to watch the ifrit at work.

"A fire-demon with anger in her heart," River murmured. "She will not emerge until that monster melts away. I chose well."

*So why do you sound so disappointed?*

More than a little scared, Melinda felt they didn't have time to wait. The trunk remained as solid and massive as a great redwood tree, but it would surely collapse under its own weight if a section melted away at its base.

"Mom!" she shouted. "It's time to go!"

Under their feet, the giant brain seemed to be waking. Light strobed and zigzagged in all directions, and the spongy surface pulsed slowly, undulating like an ocean. The pitch-black darkness all around lit up constantly as though lightning flickered nearby, and a rumble started up from deep below.

The ifrit leapt from the hole in the trunk, ablaze and triumphant. She landed on the brain and caused another flashing barrage of synapses. With flames leaping high, Melinda's mom hopped and skipped toward them. It was impossible to read her expression.

"Does she remember who we are?" Melinda gasped, gripping the faun's arm. "Or did you wipe her memory?"

She could feel the heat from the demon creature at twenty paces. And the flames roared higher still until she was a walking bonfire.

Melinda backed off, and Travis matched her step. Even the faun had to retreat.

Behind the demon, the trunk was still burning on the inside. It now glowed a bright yellow, and its outer skin bulged and began splitting, then turned black and peeled. Smoke billowed out.

When Melinda bumped into something or someone behind her, she stumbled and spun around in surprise, suddenly aware of a terrible icy-cold draft that cut all the way through her body. Panting, she watched her breath steam from her mouth and shivered as goosebumps rose on her arms.

A hooded, black-clad figure stood there, skeletal fingers wrapped around the long, wooden handle of a scythe whose shiny blade reflected the demon's flames.

"Oh no," Travis moaned. "It's the Grim Reaper."

## Chapter 32
## Death in the Air

Feeling icy-cold air in front but an inferno of heat behind, Melinda had no choice but to tear her gaze from the ghastly hooded figure. A dozen questions flitted through her mind, but right now she had a more pressing problem.

"Mom!" Melinda shouted as the demon rapidly stalked closer. "We have to go! Turn your flames off so Travis can carry you!"

She tried to keep her voice natural. Never mind that the brain was waking and had sent the Grim Reaper to dispatch them. *Just focus on normal stuff—like flying up into the darkness and plunging through a floating pool of water and out into a tower where a cauldron of potion is guarded by a griffin, a wyvern, and two male harpies . . .*

The ifrit continued advancing, slender feet dancing and leaving smoldering prints that caused a frenzied lightshow.

Melinda had no idea what to do. She glanced sideways, seeing that Travis had his wide-eyed gaze fixed on the Grim Reaper, while River seemed more interested in the rumbling coming from below.

*She's forgotten who we are,* Melinda thought as the demon raised her fiery arms. *She's gonna burn us!*

Balls of fire shot forth. Melinda screamed and ducked—but the projectiles missed her completely. They missed the faun and Travis, too. Instead, they smacked against the Grim Reaper's chest.

The hooded figure staggered backward engulfed in flames. Travis yelled something, and the faun lurched away from the raging fire. Melinda could hardly believe what was happening, but she accepted Travis's hand when he reached for her.

Abruptly, he was a mothman, wings flapping, rising off the ground and dragging Melinda with him. When her feet dangled helplessly, she yelled, "My Mom! We can't leave her!"

The faun leapt high and grabbed Travis's other hand. He kept rising, but he angled toward the ifrit, his glowing red eyes bright and fearful. "Uh," he said, "I'm not sure how we—"

The fire-demon jumped and grabbed the faun's hoof.

River screeched and struggled, but the ifrit held on. Most of her flames had died down by now; she was generating a lot of black smoke almost as though someone had doused the demon with water. Melinda stared in horror, expecting to see terrible burns spreading across the faun's leg . . . but the hand that gripped her hoof was bare and red-skinned, smoldering but no longer flaming.

Travis rose into the darkness.

Melinda looked down, seeing a mesmerizing pattern of lights flickering across the floor, and the Grim Reaper standing quite still as he stared up at them all. Though his robes let off wisps of smoke, he seemed unfazed by the attack. Perhaps just startled.

Then he vanished.

The damage to the white trunk seemed to be worsening, a hideous black scar spreading across its surface. Dark lines networked upward like ravenous ivy stems climbing a tree.

Melinda forced her gaze to what was above. The mothman's black wings pumped vigorously but not as fast as she would have expected. Still, they rose easily. With the mothman's natural flying magic and the reduced gravity, carrying three passengers apparently wasn't a big deal. *Two and a half. The ifrit is like a small child.*

She felt the heat rising from the flames and wished her mom would shut them off for good. Maybe she couldn't. The faun had to be suffering.

The rumbling subsided, lost in the darkness below. As high as they were by now, they'd left all the drama behind. Even the trunk seemed calm and unaffected up here.

"Hurry!" River snapped.

Melinda could have sworn Travis slowed his ascent just to spite her. Even so, they climbed fast. Before long, a rocky face slid into view on one side, sloping inward to meet them. They were entering the shaft. It would only get narrower from here.

"This is going to be tricky," Travis called down to them, his voice jarringly loud and echoey. "I'm feeling drops of water all around me. We're getting close."

The logistics of switching places in midair . . . Melinda tried to picture how it would play out, but she couldn't get it straight in her head. She imagined them all fumbling around, then dropping and screaming, and Travis snatching them back up and yelling at Melinda to transform and take over . . .

"Here it is," Travis said.

Melinda felt the water all around, almost like rain except the drops remained motionless in the air while the four of them ascended. Soon, water sluiced down their faces and off their bodies. Then it grew hard to breath, not much different from standing under a waterfall and looking up at it.

A muffled exclamation told her that Travis was now fully submerged. She was next, along with the faun and then the ifrit. Suddenly, floating through the air was a thing of the past. Now they were underwater, swimming upward but floundering and banging their hands against the rock on one side or the trunk on the other.

Without letting go of Travis's hand, Melinda transformed and took charge. She gave her tail a flick and shot up past him, dragging *him* now, while he continued holding onto the faun. And just like that, the switchover was complete—much easier than she'd expected.

Somewhere below, she could see flames still burning brightly even in the water. Sizzling bubbles rose all around her, something she'd just have to put up with. She gripped Travis's hand as hard as she could and forged upward, faster and faster. Giving him air on the way down had been necessary, but she hoped not to do it again—especially as he was still a mothman.

Besides, if she stopped to give him air, she'd have to do the same for the faun as well—and a flaming demon.

She cursed the narrowness of the shaft and knew her passengers were bumping against the rock. But she had to hurry.

Seeing a glimmer of light above, she put on just a little extra speed and finally broke the surface. In one smooth movement, she launched herself out of the pool and rolled onto the stone floor of the tower, giving room for the others.

They burst out one by one, a half-second apart, gasping and choking. Even her mom sputtered a lot, her flames almost doused as she gripped the rocky edge and pulled herself out after Travis and the faun. Melinda caught a glimpse of her horrible red skin. She looked like a burn victim—or someone who had been lying out in the sun for three days—or worse. But fire immediately sprang up again, hot and hungry for oxygen.

"I hope she doesn't throw fireballs at us," Melinda whispered, nodding toward the ifrit.

"Would your mother normally do such a thing?" the faun retorted.

"No, but she's forgotten who she is."

The faun shook her head. "An amnesia spell would not have helped in the circumstances, so I omitted it."

Melinda gazed at her mom, realizing the fire-demon hadn't appeared confused at all, that she'd jumped into action and helped from the very moment she'd sprung to life as an ifrit. She'd released the faun, burned the Treentacle, and shot fireballs over Melinda's head at the Grim Reaper.

"Hey, Mom," she said.

The ifrit raised a hand in greeting, but when she opened her mouth to speak, long flames licked out like a superheated tongue, so she shut it again.

As they sat and got their breath, Melinda became aware of Conrad standing there with a hefty wooden box. Motionless, he stared down at them all, his gaze moving from side to side. "What the . . ." he muttered.

Melinda realized being a mermaid didn't help. She probably looked like a fish out of water, flopping about on the floor. She shifted, adjusting her dress as her tail split in two and formed into legs.

"Did you bottle it up?" she asked, climbing to her feet and brushing herself down.

Conrad absently gave the box a tiny shake, and from inside came the gentle rattle of glass bottles. "As much as I could. But it's nowhere near enough. The cauldron is still full."

"I'll carry it back," Travis said. He picked himself up and shook his wings dry. "The weight won't be a problem." He turned to Melinda. "But let's use some right now on your mom."

At that moment, River leapt to her feet and ducked under the canopy of tentacles. A second later, they all heard her gasping and straining, and the dull thunk and scrape of metal on stone.

"Stop her!" Melinda yelled.

But her mom was already on it, a fiery mass as she went after the faun. As Melinda and Travis worked their way into the sheltered area, they just had time to see the faun heaving with all her might, the cauldron tilting, and the potion sloshing—and then the ifrit slammed into her.

The cauldron thunked back down, some of the valuable potion splashing onto the floor. River screamed as the ifrit straddled her, flames roaring . . . but then the demon leapt away, leaving the faun to bat at her smoldering clothes and scorched skin.

"Enough!" Melinda told her.

"Do not tell me what to do!" River hissed. She gave a cry of fury and crawled out of the shelter through a gap. Rather than follow her through, Melinda and Travis hurried back the way they'd come in, rushing around to meet the faun just as she rose to her feet.

Then she raised her hands and began muttering.

"No more mist!" Travis shouted, advancing on her. Then he stopped. "Wait—who exactly are you aiming that at? You know we can't be harmed. Conrad is the only one in danger here."

The man immediately set the wooden box down and bolted for the door. A second later, the door slammed shut behind him.

River's spellcasting presented itself as a vibration underfoot and a subtle movement in the air. Melinda felt the hairs on the back of her neck stand up. All around the tower above, white tendrils began to shudder and move like a nest of disturbed vipers.

"Do you think blue mist is all I can muster?" the faun said, dropping her hands to her sides. She looked exhausted but oddly triumphant.

Though she'd stopped spellcasting, the vibrations increased. Dust began to trickle from between the smooth stone blocks that made up the walls.

"Stop her, Mom!" Melinda urged.

A fireball shot forth, but the faun had been expecting it, and she ducked and rolled aside. Springing back to her feet, she crouched in a defensive position. Her coppery skin glistened in the streaming daylight from above, and the matted wet fur of her goat legs dripped water on the floor. She was so hot and bothered that steam rose from her shoulders.

Travis advanced on her from one side, and Melinda pushed closer from the other. The ifrit sprang again, landing deftly in position to complete a triangle of defense.

But defense against what? The faun wasn't doing anything now except standing there breathing hard and grinning. The vibrations continued. Dust formed into fine clouds. Cracks began appearing on the walls. High above, glass shattered. And all around, agitated tendrils wriggled and twisted.

"Why are you doing this?" Melinda demanded. "You're bringing the place down? You want to die here with us?"

"My work is done," River said with a smile. "I hope the mist spread far and wide. And this cauldron—and that box on the floor—will be destroyed when these walls come crashing down. Humans are no more. I am happy to leave this world knowing it has been repopulated. You two are the only surviving humans, and you will both—"

Her smile faded.

Travis's gaze had shifted to something over Melinda's shoulder. Maybe the ifrit's had too, but it was impossible to tell.

Feeling a blast of icy-cold air, Melinda gasped and swung around.

The Grim Reaper moved like he was sliding on ice—but at a snail's pace, his black robe billowing in slow motion. His scythe's downward-pointing blade glinted, and he tapped the long handle once or twice against the floor as he approached the faun.

"What are you doing?" the faun said, her dull-yellow eyes widening. Then she snarled. "Take *them*. Take us all if you must, but take them first!"

The Grim Reaper said nothing as he lifted his hand and pointed at her with one long, skeletal finger.

The rumbling increased all around, and a few large chunks of masonry fell from high above. A screeching of metal suggested the gantry was about to come loose.

"We have to get out of here," Travis warned.

Melinda couldn't take her eyes off the Grim Reaper. He stood there, perfectly still, pointing at the faun and following her movement as she edged sideways.

With a snarl, she bolted toward the door.

"Stop her!" Travis yelled.

The ifrit leapt—

But at that moment, more chunks of stone crashed down from high above, one of them slamming into River's skull. She folded like a ragdoll amid raining debris and dust, and lay there until the brief deluge stopped. Half buried and masked by a dirty haze, Melinda watched in horror as the faun's hand moved, fingers grasping as though trying to pull herself clear . . .

The Grim Reaper slid closer, no longer pointing but instead reaching for her, his palm turned upward as he bent over her crooked body. His skeletal hand passed through the flesh of her torso.

Her body went rigid. The Reaper retracted his hand, dragging with it a wriggling darkness that he slipped under his robes and stashed away somewhere.

Melinda let out a whimper. Rooted to the spot, she hyperventilated as the Grim Reaper turned to face them.

Then he faded away.

"Look!" Travis gasped.

Melinda swung around. Ugly black veins emerged from the rippling pool and crept up the trunk like a virus.

But as they watched the eerie demise of the Treentacle, the rumbling and vibrations worsened. More dust trickled from above, chunks of stone tumbled and smashed on the floor, glass cracked and tinkled, and rivets popped as the gantry screeched and sagged.

The ifrit let out a roar, flames shooting from her mouth. She was gesturing wildly toward the door.

"We have to go!" Travis said. "You grab that wooden box. I'll get the cauldron."

Melinda found the box far heavier than she expected. "Thanks a bunch, Conrad," she growled. Expecting to be buried under a ton of rubble at any moment, she heaved the box into her arms and staggered toward the door while Travis went to fetch the cauldron. How on earth would he drag that thing out, though?

Her mom went to help him, deftly burning through vines and clearing some space. That gave Travis the chance to flap about just above the cauldron. By the time Melinda made it to the door, the mothman was rising with the full cauldron gripped in two hands. "Piece of cake," he croaked.

More cracks appeared in the walls. A terrible groan echoed about the place.

Gasping with panic, Melinda struggled with the box while trying to get the door open. She stumbled outside and turned to see the trunk blackening all over, either burning or rotting. It began to twist and wilt, and the last thing she saw was a mass of thick tentacles swinging down and flopping heavily onto the floor.

Travis made it halfway out, the cauldron banging against the door frame. Potion splashed as he dumped it down on the step. His wings didn't fit through the opening, so he had to land. But then he couldn't move the cauldron at all. Sweating, he squeezed past it, spread his wings, took to the air again, gripped the handle in both hands, and easily raised it off the ground.

*Magic works in mysterious ways*, Melinda thought.

She stumbled away from the tower clutching the heavy wooden box. Her mom sprang free of the doorway and leapt to safety as the whole place groaned and wailed like a dying giant. Melinda heard the metal gantry finally tearing loose and clanging as it tumbled to the bottom of the tower.

"Go!" Travis shouted, flapping away over the lake, the cauldron skimming the surface.

He had his hands full. Melinda slipped into the water and transformed, and that made things much easier—she rested the wooden box half in the water and swam with it, pushing it along but holding it aloft so it didn't turn over.

She glanced back. Her mom remained on the tiny island as the tower began to crash down behind. There was no way she'd survive that if she didn't get clear.

At the last moment, the flaming ifrit took a dive. Bubbles and white steam erupted from the water.

The tower fell.

## Chapter 33
## Antidote for All

A silence fell across the lake.

Travis stood on the bank with Melinda and the flaming ifrit, looking across at the tiny island, upon which lay a mound of rubble, twisted metal, and numerous limp tentacles. Dust hung in the air.

A splash distracted him. A bit farther around the bank, a huge serpent's head rose from the water. Travis gaped. He'd never seen one of these giants before, though he'd heard stories. His dad and Robbie, when they were much younger, had taken a raft out and confronted a similar monster.

The serpent looked like it was going to slither out of the water onto the bank, but it paused—then spat something out. A figure tumbled onto the grass with a yell.

"Is that . . . Conrad?" Travis asked.

Melinda squinted. "I think so. Maybe whoever was turned into a gigantic snake still has part of his memory. Or he feels bad about killing but doesn't really know why."

"Or maybe these serpents just don't like to kill. Our dads met one just off the coast of their foggy island when they were our age. It could have eaten them, but it didn't."

"A jengu is out there somewhere," Melinda mused. "And a griffin, and a wyvern. They came splashing down."

"Yeah, they collided in midair." Travis grinned. "Maybe it knocked some sense into them." He sighed. "We have so much work to do getting everybody turned back to normal."

"Yeah, but we don't have to do it all. We just need to get it started. Then we can get teams spreading out with vials of the potion, and they can help ten people each, and those ten can spread out and help another ten each . . . It'll be all right."

Travis thought about his dad—an enormous jinn standing over Carter. "Let's get going, then."

But first, Melinda wanted to take care of her mom. The wooden box of vials lay on the ground, but the cauldron stood there also, so she dipped her fingers in and stepped closer to the fiery ifrit. "Mom, I'm gonna splash you, okay?"

When she flicked her hand at the demon, the droplets simply sizzled and evaporated. So the ifrit had to concentrate and douse her flame a little first. She ended up with her face and bald head free of flames but smoldering and red. Her eyes were utterly black, her skin eerily shiny. But her body remained on fire, and Melinda still couldn't get close.

She handed one of the vials to her mom—or rather put it on the grass so her mom could pick it up. The ifrit did so, but the glass promptly melted and shattered, and drops flew out and sizzled away.

The third attempt involved the fire-demon walking over to the cauldron, leaning over the side, and dunking her head in. She withdrew immediately; even with no flames, her hot head caused the potion to heat up and start bubbling. But the job was done; she blinked and gave a nod, then stepped back to a safe distance.

As with Conrad in the tower, the change didn't happen straight away. Rather than wait around, the three of them set off toward the village of Follen's Glen. This meant separating.

"See you soon," Travis said to them.

Melinda smiled, and the ifrit raised a hand.

Travis flew off carrying the heavy cauldron. He looked back to see Melinda struggling with the wooden box. Her mom trailed behind, setting fire to everything she touched and leaving scorch marks everywhere.

Without mothman magic, he never could have carried the full cauldron. Even with it, the thing was *heavy*. He dragged it with both hands, trying to rise up into the sky but finding himself trailing low across fields. He soldiered on, knowing it wasn't too far.

Follen's Glen was a mess. It wasn't a big place, but it surprised him how much stuff had been pulled out of the small cottages and tossed into the winding lanes. Whoever lived there now had trashed the place. He saw gargoyles and pixies, harpies and trolls, that majestic silver-scaled longma horse, even a few fauns. Confusion reigned. He figured they'd all gone home at some point, stood there puzzling over the oddly familiar junk that littered their dwelling, and thrown some of it out.

Travis landed in the middle of the village. His gaze lingered for a moment on a building with a sign out front: PORTAL. He imagined a smoky mass just inside, normally guarded by portal police. Had the mist crept into the building and through the portal as well? Had Old Earth been affected by this crisis?

Four harpies came to see what he had brought. Despite their curiosity, they remained at a cautious distance. "What's *that*?" one shrieked at him.

"Special delivery. It's the antidote."

He suddenly spotted a troll standing by a wagon, and a pixie lurking behind one of its wheels. A normal troll would have picked up that pixie and chewed off his head by now.

"Antidote for what, mothman?" a deep voice growled.

Travis turned to find a centaur glaring at him, a bushy-bearded, muscular beast. "For the mist that came through here. Everyone was infected. This is the cure."

Nobody came forward. He became aware that more and more people—creatures of all different kinds—had emerged from doorways or alleys and were standing around watching, frowns on their faces. He suspected a human would have been run out of town by now.

Travis had a feeling he'd have to get a little more creative with his sales pitch. Everyone here had lost their memory and had no idea they were supposed to be human—and they probably wouldn't *want* to be human now.

"I'm taking it to Carter," Travis said. "I'm supposed to deliver it there, let everyone get some, and then head out to the smaller villages like this one." He shrugged. "I just happened to be passing and thought I'd drop in. But I can bring it back later after everyone else has had some. *If* there's any left."

He moved toward it, reaching for the handle. The harpies leapt in front of him, and the centaur came trotting.

"We're not sick," a harpy sneered. "We don't need antidote."

"That's good. Maybe you don't need it. Like I said, I'll take it to Carter and—"

"Not so fast," the centaur said. "What kind of sickness?"

"Oh, nothing serious." Travis shrugged and stared at the ground. "People just don't feel like themselves. They lose their memory and get confused, can't remember where they live, what their name is . . ." He looked up at the centaur. "Know anyone who's been acting like that?"

Murmurs swept around the place.

"Leave the antidote," the centaur said. "We'll get ours, and *then* you can take it away."

Travis had to refrain from smiling. He put on an air of grudging acceptance. "All right—but only a couple of drops each." He stepped back and allowed a pixie to stand on tiptoes and peer into the cauldron. "One for each eye. We have a lot of people to give it to."

"One for *each eye?*" another harpy shrieked. "What kind of foolery is this?"

"Bring a cup," the centaur shouted.

"Uh, no, you don't need a cup," Travis said, feeling like he might be losing control of the situation. "You're not supposed to drink it."

"A cup!" the centaur roared.

Finally, a goblin seated next to an upturned barrel outside a cottage tutted and climbed to his feet. He picked up his metal tankard, took a last swig to finish off whatever ale was inside, and lazily threw the cup. It bounced and rolled, and the handle came off.

A female harpy leapt for it, then eagerly dipped it into the cauldron. As others looked on, she put it to her lips and—

"Stop!" Travis yelled.

Everyone jumped and looked at him.

He walked around the cauldron and held out his black-furred hand. "Let me have that cup before you do something really stupid. If you drink this stuff, you'll regret it. If you put more than a drop in each eye, you'll wish you hadn't. Just do as I say, and everything will be fine. I've seen it."

The harpy clutched the cup to her chest and snarled at him, crouching and spreading her wings. "I don't believe you, you bug-eyed freak."

Travis sighed and dropped his hand. "Then drink it. Go ahead. Let everyone else see what will happen so *they* don't make the same mistake."

Nobody moved.

"What will happen?" the centaur growled.

Travis said nothing. He folded his arms.

The harpy held out the cup—not to Travis but to her harpy friends. They all shied away.

In the end, the harpy swore under her breath and shoved the cup into Travis's hands, causing a few drops to splash out.

"A drop in each eye?" she complained. "Sounds bogus to me."

Still, the harpies leaned over the cauldron and tentatively dipped their hands in. Then one splashed herself in the face. She did it again, blinked, then once more. With her cheeks wet, she grinned and said, "I'm cured!"

The other harpies jostled to be next.

Two elves and a goblin hurried over, but a troll suddenly lunged for the goblin, taking him down with force. They rolled in the dirt in a tangle of limbs. A gargoyle slid down off a nearby roof and thudded to the ground, red eyes blazing. Travis couldn't help giving three fauns a hard stare . . . but they were clearly a harmless family, perhaps a father and two children. Where was the mother? Was she a faun as well, or one of these elves, or even the troll? Did they even realize they were a family, or were they just banding together with others of their kind?

With more and more villagers hurrying toward the cauldron, Travis felt he could probably slip away for a bit and leave them to it. If they all got some at the same time, they'd all revert to normal together as well. How long had it taken back at the lighthouse for Conrad to change? Half an hour? But the Treentacles tended to skew time, so he doubted it had really taken that long. Probably half that time, maybe less.

He noticed the centaur still seemed unsure, letting everyone else go first. "It's okay," Travis called to him. "It's safe." He turned his gaze to the spectacular, red-feathered, nine-headed bird as it flew overhead. "A word of warning, though. Make sure anyone with wings stays on the ground afterward. See that bird up there?"

"The *bird?*"

Travis sighed. It would be easier to understand once some of the villagers were human again.

The centaur gave a curt nod. "If a mothman advises it, then I cannot argue. But tell me—what did you see?"

"Huh?"

"In your vision. You said you'd seen it."

Travis frowned, thinking back. "Oh! No, when I said I'd seen it, I meant . . ." *I meant I've seen a couple of people revert back to normal. I know the potion works.* But he realized the centaur assumed something else. "What I meant was . . ."

"You had a vision," the centaur prompted. "You saw what? Is there more to this mist than mass confusion?"

Travis didn't quite know how to answer. And he didn't feel right lying, either. He picked his words carefully. "I've seen things I don't want to talk about. Things that can't be allowed to happen. I promise you, we all need to take this potion."

With another nod, the centaur turned to the gathering crowd around the cauldron and pressed forward, eager to take his turn.

Travis felt a little humbled that the centaur had taken his word for it. Or rather taken a *mothman's* word for it. But why not? As far as he knew, mothmen had always been respected for their visions. Feared and perhaps even loathed for the terrible omens they delivered, but respected nonetheless.

He glimpsed the longma standing behind a cottage, grazing on the grass there. The thing was enormous. Travis looked at the metal cup in his hand, still half filled with potion. He might as well do something to help.

The giant horse eyed Travis warily as he approached, finally lifting its head while continuing to chew the grass in its mouth. Funny how such a powerful, magnificent, scaly, fearsome dragon-like creature could be a grazer.

He spoke softly to the beast and dipped his fingers in the potion. Then, in one smooth movement, he gave a gentle flick near the horse's eye. It didn't react too strongly, but his aim was off, so he tried again. When a droplet scored a direct hit, the longma jerked backward and blinked, then turned and trotted away.

"Hey, wait, don't go!" Travis called. He went after the creature but knew he'd never get that close again. It seemed unconcerned, just not so amiable now. It turned his back on him and continued grazing. And when Travis crept closer, it gave a soft whinny and moved away.

He tried again and again, but when the longma lifted its head and turned to glare at him with a soft growl, Travis knew he needed to quit. Let the townsfolk deal with it. As a group, they could corral the beast and deliver antidote to the other eye.

Returning to the streets where the cauldron stood, he was pleased to see the harpies and gargoyles had cleared out, leaving a stream of others calmly edging forward to take their antidote. The centaur remained like a sentry, his bulging arms crossed.

Travis waited, his patience wearing thin. He felt drained of energy and emotion. He thought of Melinda struggling with the wooden box—or perhaps her mom—or both of them. It would be easier for Travis to carry. But then again, why should he bother? Besides, he had a whole cauldron of his own to cart around . . .

Then he kicked himself. All these people could help. Once they'd returned to their human forms and recovered their lost memories, they could go find lots of bottles and fill them with potion, then load up a wagon and take it all to Carter—or to other villages, since Melinda had plenty of potion in her box already. She was right. It wasn't about one or two people going around giving everyone drops in their eyes. This would be a communal effort, pitching in to restore humanity to the land.

Everything was going to be fine.

This should have made him feel better. Oddly, he felt nothing.

Soon after, the first harpy suddenly reverted to human form. She was flying low across the village at that moment, carrying a bag stuffed with stolen goods, and when she changed back, she screamed and fell, landing with a thud and rolling over several times in a cloud of dust, her bag spilling out bread rolls, chunks of cheese, apples and pears, and leftover joints of meat.

*Told you*, Travis thought. *Stay on the ground after taking the potion.*

He watched in silence. The harpy deserved a rough landing, but the human woman did not. Not that he cared one way or another . . .

*Part of my soul is missing. It's starting to affect me.*

He thought about that with a sense of detachment as he watched the events in the village.

As everyone stared in amazement, the next few harpies reverted to human form, and then the pixie, and the elves, and the fauns . . . and all amid an increasing babble of surprised yells, roars, screams, and cries.

Travis slid around the corner. Everything would be fine soon, once they were all human again. But right now, he suspected the centaur and others felt betrayed.

*Like it matters.*

He went to watch the longma. It grazed peacefully. But then it paused and lifted its head, staring into space as if sensing something.

Abruptly, it shrank and morphed into the form of a—

Apparently one drop wasn't enough. He carried his cup over to the struggling half-horse, half-woman creature whose bare backside was partially covered in silver scales. She lay awkwardly, mostly facing down but twisted a little, one side of her body like a stretched-out human and the other the size and shape of a shrunken horse. She was a pitiful, misshapen mess that fumbled around on the grass letting out a strangled noise, a cross between a nicker and a moan.

Travis grunted, "Well, that's not right."

He bent over her ghastly, twisted head and stared into the enormous horse's eye, while the other, on the stretched-human side of her face, rotated in panic. *Just like in my vision.*

He splashed his wet fingers at her, ensuring he made contact with the larger eyeball.

After that, all he could do was wait. He stroked her head, feeling a little odd since this was a person, not an animal. He felt a duty to calm her, though he didn't really understand why he should bother. "It's going to be okay. Just be patient. Ten minutes, and you'll be fine."

She whimpered.

In his vision, it had seemed like he didn't feel sorry for her. And the truth was, he didn't.

*I need to get my soul back.*

## Chapter 34
## Wandering Shells

Travis left Follen's Glen soon after. He advised the centaur—who'd reverted to a man known locally as Wily Will—to bottle up the potion and take it on a wagon to all the surrounding communities except Carter. "Split it up," Travis suggested with a shrug "Whatever. I have to go."

As he flew off, he glanced down to see if the longma had been fully restored. He saw a completely normal woman huddled in a ball, and he nodded. Then he smiled. *Longma.* There was a pun there somewhere. Was she a mother? In that half-horse, half-human state, she'd been a *long ma . . .*

He sighed. The joke was pathetic. And in pretty poor taste. He just couldn't help feeling tired and indifferent.

It seemed the blue mist had cleared at last. He had to assume the storm had stopped spreading now that the Treentacle was dead. The crisis was over.

*Great*, he thought.

It didn't take long to find Melinda and her mom. They were trudging across a field carrying the box between them. When he touched down, Melinda gave him a nod and said nothing.

"Travis!" Lauren exclaimed with a smile. "I'm so glad you came back for us." She narrowed her eyes. "Are you feeling okay?"

He shrugged. "Fine. Why?"

Lauren sighed. "Put the box down," she said to Melinda. Then she waved Travis closer. "I dragged the full story out of Melinda. We need to find Mr. Grimfoyle and get the missing pieces of your souls back. It's starting to affect you."

Travis stared off into the distance. She was right, but it didn't seem to matter so much anymore. "I guess," he muttered.

"That's exactly what Melinda said."

Melinda rolled her eyes. "Stop fussing, Mom. Having part of my soul missing bothers you *way* more than it bothers me."

Lauren reached for her. "That's precisely my point. Now let's get home."

The journey was short and quiet. Lauren carefully gripped Melinda in her talons, her harpy toes long enough to encircle her upper arms without digging into flesh. Harpies had oversized bird feet designed to carry whatever they'd plundered. Too bad she hadn't been able to carry Melinda *and* the box. Travis ended up carrying it instead.

He heard the little bottles of potion jiggling as he arrived in Carter. The gigantic jinn still towered overhead, though he seemed faint now, the mist that surrounded his invisible form a little thinner than before. Lauren, swooping around, gasped and made a comment, but Travis wasn't fully paying attention and missed what she said.

The moment he touched down, the box seemed to grow four times heavier, and he put it down on a low wall.

"What *is* that thing?" Lauren exclaimed after she'd deposited Melinda and landed. She squinted over the rooftops. "And why can't I see it now?"

Travis could barely make it out, either—a funnel cloud so indistinct that it took three or four glances just to spot it.

"I think that's Dad," he mumbled.

Lauren stared at him. Then she opened the wooden box, pulled out a vial, and said, "Go. See what you can do. I'm going to find Mason."

Feeling a little like he was dreaming, Travis took the vial and launched into the air. Glancing around, he noticed the streets in a similar disarray to Follen's Glen—things thrown out of houses in disgust. He imagined a surly goblin arriving home would find gauze curtains and fluffy pillows annoying, the first things to go. He couldn't imagine what trolls would think. They'd probably urinate on the walls to mark their territory.

The jinn came alive and reached for him, the misty funnel cloud thickening. He hadn't moved. His feet were still planted in the same spot, one in each street.

"Dad!" Travis yelled, flying closer.

He eyed the massive, sweeping hand and timed his evasive maneuver just right, ducking under and then soaring to reach the barely perceptible face before the giant reached for him again.

"Do you know who I am?" Travis shouted into the smoky face as he uncorked the vial.

The loudest, deepest rumble he'd ever heard blasted him along with a rush of wind—all emanating from the widening shadow in the lower part of the face. Travis had to let the noise subside before he could hear himself think.

"I have potion!" he said, holding up the vial. It seemed pitifully small now.

Glancing over his shoulder, he cringed at the sight of the slow-moving hand reaching for him again, the fingers spread wide.

*No time to talk*, Travis thought in panic.

All he could do was give the vial a hard flick so the potion shot out and into the dark, smoky mass where he judged one of the eyes to be. He couldn't help thinking it was never going to work. *Not enough potion! My aim is off! What if he shuts his eyes?*

Not to mention the giant hand closing over him.

He yelled and bolted through one of the gaps between the fingers. It was like escaping a collapsing cave. Darkness closed in on him as he shot through the opening—and then he was out in bright daylight again, tumbling away.

His vial was empty. He rushed away and descended on the street where Melinda waited with the wooden box. "Need more!" he shouted.

Melinda held up a vial as he slowed his descent and hovered above. Then he bolted skyward again. The jinn seemed a little more distinct now, his outline more defined and his facial features showing through. He reached for Travis again, his fingers outstretched, his mouth open wide and letting out a long, thunderous roar.

Still he didn't move. Travis considered that as he circled the giant's head looking for an opening. The jinn followed his moves, twisting around, but he couldn't turn his head all the way, so he had to snap back in the other direction—a somewhat ponderous action for one so big. *That* would be Travis's opportunity.

What stopped the giant from moving? One step, and houses would be crushed. Two steps, three steps, more houses. Maybe the fourth step would put him outside the town away from harm. But why did the jinn care what he stood on?

*Because that's my dad*, Travis thought. *He knows the damage he could do. He's trying to stand still.*

But then why was he trying to grab him?

Travis continued his circling motion, and as the giant broke eye contact and started to turn back the other way, Travis darted closer and hovered right above the colossal head. There was room to land and run around on that domed surface, though he'd be waist deep in mist if he did . . .

An ill-timed mothman vision flashed into his head:

*. . . Mr. Grimfoyle, with a smile on his face and his eyes gleaming, reached down and picked Travis up from the ground . . .*

Or so it seemed. It was such a bizarre vision. The old man's hand seemed huge, rather like the jinn's—all encompassing, each finger bigger than a grown man. Dealing with the jinn had most likely triggered the vision. Mr. Grimfoyle was portrayed as a giant . . . although the chimney looming over him suggested otherwise.

Travis shook his head and hovered there above the jinn's face, steeling himself. The jinn had turned his head all the way back around and was just now realizing his quarry had vanished—and Travis chose that moment to swoop down over his target and fling the entire vial of potion into the second eye before flying away out of range.

The jinn clawed at his eye and bellowed some more, and just for a moment the monster acted like an oversized child throwing a tantrum.

Travis almost forgot to flap his wings as the jinn tilted to one side and lifted a gigantic smoky foot. That single action caught a house on the upswing, demolishing it in an instant. A smoky vapor rolled off the bottom of the foot, and a number of goblins made a run for it.

Then the jinn's anger evaporated, and he slowly put down his foot.

*Definitely my dad,* Travis thought. *He's aware. He's in there somewhere, fighting to stand still no matter what else.*

Travis went to land, but something clanged into place in his head. With a gasp of realization, he shouted, "Melinda! Come on, we have something we need to do."

She looked completely disinterested. "Huh?"

Melinda barely had time to lift her hand before Travis snatched her up and dragged her off the ground. "We're going to get our souls back," he told her.

Just before he left the town behind and headed across the meadows, he glimpsed droves of goblins lining the streets. The stout fellows seemed to be organizing themselves into patrols, perhaps to stop the residents from trashing their own homes.

"Where are we—" Melinda started.

But Travis had already arrived. He descended on his home, circling around to the back of the property. He glimpsed a donkey standing there, but his attention focused on Mr. Grimfoyle, who was standing by the chimney. The vision had been as accurate as all the others, yet it still astonished Travis that he'd foreseen this so perfectly—and from the point of view of a blue gem lying on the grass!

He glided in, utterly silent. Mr. Grimfoyle hadn't seen him yet. He had a gleam in his eye and a smile on his face as he bent to pick up the gem . . .

Travis carefully dropped Melinda—then slammed into the old man, knocking him sideways. The gem shot into the air, sunlight dancing off its glassy blue surface. The boulder opal hit the chimney and bounced off into the grass again.

"Hey!" the old man shouted, picking himself up. "What did— Why—"

"We want our souls back," Travis said in a dull voice he felt unable to breathe life into.

Mr. Grimfoyle rolled his eyes. "Really, boy? There are things far more precious in life than a soul." He pointed. "Like that hoard, for example."

Travis blinked in surprise. There was that donkey again, staring at him from the corner of the house. A small, two-wheeled trap was hitched to it, and the compartment at the back was filled with sacks, bags, boxes, and many larger items stuff along the sides—silver candlesticks, a few gleaming swords, an ornate shield, and much more.

"That's all from Follen's Glen?" Travis said.

"Enough to keep me going for years," Mr. Grimfoyle replied with a chortle. "But the gem is probably worth far more. Help me find it."

"I'm more interested in our souls."

A feeling of exhaustion had swept in again. Travis almost didn't care about getting his soul back now. It was probably too late anyway.

The man searched the grass. "Where did it go? That gem could fetch me a fortune, you know. And I doubt the steamer dragon will come after it now."

"She's dead." Travis felt nothing for the dragon though he knew he probably should. "And you are *not* having her gem."

Mr. Grimfoyle's scowl deepened, though his gaze never left the grass. "Says who? Now look, I assume you defeated the faun and destroyed that ghastly white tentacle-plant thing. Very good, well done. But run along now. I've done my part, and I deserve a reward. My business does not concern you."

Melinda put a hand on Travis's arm. "Let him have it."

He blinked at her. "Huh?"

"Let him have it. If it weren't for him taking part of our souls, we wouldn't be here now, and the faun and my mom would still be stuck down underground. Maybe he deserves *something*."

Travis wanted to argue with her, because it felt wrong letting this wily old coot get a reward just for doing the right thing—especially as that reward was the steamer dragon's precious opal. But as his anger subsided, he realized he didn't really care as much about it as he thought.

He felt exhausted all of a sudden, and past caring. Taking a seat on the old tree stump, he leaned forward and put his head in his hands. Melinda stood off to one side, equally dejected. Mr. Grimfoyle continued to search the grass for the gem.

"Stump," Travis muttered.

He stared down at what was left of the old walnut tree. Earlier that morning, the jinn, his dad, had roared what sounded like "stop" and then "stomp"—but what if he'd been trying to say "stump"?

Almost the second Travis realized this, he knew the potion was buried right under him—*under the paving slab at his feet.* His mouth fell open at the sight of the tiny patch of grey concrete. Grass had encroached across most of its surface, so it was no wonder he'd never noticed it before.

He reached down and dug around the edges, then got down on hands and knees and started scooping with his tough, black-furred, mothman fingers.

"Travis?" Melinda called. "What are you doing?"

"Looking for the gem, I hope!" Mr. Grimfoyle snapped, prowling around in the longer patches of grass. "Where did the blasted thing go?"

Travis couldn't help thinking there was a kind of ancient omen at work here. His dad had buried the potion by the walnut tree and covered it with a paving slab. Many years later, he'd had to cut the tree down. Since then, he'd sat on the stump with his feet resting on the very spot he'd buried the potion. How many times had he thought about the faun over the years?

The slab came up easily once he got a good grip on one edge. Underneath, a tin box—and in the tin box a grey rag wrapped around a bottle of potion.

*The original potion from twenty years ago.*

He held it up, awed. Melinda knelt with him, her eyes wide.

"Bit late now," she said after a moment. "Got plenty of that stuff now."

"I know, but . . ." He stared at her, beginning to shake as he remembered something. "When we were down underground with the brain—"

He broke off. Suddenly, he knew what he had to do.

"We want our souls back," he said loudly, climbing to his feet and facing Mr. Grimfoyle.

Mr. Grimfoyle let out a heavy sigh. He gave up looking for the gem and turned to face Travis and Melinda. "Sorry. For the first time in a long time, I've started to feel . . . *joy.* Mainly the joy of coming here to claim that opal once and for all, but joy all the same. It's been a long time since I—"

"We don't care," Travis interrupted. "Give us our souls."

"You can't have them, and you can't have the gem. Now, run along."

The old man went back to searching. And, seconds later, he exclaimed loudly and pounced on the gem. He held it up to the light and squinted.

"Breathtaking! An absolute fortune!"

Travis leapt at him, his wings flapping hard. The old man quickly jammed the opal into his pocket—but Travis had no interest in that. He simply uncorked the small bottle and threw the remains of the potion in Mr. Grimfoyle's face.

"Argh!" the man yelled, wiping his eyes. He blinked and examined his glistening hands. "What the dickens was that?"

"It was potion."

Mr. Grimfoyle staggered backward in horror. "Do you have any idea what you've just done?"

Melinda nudged Travis. "What exactly *did* you do?" she whispered.

He kept his gaze on the old man but spoke sideways to Melinda. "Back at the tower, underground . . . While you were connected to your mom seeing things from her point of view, I saw what went on with the faun—and with Mr. Grimfoyle. I saw everything, and I *heard* everything. This potion heals. It's going to restore this old man to the way he should be."

"No, no, NO!" Mr Grimfoyle shouted. He stood there shaking, holding his hands up as though expecting two hundred years to catch up with him in an instant. "How long does it take for this stuff to work?"

"Just over ten minutes," Travis told him.

The man's face darkened. "If you think you're getting your souls back now, after what you just did . . ."

But, a second later, a dark vapor rose out of the man's chest, followed by another. He sagged and let out a whimper.

"They don't belong to you," Travis said. "Your natural state doesn't include two stolen souls."

"They're mine!" Mr. Grimfoyle yelled, reaching for them. But his hand passed straight through the vapors as they floated in the air.

The first partial soul zipped forward and entered Travis's chest. He let out a gasp, almost overwhelmed by the deluge of emotions that came with it. The other dark cloud plunged into Melinda's body, and she cried out.

Though Travis staggered and almost fell, the turmoil of feelings settled down quickly, and he basked in amazement at what he'd been missing. He hadn't noticed a huge difference when a third of his soul had been *taken*, but he certainly felt its return.

He and Melinda hugged in delight, then turned to find Mr. Grimfoyle.

The man had climbed onto the two-wheeled trap. He made some sharp noises and flicked the reins to get the donkey moving, then slumped in his seat. Travis and Melinda hurried around to the front of the house to watch them head off across the meadow.

"Let him go," Melinda whispered.

Although the potion was supposed to take maybe twelve minutes to kick in, it seemed the old man was already feeling its effects. His hair dropped out as he went, leaving random bald patches on the back of his head, and he hunched forward on his seat, his head lolling from side to side as the trap bounced across the grass.

Travis and Melinda watched him go, tears running down their faces.

*The problem with having my soul restored,* Travis thought in misery, *is that now I care too much about the old fraud.*

## Chapter 35
## Cleanup

Melinda had to put thoughts about the old man aside. There was too much to do, and her brother was still missing.

She hopped up and down, eager to see what would happen when the first batch of recipients morphed back to their former selves. It was a major operation, but her mom had it in hand—and she had an army of *real* goblins willing to carry out her orders.

The first batch wasn't incredibly well organized, but it was fast. Goblins crowded around to grab pocketfuls of bottled potion, then headed off and started flinging it about in the faces of naga, elves, gnomes, pixies, a sphinx or two, a wandering squonk, even an unruly troll. Melinda's mom had a few stern words and told them to use it *sparingly*, no more than a drop in each eye.

Travis added that it really did have to be a drop in *each* eye, otherwise it would only half work. The goblins gave him disbelieving looks but were a little more careful after that.

While that was going on, Melinda stood with Travis to watch the jinn. It was time. It had been shrinking bit by bit for a while now, but when the giant smoke-monster let out a mournful bellow, it dwindled rapidly, becoming more and more solid the smaller it got, leaving a wispy trail in its wake.

Travis jumped into the air—and thudded down. Frowning, he tried again, and then held up his hands to look at them. "Whoa. What happened?"

Melinda couldn't help giggling. She was finding everything amusing at the moment. "Your ability expired."

"But it's not time!"

"Maybe some potion got in your face and took away your shapeshifting ability."

Clearly disappointed, Travis took off running along the street. Melinda hurried to catch up.

By the time they arrived, the jinn had shrunk down to twice the height of a cottage—which he now straddled awkwardly, one foot at the front, one at the back. Shrinking further, he stepped away and stumbled, then righted himself in the dusty street.

"Dad!" Travis called.

The jinn turned to him. Now just twenty feet tall and a distinctly human shape, the mist solidified and formed a recognizable face. Another five seconds and he was down to normal size and clarifying further. When the blue haze finally cleared, Travis's dad stood there with a sheepish grin on his face—hiding behind a pile of rubble.

"That's *way* better! I was getting a cramp standing there like that." He surveyed the damage he'd done when he'd lifted a giant foot earlier. "I destroyed Annie Fogle's home. She's gonna kill me. Hey, find me something to wear, would you?"

Melinda couldn't help laughing at the sight of Travis's dad crouching so low that only his head and shoulders were visible.

Travis hurried into a neighboring house. He emerged seconds later dragging a bedsheet, which he handed over while saying, "I can't believe you were taken down by an ogre, Dad. He *pounded* you."

"Yeah, well, let that be a lesson," his dad said as he bundled himself up. "Never underestimate a hard punch to the face." He stood up straight and stepped into view. "That thing had a good right hook. Now, where's your mom?"

"Yeah, she's been a real hothead lately, Dad . . ."

Melinda watched them both with a smile. They were so alike. Travis was looking more like his dad every day. She turned away, thinking of her own. He was safe enough, especially with Flynn to watch over him. Then again, the presence of an empusa vampire didn't fill her with confidence. But now that Hal was back, he could fly out with some potion and deal with them quickly.

Right now, her concern was Mason. Where was he? Still with Canaan and Rez? It was doubtful. For all she knew, he might be a troll or a manticore.

She went searching. Trawling the streets, she passed dozens of unfamiliar faces. Carter would never again see so many diverse species crammed into one place. A group of naga hissed at her, a gargoyle cackled from a rooftop, three brownies ran past with black hair streaming, a cyclops lurched around the corner looking confused, the ugly squonk she'd seen earlier sobbed pitifully in an alleyway . . . She avoided its gaze, not wanting the thing to dissolve into a pool of tears, as they tended to do. It would be hard to administer potion to a creature that hated being looked at.

*All we need is one drop in each eye*, Melinda thought. *Unless you're a cyclops, in which case one drop will be plenty.*

What about the six-headed hydra in the river? That one would be a real chore to deal with.

She thought about another cyclops she'd seen, the one near Flynn's farmhouse. Maybe that had been Blair or Orson. And the female werewolf had probably been Miss Simone. Someone needed to track her down. And Flynn's father, for that matter— one of the naga. Hopefully he hadn't wandered off too far. What about the kelpie?

Then there were Darcy, Dewey, Lucas, and Canaan . . . So many to find!

Would they ever again see the residents who had slipped away into the trees like the manticore who'd emerged from the mines? What about the dozens of faeries escaping across the fields?

Rubbing her face, she realized some of her jubilance was wearing thin. Having her mom and now Travis's dad taking over operations relieved the burden from her own shoulders, and that felt great—as did having her soul returned—but the task of tracking down every single mist victim and restoring them to normal . . . It seemed impossible. Too many of those people had blended into the background or joined a tribe of their own kind.

Flynn showed up right around the time the earliest potion recipients started reverting to their human forms.

"Where's my dad?" Melinda asked. "And Abigail?"

"The gnome stayed at the house. The vampire is sleeping in the basement."

Melinda stood with the dryad and watched the confusion, the cries of horror as their memories returned and they figured out they were missing a loved one. If Melinda's mood hadn't already sunk, it did now as she imagined small children wandering off . . .

The cleanup operation was just getting started, but there was a long way to go.

"Thanks for your help," she said to Flynn. "It's time you went home to your dad."

"I don't understand what's happening," Flynn said, sounding shaky.

Melinda turned to him. "I explained everything already . . . but I guess you never truly believed it, did you? As far as you're concerned, you're actually a dryad."

"I *am* a dryad."

"Well, the potion will prove you're not. It'll put you back to normal."

"You told me all that, but I *am* normal. I'm a dryad."

"No, Flynn, you're not."

Melinda pulled out one of her own vials, but Flynn grabbed her wrist. "What if I like who I am no matter what?"

She swallowed. "I . . . I don't think you're in a position to decide. You're not yourself right now."

He stared at her for a long time. Then, grudgingly, he released her arm. "I trust you, Melinda Strickland."

She applied a drop to each of his eyes, wondering if she was in fact doing the right thing.

Then they walked together. "I like you," Flynn said in a surprisingly matter-of-fact way. "May I see you again after everything has settled down?"

"When you're human?" she said. "Sure." Then she faltered. "Wait—you want to . . . to *see* me? Like, friends? Coming to visit, that sort of thing?"

The dryad turned transparent for a moment, then fuzzed back into view. "I was thinking we could go on a date."

"A . . . a *date*? I'm only eleven!" She could see her mom now, frowning and wagging her finger. "How old are *you*?"

Flynn opened his mouth to reply, then paused. "I'm not sure."

"Well—"

But at that moment, he morphed into an ordinary human boy and stood there blinking. He was the same height as her but looked a little older, with a mop of curly brown hair and bright, clear eyes that she liked.

"Hey, Flynn," she said shakily.

He stood there with his jaw hanging open for a while. Then, slowly, he began to nod. "I *am* human."

"You are. Are you happy about that?"

He frowned. "I guess."

"And did you still want to come visit me?"

"Huh?" Flynn reddened. "Oh. Yeah, sure. That'd be . . . fun. Whatever you say."

*Funny how he sounds human now. Like a farm boy rather than a well-spoken dryad from the forest.*

Then she spotted Travis's friend Rez, already restored. Breaking into a run, she called to him through the crowd of goblins.

He turned and gave her a nod. "I'm looking, I'm looking," he assured her. "Your mom's already been on to me. Last time I saw Mason, he was holding my hand back in the mines. Then the mist came, and . . ." He spread his hands. "I don't know what he, uh . . . *became*."

"What did *you* become?"

"Me? An elf." Rez snorted. "An elf! Me!"

He didn't elaborate on his scorn, but Melinda didn't care anyway. She advanced on him. "Think. You must have some idea what he was. Who was near you when you woke? Another elf? A troll, a pixie, what? What about clothes? Was anyone wearing Mason's clothes?"

"Uh . . ."

She yanked at his shirt. "Look! You found *your* clothes okay. Seems like everyone automatically picked up their clothes and got dressed before wandering out into the sunlight. Mason probably did, too."

Rez didn't know. The three of them—Melinda, Flynn, and Rez—scoured the neighborhood, and then Rez peeled off and muttered something about going off to search somewhere else. Melinda let him go. She'd never really got along with the boy, though Travis found him hilarious.

The ogre that had attacked Hal still snoozed on a rooftop at the edge of the town. The roof had collapsed even more, so he practically lay inside the cottage with his head, arms, and feet poking up through the hole. A crowd had gathered around the cottage—goblins and humans.

"Leave him be for now," a woman said. "Maybe Robbie can talk him down."

"Yeah, when Robbie shows up. Have you seen him?"

"He should *be* here already," a man complained.

Melinda walked off before someone made a comment she didn't like.

With Flynn still in tow, she found herself yearning for the dryad again. It wasn't that she didn't like the farm boy, just that she'd grown used to the well-spoken, polite, demure woodland creature.

Hal flew overhead, his huge dragon form casting a wide shadow. Thank goodness the faun hadn't been so crazy as to populate the town with fearsome animals like him! She could have had a field day with hellhounds and a cerberus or two. It seemed she'd kept the really dangerous monsters to a minimum.

Or maybe the brain had made that decision.

Melinda knew she was walking around in circles. A group of naga lined the street ahead, the same place they'd been twenty or thirty minutes ago. They were deep in conversation, and Melinda heard grumblings about goblins subjecting them to drops of potion in their eyes . . . But as she approached, they abruptly started to change, one by one turning human and staggering about trying to hide their modesty.

Covering her eyes, Melinda made a sharp right-turn into a heavily shadowed alley. There she bumped into a small creature with tan-colored skin and large eyes. Wearing a tunic, pants, and leather boots, she stood no taller than waist-high, and her oversized pointed ears waggled whenever she turned her head. For a second, Melinda thought the childlike female was a brownie because of the distinctive long, black hair.

"Hello," she called to the shy creature. "I'm Melinda."

The diminutive figure spoke in a high, squeaky voice. "I know."

Only then did Melinda realize a second figure hid in the darkest corner of the alley—a small boy hunched into a ball and wrapped in a blanket.

Her heart leapt. "Mason!"

The boy crawled out from his corner and, keeping the blanket pulled around him, shuffled toward her. "Hello, sis. What happened? I think I was sleepwalking. I remember—"

But what he remembered was lost as Melinda wrapped her arms around him and picked him up, squeezing with all her might. "We've been looking for you! Where have you been?"

The large-eared creature tugged at Melinda's arm. "I saw your mom drop potion in the squonk's eyes and walk off, and I stuck around just to see what he'd turn into. He's your brother, isn't he?"

Melinda released her grip on Mason and looked down at the small female figure. "Yes, he is. Thank you. What about you? Have you had the drops yet?"

"I don't need them. I'm *supposed* to look like this." She glanced around, looking wary, then added, "I'm Nitwit. I'm a friend of Travis."

Startled, Melinda almost forgot about her little brother as she stared hard at the creature. If this was Nitwit, then she was an imp. But although Travis talked about Nitwit from time to time, and his mom claimed to have met her, it was highly unusual for an imp to make herself known and stick around for more than a few seconds.

"So I'm finally getting to meet you," Melinda said—

And then the imp grinned and vanished.

"She's nice," Mason said. "She gave me this blanket."

Melinda returned her full attention to the boy. "Wait—you were a *squonk*?" She realized she'd seen the thing shuffling about the place, and she cringed. The poor boy! "What was that like?"

Mason frowned. "I don't remember. I just know I was sad." Tears welled up. "Squonks are so unhappy. Can we do something to cheer them up?"

"Sure, little brother. But not right now, okay? Let's go find Mom and Dad."

## Epilogue

Three days later, normality had resumed—almost.

Travis felt nothing would ever be exactly the same, especially for certain Carter residents. Twenty-three of them: fifteen men and eight women, vanished. Thankfully, all the children of the town were accounted for. Zero bodies had been found, so the town was optimistic that the missing twenty-three would be found eventually.

Assuming of course they *wanted* to be found.

One of the missing was a manticore. Reports suggested a few others were elves who had neatly avoided the potion-giving goblins and left to join others of their kind. Canaan the elf had set off on a mission to find them, heading first to Whisper Mountain in the south.

The rest of the missing could be trolls, gnomes, pixies, faeries—literally anything. They had effectively lost their true identities and might never come back of their own volition.

"They're still human at heart," Melinda mused, squinting toward the horizon. "Maybe they'll figure it out after a while."

Travis sat with her on the hilltop in the meadow between his house and the town. "Well, they don't speak the language of whatever tribe or clan they've gone off with. A naga who doesn't speak naga is gonna be booted out, eventually. They won't stand for a fake naga. Same with elves, I would think."

"The naga might be more tolerant than you think. They seem to like Emily well enough."

Travis had heard plenty of stories about Emily the naga shapeshifter. They had accepted her in the end. But what about the others? Another manticore running about in the nearby woods, one who wasn't *really* a manticore, was a very familiar story—very much like the tale of Thomas Patten nearly thirty years ago.

"How's your dad?" he asked her.

"He's fine. Still ashamed that he spent the whole time as a gnome. What about you? How's Unc—" She paused, then shook her head. "How's Hal and Abigail?"

"Dad's pretty fed up about the whole thing—being beaten by an ogre, then having to stand perfectly still for more than a day in case he trod on anyone. And Mom wishes she'd been strong enough to break through the memory block."

"*Everybody* wishes that. And as for Miss Simone . . ."

They grimaced. The thought of Lucas tracking down Miss Simone, a *werewolf*, and fighting her for hours just to get a couple of drops in her eyes . . . Her injuries had healed with the return to normality, but Lucas had retained his wounds a bit longer even with several transformations.

Travis and Melinda watched the orange sky darken as the sun sank deeper behind the horizon. To think the storm had once stretched as far as the eye could see and was now gone without a trace. Carter had been the biggest community swallowed up in the mist, but dozens of farmsteads and settlements had been affected as well.

As for Old Earth . . . The authorities had issued warnings and given portals a wide berth. At the height of its power, the storm had started to seep through the smoky holes, but the mist dispersed soon after the tower was destroyed. The townsfolk from Carter had returned unscathed.

"So I guess we both saved the world this weekend," Melinda mused.

"Yeah, I guess we did."

The enormity of it all had crept up on them over the past few days. If they hadn't destroyed the Treentacle and stopped the mist spreading . . .

But right now, Travis had something else on his mind. "Hey," he muttered.

"Mmm?"

"In the tower, when we swam down to that place underground . . ."

"What about it?"

*The kiss!*

Travis swallowed. "I don't know. I just . . . When you did that thing and gave me air. That was kind of, uh . . ."

*Kind of nice.*

"Weird?" she said. "Yeah, sorry. I saved your life, though."

"No, it wasn't weird. I was gonna say it was, uh . . ."

*Pretty awesome.*

Melinda frowned and squinted at him. "You were going to say what?"

"Well, you know . . ."

"No, I don't." She narrowed her eyes. "Look, I breathed air into your lungs so you wouldn't die. That was all. I'm sorry if I freaked you out. Was it that horrible?"

"What? No! Not at all!" Travis wanted to reach across and squeeze her hand in a reassuring way, to show that he actually liked her quite a lot, but he felt that would be even weirder right now. "I was just going to say . . . thanks."

*Thanks? THANKS? Are you kidding?*

"And," he added, "uh, that if you ever need to do that again, it's okay. Or if I need to . . . to save *your* life like that one day . . ."

He trailed off. She stared at him with an expression he couldn't fathom. *Way to go*, he thought with a grimace. *Really slick.*

"Huh," she said at last.

Travis found her staring past him. He turned to see what she was looking at. A few rocs in the sky? A goblin shuffling up the hill? Certainly nothing of great interest.

He froze as she planted a kiss on his cheek. The cool wetness on his hot face lingered for several seconds afterward. He reached up to touch it.

When he managed to turn back to her, she was staring off in the other direction, her hands clasped tightly in her lap, sitting upright with her back stiff.

"Wh-what was that for?" Travis croaked.

After a long silence, she murmured, "That's just so you know the difference between saving your life . . . and an actual kiss."

He smiled. "Gotcha."

# AUTHOR'S NOTE

Travis and Melinda will return.

As with any long-running series, you might think an author would start to run out of story ideas. Not me! Quite the opposite. But whether these ideas are *any good* is up to you. I'll keep going for as long as readers enjoy the books.

When I'm writing, I often find myself thinking, "Hey, that would be a cool idea to explore." I end up with a list of things I could write about next. Most of those ideas don't quite make it into print, but still, coming up with the plot of the next book is not a struggle at all. The only struggle I have is finding the time to write it. I do pretty well with three books a year, but four would be better. Or five. Or six . . .

The giant brain under the ground keeps rearing its ugly head (well, you know what I mean), and one day in the future, I foresee an epic battle to destroy it once and for all. But imagine that! Is the brain the source of the magic in New Earth? Would destroying it change everything? I'll be honest: writing that story has me quaking in my boots. It would be a game-changer.

But for now, there are plenty of adventures to be had.

What decides the setting for the next book? It's usually just a general "feel" that I latch onto. In the case of *Death Storm*, I had an image (a prophecy?) of a huge wall of mist rolling across the land. I was in the library one day for a book signing, and I'd just seen Stephen King's updated movie "It" the night before, and it set me thinking. You see, that book and original movie had two timelines—one following the adults, and another flashing back to the adventures they had when they were kids. What if I wrote two books, where the first is Hal and his friends dealing with a foe, and the second is twenty years later with the new generation of shapeshifters dealing with the same foe?

I had actually ended the Island of Fog series after the ninth book, thinking I was done and needed to write something else. Well, I had a hankering to pick up where I'd left off, and I needed the tenth book to be fairly special.

So *Forest of Souls* came into existence, along with its companion *Death Storm*. I wanted to write each book to be a standalone adventure but which could be enjoyed even more when read together—and in any order. That was my goal, and I think it works.

I take great pride in continuity. Many readers have asked me how many millions of notes I must have strewn around my office. The truth is, I have *zero* notes. Nada. Zilch. But I do have my books, and if I need to remember how I previously described a pixie, I can just open up a book and do a quick search. Mostly, though, I'm just immersed in my own world. My memory isn't great for most things, but I think recollection is easier when you actually *live* something rather than just read about it. I live in the story for three months per book, and I write three books a year, so that's . . . well, most of my year living in a fantasy world! Yup. That pretty much sums me up.

My next Island of Fog book will take the shapeshifters to the edge of the planet, the sharp drop-off on the horizon. Of course, this concept is ridiculous even in New Earth where anything is possible. Yet it exists.

And the next Island of Fog Legacies book? Ideas are still brewing on that one. You'll just have to stay tuned.

**Keith Robinson**
*Sci-Fi and Fantasy Author*
https://www.unearthlytales.com


Did you enjoy **Death Storm**? If so, please consider posting a rating or review on Amazon, iTunes, Barnes & Noble, Kobo, etc. Reviews and ratings help sell books. Thank you!

# OTHER SCI-FI AND FANTASY NOVELS
## BY THE SAME AUTHOR . . .

In *Island of Fog*, a group of twelve-year-old children have never seen the world beyond the fog, never seen a blue sky or felt the warmth of the sun on their skin. And now they're starting to change into monsters!

What is the secret behind the mysterious fog? Who is the stranger that shows up one morning, and where did she come from? Hal Franklin and his friends are determined to uncover the truth about their newfound shapeshifting abilities, and their quest takes them to the forbidden lighthouse . . .

The Island of Fog series is where it all started. Go back twenty years and follow the adventures of the original shapeshifters. There are also novellas and short stories in the Island of Fog Chronicles.

In *Sleep Writer*, everything changes for twelve-year-old Liam when a girl moves in next door. Madison is fifteen, pretty, and much weirder than she seems. Sometimes when she's sound asleep, she scrawls a message on a notepad by her pillow. She finds these cryptic words when she wakes the next morning—a time and a place.

But a time and a place for what? Liam and best friend Ant join her when she goes hunting around a cemetery late one night, and life is never the same again.

This fun science fiction series is ongoing, with at least one new novel each year.

In *Fractured*, the world of Apparatum is divided. To the west lies the high-tech city of Apparati, governed by a corrupt mayor and his brutal military general. To the east, spread around the mountains and forests, the seven enclaves of Apparata are ruled by an overbearing sovereign and his evil chancellor. Between them lies the Ruins, or the Broken Lands—all that's left of a sprawling civilization before it fractured. Hundreds of years have passed, and neither world knows the other exists.

Until now.

We follow Kyle and Logan on their journey of discovery. Laws are harsh. In the city, Kyle's tech implant fails to work, rendering him worthless in the eyes of the mayor. In the enclaves, Logan is unable to tether to any of the spirits, and he is deemed an outcast. Facing execution, the two young fugitives escape their homes and set out into the wastelands to forge a new life.

But their destinies are intertwined, for the separate worlds of Apparati and Apparata are two faces of the same coin . . . and it turns out that everyone has a twin.

There are two books in this series, with a possible third (a prequel) planned for the future. This series is co-written with author Brian Clopper.

In **Quincy's Curse**, poor Quincy Flack is cursed with terrible luck. After losing his parents and later his uncle and aunt in a series of freak accidents, Megan Mugwood is a little worried about befriending him when he moves into the village of Ramshackle Bottom. But incredibly good fortune shines on him sometimes, too. Indeed, it turns out that he found a bag of valuable treasure in the woods just a few months ago!

As luck would have it, Megan has chosen the worst possible time to be around him.

This is a fantasy for all ages, a complex and rewarding tale, a little dark in places but also a lot of fun.

Go to **UnearthlyTales.com** for more information.

Printed in Great Britain
by Amazon

16081222R00181